‘Joyful, uplifting and full of heart – I loved it.’
Sarah Turner, author of *Stepping Up*

‘A thoroughly heart-warming read, full of lovable characters and a resounding message of hope for our times.’
Kate Storey, author of *The Memory Library*

‘Sweet, uplifting and deeply touching . . . a delight.’
Justin Myers, author of *The Last Romeo*

‘A tender, heartwarming story of friends, family and the unexpected joy that’s waiting in the spaces in between.’
Julietta Henderson, author of *The Funny Thing About Norman Foreman*

‘Moving and uplifting, *The Stand-in Dad* is *Heartstopper* for adults; a love letter to queerness and the family you get to choose.’ **PJ Ellis, author of *Love and Other Scams* and *We Could Be Heroes***

‘A breath of fresh air. Powered by kindness, community and love, this book is lots of fun and absolutely full of joy.’ **Eleanor Ray, author of *Everything is Beautiful***

‘A sweet and touching story that highlights that true friendship comes in many forms.’ **Charlotte Butterfield, author of *The Second Chance***

‘What a joy! A vibrant, warm and hopeful story, with a cast of characters I’d love to be friends with and a flower shop I wish was on my street. Loved it.’ **Penny Mirren, author of *The Unretirement***

‘A book with spring in its step . . . I read this with a big smile and a soaring heart.’ **Jack Strange, author of *Look Up, Handsome***

‘A gentle heart-warming story . . . with a dash of humour whisked in to delight.’ **Charlie Lyndhurst, author of *Finding Our Family***

Alex Summers is a queer and neurodivergent writer from Milton Keynes, who now lives in London with his partner. When he is not writing, he is reading or swimming. *The Stand-in Dad* is his first novel.

ALEX SUMMERS

THE STAND-IN DAD

avon.

Published by AVON
A division of HarperCollins*Publishers* Ltd
1 London Bridge Street
London SE1 9GF

www.harpercollins.co.uk

HarperCollins*Publishers*
Macken House, 39/40 Mayor Street Upper
Dublin 1, D01 C9W8, Ireland

A Paperback Original 2025
2

First published in Great Britain by HarperCollins*Publishers* 2025

A catalogue copy of this book is available from the British Library.

ISBN: 978-0-00-874066-5

Set in Sabon LT Std by HarperCollins*Publishers* India

Printed and bound in the United States

For Alison Milton
1965–2024

PROLOGUE

Meg looked up at the stars, hoping for an answer. The sky was a dark purple, the sun long gone, and she felt the cold spread around her neck and shoulders. She wished she was wearing Hannah's big pink fluffy jumper, something to comfort her. She felt restless and adrift. All she wanted was Hannah and a blanket and the breakfast they loved. A cup of tea, made by somebody else. A biscuit and a hug.

She wanted, more than anything else, to be somebody who could have a hard day and run back to their parents' house, to have her dinner made for her before curling up in fresh sheets. She wanted a mother who would stroke her face and tell her everything was going to be okay. Meg wondered, after what had happened, if she had ever had those parents. Her heart, she noticed, was beating faster than ever.

If only she could have a normal wedding. Now, if she went back in, they would be waiting for her to decide what to do, but if she went home, she'd be found there too. She didn't want to see anyone.

Breathe in for three, hold for four, breathe out for five.

She tried it but it didn't work.

The idea of returning to normal felt too much. She let the panic take her over. Maybe this was what she deserved. Screw the breathing exercises, screw calm. Maybe her parents were in the right, and maybe she had been so stupid to expect that she'd be allowed a wedding like everybody else had had. A car rushed past suddenly out of nowhere, and she pictured it driving into a puddle, the water splashing all over her.

Surely, it was one of those days.

Now, Meg began to run. She didn't know where she wanted to be, but it wasn't here in the street where anybody she knew from when she'd grown up could see her. She didn't want to be found. She wanted to be invisible.

The air braced her lungs, and there was drizzle on her face and all round her mouth as she tried to breathe. She kept going, her legs stamping into puddles on the pavement, her arms swinging, and soon she couldn't tell the rain from the teardrops streaming down her face.

1

DAVID

No matter what David tried, he couldn't get the new mixed bouquets to sit right. He must have been crouched down in the window of the shop for ten minutes before he, or maybe his knees, gave up and he moved on to the rest of the morning's list.

After clearing out some stagnant grey water from the peonies and spraying the most tricky houseplants, he returned to the window and spun the bouquets round one last time, about ninety degrees. No, this wouldn't do. He bent down again.

'Come on, little guys,' he said, under his breath.

They were beautiful, fresh from Holland, delivered at five in the morning, and arranged by his hand two hours later. A white, pink and orange mix for any occasion, lilies and chrysanthemums and snapdragons, wrapped in crisp brown paper with the shop's logo on. He continued to fiddle with some of the stems. Sometimes it only took one flower to move to make the whole collection work.

Savage Lilies, the flower shop, was his pride and joy. It had been a lifelong dream; a little slice of heaven in

Woburn Sands, one of the small towns that dotted the edge of Milton Keynes. The wooden exterior was bright green, repainted last year by his partner Mark and some of the teenagers from the youth club, and the inside was a busy vista of plants, flowers, greetings cards, café seating, and a couple of make-your-own bouquet tables he used for evening classes.

The shop had ebbs and flows but they tried to listen to customers, and to Mary Portas, to keep the shop going. *Make shopping an experience,* she always said. *Innovate.* What with Mark having a proper job too, they just about got by. It never felt like work. After more than half a century on this planet, he had something close to the perfect life.

Modernizing the shop had added several extra jobs to the morning checklist that Mark had printed and stuck up in the back room *(thanks Mary!)* but if it kept his lovely life going, then it was worth it. David turned on the PHOTO-SYNTHESIS photo booth, which began to whirr with electricity and then he stretched up towards a row of string-of-pearls plants hanging from a high shelf that needed watering. He'd never loved houseplants, but if that was what people were buying alongside flowers, it made sense for them to *branch out,* a pun Mark never failed to use where he could.

Lastly, he adjusted the volume of the shop's Plant Playlist, a kind of in-joke between him and Mark. He must have got a little too energetic earlier that morning listening to Savage Garden, since the volume was at level forty-five. He spun the dial down to thirty as 'Build Me Up Buttercup' segued into a recent addition: 'Flowers' by Miley Cyrus.

Just as David began to make a cappuccino for himself – it was around half nine when they opened that the tiredness of a five o'clock alarm would start to get to him – he noticed a woman sitting on the bench outside the front of the store. She must have been waiting to come in, or perhaps waiting for somebody, since she kept looking up and down the street and jumping at the sound of every car. She was incredibly pretty in that effortless way of someone wearing no make-up. From where David was stood, she looked to be about thirty, with medium-length black hair tied in a ponytail that rested over one shoulder. She was wearing dungarees, a piece of clothing David had noticed becoming much more popular again recently, and was checking her phone.

He walked to the store windows and poked his head out the door, pretending to need to wipe at a non-existent smudge on the glass.

'Morning!' he said. 'Lovely day.'

'Yes,' the woman said quietly. She had a kind, soft voice, but she was clearly sad, and David noticed a tiny pride-flag pin, the modern one with all the other bits on, affixed to the pouch on her dungarees. 'Summer's coming!' she added, before looking down at her phone again. He could see from where he was standing that she was just flicking between apps, nothing to do and nowhere to go.

David nodded at her, paused, and then sensing her wish to be left alone, went back inside the empty shop.

'She's been there for twenty minutes!'

'David,' Mark said, putting on the gentle voice he used whenever David had one of his big ideas. David could hear him holding back a sigh on the end of the telephone. 'You can't help everybody. Remember when you thought that boy had fallen over outside the shop but he was just sitting down?'

'Okay, that one was unfortunate,' David reluctantly agreed.

'And the old woman when you asked if she needed anything and she said she needed you to leave her alone . . .'

'Okay, Mark, I get the picture.'

'I'll have to go, my ten o'clock's here,' Mark said. 'Just give it five minutes. Why don't you . . . *pot*-ter around for a bit, distract yourself.'

Chuckling at his own joke, Mark said his goodbyes and David hung up the phone.

He glanced up again, because he couldn't help himself, and felt immediately vindicated when the woman outside began to cry. She put her head in her hands, and even now somewhat hidden by the troublesome bouquets in the window, he could see her shoulders shaking. Scrambling, nearly kicking over the empty Dutch buckets near the door in his haste, he moved quickly outside, feeling terrible that he'd had space in his brain to feel vindicated.

'Hello again,' he said, offering her a tissue in his outstretched hand.

The woman looked up.

'Oh, thank you,' she said, taking the tissue and dabbing at her eyes. She sniffed. 'That's really thoughtful of you.'

'Are you okay?'

The woman looked unsure. She checked her phone again and took a big, shaky breath in to try to control her crying.

'Maybe that's too big of a question.' David smiled at her. 'What's your name?'

'Meg.'

'Well, Meg, I'm David. What about an even easier question – do you want a coffee?'

Meg, clearly desperate to not be crying on the high street, followed him inside and sat down at the table furthest from the front of the shop. Before he set about making her a drink, David put a Viennese whirl as big as his head on a plate and brought it to the table. Meg's tears, which she had been attempting to stop, suddenly poured down her face at this act of kindness and she brought her hands up to her face again.

'It's okay,' David said, patting her on the back. 'You can cry in here. You won't be the first. Or the last.'

2
MEG

Sitting opposite the man who had now introduced himself as David, Meg was surprised at how the day had turned out. When she left the house that morning, she hadn't expected to be tear-stained and sharing her entire life story with a stranger in a flower shop.

Often, if you talked about your mum and dad without the loving tone or jokey chiding of most people, you were met with blank expressions. The majority of people, lucky them, just thought their parents were brilliant, but when Meg spoke about growing up here and moving back last year, living closer to her parents again, David seemed to be completely judgement-free. When he asked a question, he leaned forward for the answer, making it clear he was paying attention. He had bushy eyebrows and kept shifting to rearrange his corduroy trousers and sweater vest, but he was still listening to every word she said.

'So they gave no indication,' he asked, pushing his glasses to the top of his nose. 'That they wouldn't come?'

'They said they'd be here. Nine-thirty sharp. And they're punctual people. It's not like my parents have ever been amazing, but this is my *wedding*, you know. I'm worried they looked up the shop and stood me up.'

'Oh.'

'Sorry,' she added, looking around. 'It's a lovely place.'

It really was. For the first time, she appreciated the sheer volume of flowers and plants that were squeezed into this ordinary-sized building. The shop must be half the size of the small supermarket next door, and yet somehow David had managed to fit in this huge table, the café area and a photo booth. Behind the till was a huge grandfather clock made of wood, surely an antique. She remembered that this shop had been the local pharmacy when she'd been younger. Half of the high street now was made of shops she didn't recognize. Where there were now a row of bouquets in the front window, there had used to be a marketing-sized prop bottle of shampoo, and Meg remembered the day she'd grown enough to be taller than it.

Perhaps it was the nostalgia of it all that had made her so upset that her parents had stood her up. The message that had set her off crying just before ten o'clock had read: *Sorry. We can't come today. Apologies, Mum and Dad*

'Were they always like this?' David asked. He lifted his mug at her to offer another coffee, but she waved it away. He got up to make his own. 'Was it always hard?'

'They were always subtly homophobic,' she continued. 'Saying things about Graham Norton, tutting whenever they talked about gay rights on the news and, well, Lily Savage actually, they always had a problem with. Dad used to say *bring back Paul*.'

'I was concerned about the name,' David told her, turning back around and raising his voice over the sound of steaming milk. 'Lily hasn't performed in years, so I worried people wouldn't get it, but Mark, that's my partner, he said Lily was forever.'

'He's a smart man,' Meg said, remembering how fascinated she had been as a child by the big blonde wigs and Lily's spindly legs. 'How long have you been together?'

'Nearly twenty years,' David said. 'We met when we were mid-thirties, up north, through some mutual friends. The time will fly by.' David clicked his fingers. 'Enjoy everything, because soon as you know it, you'll be counting in decades.'

'And you're still happy?'

'Happier than ever, actually.' David reached out to her. 'Which you will be too. I promise, nothing lasts forever.'

'Are you married?'

'No, it's . . . We're good as we are.' David pushed his reading glasses up his nose. 'Now, you were telling me about your parents. Keep going, if you want. I always find it's better to offload.'

'Well, both my parents were teachers, and still are. They teach at St Helens.'

'Mark works there; he's the school counsellor. Maybe he knows them.'

'Maybe,' Meg said. She didn't know how she felt about other people talking about her parents. It wasn't embarrassment at their faults but that she didn't want to hear from anyone else how nice they were either. She shook the complex thought from her head. 'When I was a kid, you know, they said some bad things, when they had no idea they had a little gay child in the room, but everyone did that when I was young. It wasn't like they were the exception.'

'I see.'

'Then they were terrible when I came out, actually,' she

continued, swirling the murky dregs of her coffee around in the mug. This was always really hard to talk about but David was older than her and things must have been worse for him, she presumed, perhaps unkindly. She hoped he'd understand. 'There was lots of crying, and saying I'd disappointed them, or that I was just going through a phase. That's what Mum said. Still something she says, actually, hoping me and my teenage boyfriend will get back together.'

'Any chance?' David asked, smiling.

'No, we were never actually going out.' Meg exhaled. 'He's gay too. We kind of just let them think we were. I've never had the heart to tell them.'

David smiled at her.

'I still call him an ex, you know,' Meg said. 'We kissed; we held hands. Almost like trying it one last time, before knowing it's not for you.'

'I had some girlfriends like that.'

'He still lives around here, on Cressida Street.'

'Lovely houses on that road,' David joked. 'Don't rule him out too soon.'

Meg laughed, and wiped some tears from her face with the sleeve of her jumper as David sat back down next to her.

'Anyway, then I went off to uni,' Meg continued. 'Best years of my life. Far away from here, up in Scotland. Saw them for Christmas and birthdays. Met Hannah. The last few years, moving back, I thought we were better than ever. Hannah was happy too; obviously she doesn't want difficult in-laws. They weren't jumping up and down when we told them about the engagement, but they seemed happy. I've got a cake tasting on Monday and I guess they're probably not coming to that now either.'

'Can Hannah go instead?' David asked.

'No, she's in Italy with work,' she said. David looked confused. 'She does events,' she added.

'Oh fancy!'

'No, quite boring,' Meg said, laughing. 'Everyone thinks that, but she does the graphics for screens so she's usually on her laptop in a cupboard somewhere. We both do illustrations, but hers are more computer, graphic-design based. Anyway, that's why I was relying on them. I thought if I couldn't do it with her, it should be family.'

The word *family* nearly set Meg off crying again and so, to distract herself, she stared at what David was doing. While they were talking, David had been using some small contraption to rip leaves and thorns from the stems of his roses.

'We make the most money from roses, you know. Not a lot, mind you, but they're still the most popular.'

'What do you do with the broken ones?' Meg asked, indicating to her right a small pile of flowers where he'd accidentally broken the stems.

'We can't sell them, but I put them in a little vase on the counter usually. Take them home or give them out sometimes. It would make me too sad to bin them.'

Meg watched the pile of flowers building, thinking how David seemed to be able to turn any negative into a positive. She wished she had that skill.

He looked at her. 'What are you going to do about the cake appointment?'

'Maybe I need to rethink the whole thing,' she said. I can't do all these jobs on my own; it'll be miserable.'

'Do you have anyone else who can go?'

'We've only just moved,' Meg said. 'We've got friends

but they're all back in London and busy with husbands and kids. I haven't really made any friends in the area. I was actually thinking of getting in touch with my ex . . .'

David stared at the small pile of broken roses, deep in thought. Meg wondered if she had outstayed her welcome, whether he was keen to get on with his day, or whether she was preventing customers from coming in. She didn't know much about business but she knew seeing someone crying would stop her going into a shop.

'What if I came with you?'

'What?'

David sat up in his chair and swept the useless leaves into the bin. 'I never got married. I'd be interested to see what happens. Any of these appointments, while you sort things out with your family, I could come. I'm sure you wouldn't want to go alone.'

'But . . .' Meg said. She didn't know what to say. 'Would you . . . Don't you have the shop? I can't ask you to do that.'

'You're not asking me, I'm offering.' David smiled. 'It's different.' He got up from the table and carried the bin from behind the counter back to where they were sitting. 'Eating cake with a new friend isn't exactly a chore. We could do Monday and see how it goes. We don't open on Mondays anymore so I'm free.'

He walked around the shop, looking for a vase. 'It was actually to save money, opening for longer on the other days and . . .'

'That's really kind of you, David, but . . .'

Part of her wanted to accept this man quickly into her life, send him a wedding invitation, or even jump across the table and hug him for all the kindness he had shown a complete stranger, but this wasn't what she had pictured for her wedding. She wanted her own parents; she wanted to be normal.

'Thanks . . .' She hesitated. 'But I just need a little think about all of this. I'll be back! Well, presuming we go ahead, I mean. I'll probably be back.'

'All right, pe—' David said. 'Sorry, I nearly called you petal. Mark always says I can't call people *petal*, not in here, too silly. But, *Meg*, if you need to talk, at any point, I'll be here. Except Mondays.'

'Thanks,' said Meg. 'How much do I owe you for the coffee, and the . . .'

'It's on the house.'

'No.'

'I absolutely insist.'

'You can't.'

'I can,' David said, standing up from the chair to see her out. 'It's my shop.'

'All right,' Meg said. 'Well, thank you.'

'Good luck, Meg,' he said. When she got to the door, she turned back round to look at this kind man surrounded by plants. 'There's so much more to your life than what your parents think it should be. Remember that.'

3

DAVID

Sitting at the counter reading his book, David was enjoying a quiet day in the shop. Thursdays were always nice, before the weekend. He'd had a rush during the morning with some of the school-run mums in with their complicated coffee orders and then a late delivery of foliage that had taken six trips to bring into the stockroom at the back. That lunchtime, he'd met with the shop's accountant. Gloomy news, but best to put it to the back of his mind for now.

With the afternoon came the occasional stranger in off the high street. After an initial greeting, he liked to give people a little bit of space to enjoy the quirks of the shop without being heavy-handed. Mark had once made him perform role play, pretending to be a customer after the shop had closed. His feedback, given gladly and with the hint of a smile, had been that David could be somewhat overfamiliar.

He watched as the late March winds blew all of the trees outside back and forth, the occasional plastic bag or piece of litter making its way past the shop at speed, and people marched or sauntered past, the beginning of the school run and the commute home. It was like his own little TV show, the rectangular framing of the shop's front window his own screen, and it made it impossibly hard for him to concentrate on reading. He found himself scanning the same page again and again, his mind drifting to Meg and how upset she had been the day before. David kept wondering if she'd come back, either to buy wedding flowers or just to say hello. Had he been too intense to offer to help?

'David!' came a voice in the doorway. 'Long time, no see!'

Standing in the doorway, quickly shutting the wind away behind him, was Carl, one of David and Mark's good friends. He lived in Milton Keynes, in a modern flat by the canal, and he always looked so much more stylish than either him or Mark, who were always either covered in mud (him) or dressed casually, in order to make the kids he counselled feel like he was approachable (Mark). Carl was wearing a trench coat and heavy NHS-style designer spectacles, which he pushed up his nose as he spoke.

'I hoped you'd be in.'

'I'm always here,' David said, rising to greet his guest. They hugged, kissed each other on the cheek and he led him to a table. He wasn't technically always there, but David liked the idea anyone could come and see him whenever, and it *was* always him there before ten, dealing with deliveries and opening up.

'Well good.' Carl nodded. 'How are you doing?'

'I'm well,' David said, getting them both a drink from the fridge. 'Carrying on. Slightly slow month here,' he continued. 'But we're getting by. How's business? You had that big client come on in January?'

Carl was a copywriter for a large company who did

work for many even bigger companies, and was often off to London or to fancy awards ceremonies to celebrate their work. Matty, his slightly younger partner, was a photographer. Together, the two of them always looked like something from a catalogue.

'Gosh, Matty's right,' Carl said. 'You do have such a great memory. I am busy, yes, but it's slowing down soon, and then me and Matty are off to Greece week after next, for some early sun.'

'You booked it!'

'We finally booked it.'

'I adore Greece,' David said, dreaming of feta. 'Some of the most underrated food, I find.'

'How's Mark?'

'He's good – he's busy too. Feels like every kid is after counselling at the minute. He keeps getting back late, since they do appointments after school now too.'

'Well,' Carl said. 'I guess that's good. Not good, but good they're getting help. I wish I'd had a Mark when I was growing up.'

'Me too,' David agreed, sipping his lemonade. 'Me too.'

'How's Lilies?' Carl said. 'Busy?'

'It's been really quiet this week,' David said, thinking of that conversation with the accountant. 'I'm thinking of new ideas to get us some more custom . . . Our Valentine's idea didn't really work. I'm thinking of setting up a network of local businesses.'

'That's a great idea,' Carl said. 'Even better, why don't you connect with other queer businesses?'

'Oh, maybe.'

'Don't be shy; there's loads out there. I keep going to queer networking events. They're all the rage. Gives you more of a reason to support each other, and you can do it with companies that do events so they recommend you to their clients.'

'I guess that does make sense.'

'Lots to think about,' Carl said. 'Let me know if I can lend a hand.'

'Anyway, what are you in for? Is this a business or a pleasurable visit?'

'Both please,' Carl said. 'I wanted to pick up some roses, for Matty's birthday.'

David stood to show him the latest arrangements he had, thinking that Carl might take to one of the more unique bouquets in the window he hadn't been able to sell.

'No, no, sit down!' Carl insisted. 'Let's have a gossip about our friends first. The most important local network. Have you heard about Angie's date on Saturday?'

Carl had stayed for about forty minutes, and they had only been interrupted by customers a couple of times. After that, Martha, another old friend, came in to say hello. She taught music lessons at St Helens and was maybe one of David's more eccentric friends. He didn't know anyone like her, who cared so little what people thought. She had short blonde hair, and did her make-up with little wings around her eyes. Where Carl was curated, Martha's coolness was effortless.

After catching up about each other's lives – Martha had David rolling around laughing with an anecdote about a day she'd plugged the keyboard in wrong, thinking it was broken, when it was actually connected on Bluetooth to the main school's speakers – David realized Meg had been on his mind all day, and he wondered what Martha thought. Maybe a woman's perspective was needed.

'She ended up staying about an hour,' he said. 'I think she had calmed down by the end, but she was so upset, crying buckets.'

'She was crying?' she asked.

'She was *really* crying,' David said. 'I couldn't bear it. Sounds like it was really awful for her, her parents leaving her hanging like that.'

'Of course.'

'A wedding should be a happy event.'

'Sorry, David,' she said. 'With your parents as well, that must have been hard for you to listen to.'

David had shared with his friends what had happened with his own parents, the way they had reacted when he had come out to them at the age of sixteen, but that had been so long ago that it rarely came up. Some of that came from David himself avoiding the topic. It made him isolated and uncomfortable, even amongst his gay friends, and a large part of him simply wanted to forget.

'It was,' David admitted. 'My situation was different though . . . Mine broke all contact with me, and they never met Mark, but that was years ago! It feels like every year things get a little better, but nowhere quickly enough. It's so depressing.'

'What can you do though? Sounds like you helped her in the moment, and you offered more help.' Martha touched his hand. 'You're always hard on yourself.'

'I just . . . She deserves her family being there for her . . . I just wanted to do what her own parents are too . . . I don't know, scared to? Too ignorant?'

'Too scared,' Martha said. 'Is perhaps the kinder way of looking at it.'

'You just have to convince people; that's what I've always said,' David stated. 'Haven't I? Tides always change. It's just that some people take longer than others to wade in.'

'Just make sure you're not reaching out to help to try and get a different outcome, or to reverse what happened with you.' Martha rubbed at his shoulder. 'It might not happen.'

'It might, though.'

Martha laughed. 'You can be much too positive, sometimes, and too nice. I'd get torn apart at school if I was like you.'

'Well,' David said. 'I get away with it somehow. Talking about you being nice . . . you still never sent me the recipe for that banoffee sticky pudding, by the way. I've been telling Mark I'll get it out of you one way or another.'

'What are you going to do about Meg?' she asked. 'You're changing the subject.'

'As are you,' he said. 'I need that recipe! What does the youth club say? Oh yes, don't *gatekeep*.'

Martha looked at him, waiting for him to answer her.

'I really don't know what to do,' David continued, sighing. 'I didn't get an address or number or even last name or anything, so I hoped I'd just naturally see her again and I could check she's all right.'

'I'm sure she will be,' Martha said. 'People around here look after each other.'

'They do,' David said. 'But she's new and her partner's away. What if she doesn't have anybody?'

As he spoke, the lady from the local foodbank arrived. 'All right, sweetheart,' she said, coming into the shop. She was wearing a gilet and had her head wrapped up in a snood. 'I like these ones.' She indicated the new celebration bouquets in the window and David smiled, happy his work to get them right had finally been recognized. 'I can't stop long. What have we got?'

'Thanks so much,' he replied, standing up to get boxes from behind the counter he'd prepared earlier. 'I've only got a few bits today. Those three bouquets and I've only had a few cakes not sell, but I've put some cartons of milk in there too, on me.'

'You're too good, Davey,' the woman said, clearly on a mission and already halfway out the door. She waved. 'See you next time.'

With that, she was gone.

'Do people call you Davey?' Martha asked, putting down her cup of tea.

'No, never,' David said. 'But she did it the first time and I haven't had the heart to tell her.'

He usually closed down the shop slowly from about six o'clock, and had recently started leaving the Open sign up on the door while he did so in case they got any last-minute customers. Sometimes, it could be only a matter of tens of pounds that kept him in the black for each day, particularly during slow weekdays. As he began to sweep the floor of leaves and petals and general rubbish that had accumulated throughout the day, some of the youth group tapped lightly on the window, and started waving. They were moving in that uncontrollably energetic way teenage kids had when they were together. Whereas a few years before, they'd run around playing to get rid of it, now it came out in other, more subtly mischievous ways.

Behind the group, good-naturedly chiding them for

moving too slowly in the way of the door, Mark arrived, and they instantly cleared a path for him. They were scared of Mark in a way they weren't of David.

Since he and Mark had started being involved in the youth club, they'd now seen a couple of generations' worth of kids make their way through it. There was a man from the council, Jacob, who ran the scheme, but David and Mark helped once a fortnight or so, taking the group on socials or setting up sports or art events in the shop.

As Mark made his way into the shop, putting down his satchel, Benji, their secret favourite, was sticking the end of his nose up against the glass for comedic effect. David would have to clean that, but he didn't mind. He waved at Benji, pretending to tell him to stop, though he knew he wouldn't.

Benji had been in the youth club for a couple of years, and even though the official cut-off was fifteen, nobody had had the heart to turn him away. The group needed him as much as he needed it. He'd had a difficult upbringing involving an absent mother and an angry father, David had gleaned, and sometimes he still struggled with his emotions.

When David had first started helping with the group at Mark's suggestion eight years ago, he thought he had to discipline the kids or take on a parent role for Benji and the others, but what they needed was more of an impartial distant uncle, an approachable grown-up who could still toe the line. The main job was just listening and supporting them.

David pretended to hop down into the 'cellar' behind the counter, a joke he'd never got tired of but that the kids were already rolling their eyes about outside. Mark was shaking his head, and the group were laughing at that even more. Always willing to do something for a laugh, Mark came back behind the counter too and followed David downstairs. Then, Mark came back from the 'cellar' and pretended to find a new set of stairs next to the existing ones. He got so carried away that by the time he and David looked back to the window, the kids had gone and David and Mark were alone.

'Hello, you,' Mark said, moving towards the counter to kiss David on the cheek. 'Careful, the cellar door's open.'

David started pretending to trip over it, but thought perhaps the joke had had a beat too many, and picked up the cloth he used to wipe the windows.

'Do you mind watering these?' He pointed to some jars of flowers on the table. 'And these.' He pointed to some pots below the counter. 'Then we'll be good.'

If Mark made it home in time, they tended to close down the shop together before they went upstairs to their flat, and no matter how busy or long Mark's day had been, he always lent a hand in whatever way he could. It was a nice way to catch up and even him being there made the mundanity of jobs like cleaning the coffee machine (David must admit, he did need to do this a little more regularly) feel less taxing.

'How was your day?' he asked Mark.

'It was okay. There's a lot of sickness going round, so a couple of cancelled appointments, a lot of children struggling with low mood. I don't think the weather's helped.'

'Of course,' David said, peeking out of the window. 'It's miserable out there, for March. Bring on spring.'

'Has that girl come in?' Mark said. 'The one who cried?'

'Nothing yet,' David said. 'I can't stop thinking about her. I tried to look her up online today but I couldn't find her.'

‘Well you could barely find your search engine, to be fair.’

‘Very funny.’ He leaned against the counter. ‘I’m serious. I kept thinking about my own parents, if we’d got married . . .’

‘You can’t wish for a different outcome.’ Mark leaned against David’s shoulder. ‘This is a different situation.’

‘With her, I just kept thinking, what if that was me?’ David said. ‘Would I want me to find me, check I’m okay?’

‘Talking about finding yourself? At fifty-four?’

‘You’re not far behind.’

‘You’re not going to run away to a yoga retreat, are you?’

‘I will if you keep on, Mark.’

‘I’m sure she’s okay. She’s got a fiancée.’ Mark was holding his bag, ready to go. ‘What did you say her name was? Hannah? She’ll be able to rely on her.’ He kissed the top of David’s head and they started to get their things, ready to leave. ‘Just be patient; I’m sure she’ll pop in if she’s local.’

‘I could always undercharge her, as a gesture – give her the family discount.’

‘I’m going to tape your hand behind your back if you keep being so trigger-happy with that family discount button.’ Mark poked him in the side affectionately, pulling his satchel over his head. ‘What did the accountant say last year?’

‘She said I needed to close in a smaller ring of who I counted as friends and family . . .’

‘Yes.’

‘And that living in any surrounding postcode didn’t count.’

‘Exactly.’

'I can't help that I—' David smiled. 'That *we're* so popular round here. I'm nearly ready to go, by the way.'

'I suppose you can't,' Mark said. 'It's the weekends that I'm behind the till. The thing is, people can't resist.'

'Oh *ha ha*,' David said. He wanted to tell Mark what the accountant had said this week, much starker news than last year, but he figured it could wait. It wasn't exactly Thursday night bring-on-the-weekend news. 'Oh before I forget, Carl invited us round at the weekend, delayed birthday thing for Matty. Dinner at theirs.'

'Oh, great.' Mark was sitting on the counter, swinging his legs. He always knew when David said he was ready, it was never quite true. 'Their food is always such a treat.'

'Maybe I use this as an excuse to get Martha's banoffee sticky pudding recipe to bring,' David said. 'I asked her for it again today, but she's really resistant.'

'When are you going to have time to make that?'

'I'll find time!'

'Tell me when you've found some,' Mark said. 'I'll use it to stop my forehead wrinkles.'

'Very funny,' David said.

'I do have a request on your time, actually.'

David raised an eyebrow, stacking up everything on the counter that had, throughout the day, spread across the shop. 'What is it?'

'Benji was talking about careers at school today,' Mark said. 'He's about to do his GCSEs, and I think he's wondering about the future and what he's going to do. I took such a boring academic route into this job, I wondered if you'd talk to him? Talk about your career, jobs you've had, speak to him about whatever it is he wants to do eventually?'

'Yeah, I can do that.' David thought about all his early

jobs, and which ones Benji might find useful. A paper boy? A lifeguard? The boring admin job he'd been doing when he met Mark?

'Great,' Mark said. 'I'll get Jacob to sort a time.'

'Night, guys,' David said to the plants, as he spun around to close and lock the door behind them. 'Say it to them.'

Mark stared at him. 'Really? Every day?'

David stared back at him, and Mark poked his head back in the door. 'Bye, guys, sleep tight.'

He blew a kiss and David giggled as he closed the padlock on the shutters.

4

MEG

Milky coffee and eggs two-ways. Sometimes with spinach, rarely with hash browns, always with the poshest bread they could find, anything that could give two vegetarians the buzz of a full English. That was their special breakfast and one of the things Meg had been missing while Hannah was away, along with other niche parts of the day that were her personal highlights. She had missed the moment Hannah would make a cup of tea and serve it with a biscuit like they were at a hotel. Most of all she missed the minutes in bed facing each other just before sleep, when they chatted complete nonsense, the anonymity of the darkness allowing them to say whatever came into their minds until Hannah, and it was usually Hannah, would fall silent and Meg would look to see she had gone quietly to sleep.

As a couple, they loved going out to eat but there was something about being in their own space when reunited that to Meg felt very intimate, and much more special. It meant they could talk about anything with no self-consciousness or interruptions.

They had not lived in the flat long, and with Hannah

being away a lot, there were heaps of things waiting to be sorted. Though Meg had grown up in the area, she still felt like there was a lot of exploring to do together, of new places and routines, but they needed to sort inside the house first. There were boxes and bags pushed to the corners of each room, and strips of paint options on the wall. The living room and kitchen stretched across the first floor, looking out onto the street, and the abnormally windy season, which had seemingly got worse over the last day or so, occasionally rattled the windows in their frames with an annoyingly sudden noise. Sitting at the table with Hannah, Meg couldn't have been happier.

'How was the flight then?' she asked.

'Fine once we were on,' Hannah replied, cutting into her toast. She was wearing an old university T-shirt of Meg's, and pyjama bottoms. 'It's all the waiting around I can't stand, everybody trying to jump the queue, or pacing around.'

'Were you pacing?'

'I had headphones on, just desperate to get into my seat and eat a KitKat and try to fall asleep.'

It must have been a late one. Meg would have stayed up till eleven, maybe even midnight, to see her fiancée after a long trip, but with Hannah not tiptoeing into the bedroom until two in the morning, Meg was glad she'd gone to bed at a normal time.

'So catch me up,' Hannah said. 'What's been happening while I was away?'

Hannah had been in Italy for just five days, but it had felt like a lifetime. Meg did not usually feel needy at all, but the separation had felt interminably long this time. That was the danger, really, of working freelance and in solitude.

The night before, she had gone to the cinema alone in an attempt to prove she was independent, but without anyone to laugh at the jokes with or to hold her popcorn in the foyer while she went to the toilet, it had made her feel worse. She was worried about seeing someone from her past. It was probably the continued silence from her parents getting to her on a subconscious level, having that intense need for support and familiarity.

'It's been busy,' Meg said. 'I've been working on and off, went to the cinema last night, been to the gym in the mornings.'

'And the flower shop with your parents on Tuesday,' Hannah said, sitting back in her chair and holding the warm mug with both hands. 'How was that?'

Meg wasn't sure how to tell Hannah what had happened without getting upset again. She knew – of course – that she could cry in front of Hannah, but every part of her just wanted to say she'd had a great time with her parents, and that everything was fine. Perhaps if she said it, she might be able to make it true.

'They didn't show up.'

'They what?'

'They just didn't come,' Meg said, looking at Hannah's confused face. 'They sent a text to say they couldn't and I ended up crying outside the florist's, which was embarrassing but the nice man in there, David, he invited me in and talked to me about it, and I felt a lot better.'

'Well I'm glad someone was nice to you,' Hannah said, reaching her hand out across the table to hold Meg's. 'But that's rubbish, Meg. I can't believe they did that.'

'Maybe they're just taking a while longer to get used to it?' Meg said, knowing her face wouldn't look like even she believed that. 'We are having quite a short engagement – maybe it will just take them a second.'

'Yeah,' Hannah said, in a sad tone of voice. She got it, of course, but Meg worried often if Hannah hated the situation they were in. When deciding on the wedding plans, Meg had deliberately wanted and pushed Hannah for them to get married that summer, and part of that had been the fact she was worried about her parents' involvement in the wedding. She had hoped, perhaps uselessly, a short run-up would minimize the chances of them being difficult.

'I mean they've come round before,' Meg said. 'Remember initially when they were funny about meeting you, and now we see them, well we see them quite regularly I guess.'

'Well I think we thought we'd see them more, now we've moved back to down the road from them, to be fair.' Hannah looked at her. 'We've not been round much since Christmas.'

'I guess not.'

'Sorry, Meg, I'm not meaning to, you know . . .'

'I get it . . . I do.' Meg put down her cutlery. 'Just what if they don't come to the wedding? Or what if they say they will – like at the flower shop – then leave me there embarrassed on the day? I'd be so upset, I don't know what I'd do.'

'I know.'

They sat in silence, and Meg felt like Hannah didn't know what to say. Maybe she should have told her earlier so she'd had time to prepare a pep talk.

'Anyway,' Meg said, smiling, putting their world back how it should be on a Saturday morning with the full promise of a weekend together ahead of them. 'You're back now, so it's fine. We can sort everything without them, and fix this together. It would have been nice to pick flowers with them but that's their choice.'

Hannah put her knife and fork down. 'Are you going to call them?'

'I'm too hurt right now, I think. They know where I am, and they left me on my own. They can contact me.'

'Look, about the being away . . .' Hannah looked at Meg with the face that said she was going to tell her something she did not want to hear. Meg could suddenly tell her mouth was hanging open so she closed it.

'What?'

'I wanted to tell you in person,' Hannah said. 'They've put me on the conference I told you about, which is great! Work-wise, it's . . . it's really good for me. It would mean I'm away quite a bit before the wedding. Maybe I shouldn't take it now, not if you . . .'

'You have to take it,' Meg said. 'You're so good at your job. It's an amazing opportunity.'

'Are you sure?'

'Of course!'

'But don't you need me?'

'I need you, of course, always,' Meg said. 'And your knowledge of events will be invaluable, but you'll be across all the decisions and I'll call you about things. I guess we need to both work to pay for the wedding, so it is what it is. I'll sort stuff out here. My job's so flexible, I really don't mind. And actually, I already have an idea.'

'Okay?' Hannah said. 'I'll be in Europe so I'll be on the phone to chat to you about things, and in the right time zone. What's your idea?'

'The man in the florist's, David, he offered to come to everything with me.' Meg saw surprise on Hannah's face, that she had managed to speak to the man for long enough for this to have happened. 'I think he felt sorry for me, well he definitely *did* feel sorry for me. I mean I was crying a *lot*, but he seemed to genuinely mean it. We really seemed to get on.'

'I think that's a great idea.' Hannah got up from her chair and starting tidying up the flat, now they had finished eating.

'Do you?'

'Of course,' Hannah said, taking Meg's plate. 'He always looked nice when we walked past the shop. Might even give you a discount.'

'Hannah!'

'I'm joking,' she said. 'What's he like?'

'He must be like mid-fifties,' Meg replied. 'He lives with his partner Mark who works at St Helens as a counsellor.'

'Did you ever know Mark, at school?'

'No, they moved here around the time I went to uni, I think.'

'Well, they sound great.'

'Yeah, David was amazing. It was mostly me talking but he seemed to really understand my situation.'

'I bet he will know his stuff,' Hannah said. 'He must work on weddings all the time.'

'That's true!'

'And if you are feeling a bit . . . stranded, I guess, when I'm not here, then starting to meet people is good. I know you've said that a few times now, and you expected friends just like the ones we've left in London . . . But maybe this is good. He can introduce you to people.'

'What if we don't make any other new friends for ages?' Meg asked, her worst fear about the move.

'Oh Meg.' Hannah came and stood behind Meg, rubbing her shoulders. 'Of course we will. We made friends at university and we made friends when we moved to London. It's just about putting ourselves out there. It'll get better when I'm at home more, I promise.'

'I miss the friends I already have,' Meg said. 'Sometimes I wish they hadn't all had babies so they could come and visit every week.'

'They will though, eventually,' Hannah replied. 'And in the meantime, we'll make friends here! It's normal to take time to find your community when you move to a new area.'

'I'm just worried the community here is all people like my parents.'

'It won't be,' Hannah said. 'You've already found one person who isn't.'

'That's true.' She looked up at Hannah, the love of her life, the woman she was going to marry. 'Do you think my parents will come to the wedding? Should I mentally prepare for, I don't even know, like, walking myself down the aisle? I always pictured . . . you know, all of it.'

Hannah looked sad as she sat down at the table again. She took Meg's hand in hers. 'I don't know, Meg. They should come. I mean I think it's wrong if they don't, but I also don't want them to cause stress around what is meant to be the biggest day of our lives.'

'And it's just a small wedding,' Meg said. 'It's not like I'm kissing you on a big screen in the shopping centre! I just thought they had got it, you know. Telling them we were engaged, I thought everyone was happy.'

'Me too.'

Meg looked at her. 'What?' She could tell something was up.

'No, nothing.'

'You were going to say something.'

'I don't want to make you more upset, but when we did go over to tell them, I did notice your mum give your dad a weird look.'

'Really?'

'Yeah, I didn't want to tell you in case I upset you, and it was for no reason.'

Meg didn't know what to say.

'She kind of seemed to say, like, *see I told you*, as if they thought, or hoped, we were never going to get married. I don't know.'

Meg felt a bit dizzy.

'It will be a perfect day,' Hannah continued, reaching for her again. 'Your parents will come round in the end, Meg. I know they're difficult, but all the times I've met them, I can see they love you so much. It's not about them anyway! It's about us becoming a family, officially. As long as we're both there, that's all we need.'

'You're right.'

'While they figure things out, you'll have had a great few months planning it all with this David guy, your new friend. It's all exciting!'

Hannah was so right and always had the magic touch in terms of being able to calm Meg down. Whether it was work or friends or just worrying about the state of the world, she was always there, like a warm blanket. Neither girlfriend nor partner ever felt like enough of a description of who she was to Meg. The newer term, fiancée, was closer but not quite right either, and she still changed which one she used at will.

'I know,' Meg said. 'Got to stay positive.'

'Do you want to go now, tell him you're in?'

'I'll pop in and tell him tomorrow.'

'Great,' Hannah said. 'Do you want me to come?'

'No, I'll do it,' Meg said. 'But I'll make sure you meet him soon.'

'Okay.'

'What shall we do today then?'

The window that had been subtly rattling in the background suddenly slammed shut, and one of the handles slipped slightly from where it should have been.

'Let's fix that bloody window.'

The next day, with Hannah at home working on the next few weeks' projects to get ahead, as the sun was beginning to dip below the tree line in the park, Meg was walking back up the high street from the supermarket, ready to make a detour.

When she arrived at the flower shop, its colourful awning was still out. She peeked inside. David was there, carefully bending down to spray some leaves of the biggest plants, and he was muttering to some of them. She watched him for a moment and before she knew it, she was inside the doors of the shop.

'Hi.'

David turned to face her, and put the spray bottle down. 'Meg!'

'Are you still free on Monday?' she asked.

David looked at her, surprised for just a second, before walking silently to the door to hug her.

'Of course!' he said, arms round her, beaming. 'I'd be honoured.'

'Only if you're sure! I know it's a big ask.'

'I'd eat cake with anyone, Meg. It's really not . . .'

'Sometimes I feel like I just have to do stuff alone,' Meg continued, feeling the emotions of the wedding stir inside her. 'Because I always have . . .'

'I understand that,' David said, his hands on her shoulders. 'But this time, you don't have to be alone. I'll come with you. Really. I'd be delighted.'

'Thank you so much.'

'It will be a great way to network with other small businesses too!' David smiled at her. 'So don't worry, I'll be getting something out of it.'

It seemed like David was only saying that for her benefit, but she appreciated his help all the same.

'Meet you here, ten o'clock?'

'Perfect.' David smiled at her. 'We're going to have so much fun! Where are we going? Do you want me to drive?'

'Oh, if you could,' Meg said. 'I still can't drive!'

'No worries. We can take the van.' He gestured outside. 'She's called Daisy. I apologize to you and her in advance for my parking. Anyone else in the vicinity at the time too, actually.'

'It's in Bletchley. Let me just look up the name again.' Meg scrolled through her phone trying to find it in her emails. 'Angie's Cakes – that's it.'

'I know her!'

'Do you?'

'She makes our cakes! You had her Viennese whirl actually,' David said. 'I'll make sure you pick the right flavours too. She can be a little . . . adventurous.'

'Great,' Meg said, looking over to the cakes on the counter, one of which was an unappealing green colour. 'I'll see you tomorrow!'

For the first time, Meg noticed the music playing quietly in the shop. One of her dad's favourite songs, by Robert Plant. She smiled.

'I'll see you tomorrow,' David said, picking up the spray bottle again. 'Bye, petal.'

5

DAVID

100 Days Until the Wedding

David felt embarrassed letting a stranger into Daisy the flower van. It felt like letting someone see inside your bathroom cabinet, or your fridge. She was a large Ford van, nothing special, apart from the flowers that an early iteration of the youth club had painted onto the side many years before that were now faded and chipped, and there were some hints of rust along the edges of the vehicle. It was rare that David had a reason for anybody besides him and Mark to be in the van. The driver's seat was, he realized as he sat down, surprisingly filthy. There were crumbs all over the seats, and staring at him from the floor were paper bags, empty cans of sugary drinks and something that seemed to have been a leaf once upon a time.

'Okay,' he said, doing up his seatbelt and checking the mirrors. 'Ignore the mess. Satnav says eighteen minutes. Have we got everything we need?'

'Just the address, I think,' Meg said. 'And us.'

'And a good appetite,' David said, starting the drive

down the long hill of the high street, waving to people as they passed. 'I hope you haven't had breakfast.'

'I haven't.'

'Perfect!' Meg squirmed as they went over a speed bump. 'So tell me about the wedding, from the top. What have you done already and what have you got left?'

'So we're not going very traditional,' Meg said. 'We want to do it all in a pub, so it's relaxed and we can just enjoy it.'

'That sounds wonderful.'

'There's not a lot of time, but we wanted it like that, and we can be flexible.' Meg seemed to be checking a list on her phone. 'I've lined up a few appointments already, like this and the bridal shop. I've already got the hair and make-up person for both of us. Maybe some people would think it's quite a small wedding, but neither of us have much family, so it's about sixty people, maybe seventy if some of Hannah's cousins come. I want to see everyone, you know, and have the memory, and *be married*, but I don't want all the fuss.

'And,' Meg continued. 'We're not having hen dos, or a joint one like people sometimes do, to save money. Which kind of means we don't need to have bridesmaids or maids of honour, or best women, which should hopefully make that side of it easier.'

'I didn't realize there were so many different names for that. When all my friends got married, it was all the same.'

'I've just seen so many fights and people annoyed in WhatsApp groups,' she said. 'One time, a mother of the bride sent a list of someone's friends, ranking how long she'd known them all, in order, and ever since then I've been hesitant.'

'Gosh.'

'We just thought,' Meg said, 'if we keep it to the main wedding day, we don't give anyone the opportunity for anything like that.'

The van slowed as David stopped to let people cross the road, before realizing it was his next-door neighbours, and he waved to them enthusiastically.

'I too have seen . . .' David began, struggling for the words. 'How do you say it . . . a wedding fallout?' He instantly realized he was stepping into territory that might make Meg upset again, telling a story about someone banning their own mother from their hen do, so he created another turn in the conversation.

'Mark thinks this is funny,' David said. 'He said I'm living through you and if I want a wedding I should just ask. I *think* he was joking.'

'How come you never married?'

David checked the rear-view mirror. 'I just never pictured it. We've been together nearly twenty years. We have the home and the business and we love each other, and that's commitment enough for me. I feel quite lucky already, you know.'

'I didn't imagine this when I was younger either,' she said. 'I actually used to imagine, you know, the husband, the kids, the dog.'

'It's okay for your expectations to change. What's normal changes as well, you know,' David said, indicating the wrong way for a roundabout before correcting himself. 'I wouldn't even have thought gay marriage was a possibility growing up, for anyone, let alone a possibility for me.'

It was true. It had felt like a fever dream the day it happened, watching the first gay weddings on the television, the celebrations on the streets, then the months going to the weddings of various friends. He wondered if it had had the same impact on Meg, since she'd grown up in such a different time.

'I guess,' Meg said, looking out at the window. 'Tell me about Mark. Do you think he still wants to get married?'

'Meg, Meg, Meg,' David said, chuckling to himself. 'Does the Pope have a balcony!'

Angie's Cakes had a tiny shopfront; a glass display window and, above it, lettering in pink against a purple background. As usual, David had trouble parking, but it was even more embarrassing with somebody else in the van. Soon, a queue was piling up behind him, but he was at too awkward an angle in the space to pull out and give up.

'I don't usually do this,' David muttered.

'That's okay,' Meg said. 'I can't even drive yet.'

'No, I mean, I usually get out and get a random man to help.'

'You don't?'

'I do! You'd be surprised by how much people want to help.' He looked up and down the street. 'There doesn't seem to be anyone around.'

By the time he'd finally nestled into the space, a couple of people far back were beeping their horns, and David ignored them, encouraging Meg to do the same. As they approached Angie's shop, there were the familiarly pleasant smells David looked forward to every time her deliveries arrived at the florist's. From the road, they could see all the goods on display, and Angie was standing behind them, serving at the counter, laughing with a customer and checking some kind of allergens sheet.

'Oh here they are!' she shouted as they walked in.

David had messaged ahead to say he was coming to the appointment, and he was touched by the way Angie removed her apron to come and hug both him and Meg, despite not knowing her at all. Her cockney accent filled any room, and she always wore loud colourful outfits and big earrings.

'I'll leave you to it, Sasha. Okay?' she said to a young, petrified-looking girl behind the counter, who was fiddling nervously with a pen and nodding.

Angie led them into the back room, which was much bigger, four times the size of the small front serving area. There were long sheet pans and metal racks lined up against the walls, crashing into each other loudly as a couple of people baked around them. David felt the heat of two huge industrial-sized ovens, and boxes of all different sizes piled up against the sides. On one wall, there was a neon sign that said LIVE, LAUGH, EAT CRUFFINS. Whenever he came here, David was always blown away by the volume of work that went into the tiniest treats out there in the shop, the sheer scale of it compared to Savage Lilies.

'The control room,' Angie said as they took their seats, nodding at all the activity that surrounded them. She was trying to brush flour off her trousers, but every time she touched her leg, she seemed to spread it from her hands to a new place.

'Thanks for seeing us,' Meg said.

'Oh no trouble at all,' Angie replied. 'And when I heard David Fenton was coming . . . what else could I do?'

'Today is about Meg; pretend I'm not here,' David said.

'How long have you two known each other then?' Meg asked, looking between the two of them.

'Ten years?' David said.

'It's eleven!' Angie replied. 'Since you moved here. How dare you play me down. We met, Meg, at a local gay bar down the road. David started chatting to the woman I was seeing at the bar. She's been gone eleven years but this one's stuck around. Couldn't get rid of him, not if I tried. Not if you paid me. Well if the price is right . . .' She laughed. 'Anyway, we should get down to the cakes! You don't want us going on, do you, Meg?'

'No, it's—'

'What sort of thing are you after? Big cake? Minis? Cup? Hit me.'

David watched the exchange, in awe always of how Angie managed to persuade you into what you actually wanted, rather than show any reserve. She transformed Meg's initial hesitant thoughts around a Victoria Sponge to three tiers: strawberry, chocolate and vanilla. Neapolitan Bride, Angie kept joking. To prove her point, she brought over a small tasting platter of six different flavours.

'It's your wedding, honey,' she continued, picking at the light yellowy cream of one of them. 'Don't give a damn what other people think, or want. If no one eats any, just means there's more for you afterward.'

'And it's good you've gone for the classics,' David said, and Angie started rolling her eyes at him. 'Don't give me that look. I'll never forgive the time I ate that courgette cake, thinking it was fudge!'

'It's good for people with intolerances! It's genuinely moist!' Angie was shaking her head.

'Thank you,' Meg said. 'I'm so glad I found you. This all looks wonderful. I'll have to buy something from out the front for my partner.'

'Anything you want, darling, glad I could help. I'll give you my queer customer discount too. We've got to support each other haven't we?'

'Thank you, that's so kind. You really don't have to if—'

'If you come to the till, we can settle up, unless you've got time for a cup of tea and a catch-up? I haven't got anywhere else to be, and Meg, I want to know how you ended up with David. What terrible luck!'

She cackled. David looked at Meg and of course they stayed put, because nobody could resist Angie, or her cakes.

An hour later, they'd had two cups of tea each and finished the samples. David felt fit to burst. In terms of conversational topics, they had covered Meg's parents, a situation that Angie had been genuinely sweet and insightful over, talking about her own parents who still lived in Kingston, Jamaica. Angie shared the story of her recent bad date that Carl had mentioned earlier in the week. She never failed to make David laugh, telling him a story of getting her bag caught in a revolving door and trying to style it out.

'Do you live with anyone, Angie?' Meg asked, after Angie had mentioned her house next door.

'No, just me,' she said. 'Single Ange, that's what this lot call me.'

'No we don't,' David muttered. 'Well Mark sometimes . . .'

'I used to foster,' she explained. 'For a while, but when I opened up here, it's not the sort of hours you can do and be responsible for a child. Which is a shame. I found it was important for black kids to be put with me, you know. I got them in a way I think others didn't. I often think about starting again.'

'That's so impressive, Angie.'

'I loved it, I really did. Maybe older kids could come and stay; that could work. Maybe one day.'

'She was great with them,' David said. 'Made such a difference, as I'm sure you can imagine.'

'Oh stop it, you,' she said. 'I'll cry. I miss every single one. *They* never complained about courgette cake.'

'You know that's not true . . .'

'Anyway, I've just remembered something that can change the subject,' Angie said. 'We didn't talk about the outside of the cake! The look!'

'Oh, of course!' Meg said.

'Do you have a colour scheme for the day?'

'Not really.'

'What are the bridesmaids wearing?'

'We don't have any bridesmaids.'

'That's okay, that means you can do anything.' Angie looked around the room for inspiration. 'I could do rainbow?'

'Oh no, just plain please.'

Angie looked at her with one eyebrow up. 'Plain?'

'Erm . . .'

'You can't do plain on your wedding. Not from Angie's Cakes, at least. What's your favourite colour?'

'Green, actually.'

'We could do a green cake . . . We could make—'

'Not the avocados, Ange,' David said.

'Why don't you think about it?' Angie said. 'We've got time. Ask Hannah. I'll have a think too.'

'Okay, I will.'

'I'll send you some things we've done before, pictures and examples. I've got them in a folder. Right, I'd better go out and check on the shop,' she said, walking back into the store. 'Sasha probably left hours ago.'

'I can't believe you know all these people,' Meg said, wiping icing off her lip, as David watched Angie rejoin a relieved Sasha.

'Oh, just wait,' David said. 'There are gays everywhere round here, if you know where to look. We'll work through the rest of your list, work out who you've got left, see if I know anyone else too. I've just worked out how to start a Facebook group, so I've started inviting queer businesses in the area to join. I hadn't realized there were quite so many great places, run by such brilliant, creative people.'

'I can't imagine it's easy setting up a small business.'

'Not at all. You really have to want it, and work to keep it.'

'Like this place?'

'Like this place, exactly. Angie was working as an assistant in some boring company when I met her. First in, last out. She used to run her office bake-off, and she'd win every time. We all kept saying she had talent. Eventually this place happened. Started off half the size, did a small trade. She fought, she advertised. Knocked down that back wall, all while still fostering.'

'Where did you meet them all then, these friends?' Meg said. 'Just by chance?'

'Not really,' David said, shaking his head. 'When Mark and I moved here, we'd been together nearly ten years and we knew we wanted to set down roots, and feel part of the community. We made sure we didn't say no to things,' David said. 'I've never really said no, to be honest. I've just always benefited from letting people in. I didn't go out to make twenty friends, but then, through work and all, suddenly you've got a birthday every other weekend.'

'It's so nice. Is Mark the same?'

'We're both really social, which is good. We'd go mad, the lives we have, if one of us was an introvert. No, I love people.'

'Me too,' Meg said, smiling at him.

He really felt like he'd done something right today. Helped out someone in need and also helped his friend get a sale for her business. He felt invincible. Normally for a day like that, he'd reward himself with a sweet treat but he'd really had his fill.

'Shall we go through?'

They walked back into the main shop, where Sasha was being taught something at the coffee machine. On the counter, David spotted a Marmite roulade.

'I should warn you,' he whispered to Meg, their voices covered by the hiss of the steam wand. 'Read the labels carefully. Unless Hannah likes kidney beans.'

That afternoon, as the shop was winding down for the day, David was alone with his thoughts. Songs by the Black Eyed Peas were playing through the speakers, one of the bands or artists that due to the playlist's theme, he had become an unusually intense fan of. They, along with Blossoms, Robert Plant, Lily Allen, all had entire discographies on the playlist. Early on David had realized there weren't quite enough songs for an nine-hour day, seven days a week, that followed the theme, and he was wondering if there were any songs written about daffodils when Benji arrived for their agreed meeting.

He was wearing a sports top and jeans, with sun-white trainers without even a speck of dirt on them. Despite having turned sixteen, he had that gangly look of a teenager who thought they were the most confident they could ever be, but that you could see right through. He always seemed to be okay in motion, but awkwardly standing still in the doorway of the shop, not sure what to do with his limbs, he seemed as young as he'd been when David had first met him. He had short brown hair, cropped close to his skin, and one earring, and he smiled as David noticed him.

'Benji!'

'Your favourite one's here,' Benji said, bowing. 'Don't worry, I won't tell the others.'

'Stop it. How was your weekend?'

'Yeah, good actually,' Benji said. He put out his hand for a fist-bump and David awkwardly clasped it with his palm.

'Are you going to tell me what you got up to?'

'Oh,' Benji said, before seriously thinking. 'Nothing really.'

David couldn't work out whether he was hiding something from David he wouldn't want to hear, or whether he genuinely had had a boring time. 'Well, I'm always here, if you want somewhere to go.'

'I know, I know,' Benji said, slightly exasperated. 'Thanks, man,' he said, recognizing David's gesture.

'No worries, man,' David said.

'You can't pull that off, you know.'

'Can Mark?'

'Even less than you.'

'Well there's something,' David said, before putting a glass of Diet Coke in front of both of them.

'I know you've got beers back there.'

'And when you're eighteen, you can come buy one,' David said. 'Now, what did you want to chat about? Mark said it's getting close to deciding about careers and studying after your GCSEs.'

'Not studying,' Benji said. 'I'm done with school. I want to earn money.'

Despite a difficult upbringing and the challenges he'd faced in school, Benji seemed to be enjoying studying for his GCSEs, often talking about the books he'd read in English and his love of maths. He'd once told David he knew more than the Business Studies teacher, and made an unflattering link between the acronym for Business Studies and the man who taught it.

'That's fine,' David said. 'It's good to know what you want.'

'But I don't know how to get the kind of job I'd like,' Benji said. 'I already work at the barber's in town, but I don't want to do that forever. I want a proper job.'

'Well what would you count as a proper job?' David asked. 'Maybe we start there and work back?'

'I don't want to be a teacher,' he said. 'No offence.'

'I'm not a teacher.'

'No but you're . . . you're like a teacher.'

'I won't ask what that means Benji.'

'I wanted to be an influencer, but I think that's hard, man. Embarrassing too, some of the stuff they make you do.'

'I wouldn't know,' David said.

Benji rolled his eyes, as if he was talking to his grandad. 'Right.'

'I'd do like photography or something, like in a studio?' Benji said. 'I know I don't want to sit in an office all day, but I don't want part-time work, or like trying a job here and there. I want like money coming in each month, so I can move out.'

He looked a bit sheepish about this. There was a candidness to Benji that came out occasionally, and when it did, it felt like he was asking for something from the grown-ups in his life, something he'd never been given before.

'That makes sense, Benji,' David said. 'There's nothing wrong with just wanting to pay your bills, and not being a footballer or whatever.'

'I'm not four years old. I know I'm not gonna be a footballer.'

'I know, I know,' David said, leaning forward over the table to rest his elbows on it. 'I just meant . . . doesn't matter. You know what would be useful – why don't you come back next week, with three jobs you'd want to do, and we'll look at how people got to do them. It's hard to start with all the jobs in the world. It can be daunting.'

'Okay.'

'I'll get Jacob to arrange a time. It's all meant to go through the youth club officially.'

'Can't you just message me? I've known you for five years; I know you're not a psycho.'

'Well thank you, Benji,' David said, laughing. 'I know I'm not either, and for what it's worth I don't think you are, but there's still time to be proved wrong.'

Jacob had said that at sixteen, the kids were now allowed to contact volunteers as they wished, and Benji was right, they did genuinely know each other. He supposed that was probably fine.

'Go on, let me, Dave. What's your social media handle? I'll message you.'

'I don't have social media, Benji.'

'All right, well what's the shop's social media? I'll get you through there.'

'We don't have that either.'

'You what, man?' Benji said. He looked at him like he'd just told him he'd once landed on the moon. 'Are you joking?'

'I'm not.'

'You need social media,' Benji said decisively. 'How are people gonna find you?'

'Well they'll see the sign and . . .' David's words mumbled into nothings as Benji shook his head at him.

'Let me do it!' Benji said. 'I'll set up an account now.'

'Oh, I don't know . . .'

'I'll do it!'

'I can't pay you, Benji. I don't want you to . . .'

'I'll do it as a favour. It's honestly nothing, man. I'll take a couple pics. Chill.'

'Only if you're sure . . .'

David felt like he was letting something happen he'd have no control over, but if anything could bring a few more people into the shop that could only be a good thing. The majority of his regular older customers would probably never see it anyway, and Benji was already looking around the shop, head full of plans.

'You have to let me. I've got big ideas.'

David looked at Benji, his fervour to do things, and he wondered if channelling his energy into this would be a good thing for him. Who was David to stand in the way? He'd had that scary meeting with the accountant and they really did need to boost profits. Maybe this is what David should have been doing for a long time.

'All right, Benji. But set it up on my device as well so I

can see it too, all right? And let me know regularly what you're doing.'

Benji was laughing, shaking his head. 'Device,' he muttered, laughing, taking David's phone from his hand.

'And you can have my number,' he said. 'But don't sign it up to that toilet paper delivery thing you did with Jacob.'

'That was years ago!' Benji said. 'But it was funny . . .'

6

MEG

95 Days Until the Wedding

Meg arrived at David's shop after a long day of drawing. People always asked if her hand hurt from the strain, but she must have built up the right muscles. No, it was her brain, rather than her body, that seemed spent from the effort of concentrating in that way all day.

She took a moment before going in. She had never really stopped and looked at the shop from this angle but it was as inviting as a place was possible to be. Green, luscious plants filled the windows, dotted with flowers providing drops of colour, and the gold-foil sign on the door, *Savage Lilies*, was classy but modern. Even from the outside, everything felt fresh and real, so different to how some of the other, more boring shops presented themselves. You wanted to reach in and touch what was on display and the bright green paint and the strips of pride-flag stripes brought the place to life.

'You must be so proud of this place,' Meg said as David came to the door. She stepped over a bit of felled fence that

David seemed to have driven over. 'It's so nice to have a proper florist's round here.'

'It's everything to me,' David said. 'It's the kind of place people would be sad to miss . . .'

'Are you always busy?'

'We get a lot of browsing but not enough buying. We've lost so much custom to the internet, you know. Order now from home and it's there tomorrow, or there in nine hours. We're hoping our approach is different enough to keep us relevant. I guess we'll wait and see.'

Inside, a young man was behind the till, quietly on his phone, and David led Meg towards the back of the shop, patting the boy on the shoulder as he passed.

'That's Ray,' David said. 'Used to be in the youth club; now he's at college but he works around us when we need.'

'That's nice,' Meg said. 'How long have you been involved with the club?'

'Eight years ago. We'd been living here a few years. Mark was already helping. This town . . . there are lots of different kinds of people. Some of the parents, through no fault of their own, aren't there for their kids. For others, it's an additional social thing outside of school and sports and things. That's what a community is, I guess. Everyone mixing. It's not always easy, but every year, it's worth it.'

Meg wondered how she might be able to get involved in something like that. Best get the wedding out of the way, she thought, and then embed herself here. She wondered what she might be able to offer; their flat wasn't big enough, and at thirty, did she really have any wisdom to impart?

'Anyway *finally* it's my expertise,' David said, rolling out a notepad in front of him. 'Well cakes are too, but flowers, that's what I really know about. Flowers for *your wedding*. What would you like?'

'I actually really don't know,' Meg said. 'Sorry.' She laughed. 'I'm happy to be guided. I don't really know flowers. Just like I don't know cake, or candles, or dresses, really. It's all a bit of a learning curve, this, isn't it?'

'Okay, maybe we start a different way.'

'How do you usually start?' Meg asked. She thought back to all the weddings she had been to over the years. They were definitely the last of her and Hannah's friends to take the plunge, and the two of them had been to a variety of weddings over the last year alone, in London, Edinburgh and Cornwall. They had always been classy, and in terms of flowers, there'd been some in the ceremony, some on the tables, and the bouquet, of course. They had seemed to match, but she had never really known how people knew what they wanted. All those weddings had been for straight couples, and she hadn't really thought about where hers and Hannah's wedding might fit in.

'You can start with a few things,' David said. 'Budget, colours, size, or a type of flower you really like. I mean, you can start anywhere really. I normally suggest people wander round the shop, pick up on the things they like, the things they don't; that's equally important. Then we can put things together if they work or I'll show you what goes with each flower and what each thing might look like. Is there anything Hannah wanted in particular?'

'She wanted colourful,' Meg said. 'But I think our tastes meet somewhere in between. I don't want it to look, well you know, you don't want it all clashing, do you?'

David looked at her, and she wondered what he was about to suggest. He looked like he was sizing her up.

'Why don't you tell me what you're drawn to?'

They stood up and walked round the shop. Meg felt a bit silly, wondering what her preferences said about her to this man she was only just getting to know. She said no to the 'queer bouquets' he had in a bucket in the window, which were tied with thin pride-flag ribbons. 'I just want,' she said. 'Like . . . these are nice?' She pointed out the mixed-colour roses, reds, whites and pinks, which looked like what people had for weddings. 'I know Hannah said not boring,' she continued. 'But some white roses, too, in the mix, I think would be nice and classic.'

'Okay.'

'These are nice.' She pointed to the table in the middle of the room, paint-spattered and covered with crumbs of mud. There were small jam-jars of cartoon-like orange flowers, and round dandelion-like plants in a dark purple. 'Would this all be too many colours? Or is it nice?'

'Not if you like them,' David said. 'And if Hannah wants colour, a lot of these might work, in with the roses?'

'Oh those are nice.'

'You're saying nice a lot.'

'I thought flowers were supposed to be nice!'

'They can be,' David said. 'But some can be unpalatable to people who don't like them. Some people hate lilies; some people hate roses. Flowers can be a burst of expression, or a real huge show of a feeling, or of so many different feelings. Flowers can mean anything, really.'

'Do you think what flowers you have . . . does it say much about you?' Meg asked. 'Like do people know that roses mean something, or whatever these ones are?'

'I'd say, first of all, don't ever worry about what other people think,' David said, smiling. Meg flushed with embarrassment. She couldn't help herself; she always thought of what other people might say, and it wasn't even the first time today somebody had said that to her. Her friend Ailie had been on the phone at lunch and told her to stop thinking so much about what her parents thought. 'Mark always says: *those who mind don't matter, and those who matter don't mind*. He loves a phrase. It's annoying, and don't tell him this, not even once, but he *is* always right.'

Meg smiled.

'But that gets easier with age . . . Anyway, flowers do have meanings!' he continued. 'But most people won't know the backstory; they'll just know the flower makes them feel a certain way. It's almost like astrology, how deep you can go into it. In Victorian times, you could answer yes-or-no questions with flowers, with how you passed them to people, for example. Now, that's all fallen away, but different flowers have different associations still. Roses are romantic, of course, but they've been known to indicate the lines between pleasure and pain. A yellow rose is actually supposed to signify infidelity.'

'Gosh.'

'So maybe not those,' David said laughing. 'They're a bit obvious too. Zinnia's a good one for weddings. It means absent friends and lasting affection, and salvias actually, they're about everlasting love. Camellias are for inner strength. Maybe those?'

David indicated towards a batch of flowers in another bucket on the other side of the room. They weren't packaged in a perfect bouquet, but loose and ready to be made into something beautiful. Their petals were a kind of textured white, like bed sheets.

'I like these.'

'I've always liked them,' David said. 'Not a big seller, but I try to get people to include them where I can. Actually, I might have . . .'

He looked under the counter before walking into the back room. After a minute, he came back in holding a big dusty laminated book, which he thumped down onto the table.

'I got this when I first got serious about opening Lilies,' he said. 'Mark was encouraging me, said I'd need to know stuff like this. Pick a flower for you and Hannah, then I'll show you mine and Mark's.'

Meg sat for a few minutes, looking at the book. It had a full page for every major flower, with a big index at the back, and she took her time to pick things with meanings that she liked. For Hannah, she chose a freesia, which represented friendship and trust. Hannah was really loyal, and trusting in people, so it fitted. For herself, Meg chose lavender, which she had always loved. Amongst the obvious things like calm and serenity, the book said the plant represented luxury, and Meg always thought that was what she liked about them. They felt like a treat, whether in flower form or in the pillow mist Hannah always bought her for Christmas, and if there was any day to feel like you were being treated to luxury, it had to be your wedding day.

'What are yours and Mark's?'

'His is tulips,' David said. 'They're about fame and true love. I feel like Mark's semi-famous around here. Everyone knows him, and everyone thinks he's so funny. He does have that kind of star quality. That's what drew me to him in the first place.'

'And yours?'

'I'm a bit of a daffodil,' David said, smiling. 'New

beginnings and sunshine. They always remind me it's never too late to start again.'

'That's lovely.'

'People think Mark and I are both tulips,' he said. 'Our friend Matty said that when we played this game, but Mark's the tulip, really. He's the one that's unfailingly optimistic. I can be a little more melancholy. Not often, but sometimes.'

David said he'd order in some of the plants she'd liked and she could pick from there. Meg was impressed at how easily he alleviated the stress of the wedding and how well they worked together.

With business out of the way, Meg offered to help David close down the shop. It was the least she could do. Ray had finished a long time ago. 'Seems a waste to pay him for stuff I could just do, you know, with how much everything costs nowadays,' he said. He waved away Meg's suggestion.

'Go on, let me help.'

When she insisted, he passed her a broom. 'Closing down is my least favourite part of the job.'

'How so?' she asked.

'I like the morning, when everything's possible, and you're making it all more exciting. In the evening, you're packing down. You're making the shop more boring.'

'My parents have an old friend who's a florist,' Meg said, a memory she'd entirely forgotten until she remembered him turning up to her parents' place, a large bouquet of almost comically large sunflowers flung over his arm. 'William. He's a bit more serious though, does it all out of his house, no café; always made it feel like much more of a job, much more of something you can do well or badly.'

'I like to make it fun,' David said. 'Got to give people a reason to come in. Flowers can be the first thing to cut when times get tough, but the way they can brighten up a day? There's nothing more important.'

'I agree with you there.'

They must be coming to the end of it now, since David was cleaning the floor and she had nothing left to tidy.

'So before last week happened, did you see your parents much? Their friends, people like that?'

'We've been living in London ever since I graduated so we'd see them, you know, birthdays and Christmas, come to stay in summer and stuff. We didn't do that all the time. They never came to us. They're quite . . . what's the word? They're homebodies.'

'That happens as you get older,' David said.

'They've always been like that.'

'Oh.'

Meg remembered Saturday nights at home and how if they ever went to the cinema, it was only in the daytime. What had felt like normal life to her was actually a fairly rigid routine, with set mealtimes and unmovable rules. It was only at university that she had ever had the experience of getting home after dark, or planning to do something that day that she hadn't known about when she woke up.

'I didn't move back here expecting to be at theirs every night, but we thought it would be nice, me and Hannah, to be somewhere one of us had grown up. Of course, you get more for your money than in London, so we could finally buy a place too.'

'How have you found it, since you moved back?'

'It feels the same to me as ten years ago,' she said. 'I'm sure we'll make it homely, and I'm sure we'll meet more people, but those things take time, right? For now, it feels a little like I've gone backwards. Annoyed at my parents, seeing the same old sights.' She put the broom in its place behind the counter and hung up her apron. 'All done?'

'I should move the van,' David said. 'So there's space for the delivery driver in the morning, but I can do that later. Or, better yet, I can make Mark do it.'

'Where did you grow up?' Meg said. 'I realized I never asked.'

'I've lived all over,' David said. 'Many places, many lives. Grew up near Glastonbury, actually. Then I was in Manchester, and all over there, working different jobs for many years. Then I was in Wakefield, and met Mark. We lived in Sheffield for a little bit, then Chester, then here we are. The accents seem to have all balanced each other out.'

'Would you ever move again?'

'I still get itchy,' he said. 'But not now we have the shop. I'd never give this up.'

'Oh, hello? Sorry I'm late.'

The voice came from the doorway and it followed round to where they were standing, and Meg assumed the man now standing in front of them must be Mark. He was taller than David, and thinner, with thick-set dimples on both his cheeks. His smile was infectious, and he had well-groomed dark hair combed to the side. In one ear was a tiny gold pearl-shaped earring, and he was carrying a tiny bag over one shoulder.

'Hi, I'm Mark,' he said, coming closer to shake her hand.

'I'm Meg,' she said. 'I feel like I know you already, but it's so nice to meet you.'

'I feel the same,' he said, beaming. 'Congratulations on the wedding! How did today go?'

'Oh we've been busy,' said David, coming round to kiss Mark on the cheek, and he stood with his arm protectively around his waist. 'Cakes, flowers, coffee.'

'Sounds awful,' Mark said. 'Such hardship.'

Meg watched and, despite being together for about twice as long as her and Hannah, the pair were tactile and still clearly obsessed with each other. When each spoke, the other watched expectantly and with a smile, like they were encouraging them. There was a lightness about the two of them, like they knew what they had was good and that in here, they were entirely relaxed.

'So, Meg,' Mark said. 'Tell me everything. How did you and Hannah meet, and how long have you been together?'

'Oh it's a lovely story,' David said. 'They—'

'Maybe Meg would like to tell it,' Mark said, smiling at Meg.

'I don't mind,' Meg said, laughing. 'Feel like we've told each other our life stories the last few days.'

'Don't get David started; he'll get the memoirs out. And at our age, there's a few books to get through. No, Meg, tell me about *you!* I've heard such nice things.'

Mark was clearly tired from a long week, but seeing a stranger, someone important to David, meant he stopped and asked questions and threw himself into somebody else's life. She could imagine it took effort and patience to do that, rather than rushing to lie down at the end of the day, like Meg knew she would be keen to in his shoes.

'We were both on the same course at university,' she said. 'So young, even though you don't feel it then, and illustration is very . . . there's a few hours a week together but you're left to do your own work most of the time. So you don't really see your course mates. We bumped into each other in a café off-campus where we were both trying to get our heads down and work, and then that became every Thursday morning for a few weeks. I thought we were just friends, but she thought we were flirting.'

'I know that feeling,' Mark said.

'Seems like we have the same story,' David said.

'You can slow burn at eighteen; you can't at thirty-five . . .'

'We didn't slow-burn Mark. We were . . . anyway.'

'Yes, anyway, Meg,' Mark said. 'So then how did it change?'

'It wasn't until one really miserable day in February when she asked me to get dinner with her that evening, and then I knew it was a date. I had a few hours to completely freak out, since it was my first date with a girl. I had no idea what to wear, but it was so great.'

'And then you were girlfriends?' Mark said.

'Pretty much,' Meg said. 'Now, a decade-ish later, fiancées. The engagement was very low-key, but it was perfect.'

'That's lovely, Meg,' Mark said, who was now resting against a chair in the window. 'I'm sorry about your parents too, if you don't mind me saying that. They'll come around. David might have mentioned, I work at St Helens.'

'Of course! So do you know them?'

'No, no,' he said. 'I mean the counsellor works very separately from the teachers. I just know they've both been really nice whenever I've dealt with any of their pupils and we've had to talk. I'm just sorry it's all been so . . . I don't know, is "difficult" the right word?'

Meg smirked. 'You could say that.' She felt strange. It was one thing to be talking about her parents in the abstract, it was another to talk about them with someone who had more daily contact with them than her. Anything could be happening with them, and she wouldn't know.

'Are you okay?' David asked.

'Yeah, I just think . . . they are nice, that's the problem. They're so good with kids. I've seen it. I just think it's different with your own child, you know. You have blind spots. I don't think they've ever known how to deal with me.'

It was hard to know what to do but the thought of her parents invaded every section of her life. Just when she'd distracted herself enough, here they were again, with the ongoing problem that was going to be hers to solve.

'Have you spoken to them since that day at the shop?' Mark asked.

'Still nothing, and I still don't feel like I should text them first.'

'I think that's fair.'

'It makes me worried. What if when me and Hannah start a family, like when I want our kids to have their grandparents in their lives . . . And what if it means I'll be a bad parent?'

They both moved towards her. 'That won't happen,' Mark said.

'You'd be an amazing parent,' David added.

'Thank you,' Meg said, wiping tears from her face. 'God, crying again!'

'They'll come round,' David said. 'And until then, for your sins, you've got me.'

'Thanks, David.'

'And we've just met of course,' Mark said. 'But you've got me too.'

'Thank you.' She exhaled, and shook her head. 'Right, I'd best be off. Thanks for today. I'll leave you both to it.'

'I'll message you,' David said. 'About the food festival.'

'That sounds good,' Mark said.

'You'll need to cover the shop so I can go, Mark.'

'Oh.'

'Oh, and Meg,' David said. 'I should book your wedding in! I can't believe I've forgotten the most important bit. Make sure I'm around on the day itself to deliver and come and do all the flowers . . . Give me the date again?'

'It's the last day of June,' she said. 'It's a Sunday.'

'That's what? About three months away!' Mark said. 'How exciting!'

'Obviously come to the actual day too, if you can? I'll give you two spaces.'

'Thank you,' Mark said. 'That's very kind.'

'I'll message when those orders come in,' David said, checking his phone. 'I use this weather app; it's the most accurate one. I tested them all, don't worry.'

Meg could see Mark rolling his eyes affectionately: 'He checks this at least once an hour.'

'Everything is always slightly weather-dependent, but all looks good for everything you wanted, seasonally, and we can always tweak the week of, forecast-dependent.'

'Thanks, David.'

'Oh Mark, Benji came in for that meeting,' David said, turning to his partner. 'We're having another chat next week, but he actually offered to do social media for the shop.'

'And you said yes?' Mark said.

'I couldn't exactly say no!'

'David . . .'

'Who's Benji? Meg asked. She got her phone out of her pocket and flashed up the shop's Instagram page for them. 'I saw this earlier,' she said. 'I thought it was you, David.'

'He's from the youth club,' Mark said, taking the phone and looking at it. 'I wouldn't think this is David. I've never seen him manage to download an app by himself.'

'Well I did think you'd probably had help with the caption,' Meg said. 'I didn't think you'd call something "lit".'

'Do you think it's a good idea, Meg?' Mark said.

'Yeah of course,' she said. 'Everywhere has social media now.'

'But probably from a professional,' Mark said.

'Why don't you give it a few weeks?' Meg said. 'You were saying the shop needed more customers; hopefully this helps. If nothing happens, you can suggest he stop. He might get bored anyway, if he's what, a teenager?'

'That's true,' Mark said.

'Anyway, I'd better go. Work to do at home. Bye, guys,' Meg said. 'Have a good night.'

She walked to the door and left, closing it softly behind her. She turned back quickly to wave to David who had followed her to the door to turn the sign – a daffodil with a small chalkboard in the middle section – from OPEN to CLOSED.

Against all the odds, another successful day.

7

DAVID

Back in the flat, David and Mark were surrounded by the smells of an open jar of crushed garlic, fresh chillies from the garden herb pots on the windowsill and sizzling sesame oil that Mark was heating up in the pan. They cooked together every evening, or most evenings, in a synchronicity that had surprised each of them when it first started. It was only for a treat that one of them would get to relax while the other prepared a full meal, or if Mark had to stay much later at work, or David was running an event downstairs. Birthdays, sometimes. There was something about it that made the best jobs (slicing) twice as fun and the worst jobs (washing up pans) half as hard.

'So Meg's lovely,' Mark said, beginning to stir finely diced spring onions and garlic into the pan.

'Isn't she!' David replied, running carrots across a mandoline. 'I feel so sorry for the stuff with her parents, but she'll have a great day. I'll make sure of it.'

The flat was a good size, for the two of them. When they had been looking for a place to live and a location for the shop, at first they had thought it would be nice to live separately from the business, and to be able to escape a little. When Number Fifty-Six had come up, they had both decided it felt right, and now they were happy they'd made the choice to have everything on their doorstep. They could so easily go for a drink, and their fish and chips was always warm when they got it home because it was, David had calculated, just a forty-two-second walk from shop to sofa.

The kitchen was painted white and opened onto the living room, which had two large windows that were great for people-watching onto the street. Some people might call it busy, the way they liked to have everything on show in the house, but there was a reason, David thought, for all their knick-knacks and photos and all the parts that made up their lives to be on full display. Off the hall were two bedrooms; one for them, and another which always had a clothes horse up ready for the change of sheets for their ever-rotating cast of friends who came to stay.

'Do you think you might be so keen to help her because it reminds you of your parents?'

David knew Mark had been thinking that thought downstairs. There were very few subtleties you could get past a partner of nearly twenty years, and he had been wondering when Mark was going to bring this up.

'I guess it just makes me more likely than your average Joe to help her, since I've been through a similar thing.'

'And Joe wasn't available.'

'Exactly.'

David rolled his eyes.

There was a pause, and then Mark looked at David and spoke again. 'Just make sure you're looking after yourself and not taking on too much.' He reached out a hand to David. 'This feels very much like repeating your childhood, and what if they suddenly come around and then you're out of the picture?'

'We always say it's more important to help someone in need, more important than anything else.'

'I know, David, but we're getting older,' Mark said, putting down the wooden spoon into its little resting spot on the counter. 'We're already so busy with the youth club. It's nearly summer, and that means marshalling the Race For Life, that school fete you usually do. You can do anything, but you can't do everything.'

'I'll be okay,' David said, stroking Mark's arm. It was another of the sayings Mark loved that he had heard a million times. 'I appreciate the concern, but it'll be a few hours a week. You never know, her parents might change their minds tomorrow.'

'As long as you're not upset if they do that . . .'

'I won't be.'

'From what I know of Mr and Mrs Kirby, I don't know how likely it is that they will change their minds. They're quite scary at school, and she can be quite stubborn. I didn't want to say that in front of Meg.'

Mark continued to stir and though David sensed there was something else he wanted to say, he changed the subject instead.

'How's business?'

'What was that?' David had definitely heard, but sometimes he found himself answering as if he hadn't, in order to buy himself a little more time.

'The shop, the floristry side . . . is it picking up?' Mark asked, now concentrating on cooking strips of chicken so they were browned enough, but not too much. 'I know you said the accountant was a bit full on when you saw her, but I haven't had the full story. Meg made it sound like you were worried?'

David sighed. He hated to worry Mark, or to make the shop his problem, but he knew it was the right thing to do and he knew Mark, of course, would want to help him. 'It's bad, Harry said. You know I've been trying so many different things, but nothing's really taken off. I keep wasting the seasonal bouquets. I only ever sell a couple.'

'What else did Harry say?'

'I think she enjoyed the whoopie pie from Angie more than she enjoyed sorting through my filing system but . . .'

'Did you charge her for that?'

'Who are you, HMRC?'

'David . . .'

'It's all fine! Anyway, the numbers. The topline is that the events that were keeping us steady are falling, but we can't just increase prices anymore. We're down on funeral flowers, so I've been looking at what we can do.'

'Well down on funeral flowers . . . I guess I can only say that's a good thing.'

'But also down on weddings and christenings. Birthdays too. Valentine's was down a quarter on the year before.'

'Sorry David.'

'Houseplants are holding strong,' David said. 'But the margins on those are tiny. Day-to-day buying is a bit down, across everything. I've put on more events and am looking at what other businesses might want to use the space. I'm going to reach out on that queer business network I'm building.'

'That's a good idea,' Mark said. He was shaking the pan vigorously to coat the contents evenly in the sauce he'd made, but his voice was calming and tender. He reached out his arm towards David. 'It might take time, but you'll get there. What's the network called?'

'I don't have a name yet. Let me know if you think of one.' David had finished laying the table. 'Benji said opening the network up to allies too might help with forming *collabs* or whatever he called them. I thought it might also be a good way to meet people for Meg's wedding, as well as the shop.'

'It's a good idea,' Mark said. 'As long as it doesn't distract from the shop. The social media thing could be good too I guess, but don't just follow what Benji says without thinking about it. It's your shop and you know it better than anyone. What if we alienate the older crowd that have been buying from you for over a decade?'

'Is this because Benji told you you couldn't pull off a backwards cap?'

Mark flashed him a grin. 'It's possible.'

David came to hug Mark from behind, resting his head on his partner's shoulder.

'I know Benji's a bit, I don't know, unpredictable,' David said. 'But he's older now and I think this will be good for him. We might go viral!'

'That doesn't sound good.'

'Mark, viral is a good thing.'

'Like when things are sick now?'

'Exactly.'

'Or when Benji said something was dope and you had that conversation with Jacob about drugs?'

'Trust me,' David said. 'I'm trying things. Harry said at current estimations I've got about five months and then we'd have to start winding things down.'

Mark was shocked. 'I had no idea it was this bad . . .'

'Everywhere's struggling, but with everything we do in the shop, the margins are so tight . . . But . . . I'm not going down without a fight.'

'I'm sure you're not, David, but—'

'No buts,' David interrupted. 'I've got Ray, Benji, the business network, you. How could I fail with that dream team?'

'All right.' Mark put the plates of steaming food down on the table. 'Just earmark that money we wanted for a holiday next year . . . I think we could both do with one.'

They sat down to eat, as they always did: a candle lit in the middle of the table, and no music, just the two of them together. They chatted about the news and the book David was struggling to finish. Mark talked about his sister's new job, and how his mum was persuading her to go part-time, so she could spend more time with her children, his niece and nephew, in their teenage years before they left the house.

After they were finished, they both stood up to complete the task of the clean-up. David began to wash up, since Mark had done the bulk of the cooking.

'Oh and remember Saturday next week, we've got the youth club careers night downstairs,' Mark said. 'You said you'd prepare something.'

'Yeah, of course. I won't forget,' David said, though he definitely had. 'Looking forward to it.'

'Okay, thanks.'

'Since I'm doing the washing-up,' David said tentatively. 'I guess someone else needs to take the bin out.'

'I hate taking the bin out!'

'So do I, Mark, but I'm preoccupied with all this, and everything with Lilies.' He indicated the chopping boards and pans. 'I can do *anything*,' he said. 'But I can't do *everything*.'

Mark threw the tea towel at him and went to get his shoes.

8

MEG

83 Days Until the Wedding

Campbell Park was about twenty minutes from Meg's, right in the centre of Milton Keynes. It sat just down from the shopping centre and the main blocks that made up the city and, in contrast to the grey industrial vibe of the city centre, all concrete and road, the park was lush and green, manicured into sections and pathways, and, mercifully for David, the parking was easy.

Meg was walking with David down into the middle where there was a small business and street food festival happening over the next few weekends. Already, Meg could smell some sort of tomato and cheese scent on the air, and offset against the calm natural green of the park's trees were bright, loud neon signs, sizzling food and booming speakers.

Meg had wondered whether she had dreamed the last three weeks. She wondered whether she might wake up tomorrow and her parents would be knocking on her door, and everything would be as she hoped. Instead, she'd had occasional messages from David, reminding her about their appointments and asking if she had thought about certain things, like veil weights or table plan signage or colouring books for any children attending. She had nothing, no emails, texts or calls, from either of her parents, and she still didn't want to be the one to message first.

Hannah was gone again, in Madrid and then to Rome for ten days in total, and Meg felt a renewed sense of purpose in her role of giving them both the wedding day they deserved. Today, they were to have a general browse for smaller details and the main mission was to look for food options for the day, and David also wanted to find more recruits for his queer business network, now called Work with Pride – Mark's brilliant idea. There was pressure, given how little time they had until the wedding, and often Meg wondered if she had bitten off more than she could chew, but when she said this to David, he seemed to mellow out the more neurotic parts of her brain.

'People need to be fed, watered, and for you two to be there,' David explained. 'Then it'll all fall into place. The basics are nearly there. That's all people care about – nice wine and decent music. Trust me. At fifty-four, I've been to quite a few weddings.'

'Oh God, I forgot we need to find a DJ!'

'One thing at a time,' David said. 'Let's think about food.'

'You're always thinking about food.'

'And so will your guests!'

The pubs they were choosing between couldn't do catering for the number of people they wanted, so David had suggested a food truck being a fun way of serving all their guests easily. They were walking together, but his path kept veering towards a big hut that served something called a cragel, a hybrid creation of a croissant and a bagel.

'Shall we get a coffee and take a walk round, first?' Meg said. 'It's a little overwhelming.'

'Okay,' David said. 'My third of the day, then I'll have to stop.'

Meg wondered if coffee ever affected David. He seemed level and alert no matter what time of day it was. Not wanting to change his mind, since a nice cappuccino would help keep her warm, they found a coffee cart, painted beige and brown, and Meg realized she didn't know her friend's coffee order. She turned to him. 'What would you like?'

'Cappuccino please,' David said, adding 'of course' when the man asked if he'd like chocolate.

'And a flat white for me please,' Meg said.

'I've had to get to grips with flat whites,' David said. 'They're the new thing right?'

'Kind of,' Meg said. 'I feel like they're better at waking me up.'

Now she had the comfort of a warm paper cup in her hand, they wandered through families and couples, all browsing and tasting and sitting on picnic benches to enjoy what they'd bought. There was a young girl in a green dress trying to do a perfect cartwheel, and her parents clapping every time, regardless of her result.

They wandered through the stalls, tried a free piece of fudge each, and stood by a candle stall.

'These are lovely,' David said to the owner, sniffing one of them. 'What's the scent?'

The woman sitting behind the stall in a fold-up chair stood and began to explain each candle – the ones made of sage and patchouli, and lime and honey – and Meg watched as David listened attentively, learning all about the techniques they used for the different shapes. He smelt every single one, offering them to Meg too.

'My friend here is getting married,' he said.

'Congratulations!'

'Thank you,' Meg said.

'Do you need candles, Meg?' he said. 'I think that was on the spreadsheet.'

'Probably a few for the tables,' Meg said. 'But not with an overwhelming smell. What do you recommend?'

The woman talked Meg through the two options she'd recommend, linen and rose, which she said were subtle scents that would not overpower the room, and she suggested having one for every eight people along the table. She said she'd had the rose at her own wedding.

'I'll think about it,' Meg said, taking the business card from a small stack the owner was holding. 'I'll chat to my partner and get back to you.'

'No worries, sweetheart.'

'I've got a card too actually,' David said, offering a small rectangle from his rain jacket's pocket. 'I've started a queer local business network called Work with Pride. As the name suggests, you don't have to be queer yourself, just an ally perhaps, and I thought we could all help each other out. I run Savage Lilies, in Woburn.'

'Oh yes I know of you,' the woman said, smiling. 'I'll join for sure. That's a great idea.'

Meg was stunned at how easily David seemed to win people over. They kept wandering, looking at small embroidered bags, children's clothing, and a company that framed old photos.

'Did you not like them?' David said. 'The candles.'

'Yeah, they were nice,' Meg said. 'I just need to think about it.'

'I wouldn't go for the sage . . .' David said. 'That one smelt too much like stuffing.'

'You told her it was your favourite!'

'I didn't want to hurt her feelings.'

'Are you hungry?' Meg said. 'I could do with some food now.'

'Go on then.'

They walked back up the hill towards the row of food vendors.

'If you want to try a few, to get a sense of who you might book, well I guess that's okay with me,' David said. 'I'll make room, somehow.'

'Why don't we start from the left and do any we think would work? Ooh tacos!' Meg pointed towards a rounded-edge van with a tall basic sign that just read TACOS. 'Does what it says on the tin.'

'They smell good,' David said. 'I'd buy their candle.'

They walked up to the till, and the young man inside smiled widely at them. He had dark hair and skin, and was wearing an apron and a hairnet. When he spoke, he gestured widely with his arms, and he spoke with a thick Mexican accent. He was very attractive, and she could tell David thought the same.

'My first customers of the day!' he said. 'What do you want? It's on the house.'

'Oh you don't have to do that!' David protested. 'We're not that special!'

'No but I want to,' he said. 'It's a little tradition.'

'Only if you're sure?' Meg said. They deliberated over the menu, both being much more expressive about how great everything looked, owing to the man's nice gesture. Meg felt like she couldn't order anything too expensive, so she suggested a standard taco each, rather than the more expensive quesadillas and dips. David chose the chicken and Meg asked for the tofu, and while the man heated up the fillings on a hot plate, he asked what brought them to the festival.

'I'm getting married,' Meg said. 'Do you do weddings?'

'Yes, we do!' he said excitedly. 'I haven't yet, I mean . . . we've done . . . sorry I probably shouldn't have said that. We haven't before but I would like to!'

'That's okay,' Meg said, finding this man's nervousness utterly charming. 'I've never planned one before either! What's your name?'

'I'm Ramon.'

'I'm Meg, and this is David.'

'When is the wedding?' Ramon asked. 'And what is your partner's name?'

'She's called Hannah,' Meg said, glad for the recognition, rather than the automatic jump to 'his' or 'groom'.

'And are you . . . how do they say it? Father of the bride?' Ramon asked.

David laughed.

'No, no,' Meg said. 'Well, kind of a father figure.'

'Sorry, my mistake,' Ramon said, holding up his hands. 'Here, take my number and get in touch if you want. No pressure at all.' He had finished compiling the tacos and he handed them over, and Meg took his number down in her phone. 'I've not been open long, but the food's great. If you like it, message me.'

'Do you do this full-time?'

'Not yet,' he said. 'I work in the shopping centre during the week, but I'm trying to get this to take off.'

Meg looked up at the sign, and the menus printed out from Word and posted on the flaps of the van that opened up. She instantly envisaged how she might help him and draw a logo that enticed people, but she could always offer to help him later, if they booked him. You couldn't exactly take a free taco and then critique somebody's business model.

'Okay, thanks, Ramon.'

David handed him his card too and quickly explained the concept of the network. Ramon looked delighted to have been asked.

They walked away to find a picnic bench where they could sit and enjoy the food and Meg immediately made a noise with the first bite.

'Wow,' said David.

Meg was staring at the gooey inside of the tacos. 'These are really, really good.'

'They're great.'

'Good to have different options for veggies too,' Meg said.

'And he was nice,' David said. 'Which you want, you know, nice people at the wedding.'

'I worry my parents would expect a traditional sit-down meal.'

'Don't worry about that,' David said. 'You only get married once, and you said you and Hannah love Mexican. It's your day, not anyone else's.'

'Do you think people like tacos?'

'I'm sure they do,' David said. 'And how could anyone

resist these?' David had already finished his portion and was putting his box in the bin.

'They're great,' Meg said.

'They *were* absolutely incredible.'

Afterwards, they wandered to some of the other food places, and tried a small pot of ice cream and then some crackers, which were being given out as samples.

'Ice cream doesn't count as a sweet, right?' Meg said. 'I can't betray Angie.'

'If you see her, head down, keep walking,' David said. 'I'm not joking.'

One of the vendors from the jacket potato stand had been particularly pushy about the wedding. She was asking for dates, and a number of guests, and almost pinning Meg down to confirm, on the spot, with a queue of four people behind her.

'I need more time to decide,' Meg had insisted, as firmly as was natural to her, and David started to lead her away, while the woman muttered something about getting booked up very quickly in the summer. She noticed that David had tactfully not offered her a card for Work with Pride.

They walked far away to the other side of the park. Here, next to another coffee cart and a bar, there was a small stage, with a screen either side. They inspected the line-up of local artists who would be performing from four o'clock, in a couple of hours' time.

'David Fenton!'

Before Meg knew it, a woman was hugging David from behind, squeezing him so tight she was sure he was going a little red.

'Oh, it's my second favourite Martha,' he said, hugging

this woman who was clearly his friend. She had short blonde hair, shaved round the back and sides, and she was wearing a sleeveless denim vest and jeans. Underneath was a red T-shirt, with a slogan on that said something about America. She seemed familiar, and yet Meg was struggling to place her.

'Who's the first?'

'Martha Stewart of course! She always shares her recipes.'

Martha rolled her eyes. 'I'm Martha,' she said to Meg. 'Are you Meg?'

'Yes!'

'Lovely to meet you.'

'I've told Martha about you,' David explained.

'Good things I hope,' Meg said. 'Well David's been a big help to me already. How do you two know each other?'

'We go quite far back, don't we?' Martha said.

'Martha was one of our first neighbours when we moved to Woburn,' he said. 'She popped round to say hello and we've been friends ever since. Martha does some stuff for the youth club, sometimes.'

'Well, it's very nice to meet you,' Meg said.

'We've not met before, have we?' Martha said. 'You look familiar.'

'I was going to say . . .'

'Well,' David said. 'Meg grew up here, maybe you taught her?'

Meg looked at the woman again, and David was right; that was it.

'You taught music at St Helens!' Meg said. 'Mrs . . .'

'Miss Apoline.' She smiled at Meg. 'I remember you now,' Martha said. 'You briefly tried the piano.'

'Unsuccessfully.'

Meg pictured Martha in school, looking completely

different to now. In Meg's memory, she was wearing jeans or a long skirt, and plain shirts. It was amazing how little you really knew of your teachers outside of school hours; she could never have imagined a teacher, even a substitute, in double denim. She may well have had a different haircut at the school too. She remembered kids whispering about Miss Apoline and her aloofness, the fact she might have been gay. Meg remembered just listening and saying nothing whenever the kids were mean. Of course, even as a child, she had recognized parts of the woman in herself, and the way people had mocked her scared her greatly. Now, an adult and a proud gay woman herself, it was so effortless to recognize one of her own.

'Do you still teach?'

'I'm part-time now,' Martha said, smiling. 'Which is a blessing. What do you have left to sort for the wedding then?'

This woman would definitely remember that Meg's parents taught at the school, and maybe David had mentioned her situation. Tactfully, she seemed to be moving the conversation on. Suddenly, Meg was struck by panic. What would she do if she bumped into her parents today?

'Oh,' David said, putting on his reading glasses and checking the list on his phone. 'Trying different foods.'

'Of course,' Martha said, laughing. 'You must be hating it, David.'

'Candles we might go back to; tablecloths you were after. We need a DJ too.' David looked around as if he might see Sara Cox standing behind one of the stalls.

'You know I DJ now?'

'No, you don't!' Meg said.

'I'd completely forgotten that!' David said. 'Wait, have you done weddings yet?'

'Only a couple, but they're my favourite,' Martha said proudly. 'I can show you some reviews. I've been teaching myself, have done a couple of events. Did one christening. Never again. But yes, weddings! Everyone's there for a good time. Let me know. I'm not charging while I practise, but you can literally give me the songs you do and don't want. I promise I won't play all the straight songs, like "Sweet Caroline", and "Mr Brightside". Unless you want me to!'

'Oh, are you sure?' Meg said. 'I mean that sounds amazing, and I did want queer businesses and people involved.'

'Well that's sorted then!' David said, pretending to cross it off his list. 'Tick!'

'Will you give Meg my number and we can sort it, David?'

'Of course,' he said. 'I'm starting a queer business group as well, for us to all promote each other. I'll add you to that too, for DJing and for the music lessons.'

'Thanks, David,' Martha said. 'God you're good at stuff like that.'

'We're racing through this,' David said. 'We'll be done soon. Anyway, Martha, what food have you tried? Any chance of that banoffee pudding recipe? I'll buy you a candle.'

Another hour later, and a quick trip had turned into a full day out. It was after they'd had a second lunch of dumplings and spring rolls that Meg spotted her secondary school boyfriend, Angus, the one her parents still talked about, the one she had barely really dated. He was on his own, standing in front of the ice cream truck, deliberating, hands in the pockets of a huge oversized Taylor Swift hoodie. He was taller than she remembered, taller than most people around, and she wondered if he'd had a late growth spurt after they'd stopped speaking.

'Hello, you,' she said, coming over to him, arms outstretched.

'Meg! Oh my God!'

They hugged, and whereas Meg had expected a brief hello, he was holding her tight so she relaxed back into the hug. He pulled back, and she saw his huge genuine smile, and smelt his aftershave, which had developed from the Lynx Africa of twelve years ago to something subtle and sweet-smelling. 'It's so nice to see you.'

'This is my friend David,' Meg said, introducing David and they quickly shook hands.

'Nice to meet you,' Angus said.

'How do you know Meg?' David asked.

'Well . . .' Meg said. She didn't feel embarrassed; it just felt like an odd thing to say.

'We dated, briefly, in school.' Angus took charge of the situation. 'Very briefly, and we both turned out to be gay, so not a perfect match.'

'But then we were friends,' Meg said.

'Why don't I leave you both to catch up?'

'Are you sure, David?'

'I was going to spy on the flower stalls anyway.' David started walking away. 'You two don't need to see me tutting at what other people do with chrysanthemums. I'll do a lap; take as long as you need.'

Meg was slightly unsure about being left alone with someone she hadn't spoken to in over a decade, but in David's spirit of meeting new people in what was now her community, she felt it was the right thing to do. Angus had always been great and she felt bad about how their friendship had ended. She'd been considering messaging him when they moved back, but she'd been too scared of being ignored. Maybe, she thought, this meeting was a sign.

'Oh my God,' Angus said, grabbing her left hand. 'Are you engaged? When did that happen?'

He screamed with excitement for her, and suddenly she was back to being seventeen and gossiping with him in the school corridors. The twelve years since they had finished school, when they had vowed to remain friends forever but hadn't made it past Meg's first year of university, all melted away. Maybe if she had messaged when they moved back, they might have rekindled a friendship. But, her ex-boyfriend jumping up and down at her news seemed to erase the last few months into nothing, and she felt the pull of home, in its own unique way.

9

DAVID

When community spirit was this high, it was easy to imagine it was the height of summer, but as the afternoon came, and David meandered alone to fill the time, there was a slight chill in the air as if the weather wanted to remind people it was still early on. Spring had sprung, but only slightly. *Let's not get ahead of ourselves,* the sky seemed to say.

If he had kids, maybe there would be a more obvious demarcation of the months and years passing than just the weather. Plants, of course, had their own rhythm and calendar, which felt almost musical to David, but most weeks in the shop did run into each other in a not unpleasant way. Plants didn't mind if you were a few weeks early or late. They didn't need feeding on the dot. They were very adaptable, or maybe they just had to be, and their rhythms suited David's pace of life.

He bought a hot chocolate to warm himself up – he'd also had two lunches, but it was the weekend after all and he *was* supporting local business – and took a seat at the top of the hill. Perhaps he didn't need the sprinkles, the flake or the marshmallows, but it wouldn't be a hot chocolate without them, would it?

A few people passed and recognized him, chatting briefly or just waving. There was a family from down the road who always came in for flowers on birthdays, and there was David's plumber who had done excellent work updating some of the old pipes in the first flat they had moved to in the area, before they had found the shop and the flat upstairs. He had a gay daughter, David knew, and so he recruited him for the business network.

David had a lengthy catch-up with a couple of women who were involved in the town's queer crafting club, something David had attended when they first moved, but eventually had to abandon when the flower shop became such a huge part of his week, along with everything else. He wanted to go over and tell them he'd rejoin but Mark's sensible words rang in his ears. *You can't do everything*. But maybe they could hold their meetings in the shop. Maybe running his own events wasn't enough, and hiring out the space and getting the money from food and drinks was a way to increase profits. They said they'd be in touch.

All this planning for Meg's wedding made him wonder what might have happened if, years before, he and Mark had decided to get married. He knew Mark was keener on it than him, and still was, but no part of him had ever wanted that many eyes on a performance of their relationship and Mark hadn't brought it up in years. They were happy. What was there to prove?

David felt strongly their moment, if there had been one, had passed. Their lives were full, and what good would it do to throw a party when a lot of the trappings of a wedding were impossible with him having no family?

From all that was here today, what would he put together for the perfect wedding, if they did have one? It was fun to think about it, he thought. It didn't mean anything.

He'd do his own flowers, of course. The stalls he'd looked at had bouquets well past the point David would sell them, the leaves drooping and faded, the soil dry and harsh. The DJ – Martha, not whoever was playing songs from the stage now – would play the songs that reminded him of his youth. Not his teens or twenties, which he looked back on with some sadness, but his thirties. The music that got him up and dancing in the clubs when he knew who he was, and where he had first met Mark. Pet Shop Boys, Erasure, Kylie. It was funny, at his age, that he had stages of youth rather than just the division of before and now.

Maybe it was the cold but he was hungry again. He'd have to talk to Meg about portions, since nobody wanted to be hungry at a wedding. He was entranced by Raclette A Manger, whose owners were melting and pouring molten cheese onto cubes of potato. The Pad Thai stand, Breaking Pad, was another that intrigued him. Maybe he could buy some and eat it for lunch tomorrow. Maybe it would be worth getting married if he could have a five-course dinner from this line of vendors.

He'd make a speech, if he got married, of course, and Mark would definitely want to, since he thrived on being able to share his jokes with a wider audience. David imagined they might both be a little competitive with their speeches, actually.

If they had married a decade before, when it first became possible, they would have had no money, but maybe that would have been better. Just them, the people who were important to them. David had been to so many weddings where all people did, before and after, was moan about how much they had spent. He had always felt like any gift he gave was just plugging a credit card debt.

With the shop the way it was, how would he afford a wedding now? Life was supposed to get easier as you got older. It was fine. No part of David felt he needed a wedding to consolidate or put onto paper what he had felt over the last two decades and still did, or how important Mark was to him. Mark's parents could hardly be realistically expecting a wedding, could they?

He sat for a while longer to give Meg time to catch up with her ex, wondering about his own ex-boyfriends who he was unlikely to see in the area. David thought, in a somewhat melancholic way, about what had become of them, but that was all in the past. He wished, more than he wished for a wedding, that he and Mark had had more time together, in whatever form. All those wasted years. If only they had met at nineteen like Meg and Hannah, and all of the rush of David's twenties had been with fun but dependable Mark.

Stop being a sentimental old fool, he told himself. Maybe it was the music that was doing it to him. The DJ had handed over the mic and a young man wearing a short-cropped white T-shirt was singing and playing guitar, a slow song about the passage of time. That would be it. He always found it hard to remain unmoved in the presence of live music. Maybe he could host an open mic night at Lilies!

David headed over to the stage to enjoy the music up close, and see if he could assess interest in a night at the shop, and when he was closer he could feel the vibrations of the speakers in his bones. He wondered if he should wear earplugs. It certainly felt loud enough he could imagine his doctor telling him to protect his hearing. Another hassle of age. There was a small crowd in front of the stage, obviously friends of the performer cheering near the front, and other groups stood, or sat on picnic blankets on the grass, enjoying it from a distance. He put on a large encouraging smile, in case the singer on the stage was nervous.

Slightly off to the left of the stage, a small boy, who was probably five or six, was with his parents, dancing to the music. The way he moved, the way he spun his hands around his wrists, and the way he fixed his mouth into a pout, was decidedly effeminate, and rather than laugh, he watched how the boy's parents seemed to encourage him. His mum took each of the boy's hands in his, and began to twirl him round. His dad was dancing, in his own more reserved way, but beaming with pride at his son. As the song changed, somehow without communicating, they all crouched down onto the ground as if hidden, before bursting back into movement when the next song started.

Back down memory lane – what was it about today? – and David was standing in his parents' living room at sixteen, after finally deciding he had to come out, facing two stony-faced parents who were surprised when he told them he had something to tell them. He wondered what they'd thought it might be: failed grades, he'd got into a fight, maybe he'd gotten a girl pregnant. He sat on the settee opposite them, adversarial from the off, watching their faces scanning him for a clue, in front of the Seventies-style floral curtains behind them. Their faces almost dared him to ruin their perfect suburbia. He remembered the moment he opened his mouth, and the moment he had gone too far, and the Pandora's box he had opened was never going to be closed again.

David had been the polar opposite of this happy child dancing now, his whole body seized with panic and the noise of his parents' anger washing over him. He felt the tendons in his limbs strain with stress at the memory of how he had run out of that room before they could see him cry, and how he remembered he had never looked back. He had never seen them again. Flight, indeed, rather than fight.

10
MEG

'It's been what, eleven years? That's crazy.'

'Eleven and a half,' Angus said. 'I remember that September you left . . . Everyone went, all at once.'

They were sitting on a couple of outdoor beanbags that were dotted around the park. They were bright purple, and contrasted against the somewhat faded grass struggling to become its spring green. As she caught him up on the events of the last few weeks, Meg kept having to readjust herself and the way she sat in order not to slide off onto the ground.

'So catch me up!' Angus said. 'Who's David, then? And your fiancée! It's Hannah, isn't it?'

'Yeah, Hannah. We've been together ten years now,' she said, wondering how much of her life he'd know, or supposed he did, from her online profiles. 'And that's David who owns the florist's in Woburn. I met him recently and he's going to come to my appointments and stuff while Hannah's away with work. Until my parents come round to it all.'

'That's so nice of him,' said Angus, offering her a chip

from his cone. They were loaded with purple mayonnaise and crispy bits of onion. 'What's in it for him?'

Meg hesitated before answering, wondering whether that was something she had even thought about before. She had just assumed David was being nice.

'I'm not sure,' she said. 'He helps run the youth club with his partner, Mark, and does community work, helps the food bank, that sort of thing. He's setting up a queer business network too, so that's part of it. I ended up crying in the florist's, so he kind of took me under his wing, which has been nice, you know, since we moved back, to have someone be so friendly.'

'He sounds amazing,' Angus said. 'Like one of those people who wins an award for being a community beacon on *The One Show* or something.'

'Yeah, he's great.'

'Do you worry if your parents came round and came to all these things with you, he'd suddenly feel left out again?'

'I hadn't thought about it like that,' Meg said. 'I'd hope he wouldn't mind. Who knows what'll happen.'

Angus smiled at her. He had always been like that when they were young: never doing anything without thinking about everybody else and what it might mean for them. He'd never stay too late at a party, knowing his mum would be worrying; he'd never be mean about anyone at school, knowing he wouldn't want somebody to do the same to him.

'So, Angus,' Meg said. 'Tell me about round here, your life . . . work, dating, everything.'

'Well, firstly, I'm actually going by Gus now,' he said. 'Angus always felt so *formal*.'

'I like that,' Meg said. He really was different from the boy she had known for the seven years of secondary school.

His curls were the same, and his large green eyes. Different though, was the way he held himself. At school they'd both known the other was queer from maybe sixteen, though they didn't say it to each other until a year later once they'd let people think they were dating and had to stage a fake break-up. Now, Gus was less awkward, as they all probably were, but it was so noticeable with him after a long absence. Shoulders not hunched up, hands waving freely as he spoke. His skin had cleared and seemed unnaturally tanned for this time of year, but in a way that looked completely real. 'Anyway, *tell me about you!* That's the problem when you get engaged. Everybody has so many questions for you, but I still want to know about everyone else.'

'I'm single,' he said, sadly, like it was a deficit or a problem to solve. 'Have never really had anything too serious . . . I feel like it always all moves too fast, and then turns to nothing. It's such a small dating pool here, not like what it must be in London.'

'Are you on the apps?' Meg said. Luckily, she had met Hannah before the boom of dating apps, so had never been on one herself, but she had friends who'd had successes. Her friend Sophie had just got married, and she had met her husband after just a week on Tinder.

'I go on and off them,' Gus said. 'I'll have a series of dates and then I get bored and cancel my accounts.'

'Oh, it'll happen,' she said. 'I know that's annoying when people in couples say that . . . But it's always when you least expect it. Genuinely. I never turned up to university thinking I'd meet my wife in my first term.'

'That's what everybody says to me,' Gus said. 'But I'm nearly thirty . . . I'm beginning to lose hope.'

Meg looked at him. He was such a positive person, and

always had been, but he looked so sad she wanted to hug him. Instead, she put her hand on his knee. 'If you want to get out there, go to events and stuff to meet people, I could always come with. We could join a running club or something.'

'I'd like that,' Gus said. 'It's so nice to have you back.' He leaned across and hugged her, and it felt completely natural. 'Why did you move back? I always thought you hated it here.'

'I didn't hate it here,' she said. 'I just . . . needed to leave when I did. It's so nice you stayed. I always wonder, if I'd been closer, whether they'd have got on board with the gay thing more. If they'd had to.'

'I get that,' Gus said. 'It must be the grass is always greener thing . . . I always thought about leaving. Still do. What pulled you back?'

'We wanted somewhere more affordable, where we can still get into London for work . . . But somewhere I knew and being near family, that felt nice. Woburn is lovely too, and it's so different from when we were at school. There would never have been a proud gay flower shop like David's then . . . Do you remember that old antiques shop where the old man used to yell at everyone?'

She thought fondly, for the first time in a long time, of her years as a teenager here. She and Gus had come to Campbell Park for a gig once, but they'd never have come to something like this. When she was younger, it had felt like nothing like this existed for miles around her, and if it did, nobody had had the grace to tell her.

Meg couldn't help but be brought back to those years at school when she'd felt like she'd been born in the wrong town or the wrong family. She and Angus had never really officially dated; it had been more that they'd been each other's lifeboats, she thought. At the time, she had believed they must have both known what was going on – that they were both discovering their sexuality, and it was a good subterfuge to avoid questioning – but with hindsight, maybe it hadn't all been so clear-cut, or so linear for them both. Meg had liked being seen together, and liked that her parents had assumed they were in a relationship, until she hadn't.

It was a ruse that had lasted for perhaps the entirety of Sixth Form when, towards the end, they'd started to go into London together to hang around gay pubs and clubs, too scared to go in, but feeling brave that they'd made it to the area, at least. Their parents thought they were going on dates.

'So do you still talk to anyone from school?' she asked him, the classic question that always returned when you caught up with someone from your past.

'Not really,' he said. 'The old group of boys, I see usually when everyone's back for Christmas. Kirsty, she's still around, works in town.'

'I just bumped into Miss Apoline,' Meg told him. 'You know, the old music teacher?'

'She was gay, right?'

'Yeah,' she said. 'I could tell now but I don't know if we actually knew that at the time. She knows David.'

'I can't believe how many gay teachers there were,' he said. 'I bumped into Mr Martin at Pinks a few years ago. If only we'd known when we were young that there were gay people round here, and they were having a nice time! Imagine what that would have meant.'

'I know!' Meg said. 'I think about that all the time, actually.'

Gus put down his rubbish. 'I feel worse for you. At least I could come into school and not hide myself as much . . .

But you had the trouble of not being yourself at home, and then coming into school and your parents were there too. At least I had a break.'

'But your parents were like mine right?' Meg said. 'A bit homophobic, but in the way that everyone was?'

'Yeah, I guess,' Gus said. 'A year ago we had a big talk about it, and they apologized. Dad said he regretted for years telling me I'd grow out of it, and said they should have known and been better, which meant a lot. I think it's worse when it's unspoken. Knowing your parents, and actually remembering your dad tell me off once, I get that it's scary. But you've got time. I hope they come around. They're teachers, they must see how much the world has changed.'

'Yeah,' Meg said, feeling herself well up. She'd found since that day at the shop that any mention of weddings or relationships or parents or children brought her close to tears. She'd do anything – literally anything – for a conversation like that with her parents. The problem was, she wanted them to want to have it.

'It'll all work out like it should,' Gus said. 'I promise.'

'Do you want to come to my wedding?'

It was out of Meg's mouth before she had really thought about it, or indeed told Hannah, but it wasn't like it was an ex-boyfriend or girlfriend she might still be interested in, and they had space. Sitting with Gus, she felt incredibly attached to her past. It was a part of her, and she realized that if her parents were going to be how they were, other people from her history might be able to fill the gap.

'I'd love to! Oh Meg that's so nice,' he said, hugging her. 'I'd be delighted to come!'

As they were hugging, Ramon from the taco truck walked past, and waved at both of them. It seemed to Meg like he hesitated, not wanting to overstep a boundary, but she found herself waving him over.

'Hello again!' he said.

'Hi, Ramon,' Meg said. 'How's the day going? This is my friend Gus.'

They introduced themselves to each other and had an overly formal handshake. Meg made a joke about not having been to any other food trucks, trying to hide their wrappers, and Ramon insisted she try the tiramisu stand.

'That one's fine,' Ramon said. 'Desserts aren't direct competition with tacos.'

As they spoke, David appeared, and suddenly Meg wondered what time it was. It felt slightly darker than it had before, and the group on the stage that had been rapping had now been replaced by a duo who were singing and dancing in perfect rhythm.

'We're late!' David said. 'Do you mind if we go? I'm sorry.'

'For what?' Meg asked.

'I completely forgot . . . Time . . . I thought six o'clock was four o'clock, and . . . Sorry, hi again, Ramon! Hi, Gus.'

She and David made their excuses quickly and started to walk towards the van, leaving Gus and Ramon alone.

'Where do you need to get to?' Meg asked. 'I thought you just had to get back at some point . . .'

'No, it's a youth club thing at the shop . . . Mark's going to be mad if we're late.'

'Oh I'm sorry,' she said, thighs burning. 'I should have come to find you. I completely forgot about the time.'

'That's okay,' he said. 'I did exactly the same.'

'Where did you go, anyway?'

'Oh, I just went for a walk, some thinking time, you know.'

He was walking so fast, Meg was losing her breath trying to keep up with him storming up the hill and still holding a conversation.

'Yeah.'

'I was going to ask if you're okay, Meg.'

'What do you mean?'

'I noticed with the cakes, and with Martha and some food today,' David said. 'You were hesitant to fully confirm things. Is that . . . are you just like that, or do you think part of you is delaying committing to things without knowing your parents are okay about it?'

Meg hadn't really thought about that, but she supposed there was a small part of her holding herself back.

'A little bit of both,' she said. 'It does all feel a bit weird.'

'That's normal,' he said.

'Do you think?'

'Yeah,' he continued. 'Just do it anyway. Our friends Carl and Matty, they got married as soon as it was legal, and they said it all felt so strange. It's not like you get married every day. It's supposed to feel weird.'

'Oh that's good to know.'

They had got to the top of the hill, but David didn't slow down, breathing loudly as he made his way to the van, Meg trailing behind.

'But there is one thing,' David said when they reached the van.

'What?'

'If you don't get Ramon to make those tacos, I know a Pad Thai stand that's not too shabby.'

'I'll keep it in mind.' The van beeped as David unlocked it. 'What's tonight?' Meg climbed into the passenger seat and David set off immediately.

'We do these careers nights, people talking about what they do, their path, and talking to the kids about jobs and exams and things.'

Suddenly, David gasped, and Meg worried he'd seen something on the road that she hadn't.

'What?'

'I was supposed to prepare a presentation!' he said. 'Oh Mark's going to be mad . . . I promised I wouldn't forget.'

'Don't worry,' Meg said. 'We'll sort it together.'

As the streetlights switched on above them, whizzing past their heads in lines of yellow and white, Meg felt nostalgic about the place. Years before, she'd been a shy teenager and now she was heading back to a youth club made up of people of that age. How far she'd come. Suddenly, she had an idea. 'Hey, maybe I could talk about my job?'

11

DAVID

David could not believe he had never thought to ask Meg about her work. He knew she was available at odd times of the day, so he assumed she must have flexible work or was perhaps freelance in some capacity, but he was surprised it hadn't come up in all the time they spent together.

People's jobs, he thought, told you so much about a person. The flower shop, for example, showed David's creativity, and his appreciation for small gestures. He loved what gifting flowers meant, and how memorable the gesture could be in tough times. Mark's role as a counsellor for young people showed how much he wanted to help people, and how much he cared about the next generation. Meg's job, he supposed, displayed creativity and a flair for storytelling; the competitiveness of the field showed that despite her current lack of self-esteem, she actually must be incredibly robust.

In the car back to Woburn, Meg gave him a whistle-stop tour through her career in illustration. The years after studying, when she would take any work and eventually got hired on a CBBC show to do storyboards; the years in London, her transitioning from that long-running hit to trying to get her own projects off the ground, completing the drawings for picture books from random authors and any other projects she could get her hands on. Then there was the recent past, mainly getting hired for national and international work on adverts and other short-form online work, which she said paid well, though it wasn't the most creative thing in the world. Meg seemed effusive about how she'd managed her career and said she loved being on her own hours, never having to answer to anyone, or having to sit in an office for hours on end, which David related to.

He listened attentively, distracting himself from the impending telling-off from Mark. He took a roundabout a little haphazardly and heard a driver beep their horn at him; in the rear-view mirror, a man was shaking his fist and shouting something. He imagined Mark in the passenger seat next to him doing his regular joke. *I think he's saying something nice!*

'Oopsie,' David said.

'It'll be okay,' Meg said, looking behind her. 'There genuinely is traffic.'

'Yes.'

'And, I do these talks quite a lot, at schools and universities,' Meg said. 'The kids will love it, I promise. I've got a presentation I can stick on, if there's a projector I can use?'

'There is!'

'Okay,' she said, fiddling with her phone. 'I'll just edit so it looks like I made it for today. A white lie.'

When they did finally arrive, they were about twenty minutes after the arranged starting time of the event. David tried to pull perfectly into the space in front of Savage Lilies before giving up and leaving the van halfway up the kerb. Inside, he could see about fifteen or twenty kids on chairs dotted around the shop, in casual clothes, attentive to what Mark was saying at the front but occasionally leaning in to whisper to the person closest to them. Meg patted David on the back in an act of solidarity as they entered.

'And here they are, our special guests!' Mark said.

'Fabulously late,' David said.

'Mark's been waiting!' Benji shouted, and a few kids laughed. 'He's mad at you!'

Mark was standing at the front of the shop, wearing a shirt with a sweatshirt over the top of it. The kids were smiling, sensing a playful irritation at David's tardiness.

'Right, hi, everyone,' David said. '*Thank you, Benji.* Terrible traffic, I'm very sorry.'

He looked at Mark who was trying not to look at him.

'We've all been talking about who the group prefer, me or you,' Mark said.

'What were the results?'

'They weren't good for you,' he replied, not looking at him. 'I can tell you that much.'

The group seemed to be enjoying their bickering, and he knew despite the fact Mark was genuinely annoyed that they were both playing up to it, talking out to an audience rather than facing each other.

'We'll run the vote again at the end of the night,' David said. 'And I'll slip you all a fiver. Anyway, I think we're supposed to be talking about futures and careers and so I have prepared a little something.'

'What have you prepared, David?' Mark asked, patiently.

'My new friend, Meg, is an illustrator,' he stated proudly, gesturing over to Meg who was standing somewhat nervously at the back of the shop avoiding Mark's stare. 'So she's going to talk a little bit about her job, and how she got into it, what she studied . . . Can everybody give her a little round of applause?'

Mark pointed her towards a stain on the floor. '*Plant* yourself there so everyone can see you.'

He winked at the crowd and Fred, one of the boys sitting with Benji, shouted, 'No more puns! Please!'

Meg took a deep breath in, and David and Mark moved to sit down at the back of the room, next to Jacob. David could see Mark looking at him out of the sides of his eyes.

'What?' he whispered to him.

'You genuinely planned for Meg to speak?' Mark muttered. 'You didn't just forget?'

'No!' David whispered back, hoping Meg's existing talk she had done before seemed pre-planned. He stared straight ahead and clenched his jaw so Mark couldn't see him flailing. 'I am sorry we're late though.'

'Hi, everyone,' Meg said, after the applause had died down. 'Now, first thing, can everybody tell me their favourite animated character?'

'That was so cool!'

David could hear Benji talking to his friends as Meg wound down her speech and talked about a couple of the websites she would send round via Jacob. He was now sitting with Fred and a girl called Salma, who always seemed to find each other. Together they formed a trio of the most influential, or perhaps just the loudest, members of the club. Maybe it was also because they were the oldest, but David felt relieved. A sign of positivity from them was always a good indication the rest of the group would have enjoyed something; whether the three of them were reflective of the group or whether people just followed what they said, he was never sure.

He went over to congratulate Meg as the kids continued to chat, and he heard one of the new girls who loved performing arts telling a new member of the club which one was David and which was Mark: 'Mark's the smarter-dressed one. No, on the left; no, *stage* left.'

'You did amazingly,' David said to Meg. 'The kids loved it. Well done.'

'Oh thank you,' she said. 'I'm a bit rusty. It's been ages.'

'You were so good with them, the questions, the interactive elements. I loved it.' David smiled and pointed at the kids, who were now looking at each other's drawings they had been scribbling as she spoke. 'They did too. You might only get a couple of thank yous, but don't take it personally.'

'Thanks, Meg,' said Mark, who came to stand with them. 'That was great.'

'Did you think so?'

'Yeah, it was brilliant,' he said. 'Thanks for getting involved. If you ever want to—'

'David and Mark and Meg,' came a voice from behind them. They parted their group slightly to see Salma standing behind them. She was wearing black leggings and an oversized T-shirt that had rips in it.

'Hi, Salma,' he said. 'You've torn your shirt!'

'It's supposed to be like that,' she said, rolling her eyes. 'Have you heard the new Dua Lipa song?'

'No, I haven't,' David said.

'Me neither,' added Mark.

'It's *very* good.' She nodded her head, like there was no

more to say on the matter. 'You need to put on Radio 1 instead of that stuff you play in here.'

'Hey,' David said. 'That's a very bespoke playlist.'

'Maybe she's just *pollen* your leg,' Mark said, and Salma walked away without saying anything.

'You'll soon be introduced to all of Mark's dad jokes,' David warned Meg. 'Buckle up. Sometimes they enjoy them, sometimes, well, they walk off.'

'Make sure you laugh,' Mark said. 'Please.'

'I'll make sure I . . . Rise to the occasion.'

'What?' David said.

'*Rose* to the occasion,' Meg said, before pausing. 'Did that work?'

'Nearly,' Mark said.

'Hmm,' David said.

A few people were peering into the shop from the street outside and suddenly, David felt like he shouldn't be closing the shop for events like this. What if they were losing out on valuable custom? They needed to make sure they got any money they could, any time of day. He knew Mark wanted him to be more business-minded, as did his accountant, but he also knew the youth club was a priority for both of them, so what was the solution? He couldn't renege on an existing commitment.

'Do you know all the kids here?' Meg asked, looking out at the shop.

'Mostly,' Mark said. 'I can see a few new faces. Jacob there runs it, and he takes them to different things. He works at the council. We like doing the careers evening because they meet other people in the community and see all sorts of different jobs, but we sometimes help with days out and some of the sports sessions. Keeps us fit, running around. I don't envy the days David is the referee at the football games.'

'I'm not sure I really understand the offside rule,' David said. 'And they don't really like that. But they're good kids. It keeps us young. We always know what Dua Lipa's up to, thanks to Salma, and Fred always gives us language lessons. We always know what's ace, you know. Everything's *ace*; anything rubbish *gives them the ick*.'

'I had heard that one,' Meg said.

'Well you're actually young. You don't need the help,' David said. 'But we do sometimes. We now know all about Stormzy and Maya Jama, and Rio was telling us the other day about something called *rizz*.'

'Does the evening usually run late?' Meg said.

'No, no,' Mark said. 'We leave them to chat; maybe if they have any questions, they'll come and find you. I've laid out some fizzy drinks. We usually just give them some time to socialize and catch up, and we'll clear them out by seven, quarter past. What are you doing this evening?'

'Hannah's back,' she said. 'So I think we might go for a drink, or get a takeaway. Nothing too wild, but I'm just so excited to see her.' She glanced at the tired old grandfather clock in the corner. 'She'll be wondering where I am actually.'

'Oh well, head home if you want,' David said. 'You don't have to stay.'

'Okay, great,' Meg said. 'I'll slip out. What are you both doing tonight?'

'We were going to watch a film the kids are all talking about, something action-packed,' David said. 'I can't remember the name.'

'David's cooking dinner for us,' Mark added.

‘Since when?’ David said.

‘It’s just that you said Meg had been primed to do this all week?’

‘She had,’ David said, suddenly panicked.

‘Yes,’ Meg added convincingly.

‘But then you were late,’ Mark said. ‘Meg just said she actually had plans this evening, and I noticed page six of your presentation said in the corner it was last year, and for a school in London.’

‘Oh,’ he said.

‘Oh,’ Meg said.

‘You missed a page,’ David whispered to Meg.

‘Well it’s hard using PowerPoint on your phone,’ she whispered back.

‘I can hear you,’ Mark said, but he was smiling. He could never stay mad for long. He turned to David. ‘I’d love you to make me a nice drink as well.’

David knew he and Meg looked sheepish, and he tried to get Mark to smile.

‘Okay, deal,’ he said, gathering his things up as the party started to leave in groups. ‘But it all worked out okay in the end!’

12

MEG

'And then,' Hannah said. 'It had been there the whole time, so I just switched it on and showed them! They were blown away!'

Meg had been watching as Hannah spoke about some work drama, some close-to-the-wire stress that seemed a daily part of her work life, something Meg would absolutely hate to happen to her as regularly as it did for Hannah, but that her partner found so fulfilling to solve. She had been watching her girlfriend, no, her *fiancée*, speak for ages and was it usual that in the run-up to a wedding you became more and more obsessed with your partner? Every time Hannah returned home – maybe it was also her absence that was making Meg's heart grow fonder – Meg was struck in a visceral way by how lucky she was.

'What are you looking at?' Hannah said. 'Am I boring you?'

'I'm just in love with you!' Meg said.

Hannah smiled at her and pushed Meg's foot with her own under the table.

They had come out on a Sunday night to a pub in another

village; its outside was run-down and uninviting, but since moving back to the area, it was the best Sunday roast they had found. After sharing bread as a starter to save space, they were both struggling to get near the end of a veggie wellington that was full of broccoli, cauliflower, nuts and pulses. Thick gravy sat in a boat on the table unfinished.

'It's rare they give you too much gravy,' Hannah said. 'This is amazing.'

'And the reason why we're never going anywhere else.'

'Do you remember when we used to drink a bottle each, no problem?' Hannah asked, gesturing to their drinks. Hannah was drinking sparkling water, and Meg had no work to do the next day so she had ordered a small glass of red wine.

'I do remember,' Meg replied, rubbing her temples at the idea of a hangover. 'But it seems like a lifetime ago.'

'And in that student union bar, do you remember, we used to do that shot of . . . What was it? Before every night out?'

'Baby Guinness! Those were disgusting, really.'

'Yeah, don't know what we were thinking.'

Perhaps it was normal, too, in the run-up to a wedding, to be reminiscent of all the time you had shared together, but particularly the first year you met. Rarely did a conversation go by when they did not talk about how much things had changed since then. Often, Hannah would find and send pictures of the two of them from that time that popped up on her phone or on her social media pages. In the photos there was always Meg, in her glasses because she hadn't yet discovered contact lenses, and Hannah, her hair more curly and uncontrollable than it had ever been, before she had found the products and online tutorials that made up her extensive routine.

There were photos from before they got together; on opposite sides of group pictures on course nights out, when Hannah would bring out her old digital camera and take hundreds of photos. In the selection they always looked at, the two of them got closer and closer together as the terms progressed, until the photos were just of the two of them, smiling, hugging, kissing each other on the cheek. You could see, like a flip animation, the relationship build in real time.

'Do you remember that old digital camera you used to have?' Meg asked. 'Before we had phones and I used to take it everywhere?'

'I do!' Hannah said. She said it so exuberantly it sounded like they were at the end of an aisle, on a day that was now less than three months away, and they both laughed. 'I'm glad, or we wouldn't have memories of that time. Well, we'd have the memories, but not, you know, the hundreds of photos of evidence.'

The pictures did seem like evidence, required proof of a time Meg could only faintly remember, more as a feeling than as a concrete set of full scenes. Maybe she'd print some of the photos out for the wedding, for on the tables or something.

They stayed for another drink. Neither of them could fit in a dessert, but they didn't want the night to end (going to sleep meant another day closer to when Hannah would be off on a flight again) and Meg was glad they did because in the bar area of the pub, she bumped into Martha coming back from the toilets, dressed in leather trousers and a short T-shirt.

'Hello!'

'Martha, hi!' Meg said, after just passing her and not

realizing. Martha stood to give her a huge hug. 'Sorry, it's so dark in here.'

'Who are you here with?'

'My fiancée Hannah!' Meg said. 'Will you come and meet her?'

Martha separated from a group of five people her age, who all waved at Meg though she recognized no one, and followed Meg back over to their table.

'Hannah, this is Martha who I was telling you about! The music teacher from my old school . . . and the DJ at our wedding!'

Hannah looked slightly shocked at the intake of all this information, but warmly greeted Martha and invited her to take a chair at their table. 'Only if you have time,' Hannah said.

'Yes, of course,' she said. 'I'm with some very old friends and we've got nothing left to say to each other so don't worry.'

'So . . . our wedding,' Hannah said. 'Thank you so much! I can't tell you how appreciative we are. It's so nice to have so many queer people involved. That's really important to us.'

She smiled and reached her hand out between her armchair and Meg to take Meg's hand in hers.

'It's an absolute pleasure,' she said. 'I enjoy teaching at St Helens, but I get so much more from the DJing.'

'How come you did learn?' Meg asked. 'In the end?'

'It was David, actually,' Martha said. 'Though I think he's forgotten. I kept saying it would be my new year's resolution, and one time he just said to me, "You know you've mentioned that every year we've known each other." That did it for me. I thought that was crazy! And I'd better follow through. If one of my friends was saying this, I'd be telling them to do it, so why not me?'

'That's so cool,' Meg said.

'So if you have any hobbies, any dreams,' Martha said, running a hand over her short hair. 'Then I say, just do it! No regrets, that's my motto.'

'How's the teaching?' Hannah said. 'I bet it's hard to do that and work at the weekend too, and late nights.'

'It's okay,' she said. 'The older I've got, I actually have more energy, because I don't waste it on stupid things. The thing with school, you're never not busy, that's for sure, but that's how I like it. I'd be bored otherwise. I love teaching, and you know what, it's a different place from when we were at school, and, Meg, from when you were there. I don't think you'd recognize it.'

'In what way?' Meg said.

'Kids are nicer, about most things.' She looked somewhat emotional. 'There will always be bullying in schools, sure, but everyone's much more aware of what everyone else might be going through. I've found that even goes for teachers, which is crazy. A student having sympathy for their teacher!'

'So would you know Meg's parents then, at the school?' Hannah asked, and Meg could hear the tentativeness in her voice, as if she wanted to ask but would stop if Meg didn't want to hear. 'Mr and Mrs Kirby?'

'Yeah,' Martha said. 'They're old-school, but you probably know that better than me, Meg. Keep themselves to themselves, stay in their classrooms or in each other's, rather than mix. They teach proper subjects,' Martha added. 'So you do have to be a little more serious, getting judged on your exam results and things. No wonder they don't have time to sit and talk rubbish in the staffroom like me and Mark.'

Martha looked at Meg, as if to see if what she said was okay.

'They were always very serious,' Meg said.

'Some people have to be, I guess,' she replied. 'We never know what's going on in people's heads. Anyway, I'd better get back to my friends.'

'No worries,' Hannah said.

'Send me a list of music you like, whenever you get a minute,' she said. 'Then I usually put together a playlist for different parts of the day, hoping it's things you'd like. But you can say yes or no, go through it with a big red pen you know, do crosses and ticks. Like a teacher! It's quite fun, I always think. Nothing's off-limits; it's your day. I won't judge.'

Meg smiled. She couldn't imagine Miss Apoline being a fan of B*Witched, but she was willing to be surprised. 'Lovely to see you.'

'Angie might be in later, if you're still around,' Martha said. 'David said you'd met her. Nice to meet you, Hannah!'

She walked away and after a moment Hannah turned to her and slapped her hand playfully.

'When did you get so bloody popular?'

On the walk home, sleepy and full, conversation turned back to the wedding; what was left and what had been done.

'Do you need help with anything?' Hannah said. 'I know I fly on Tuesday but anything I can do remotely, do let me help. Shall I make that playlist?'

'Oh yes please!' Meg said. 'I'll give you Miss Apoline's number.'

'It's so funny you still talk about her like she's a teacher.'

'She is a teacher!' Meg shoved her playfully. 'Otherwise we're on it, I think. David's been such a help, and we've got all these new people and his friends taking care of certain things. My spreadsheet is nearly full! I've found a couple of the vendors from his new business network. There's a décor person I've sorted a meeting with.'

'I was taking a look . . . The tacos look great too,' Hannah said. 'Such a great idea and we never wanted a sit-down meal anyway, did we?'

'No,' Meg said. 'But do you think it's enough food, like proper food?'

'Of course! And if he does those little nacho cups you mentioned as a sort of canapé, I think that's perfect, since there'll be all the cake later too.' Hannah watched her face out of the sides of her eyes as they turned onto their street.

'I just worry if people think it's weird when we have non-traditional things,' she said. 'Like if people expect a sit-down meal.'

'And by people you mean your parents?'

'Well, yeah.'

'They haven't got in touch, so once they've RSVP'd they can have opinions on the food.'

'Hannah!'

'Sorry, you know what I mean. We need to not care what people think. Everyone's weddings are different, because everyone's different.'

'You've got me worried now, I realized they actually never RSVP'd. Should I have known?'

‘They’re your parents, Meg; we assumed they’d just be there. I don’t think mine did either. Has there been anything since that message?’

The day before, they’d sent a text saying they were sorry to have missed the appointment but they were finding the situation difficult. They didn’t say why, and when Meg replied saying they should talk about it, they didn’t respond.

‘No nothing,’ Meg said. ‘And I’m not double-texting.’

‘Just leave it,’ Hannah said. ‘The ball’s in their court again. I love you, Meg. I’m sorry this is happening.’

She reached over to hug her as they walked.

‘Everyone’s right though: we’ve just got to focus on the good stuff . . . Like, and I was meaning to ask, when are you going to buy your outfit?’ Meg said. ‘You can’t wear this.’

Hannah was wearing jeans and a big fluffy pink jumper, which was worn at the elbows and around the cuffs.

‘Why not?’ Hannah said. ‘It’s untraditional!’

Meg raised an eyebrow at her.

‘Mum’s coming down next month, the second or the third, I think it is,’ Hannah said. ‘She’s very excited, I’ve found a couple of shops I want to try.’

‘And you’re still not going to let me know . . .’ Meg said. ‘Dress or suit, or any other information?’

‘I really think it should be a surprise!’

‘Okay.’

‘You’re not telling me about yours, or showing me.’

‘Yes but you know I’m getting a white dress!’ Meg said.

‘When are you going to go?’

‘I think it’s on David’s list,’ Meg said. ‘This week actually. I don’t want to overthink it, I just want something nice I can eat tacos and Angie’s cakes and dance in.’

'None of that dieting rubbish.'

'On that subject,' Meg said, 'do we have the Dairy Milk left in the fridge for when we get home?'

Hannah nodded, and, holding hands, they sprinted down the rest of their road to get to it quicker.

13

DAVID

74 Days Until the Wedding

'Hello, you.'

Meg looked sheepish as she stood outside Savage Lilies waving. She was looking oddly at him, and perhaps it was because he wearing a large brown suede jacket with a shirt underneath, a smarter combination than anything she had usually seen him wear.

'What's with the clothes?' she asked. 'You look fancy.'

'Meg, I can't dress how I normally dress for a bridal shop.' He spun round. 'I made an effort.'

'Well, thank you.'

He looked at the grandfather clock behind the counter. 'Best be off.'

'Where's that clock from? It's wonderful,' Meg said, as they started to walk to the bridal place.

'It was my parents',' he said. 'The one thing I kept of theirs. Been in the family for years, I think. Costs a fortune to repair.'

He paused for a minute, remembering where it used to

stand, in the doorway between the kitchen and living room in his family home.

'How are you feeling?' he asked. 'It's dress day! One of the big ones.' Meg was silent. 'All okay?'

'Yeah, yeah,' Meg said. 'Just hope we can find the perfect one!'

'No pressure, then.'

'It's just up here,' Meg said, pointing to a cream-bannered shop. 'I actually worked in the shop next door as a teenager. It used to be a gift shop.'

David looked sadly at the now vacant shop, and feared the same for Lilies. He put the thought out of his mind. Today wasn't about him; today was about the dress.

He had often seen people going in and out of the bridal shop on the high street, groups of friends, daughters and mothers and sisters, all arm-in-arm outside the shop, the bride holding the huge dress in its protective casing, posing for pictures. He had never been inside. It felt like a space for women, and he felt somewhat hesitant about going in, which is why he'd made sure he and Meg were okay to meet and go in together.

'I guess this is one of the only people in the town you don't know? The only one of our appointments?' Meg asked as they walked in the doors.

'Pretty much.' He was hoping with the launch of Work with Pride, that even those he hadn't yet met, or wasn't aware of, would soon be familiar to him. 'I'm popular, what can I say?'

Inside, the shop was pink and white, with black signage that said, 'I said yes to the dress!' against a wall with flowery wallpaper. Through into another room, white dresses lined three of the walls on sturdy-looking rails, which were weighted down with black sandbags hidden beneath them. There was a huge mirror and sofa, with a ring light in front of the mirror, and there was a smell of sugary cleanliness from a tiny bar in the corner, with a fridge that seemed to only contain Prosecco.

Meg looked somewhat unconfident, and David wondered whether it was this, more than any other appointment, that she had envisaged completing with her mother.

'You must be Meg,' said the woman behind the counter. She had short dark hair, and a stern expression. Her skin looked soft and polished, effortlessly perfect, and she could be nearly any age. David had always wondered what you wore to sell a wedding dress, and it turned out the answer was a blazer, T-shirt and trousers, which brushed the floor just above her high heels, at exactly the right height.

'Yes, hi.' Meg was looking round the shop, and seemed somewhat overwhelmed. 'Hi.'

'Don't worry, you don't have to try them all on,' the woman said, smiling. 'I'm Susan,' she added, shaking David's hand.

'David.'

'Are you . . .'

'A friend of Meg's,' he said. 'Here to support.'

'Lovely,' Susan said. 'Welcome. So, Meg, I've got your deposit, you've got the next hour for whatever you'd prefer. The way we usually do it, you pick five dresses. Hang them here, try them all on, and then we see whether you swap them all out, look for more of a certain type, whatever. Anything here, we tailor to your body shape obviously. I've been a seamstress forty years, do it all myself. That bit takes time but it's so we can get it exactly right, and it works with your timeline. You'd come in for a fitting closer to the time anyway, so we make sure it's perfect.'

'That's amazing,' David said.

'I can stand and say nothing, or I can give you my opinions,' she suggested.

'Maybe light-touch,' Meg said.

'Okay,' Susan said, smiling. 'And you mentioned your partner in the email, do you know what she's wearing?'

'No, we're keeping it a secret.'

'Better that way.'

'Do you think?' David said.

Susan nodded. 'Means you can just do what you want, which is what's important. Right, shall we get going? Can I get you both a drink?'

David enjoyed a cold Diet Coke from somewhere in the back room, careful not to move from his designated spot a few metres away from any fabric, as he chatted to Susan about the joys and trials of running a small business in the area. Meg circled the room, picking out dresses. David could see from the way she carried each one that they were heavy, and she was deliberating on each one she liked for a long time before adding it to the rail.

'Do you need a hand?' he asked.

'No, all good,' Meg replied. 'I'm going to put this one on,' she said, pointing to an embroidered flowery one.

'That's kind of like the dress I wore to my wedding,' Susan said, as Meg headed into the changing area.

'What did your partner wear?' David said. 'Did you attempt to match?'

'He went traditional . . . navy suit, brown shoes. You know the type.' Susan sighed. 'Men's clothes can be so boring.'

'I need to figure out what I'm going to wear,' David said.

'We could always help. I know a few tailors,' Susan said,

smiling. 'Other local businesses. Let me just check if Meg needs a hand.'

She put her head next to the changing area and called to Meg. 'All good, thanks,' Meg replied, and Susan came back to stand with him.

'It's nice to have gay people coming in to get their dresses now; makes for a whole different experience I find.'

'In what way?'

'Sometimes two brides come in together and I worry they might fight over the same dress, but mostly it's so lovely. I find there's a lot more emotion attached to it, and the options we've got in, we've got quite a few different things now, with how different all our brides are.'

'I'm ready!'

Meg's wavering voice rang out across the shop as she stepped out from the changing room and was guided onto the small circular platform in front of the mirror. The dress was huge and you could see her back muscles clenching as she tried to move in it. The back was baggy too, so she had stuffed a cushion in it to make it fit. After a second of looking at herself, she caught David's eye in the mirror and they both smiled, before starting to laugh.

Before they knew it, they had the giggles.

'So, not this one then?' Susan said.

'It really doesn't suit me . . . I wanted to start with something traditional, sorry,' Meg said. 'I don't know why this is so funny.'

'I think it's not the most flattering shape,' Susan said.

'I think it's the back . . . Why have you put a cushion there?' David said.

'It was in the changing room on this stool. I'd read people do that somewhere.'

Susan stepped forward holding two large clasps. 'We actually use these. That cushion is . . . décor.'

Before they knew it, they were all laughing.

'Sorry, Susan,' David said.

'Whatever works for the bride,' Susan said, in that reluctant way people are when they're enjoying a joke but shouldn't, like a tired father trying to put naughty children to bed. She was smiling but stern. 'You should all be comfortable enough to say what you like, or don't, in here. That's the aim. You're spending your own money.'

Next, Meg came out in three other dresses one by one. Initially, David felt like he was in the montage of a film. One was shorter, one had lacy sleeves and another had a sheer corset-type waist that looked uncomfortable. After each one, as soon as Meg looked in the mirror, she seemed to immediately know it was not for her, and did not even want to hear David or Susan's comments. Often, it took one look and she knew, though Susan made her reluctantly spin around. She became sullen and quiet, and David could tell something was up. This was surely not what either of them had expected from the day. Tactfully, Susan went to busy herself at the front of the store, and David almost felt like looking around for support, before realizing that that was what he was there for. It had all been so easy in Savage Lilies that first day helping a stranger, but now he couldn't help Meg without feeling the weight of her sadness himself.

'Are you okay?' he asked.

She looked at him, sniffed, and shook her head.

'You know you don't need to find one today,' David said. 'We can come back.' He lowered his voice. 'We can go somewhere else. It'll be trying a few, and seeing which styles work, and even then there'll be so many different versions.' Meg looked at him, still not speaking. 'Tell me how you're feeling.'

'I don't feel like a bride.' Meg's lip was doing that wobbly thing that happened when you were a word or two from letting go of what you had been holding together. 'You're meant to be feeling amazing, and the best your life's ever been, but . . . my parents still haven't replied to that message about talking.'

'I was going to ask whether . . .'

'Yeah,' Meg said, wiping her eyes. 'I wasn't going to say anything, but like, I don't feel like it's my *wedding*, you know. They should be here.'

David paused. He'd made a private pact with himself not to criticize Meg's parents while being a kind of temporary father figure. He felt even more protective of her than before, but he knew she needed support, rather than not understanding how complex a parental relationship could be.

'It'll be okay.' He moved closer to her. 'Trust me, whatever happens, you've done what you can; you know that. You've behaved impeccably. Hey, why don't you try that last one, since you got it out. You do need a dress and this shop is great. I think you've looked beautiful in all of them, but if you don't like any, we can come back, go elsewhere, or you don't actually even have to wear a dress! If you decide that isn't right.'

'I guess.'

'I know it . . . I promise you, you can do whatever you like to make it feel right. We'll sort it.'

He passed her a tissue quickly. The boxes of them dotted around were, presumably, for a more happy occasion, but they did their job.

'Okay, I'll try this one on,' she said. 'Only because Susan's scary,' she added, in a whisper, which made them both laugh.

'Take your time.'

Meg went back into the changing corner, and it felt like ten minutes before she came back out. She had wiped the tears from her face, and her skin had a dewy soft tone to it. She had put her hair up and out of her face in a ponytail and she held her hands in front of her. The dress was beautiful. It had tiny straps on her shoulders, which seemed like they shouldn't be able to support the dress and its train, which puffed out slightly but subtly from her frame. It was completely plain. No dramatic buttons, no corset, no detailing other than stitching in the places there had to be stitching, which meant that Meg was the focus, rather than the dress itself.

'I think this is actually it.'

David smiled, and before long, realized he hadn't actually said anything, since he'd been trying not to cry. She looked magnificent. He was glad she had decided it was the right one because otherwise he was going to have to convince her.

'Do you?'

'You look amazing,' David said.

'This feels much more you,' Susan said, walking over from the front desk.

'Do you think?'

'Fits you really well already,' she said. 'Let me get the clasps. Are you having your hair up?'

'I think so.'

Meg was smiling again, David was glad to see, and cautiously, just slightly, she seemed to be smiling at and admiring herself in the mirror.

Like the youth club would say, this was *ace*, David thought to himself.

He said he'd leave her to change back, and he went to speak to Susan. *Be brave,* he imagined Mary Portas saying in his ear, as he approached her with a stack of cards that he was hoping to leave in her window. He wanted to invite her to join his business network too. He hoped she'd say yes.

By the time he got home, David was exhausted. He had only been out of the flat for a couple of hours, but emotionally, he felt absolutely spent.

He came to hug Mark who was sitting on the sofa reading and as he started to talk about his day, Mark put the book down and lay down while David spoke.

'And after those four dresses,' David said, catching him up, 'I was really worried.'

'Well of course.'

'But then, we had a bit of a pep talk – you know when you just take all the pressure off. The next one, she loved it. She absolutely loved it, and she was right to. She looked amazing. And I was thinking, you know, Matty could be the photographer for the wedding? I know he doesn't do weddings, but maybe he would for this. I'll have to ask him.'

'Okay, yeah,' Mark said. 'Maybe.'

'Next we need to do décor, and actually confirm the venue.'

'You know Matty's dad is in hospital?'

'What?'

'He's okay, but he had a serious scare with his heart.'

'Oh, that's awful.'

'I know,' Mark said. 'So maybe don't message yet. And if you weren't so obsessed with this wedding, maybe you would have spoken to him.'

'Sorry, I didn't even realize . . .'

'I know you didn't.'

David looked at Mark. It wasn't like he was picking a fight; neither of them ever did that. His voice was level. It was clear, though, that he was upset.

'Is what I'm doing with Meg a problem?' David said. 'I didn't even know you were annoyed . . .'

'I'm not *annoyed*,' Mark said, before sighing. 'I'm a little frustrated that all you've talked about since you got in is somebody else's wedding. You were late on Saturday and you didn't prep anything like you promised you would. I'm worried about you too. This is a lot to take on with everything that's happened to you.'

'Okay but I solved Saturday, and I thought we were okay . . . I'm fine, I promise.'

Mark sat up and leaned against the arm of the sofa. 'I'm deadly serious, David. I've not mentioned it for years but it's been on my mind recently and I think it must be on yours, with all of this. I would like to get married. I would, before we're old and we've got other priorities or life happens to us. I would like you to consider it properly, and work through whatever it is that just makes you shut down when we talk about it. Your parents can't stop you doing certain things forever, not if those things are important to me too.'

'Mark, I . . .'

'It hurts to see you spend all this time on a stranger's wedding when you won't even talk to me about the possibility of us getting married. That's the bottom line.'

'It's . . . Meg's not a stranger.'

'She was,' Mark said. 'Literally, what, three weeks ago, she was someone you didn't know existed, and now it's like you're doing something every day for her. And the money problems at Lilies, David, you need to take them seriously. The shop has to break even. It's not a game, it's real life. I'd like to go on holiday this year . . . And if we got married, how would we pay for it?'

'I know about the shop,' David said.

'I'd like to get married while my parents are alive,' Mark said. 'And it feels awful saying that to you that I might get a wedding where that does happen, and you won't have that, but I really think we should do it.'

'But our life is good!' David said. He stood up, since sitting on the edge of the armchair was beginning to make his thigh ache. 'Do you not think marriage is . . . for young people? What do you think people will think?'

'What happened to not caring what people think? You have to practise what you preach. People would be happy! Who do you know in our lives who would be upset, or laugh at the idea of us getting married?'

'Well, nobody.'

'Exactly!' Mark said. 'David, please, just think about it seriously. And be mindful not to let Meg's wedding take over. I know it's exciting and it's a nice thing for you to be doing. I get it; I really do. Meg is lovely. You just have other commitments too. Remember that.'

'Okay,' David said. 'I'll think about the marriage thing.'

'You promise?'

David set his face straight and reached out to hold Mark's hands. 'I do.'

'God, you're annoying.'

They sat on the sofa together, in comfortable silence, and David couldn't help but think of the first promise he'd made Mark, two decades earlier.

David was living in Wakefield, working as a teaching assistant. He had a few friends in the town from work, and a couple of others who had moved from Leeds. He was out at the town's one gay bar with a friend, and was introduced to a number of other men, who all seemed to know each other, bringing friends of their friends to the table, until there were about a dozen or so of them. David had been seated next to Mark, and though they had chatted the entire night, everybody else fading to dust in his peripheral vision, David had not realized Mark had been flirting. Years later, Mark always told this story: David friendly but oblivious, him not knowing where he stood either.

They had kept talking, till the others were bored and went to dance, or get drinks, or went home, and it was just the two of them. David had kept telling Mark he was free to go dance, or go home, sorry if he was keeping him, and his complete lack of awareness was oddly charming, Mark also said later.

Much later in the evening, Mark's friends had all left and he finally told David he'd like his number.

'Why?' David had said.

'To call you.'

'Why would you call me?'

'To ask you out.'

'Oh.'

The penny dropped, and David had scrambled for his recently purchased smartphone. They did not kiss that evening, just left on a note of hope and potential. Mark's friends who he was staying with (turned out he was living in Leeds, not Wakefield, at the time) were heading home, and he couldn't change plans as they'd worry, so rather than a kiss or anything more, they left on a promise.

'You promise you'll call me?' Mark said.

'Of course,' David said, and he meant it. He knew, without doubt, that he would. 'I promise.'

When Mark left, he wrote the number on his hand too, just in case anything went wrong with his phone, and the next day, he had called. The last nineteen years, ten months and five days, the best of his life, had all hinged on that promise.

14

MEG

62 Days Until the Wedding

Meg was tired. She had been up late the night before finishing an illustration project for a breakfast cereal brand's new advertising campaign. She had been drawing pieces of cereal for so long she had become almost like a factory manufacturing line, and by two o'clock, because she was almost done and why not, she had stayed up another half an hour to finish.

Later that day, she knew she needed to fit in some time looking at Ramon's taco truck branding. She'd talked about it with Gus, who'd said he'd been texting Ramon and when he mentioned it to him, he had been really keen. She was happy to help, now she'd confirmed the truck for the wedding, and said she'd draw up a couple of mood boards.

She needed to catch up with Hannah too; it was tough, her being away, and trying to make her feel like she was involved in all the decisions. Since she worked in events, her input was genuinely so helpful, and she knew at some point today she needed to update the wedding spreadsheet and send it to her.

David was picking her up at eight-thirty that morning, so, thinking back to all her work yesterday and the work that was to come, it was with heavy legs and tired eyes that she climbed into his van, heaving herself up the small step, careful not to make a groaning noise. Another thing for the list – she really needed to start learning to drive.

'I brought you a coffee,' he said, passing her one of the Savage Lilies-branded cups, bright green with striped lettering. 'A flat white. Have I got that right? Oh it rhymes!'

'Thanks so much,' she said, taking it gratefully and balancing it between her legs. It was needed, and likely the only way she would make it through today's appointments. She'd had two pubs in the area save the date for her, and she would pick between them when they had a chance to meet the owners. However, she was aware their idea of a simple wedding in a pub would need a level of decoration to feel simple, and so she had found Jacques, an interior designer and event specialist who had invited her and David to his home in order to talk through her ideas and what he might be able to offer. The appointment was free, he'd said on the phone, as it was important to make sure their ideas matched, and that they had *synergy.*

He lived in one of the new builds on the other side of town, in a huge area that Meg remembered going to on a school trip once when it was just fields, when they had been learning about local wildlife. When they arrived, they instantly knew which was his door, as it had the number of the house but a small plaque next to it, which read *Jacques: Event Visuals and Interior Design.*

Once inside, Jacques didn't waste much time. Meg had barely taken in the design of the house itself before he had begun interrogating her about the wedding. Briefly, she took in wood panelling on one wall, a marble light fitting and, in the garden, a sunken conversation pit. It was in no way what you might expect from the uniformity you were greeted with from the road, and though the décor was loud, it was all very charming and fitted together.

'So,' he said. He was tall and thin, and was wearing a fitted shirt and chinos that were pin-straight down to his feet where he wore duck-patterned socks. 'There are such simple things you can do to make a venue look great. Nowadays, it's all about the visuals. You want every photo, every angle, to be perfect. You only get one shot at this, for all the shots to be flawless.'

It felt like a rehearsed line. He was evidently much more serious than the vendors they had seen before. David was refusing to meet her eye.

'The visuals need to be unique, but comfortable on people's eyes,' Jacques said. 'They need to let people know, you know, that this is a wedding. No, that this is *the* wedding.'

'Exactly,' David said, nodding.

Meg turned sideways and looked at him.

'The things I'd like to focus on,' Jacques continued, 'with what you've shown me, is a photo wall. Not with flowers – that's a bit passé – but imagery.' David stiffened next to her. 'Something different. We need to unite the space, so again, flowers, if used sparingly, could do that, but I'm more interested in linens, and cushions, and *colour.* The arch at the end of the aisle, that's always really clearly setting out your stall. I'll need to see what you're wearing, and the outfit of who's walking you down the aisle, to make sure everything matches.'

'Erm yes,' Meg said. She didn't want to think about her dad still not confirming he was coming and therefore that he would walk her down the aisle. In front of Jacques, and for now, she just pretended. 'Yes, that'll be fine.'

'Good,' Jacques continued. 'And again, that's just more of the linens, the way I usually do them. If you hire in, that's actually not too expensive. Linens look much better than anything else.'

'But flowers are important, right?' David said. 'Sorry, I should have said. I'm her florist.'

'Oh.' Jacques paused. 'People don't usually bring their florists.'

'Oh, he's also my . . .' Meg said '. . . friend.'

David smiled at her.

'Flowers are great,' he said, correcting himself. 'Don't get me wrong. We love a florist! Well done you. Florals can be very . . . impactful, when used sparingly.' He was flitting about the room, grabbing different materials to show her. 'You said about non-traditional weddings, well I like to use flowers slightly less than for a traditional service. I like to think of visuals as made up of, say, fifty things, rather than just flowers, like everyone else thinks of.'

Meg slightly got it, but she was in no way going to alienate David, and she could see how you could have multiple flowers alongside whatever décor Jacques would plan. Distractingly, Meg couldn't count the number of times he had said the word *visuals*.

'Look, let me show you,' he said, sitting down between them with a big book with his name embossed on the front. 'The pictures speak for themselves.'

Meg breathed in, perhaps expecting some kind of friction here over the differing tastes of the three of them, but from the first page of the book, she was hugely impressed.

'These are . . .' Meg began.

'Amazing,' David said, finishing her sentence.

Each page had a before and after, and he had managed to turn a lot of familiar locations across the city and its surrounding towns into bespoke, modern venues. There was a town hall where she'd been to birthday parties years ago as a child that had been turned into what looked like a sun-drenched Italian cottage, or there was an installation in the shopping centre Meg had spent countless weekends hanging around in that had turned a marble-floored concrete square into a bright cartoony beach. It was uncanny, the places of Meg's childhood made into something completely different.

'That one wasn't a wedding,' Jacques said. 'I had to work with . . . a lot of children.' He looked like he'd eaten something sour.

'Oh, I love this one!' Meg said, pointing at the book. It was a hotel near where her parents had once lived, and with just white, pink and blue, Jacques had turned the space into an elegant sort of room that seemed to go on as far as the eye could see, which was then transformed again when the lights went down, and fairy lights in opposing colours turned it into a kind of linen-draped club. Meg remembered having a tenth birthday party there, with an S Club 7 theme.

'We can use that as the blueprint,' Jacques said. 'That's within the budget you mentioned to me.'

'Okay, perfect,' Meg said, nodding. 'Oh I'm so excited now! And it's so important to me to support queer-owned businesses in the area.' She turned and beamed at him.

'You're just assuming I'm gay?'

'Oh,' Meg said. 'I—'

'No, we didn't—' David started.

'Because my sign says interior design?' Jacques stared at both of them. He grinned. 'I'm just playing, of course I am. Imagine the alternative!'

He laughed to himself and, relieved, Meg and David did the same. He was odd, this man, but Meg liked his work and was intrigued by him. The photos spoke better than he did. As they relaxed, she let her eyes wander around the rooms of his home, and she saw in the kitchen that he had a breakfast bar with hanging saucepans in a way that reminded her of a home completely different to this one, like an old farmhouse. It was clever, really clever, what he'd done with the place.

'I should say then,' David began, 'I've started a queer small business network, Work with Pride. For us to share learnings, but also to recommend each other. Would you like to join?'

Jacques paused. For the first time since they had arrived, he'd stopped speaking and he looked genuinely thankful. 'That's a great idea,' he said. 'Thanks so much.'

'No worries,' David said, passing him a card. 'I wondered too if you might come and look at the design of my shop? We could do with fitting more people in for events and there's a few things that could do with a refresh.'

'I'd love to!'

They discussed dates, costs and next steps, and before too long, David and Meg were back in the van, returning to start their days.

'All this and it's only nine-thirty,' David said. 'We're doing well.'

'Aren't we just?' Meg said. 'I've got a few more work bits to do, then I want to try the Lido at some point. I keep meaning to go.'

'So, Jacques.' David turned off the main road onto the street before the High Street. 'Did you like him? Happy to go ahead?'

'Yeah, I think so,' Meg said. 'I know he made that little joke but I liked how proud he was, you know, and I feel like he'll do a good job. Not everyone who does something for the wedding has to be a new friend. Maybe we've just struck lucky so far.'

'Maybe,' David said. 'He'll do a good job, but don't you dare cut back on any flowers.'

'David,' Meg said. 'That idea is *unthinkable* to me, trust me.'

'Good,' he replied, pulling into his usual parking spot in front of the shop. Meg heard a squeak under one of the wheels but didn't say anything.

'Do you think Hannah will like the one I picked out?' Meg asked. 'I'll check with her obviously.'

'I can't see why not,' he said. 'It's simple but really nice, and it has a lot of colour like she wanted.'

'Yeah.'

'Do you tend to have the same taste?'

'I think so,' Meg said. 'We always pick the same things for the house, so, yeah.'

'Do you think you're similar generally?' David said. They were standing by the van outside the shop and with Ray inside manning the till. David seemed in no rush to leave. 'I always wonder how different you can or should be as a couple.'

'I think so,' Meg said. 'Hannah's maybe more

adventurous than me. I like going out and doing things but I love a home comfort, and I'm really happy at home with my things, having a quiet one. She needs a little more excitement – new people, new places, you know, which her work gives her. I guess we're the same with the big picture though, like neither of us want to work ourselves into the ground. We like that we do something we enjoy for our careers but we still want work to fit into our lives and not the other way around.'

'That makes sense. I try to be the same.'

'How about you and Mark?'

'I think we were more different when we were younger,' David said. 'Mark always wanted to stay till the end of the evening, and he was definitely always more demonstrative in public, which I never was. But with everybody, when you get older, your life slows down in a pleasant way, and we're probably the same as you in terms of liking the simple things. We have a routine that has enough variation in it to be exciting but enough stability for us to feel really strong.'

'And do you think you're different?'

'Our upbringings were very different,' David said. 'I rush into things, whereas Mark takes his time, which I guess . . . He was brought up with really involved parents, whereas I was left to my own devices. I'm not very used to getting everyone's opinion; I'm more used to being a lone ranger. He has to stop me jumping into things quite impulsively, but I think we balance each other out, like that.'

'Were his parents good when he came out then?'

'Yes,' David said. 'He's only told me that story maybe once, since it's so boring! They both already kind of knew, and were supportive. Mine were awful, but you know that.'

'Oh I'm so sorry, David. You've told me the basics, but I'm here if you want to talk about it.'

'That's okay,' he said. 'I know you get it, you know, how tricky it can be.'

'Do you ever . . . ?'

'No, I never got round to it and it's not an option now,' he continued. 'They died quite young. I'd just met Mark and my mum got ill, a complication with her lungs, then she died so suddenly before I'd got my head around going to see them. Then Dad died really quickly after that. A broken heart, I think. I was devastated obviously, but kind of removed from it. It was only in the years after I dealt with it properly. Mark recommended a therapist.'

'I'm so sorry.'

'Not much you can do about the past though,' David said. 'You can only affect the present. Like I do wish I'd gone to the funerals. That's a big regret, but . . .' He sighed. 'What can you do?' He looked up oddly at the shop, as if he was going to say something about it. 'Anyway, I'd better go and relieve Ray because I can see he needs to go to the toilet but is too polite to ask or leave the counter. I'll see you tomorrow.'

With that, the positivity back on his face, David was gone, and Meg was left feeling optimistic about the wedding but sad for her friend, and wondering about her own parents and her own regrets. How would she feel in twenty years if they didn't come to the wedding?

15

DAVID

47 Days Until the Wedding

David invited Meg to the shop for lunch before they went to see wedding venues. He felt they were true friends now. She often spent her lunchtimes, she had said, watching television with food on her lap, or eating a sandwich while she worked, so he thought she might enjoy the company. Savage Lilies only had two lunch options, unless you wanted one of your three meals a day to be a chocolate muffin, and so the choice was the savoury pastry or cheese and Marmite roll he ordered in from Angie. While they ate, they caught up, and despite the fact he should be wishing for customers, it felt good to talk alone.

David wanted to talk to Meg about what Mark had said about them marrying. He wanted to be able to give Mark a definitive answer but there wasn't any definitive answer in his head. How did you know if you wanted to get married? How had Meg known?

However, they talked about the venues and then they spoke about options for décor and what Meg thought about Hannah's playlist choices, and he hadn't worked out what to say. He asked instead, wondering if it might come up naturally, about their engagement.

'It was very casual,' Meg explained. 'We both knew we wanted to marry, and she said she wanted to propose so I was just waiting. Then, one day, on a walk by the canal where we used to live, she just did it. I didn't expect it, not then or like that. She had a lovely speech ready and I said yes and a few random people cheered. It was nice. We went for dinner, called all our friends when we came home. Told our parents.'

David felt strange at the thought of doing something similarly low-key with Mark and he didn't know what to say. He wondered if their after-dinner walk would work. Would Mark want it in public, or private? Too much to think about. Instead, he said, 'Shall we get going? Don't want to be late.'

The first appointment with a venue was at David's preferred pub, The Sheep's Inn. It took just twenty minutes to have a tour and discuss prices, and then around three o'clock, they walked together to the other pub on the high street. It was called The Old Oak, and sat neatly at the bottom of the hill. In the front parking area, there was a large tree that shadowed and protected the building itself, and then round the back was a huge garden area, which was where Meg would want to erect a marquee.

Hanging around outside the front were a group from the youth club, all finished school for the day, and seemingly daring each other to try and go in and get served. Benji was laughing, and Salma was standing closest to the door, as if she might try.

'All right, everyone?' David said. 'What are you doing here?'

'Oh, not much.' Fred was laughing.

Salma looked sheepish, but Benji looked more confident.

'Maybe if we go in with David, they'll serve us,' he said. 'Or let us have a drink with a meal.'

'I don't think so,' David said. 'You guys be careful.'

He heard one of the others mutter that they should go to The Sheep's Inn, the other pub, but David laughed because that was the one he would count as his regular, and the one where he and Mark were much more likely to see them.

'Do they try this a lot?' Meg asked.

'I think it's more like something to do,' David said. 'Whether they get in or not doesn't matter. I mean, there's not a lot to do round here and this'll pass an hour or so.'

'I won't tell them but it's much easier at The Hope, in the village over.'

'Meg! Definitely don't tell them that.'

'We only did it once or twice.' Meg sighed. 'There was so much more here for kids when I was young.'

'Was there?'

He and Mark must have moved here around the time Meg had left, and David had felt curious about how the town compared from when Meg had grown up here to now but he didn't want to upset her by asking.

'Yeah, there was the pool with the slide, and that only cost a pound to get in,' Meg said. 'The park was better before too. They've got rid of the bus route I used to get into town – I noticed the other day when I wanted to go shopping. I would have hated if that had happened when I was in Sixth Form, I'd have had no way to get into town without relying on Mum and Dad, or Gus when he learned to drive.'

'That's rubbish,' David said. 'I really feel for the kids.'

'I guess you don't miss what you didn't know existed before, but, yeah, it's tough. I get why the club is so valuable.'

Inside, they were greeted by Rod, who ran the pub, and who sat with them at a table in the corner.

He was a large man, with a loud voice. He was wearing boat shoes, jeans, and a polo shirt in a dark green colour and he was wearing a big metal watch on his wrist. When he spoke, his face broke into a smile, and David noticed he had combed his hair over to cover a receding hairline. He must also, thought David, be somewhere in his fifties.

'So, a wedding,' he said, getting out an old binder. 'That's exciting. We never normally do weddings.'

'Yeah, it's . . .' Meg looked at David as if he were better placed to describe her wedding to this stranger, but of course this was her job and he let her explain. 'It's not very traditional. We don't want a big thing. Me and my partner, Hannah, she and I would like something intimate, and easy and casual.'

David noticed her deliberate pronoun use, something familiar to him, the taking of the power out of the hands of someone else to force you to come out and to do it instead on your own terms.

'Great,' Rod said. 'Well that's no problem and we can certainly host it. We've got the date saved. What would you need on the day?'

'I'd want the marquee outside, for the ceremony, and that can turn into where people sit and eat. We might need to hire some chairs in, but that's fine. Fingers crossed, it'll be sunny, in June. We'd want a microphone, and a DJ will be coming until, what . . . midnight, or one o'clock? Whenever you can be open until, really. We have a food truck we'd like to bring in, since I know you said you can't do food on that scale, but looks like they could drive into the garden from the road?'

'Yeah, sorry about that.'

'No problem at all,' Meg said, smiling at him. 'I think that's everything. We've got a bit of money for a bar tab and then people can order themselves at the bar afterwards.'

'Great,' he replied. 'We also have a small outside bar we could open. So you can make that just a second bar, or a cocktail station or whatever. That sound good?'

'Okay.'

'We also have a storage room in the basement, which is good for events and things. We can clear it out slightly, give you more space, put anything in there the week before.'

'That would be great,' David said. 'Save us carrying things back and forth on the day.'

'It's quite short notice for a wedding, isn't it?' Rod said.

'Yes.'

'It's no problem. A tight deadline, but we can make it work. I just have to make sure the regulars don't turn up annoyed we're closed. Can you let me know in the next week?'

'Brilliant,' Meg replied. 'I'll come back to you as soon as I can.'

'How are you feeling then?' Rod asked, turning to David. 'Daughter getting married – it's a big day. I remember my wedding day. The in-laws were all over the place.'

'Oh,' Meg said.

'I'm actually not her father.'

'Uncle?'

'No.'

'. . . Grandad?' Rod said tentatively.

'No, none of those.'

'Sorry, I'll stop guessing.' Rod put his hands up in

surrender, in a way that annoyed David, like he was mocking him. 'It doesn't matter.'

'It does matter, actually.' David could feel his chest tighten. He, as happened incredibly rarely, was getting angry. Meg was looking at him strangely from across the table.

'Okay, how do you . . . know Meg?'

'I'm a friend of hers and I'm . . . I guess you could say standing in for her father.'

'Why's that then?'

'Because she's gay and her parents are currently not looking like they'll attend the wedding,' David said. 'And I'm gay too.'

They all looked at each other for a moment, and then Rod spoke again. 'Sorry,' he said. 'You just didn't look gay.'

David was stunned. 'What does gay look like then?'

'David . . .' Meg said.

David could feel bile rising in his throat, his whole body tensed with the stress of confrontation. He was already too warm in his jumper, and now he could feel sweat pooling at the base of his back.

'Why are you getting so mad, mate?' Rod asked. He had pushed his chair back slightly away from the table.

'Because I am gay,' David said. 'Whether you think it or not! *Mate!*'

David worried too he shouldn't have said about Meg's parents. She was looking at him funny, like he'd let her down, and that she wished she was anywhere else.

Rod was fumbling with how to fix the situation. 'I literally never said . . .'

'Maybe we should go,' Meg said.

'Maybe we should,' David said, taking Meg's hand. She waved it off.

'I'm really sorry,' Rod said. 'I genuinely didn't mean to offend, or to upset anyone . . .'

Suddenly their small table felt much too cramped. David was desperate to get up, to be anywhere but here.

'I know,' Meg said, turning back to him when they were already steps away from the table.

'No, don't say that, Meg,' David said, looking at Meg. 'He didn't say it to you.'

Meg looked up at him, with surprise and hurt in her eyes. 'Let's just go.'

'I *really* didn't mean to upset—' Rod tried to speak, but they were already several feet away.

'Well you did,' David said.

'Sorry,' he said again, as David pushed open the door.

They got outside, and David took his jumper off, stood underneath the tree in the car park taking in big gasps of air.

'Are you okay?' Meg asked him.

'I don't know,' he said, shaking his head, pushing her away. 'I didn't expect . . . I need to sit down.'

16

MEG

'I just didn't expect it. I mean every day I get up and get on with my life, and now I have to prove myself to a man in a pub I've never met?'

Meg was surprised both at how angry David had been, and how long-lasting the feeling seemed to be. She guessed his response stemmed from how his parents had been when he'd been growing up and when he came out to them, but she hadn't thought before about someone's childhood still affecting them at David's age. It made her worried. He'd said bits and pieces as they'd got to know each other, but the way he'd spoken about his parents had always been factual and as if it were all a long-ago memory, compartmentalized and neutralized. After leaving the pub, he had gone silent on the walk back up the hill but now inside Savage Lilies, he still seemed upset. She had sat him down with a mint tea in the back room and was trying to provide for him what he had provided for her the last few weeks, with the niggling thought at the back of her head: *You need to speak to your parents.*

'I know, David,' she said. 'It was thoughtless of him, and he shouldn't have said it. I completely agree.'

'I just wish something like that wasn't enough to . . . You know, to ruin my day.'

David wasn't crying, but his cheeks were red and he was breathing in that way where someone is trying to slow their body down to calm themselves.

'I know,' Meg said. 'I would have been the same. People can be cruel, but I really think he didn't mean to be, and I believe he was sorry he upset you.'

'Yeah,' David said. 'I was just too caught up in there.'

'Obviously if you're really offended and you don't want to see him again,' Meg said. 'We can just go with the other pub.'

'No, Meg, it's your day,' David said. 'It's nothing to do with me.'

'I wouldn't want you uncomfortable.'

'But that's on me, not him.'

'The Sheep's Inn was our favourite, anyway, I thought.'

'It was,' David said.

'Okay then, that's settled.'

'Only if you're sure.'

'I am.'

He smiled at her and she rubbed her hand up and down his arms. David was still a strong man, physically and mentally, and she was surprised to see how something like this had been the thing to shake him. He wiped at his eyes with a dotted handkerchief. 'You're not angry I told him about your parents? As soon as I said it, I realized it wasn't my news to share.'

'That's okay,' Meg said. 'I'm not embarrassed. It's not about me. I was just worried you were upset.'

'It's just . . . I don't know.' He was fiddling with the polka dot fabric in his hands. 'I feel like I've worked so hard, since my parents and everything that happened, well since I came out to them, I've worked so hard to be proud, and to be myself, and to go into all situations with nothing to hide. Things like that, they make me feel like I'm causing a fuss. Like I should just easily pass for a straight old man and make everything easier for everyone else, so they don't have to deal with difference. But why should I?' He threw his hands in the air.

'You shouldn't!'

'It's easier when you're young – you can show it in your fashion. You can, I don't know, you can talk about dating and things . . . Unless I'm standing with Mark, people don't know. Even then, they sometimes assume we're brothers or friends or whatever. We looked after his niece and nephew and someone assumed we were two dad-friends with our own kids. People just love to not believe you.'

'I get that.' Meg smiled. 'We went away for a night to celebrate our engagement and they asked why sisters at our age wanted to share a bed.'

'That's awful.'

'Yeah.'

'It brings me back round every time, to me coming out to my parents,' David said. 'Them sat in the living room, just not accepting it. Point-blank, my dad said *no you're not*. My mum said it was a phase, when I pushed them and I said no it wasn't, and then my dad said well you need to choose to make it not what you are, or we don't want you under this roof.'

'Bloody hell. I'm sorry, David. I can't believe . . . I didn't know it had been that bad.'

'It's okay.'

'I really am sorry,' she said. 'That shouldn't have happened to you, and you were so young.'

She stroked the side of his neck. It felt weirdly intimate but she felt close to him, and she knew, selfishly, that David was the right person to see her through all of this, and that maybe she could repay him by doing the same in the other direction. She leaned over to hug him fully, until he was okay again.

An hour later, she walked back to hers, to prep the house for Hannah's arrival. It was at times like this she wished she drove, walking through the drizzly grey May streets, face steeled against the oncoming rain.

She had left David in okay spirits. He said he would ring and confirm the other pub, The Sheep's Inn, before the deadline of midnight tonight in order to secure the booking, and she had headed to hers, hoping Mark would be home soon to give David some more support too. She genuinely didn't care too much about the venue, since both pubs were fine and their guests would barely notice a difference. She was just worried about David.

On the street, she saw a few members of the youth club outside the small corner shop, playing with a bike and pushing each other around. She guessed they hadn't got served. She waved and Salma shouted her name, so she went over to quickly say hello. They were standing under the shop's awning and it was a welcome respite from the rain.

'Hey,' she said.

'It's Meg!' Salma said, shouting to the others. 'Gio, you missed her talk on her job. She used to work for CBBC.'

'That's so cool!' the boy, presumably Gio, said.

'Well, not anymore . . .' Meg said.

'Yeah, she's now *freelance*,' Fred said. 'Which means you do your own hours. I want to do that.'

Meg was surprised and touched the kids seemed to have listened to her talk. She didn't know how it had gone down. In the moment, in the shop, she had been purely focused on continuing the talk and not losing the group's attention.

'Are you doing another talk, Meg?' Benji asked.

'No, I don't think so.'

'Oh!' Salma said.

'Unless,' Meg said. She thought back to her boredom round here when she was a kid, and what David had said earlier. Would this be a way of paying him back for all the help he was giving her? 'Would you like one?'

'Yes please!' Salma said.

'Yes!' Gio said. 'I promise I won't miss this one.'

'Well maybe I'll talk to Jacob, see if David can give us the florist's,' Meg said. She saw a few of the kids slap each other's hands excitedly. 'I could do a drawing class?'

'Thanks, man,' Benji said. 'I could do with working on my skills.'

'Okay, decided then.' Meg smiled at them, and looked out at the rain, which seemed to have eased off, just slightly. 'As long as David says yes.'

'He will,' Salma said. 'He loves us!'

'Yeah, he's sound,' Fred said.

'Well, I know he doesn't always feel like he's sound,' Meg said. 'So make sure you're good to him.'

'What do you mean?' Fred asked.

'It's just sometimes . . .' Meg paused. It had been a throwaway comment, but the group were old enough to understand. 'When you're a kid, you assume adults know everything and that they're always fine,' she said. 'And actually . . . they find life hard too. We're all just figuring it out.'

'Even Dua?' Salma asked.

'Especially Dua.'

Meg waved and ran out into the rain, feeling every day like she was embedding herself with another anchor in this community, and she positively sprinted down the road. She was getting soaked, but it was worth it because she was running towards Hannah, who'd be home so very soon.

17

DAVID

46 Days Until the Wedding

That Thursday, David had no deliveries, because he'd consolidated the weekday and weekend orders in order to save money. So, he treated himself to a small lie-in, sitting in bed listening to Radio 1 – he was keen to hear that Beyoncé song Salma kept talking about – and eating Cheerios. After a long shower, and putting on one of his favourite T-shirts, it was half-eight by the time he was downstairs and he began to whizz through the usual opening jobs in record time in order to be able to open for nine-thirty. Without the usual five o'clock wake-up, he actually felt more tired, which was perhaps because on a normal day, he would have already been on his fourth coffee, not his first.

No, that Thursday, he was all out of sorts.

A woman wearing a cap knocked on the glass of the door. 'Are you open?'

'Yes!' David said. They had been for half an hour.

'Okay,' the woman said. She peered round for a few minutes and left pretty much immediately. David sat back behind the counter, and wondered what it was all for. All week, his mind had been taken up with what Mark had said about considering seriously the question of them marrying. He hadn't given an ultimatum exactly, but it wasn't fair on your partner to only respond if there was a loss of your own to be had. He knew he had to give it proper attention, but he still couldn't work out how to work out what he felt. Would it be easier to just say yes? No, that wouldn't be fair either.

Mark had come home late the night before and needed to vent about a new workplace initiative, which he said was about management, nothing to do with helping young people. Some of the teachers – David couldn't help but imagine Meg's parents among them – had complained about time and resources being taken away from teaching and being given to something as 'extracurricular' as counselling. While chatting, David had cooked them dinner and needed to pop down to the shop to get some basil and to set something out for the morning. By the time he remembered about calling the pub, it had been a bit late to get in touch, and having a bit of a headache, he'd gone to bed early, noting that he would phone in the morning. A few hours wouldn't make a difference.

Then today, he hadn't called whilst upstairs, thinking he should get his jobs going so they could open, and so he knew it was something he should do before lunch. He thought about writing it on his to-do list. He realized no music was playing so he pressed shuffle on the shop's playlist, and 'Roses' by OutKast blared loudly from the speakers so he started to fiddle with the volume to make it right.

Another knock at the window, which he thought might be a customer, turned out to be Benji, Salma and Fred, who were waving vigorously, all in school uniform, which made him walk away from his list and to the front of the shop.

'What do you all want?' David asked. 'So early!'

'We're running late for school,' Fred said.

'Well off you go then,' David said. 'Don't get in trouble on my account.'

'We wanted to bring you something,' Salma said, and from her bag she produced a Tupperware box full of brownies, which seemed to have been stacked on top of each other and had all blended into one. On top, in green icing, were some words David couldn't make out.

At the same time, Benji was walking round the shop with his phone, filming.

'What are you doing there?' he asked him.

'Don't mind me,' Benji said. 'It's for your socials.'

'More than one?' David said. 'I thought each person had one social media.'

'Come on, man,' Benji muttered.

'We made these together last night,' Salma said, pointing again to the brownies.

'We appreciate you,' Fred said. 'Not to be intense.'

'Oh, guys, what brought this on? You didn't have to do this!' David said, peering into the Tupperware and still keeping an eye on Benji bouncing around the store.

'You always do stuff for us.' Benji looked proud, perhaps the ringleader of this plan, as he seemed to be for so many others. 'We wanted to do something. Hope they don't taste bad, we've never made them before.'

'I'm sure they're great,' David said.

'You've got two hundred followers on Instagram now, by the way.' Benji was bent down, filming some kind of reveal from the bottom of a string of nickels plant from the end of its tendrils to its pot hanging from the ceiling. He said it casually, but David could tell he was proud of himself, and seeking positive feedback.

'What?'

'Followers are like, when . . .'

'I know what followers are!' David said. 'I'm not one hundred and fifty. I mean, that's great, surely, Benji? Not great, but amazing. If two hundred people came and used the florist's, I'd love it.'

'There's three hundred thousand people in Milton Keynes,' Fred said. 'That was in a geography test.'

'So a few more people to go then?' David said.

'It's not bad,' Salma said. 'But it's nowhere near . . . I mean Taylor Swift has two hundred and eighty-four million.'

'Shut up, Salma,' Benji said.

'Hey, guys—'

'David Beckham has seventy-one million,' Fred added.

'Well I don't think we're competing with them, thankfully.'

'Anyway,' Benji said. 'I've got ideas. I'll come in one day and film some stuff. Not tonight though.'

'He's going on a date,' Salma said.

'A date! Who with?'

'I don't know!' Fred said.

Salma crossed her arms. 'He won't tell us.'

'It's just the cinema,' Benji said. 'I mean . . .'

'Which cinema?' Salma said.

'That's okay,' David said. 'You don't have to share.'

'I'll tell people sometime . . .' Benji said. 'If it goes well.'

'Well it won't go well if you have a detention and can't go, so why don't you all get to school?'

'Thanks, David,' Fred said.

'Thanks for the cakes!'

'Bye, Dave man . . . don't eat them all, they're for Mark too!' Benji said.

'Hurry up,' shouted David, laughing. 'You're making me feel like I'm late!'

Later, David was sitting behind the counter and he knew he wasn't even going to be able to get through a page of the book. He was distracted by the thought that ideally he wouldn't be reading because there'd be customers, and whether there was anything else he should be doing to get more custom. Should he be planning more events? Should he be standing outside the shop shouting at people to come in? They usually did the wreath-making classes at Christmas but maybe he should do more than one, since it always sold out. Was there something he could do for New Year's? What was the Halloween equivalent? Would he even make it to the end of the year? Why were there no obvious summer events?

At that moment, his phone rang, Mark calling.

'Hey, honey,' Mark said.

'Hello, you,' David said.

'All okay?'

'I'm okay, a little bored, bit sleepy, but what can you do?'

'The post-lunch slump. Did you eat that cheese and Marmite thing again? I told you . . . Anyway, many people in?' Mark's voice sounded strained asking about the shop's business, as if he'd made it sound deliberately hopeful. 'I had a spare ten minutes; thought I'd call.'

'Not this afternoon.' David fiddled with a pen in his hand. 'Hey, I was thinking, maybe the flower-arranging classes should be monthly. Rather than just around a holiday, they could also be generally about learning the skill, you know, or maybe hen dos?'

'Hen dos is a good idea,' Mark said. 'Though you can't discriminate. Maybe some manly stags would like a flower class.' He sighed on the other end of the line. 'It takes so much to make this a success, doesn't it?'

'What do you mean?'

'It just feels like you're pouring so much of yourself and your time into this. When you started . . . It never used to be this hard. It's not a job, it's a life.'

'I know, Mark, but I love it.'

'I know, I do too.'

There was silence for a minute.

'You feeling okay about the pub yesterday?'

'Yeah,' David said. 'I was being silly.'

'No, you weren't.'

'Well, not silly, but . . . it was a small thing."

'If it's not small to you, then it's not small to me, David.'

'I appreciate that, but I am okay.'

At that moment, a delivery man knocked on the door, and was waving at David.

'Sorry, I've got to let someone in.'

'That's okay, see you this evening,' Mark said. 'Are we still having sausage and mash?'

'Yeah, if you want.'

'The perfect dinner,' he said, before hanging up.

It turned out the man was delivering the takeaway coffee cups they normally used, but with more than usual still left in the shop, David was going to have to find somewhere for them to go. He wondered if this was more than he normally ordered, or whether coffee sales were now down on top of everything else, and so when the man had left, he sat on the computer and went back through his invoices and called the company to see what they could do. They couldn't let him order ad-hoc (well, they would but it would cost more) and so he reduced his monthly deliveries, assuring them he'd ring to increase them again if needs be. When that was done, he realized he hadn't changed the water for the lilies behind the till, and so he did that too.

It was half-five before he sat down again, after a flurry of anniversaries and birthdays people were coming in for. At the moment he was considering what to do first to shut down, Meg came into the front of the store. She was wearing a big fluffy pink jumper and jeans. Her shoes were white, with big metallic silver stars on. Seeing her, David instantly realized that he hadn't phoned the pub to confirm the wedding date.

'Hello,' he said, his mind spiralling.

'Hi,' Meg replied. 'Just you?'

'Just me for now,' David said. 'How was your day?'

'Good, I went to work from that café, Marcus's – you can get to it on the bus?'

'Oh, I know the place,' David said. 'There's no Marcus though; that's just the name.'

'Is it? Oh that's boring.'

'I think he's called Kevin.'

'Doesn't have the same ring.'

'I suppose we're just as bad. Lily's not here either.' He sighed, pointing to the sign in the window, hoping she might leave and he could call the pub or head down there. 'Anyway, what can I help with? We didn't have anything planned today did we?'

'No, I just wanted to check all was okay when you called the pub?'

'Oh Meg!' David said. A shiver ran down his back.

'Sorry, I kept meaning to do it today and I forgot! I just remembered as soon as you came in. Let me call now. I'm sure it'll be fine.'

'I can just do it,' Meg said. She was talking slowly. 'Hopefully they're not booked up.'

'No, I can. Let me do it, Meg. One sec.'

He grabbed the phone and walked into the back room to avoid the sting of annoyance he could tell Meg was, willingly or not, directing at him.

'Hey, hi, it's David Fenton calling. We spoke earlier this week about a wedding.'

'Yes, on the . . .'

'Oh, well that's . . .'

'Is there any . . . ?'

'Okay, I understand, anyway, have a nice day.'

He came back slowly into the front of the shop.

'Meg, I'm so sorry, I . . . they've given the day away. They must have had somebody else waiting. I'm so sorry, but we'll sort it out. I'll do anything we need. We . . .'

Meg stared at him. She wasn't saying anything, but David noticed her nostrils flare slightly. It was almost worse that she wasn't reacting. If only he'd not been so busy this morning, or not let himself have a lie-in, maybe he would have done it, and this wouldn't be happening.

'I can call Rod and check the other one's still free?' David asked. 'I genuinely think it will be. That would be too unlucky.'

Meg was silent for a moment, before adding: 'Sure.'

David looked at his phone and realized he didn't know the number to The Old Oak, or for Rod.

'Do you have the number?'

There was a pause.

'I'll just do it,' Meg said.

'No, I don't mind speaking to Rod.'

'I know, but I can't let you do that.'

'Well I want to—'

'Well I don't want you to. I'll just call, honestly!'

He didn't know what to say, and he realized, perhaps, he hadn't said anything back to her for quite a while.

'I'm going to go,' Meg said.

'Are you sure?'

Before he knew it, Meg had walked out of the door and it was swinging shut. First not knowing what to say to Mark, then the shop's cashflow problems, and now he'd messed everything up with Meg. Why couldn't things ever just go well? David sat down behind the counter and threw his book to the floor and imagined what would happen next, probably Meg uninviting him from the wedding, and saying she never wanted to see him again, because he had one job, and he'd screwed it up. He'd disappointed and failed her, just like everybody else who was supposed to be helping.

18

MEG

As soon as Meg got into the house, she burst into tears, and Hannah came running towards her. There was music playing quietly, and from the kitchen Meg could hear the kettle pop to show it had finished boiling. Steam was rising from something on the hob. The comfort of being home enveloped her, and she felt able to release the feeling she'd had since she left the florist's, of being a bad person, or ungrateful, or unable to control her anger.

'Meg?'

'I'm here,' she said. 'Sorry, I . . . I saw David and . . .'

'What's happened? Are you okay?'

Hannah had put both her hands on Meg's shoulders and was staring into her face, trying to see what she could do, or say, that might help.

'What's happened? Meg?'

'Can we sit down?'

Hannah led Meg into the kitchen and she sat at the table, and immediately started to play with the tablecloth in front of her.

'I just feel awful,' Meg said.

'Why?'

'We've lost the pub we wanted,' Meg said. 'Everything keeps going wrong and I don't know why!'

'Well that's okay,' Hannah replied. 'We can . . . What happened? Why did we—'

Hannah had her hand on Meg's shoulder and Meg could feel her heartbeat lowering.

'David was supposed to ring the pub yesterday,' Meg said. 'To confirm the booking or they were going to release it, and I showed up today and he hadn't. Which is really annoying but I didn't hide that I was frustrated and he looked so sad and I was horrible to him! The only person who will actually come to all these things with me and I've . . .'

'Oh Meg. What happened?'

'I've pushed him away! He called them and now they're booked, so we're going to have to go with the other one, presuming they even have space, which I'm not even sure they will now, given our luck. I just walked out, and was obviously annoyed at him, but why would I do that to him? Should I go back?'

'It's okay, Meg, it's all stressful. He'll—'

'But why?' Meg said. 'Nobody made us get married and now I'm having a go at some kind man who's just trying to help? Is that who I am now?'

'You're not who you are for one minute in a really stressful situation,' Hannah said. 'You know that.'

'I'm not sure anymore.'

'Meg!' Hannah said, louder than before. She stared into her eyes. 'Promise me you won't take this on as some big moral failing. He didn't do something, by accident, but the result was stressful. It's not like you shouted or anything?'

'No, I didn't. I was talking normally.'

'Then I think it'll be okay,' Hannah said, stroking her leg. 'Honestly.'

'Do you think?'

'I wouldn't say that if I didn't think it would be.'

'Okay.'

'You said that David was the only one who'd come to everything . . . Meg, I'll drop the job and come if it's important to you; you do know that?' Hannah was looking at her sadly, expecting an answer. 'Do you?'

'I do,' Meg said, taking Hannah's hand. 'I . . . I know it's for practical reasons that you're away and you've not *chosen* to not be here. David's great and I genuinely didn't mind the situation we were in. I was really enjoying it! I'm just . . . I'm so sad today has happened. I'd been kidding myself that everything was fine.'

'Your parents?'

'Not just that,' Meg said. 'I'm so stressed all the time, thinking about the situation, and the whole wedding. I can tell I'm not really concentrating on work and just phoning it in. Like, I'm not booking in any new work or looking for it, and the stuff I've got going on at the moment I just go into the zone and get it done, but all I'm thinking about is what we need to do, and what'll go wrong. Every time that happens, I think about how my parents will be vindicated as soon as something does go wrong, because it'll show them we never should have got married. That's if they even come!'

'You think we never should have got engaged?'

'Obviously, I don't think that, Han,' Meg said, her hand on Hannah's shoulder. 'I just think that's how they'll feel.'

'Let's think practically about your parents.' Hannah stood up. 'Let me just do the next stage of dinner. One second.'

She put the pasta on to boil, balancing a wooden spoon across the top of the pan, and then came back to sit next to her on the sofa.

'Have you had any more contact with them?'

'No,' Meg said. 'Not since I texted Mum about the wedding dress shopping.'

Hannah knew about what had happened with her parents, how they hadn't responded about speaking and about their no-show at Savage Lilies. Meg had messaged about finding her wedding dress, and her mum had replied saying congratulations, but not anything else. It was formal, like Meg was one of their pupils, and it made Meg feel even more isolated.

'Sorry,' Hannah said.

'I know.'

'They'll get in touch. It hasn't been that long since all this started, and we've got time until the wedding. They're old-fashioned. They won't not RSVP at all, surely? I was thinking about that since the other day . . . They're traditional. The save-the-date will be on the sideboard. They'll know they have to say something.'

'Han, what if they don't?'

Hannah paused. 'If they don't,' she said, 'we go ahead with it, and we have an amazing day, and from then on you're my wife. I'm your family. And we'll have an excuse to have Christmas at ours, meaning we won't have to eat that blancmange your mum makes anymore.'

'Stop.'

'Sorry, is it a good time to make jokes?'

'I'm not sure,' Meg said, but she knew she was smiling, and she wiped the tears from her face.

'Okay,' Hannah said. She smiled at Hannah who got

up from the sofa and kissed her on the forehead. 'Now, sit there for a second while I finish tea.'

From where she sat on the sofa, Meg watched as Hannah stirred the pasta in its water, before adding salt, and then getting pesto from the fridge and the roasted vegetables from the oven. She drained the pasta, tapping her foot in time to whatever was going through her mind. Meg watched transfixed as Hannah poured ribbons of leeks and courgette down into the pan. She poured in a length of brilliant white double cream, and began to stir.

'That smells amazing,' Meg said.

'Simple,' Hannah said. 'But delicious.'

'Comfort food, hopefully,' Meg mumbled.

Hannah divided the pot into two bowls, and grated parmesan generously over the top. By the time she had brought Meg's bowl over to her, the parmesan was melting into a nutty-smelling crusty layer on the top of the meal.

'Thank you.'

'You're welcome,' Hannah replied. 'Is there anything I can do after this to make things less stressful? After the next trip, I'm back for good. Until the honeymoon, of course.'

'I know . . . nearly there. We can call the other pub maybe, just make sure we can book in. I also feel bad because that's the guy who made David upset, but I don't think he meant anything bad, so I can't really not book . . .'

'David will understand.'

'Once the venue's booked in, that's fine.' Meg spoke between spoonfuls of the meal that were pleasantly burning at the roof of her mouth. 'I think everything else matters, but the only thing you really need is the venue, the legal part, guests, you know.'

'Yeah.'

'We'll send out the proper invites too,' Meg said. 'I know everyone knows the date, but it's so nice to have the proper paper invitations.'

'I agree – makes it feel official.'

Meg was reminded, once again, that even the concept of guests included the obvious question. *Will my parents come?* She looked at Hannah, who seemed deep in thought.

'What?'

'I was just thinking . . .' Hannah said. '*I* could always go and see Ava and George and try to talk to them before I leave? I'd be happy to come with you, obviously, but I wonder whether that stops you having to get upset with whatever they say, and I can just find out how they're feeling, and then we can work out what to do. I can do the practical, rather than the emotional.'

Meg looked at her, not sure if the idea she was suggesting was brilliance or madness.

Hannah had finished eating and put her hair up in a ponytail behind her. 'We both need to know, really. You'd be less stressed knowing. Table plans, these appointments, what to do about other family members. What do you think?'

Meg was unsure, but too emotional to think straight. 'I'll think about it.'

'Okay,' Hannah said. 'Absolutely no pressure.'

'Thank you for thinking about that.'

'Of course. What else am I here for?'

Meg kissed Hannah on the cheek. 'Well, to cook dinner,' Meg said.

'What do I get in return?' Hannah asked. 'A kiss?'

At that second, the doorbell rang. Smiling at Hannah, who rolled her eyes, Meg walked to the front of the house to get it, and standing in front of her was David. He was a couple of feet back from the door, and had thrown a grey hoody over the T-shirt he'd been wearing in the shop. It was cold outside, and in his shivering hands, he was holding a small bunch of off-shoot roses, wrapped in red paper.

'Hi,' he said. 'Me again.'

19

DAVID

'David!'

Meg greeted him at the door and hurried him inside out of the cold, for which he was very grateful, as he wasn't sure when he'd stopped being able to feel his thumbs. He'd rushed out of the shop without a proper coat. Meg and Hannah's home smelt of candles and pesto. The light coming from the yellowy living room was inviting and they stepped forward down the hall. Hannah smiled at him and carried on pottering around clearing up.

'How are you doing?' he asked Meg.

'I'm okay,' she said. It was weird; he'd never been in this house before and Meg was upset with him, but he felt the familiarity between them wash over him, and he felt like everything was going to be okay. She smiled at him, and he knew they would be.

'I'm sorry.' It was out before he'd had a chance to say anything else.

'No, I'm sorry.' Meg put a hand on his arm. 'I shouldn't have behaved like that. You were only trying to help.

You're not a wedding planner; I can't hold you to things like that.'

'Yes,' David said. 'But I said I'd do it and I should have . . . That's on me and I apologize for that.'

'You don't have to.'

'Hug?'

'Go on.'

They embraced in the hallway, and David felt instantly relieved.

'I felt so bad,' he said.

'I don't want you to feel like that.'

'Hey,' Hannah said, poking her head back into the room. She had clearly gone and busied herself as they'd started talking. 'Do you want any pasta, David? There's some left if you'd like some.'

They followed her through into the living room. It was a bright room, with yellow-painted walls and dark blue cabinets. The TV was on, with no volume, and there was a book upside down on the coffee table.

'We're going to paint,' Hannah said. 'We didn't choose this colour; I need you to know that.'

'I like it!' David said. 'It's fun.'

Meg took the roses from him and put them into a small vase by the sink.

'Those are lovely,' Hannah said, sitting back down on the sofa. 'Thank you.'

'So.' He sat on the edge of the sofa and looked at them both. 'Everything's sorted. I called The Old Oak, and that's confirmed; you're booked in.'

'Oh, thank you.'

'You didn't have to do that,' Hannah said.

'All done, no bother,' David said. 'Sorry again. Rod

and I had a little heart-to-heart on the phone. We both apologized, and he's going to order in some flowers for some other events, so that was nice. We're okay.'

'Thanks, David.'

'Right, thank you for the pasta offer but I'm not stopping. I'd better get back to close up the shop.'

'How is Lilies doing?' Hannah asked.

'We're . . .' David paused. He had been planning to lie, say how wonderful everything was, but they had a class so underbooked planned for tomorrow that he'd had to cancel or he'd have lost money, and now their cake sales weren't breaking even and he worried he might have to stop buying from Angie. He sat down again. 'We're struggling, to tell you the truth. I think that's part of why I'm so stressed and forgetful. People always need flowers for weddings and things but . . . day-to-day, it's one of those luxuries that's so easy to lose with everything else going on. I just want to get through the weekend and then I need to sit down and properly make a plan.'

'Oh, David,' Meg said. 'I didn't realize. I thought it was all good.'

'It's not bad-bad,' he replied. 'I just . . . we could be doing better. We *should* be doing better.' These two didn't need to know what the accountant had said about five months, not with all they had going on. 'All the wholesale prices have gone up, and I don't want to pass those on. So I need to find other ways.'

'Have you thought about subscriptions?' Hannah said. 'That's a thing people like: deliveries to the door, a monthly treat they just make part of their regular spending.'

'We have one for coffee beans,' Meg said. 'And I used to do one for bath bombs, but Hannah made me divert that into the wedding fund.'

Hannah looked at David. 'She was spending forty pounds a month on baths!'

'That's not a bad idea,' David said. 'Me and Mark were talking about how to turn one sale into many. There's some kind of business studies name for that but I can't remember it. Benji'll tell me. Anyway, maybe I can put flyers in with purchases, give some money off or something, put it on social media.'

'That's a nice idea,' Meg said. 'We could always design something for you?'

'Would you really do that?'

'Of course! You've done so much for me, I'd love to. We can't print them or anything but we can make them look nice.'

'I'd really appreciate that,' David said. 'If that's no trouble?'

'Not at all,' Meg said.

'Are you sure you don't want some pasta, David?' Hannah said. 'It'll only be going in the fridge?'

'Oh, if you insist,' David said, and he accepted a small bowl dished out by Hannah, sprinkled with cheese. 'Thanks, this looks delicious.'

'Thanks, it's one of our comfort dishes.'

'Mine's toad in the hole,' David said. 'Or a roast dinner, or a barbecue, actually.'

'Is there anything else you need help with, with the shop?' Hannah asked. 'You've done so much for us. I'd love to help you out in return.'

'Not really,' David said. 'Like I said, Benji's doing our social media. I've kind of left him to it.'

'I mentioned to some of the youth club about a drawing class,' Meg said. 'I know that doesn't make money but the kids seemed keen.'

'Perhaps you could do that as a trial run, Meg, but you could always adapt that into an adults class, that people do pay for?' Hannah said.

'Meg, that's perfect!' David said. 'I was looking at more events.'

Hannah smiled. 'And, Meg, you wanted some more work that wasn't solitary.'

'Count me in!' Meg said. 'Let's start with the youth club so I can work out what we'd need, size and length of the session and stuff.'

'Shall we have a look at what Benji's up to?' Hannah said. 'I'm intrigued.'

Meg got out her phone and began to look at the shop's social media.

'Oh wow,' Meg said.

'This is actually really good,' Hannah said, also looking at her phone.

Meg showed him a small video posted on the shop's profile, which had the date and time, and a series of shots of dewy, fresh flowers in the windows and plants dotted elsewhere around the shop. It was what Benji had been filming the day before, he realized. The music playing on top of the clip was a song he'd taken from the Plant Playlist, Taylor Swift's 'Never Grow Up', and the shop's new opening times were super-imposed on it, in bright white font.

'Are you sure this is a good idea? I was worried when he suggested it.'

'Of course, David!' Meg said. She was now showing him something called TikTok, where everything was moving very quickly. 'Even if it brings one person in, and you've not had to do anything to get them in, then they'll recommend it.'

'This TikTok's got six hundred and fifty views,' Hannah said.

'WHAT!' David nearly dropped his bowl. 'That's crazy.'

'That's good,' Meg said. 'And it's only been a few hours.'

'I thought it was really more for his benefit than mine,' David said. 'But maybe this is a really good thing.'

'Definitely!'

David stayed for another half an hour, talking about the shop and what Hannah had learned about events at her own work. She talked about creating a buzz around ticket release dates, and publicizing when you were sold out, so people felt they were missing out on something. She talked about visual identities online and then told David that something as simple as a candle could make a live event feel premium. He didn't realize how late it was until a text from Mark reminded him he was home and that David should probably join him.

'Don't tell Mark I had a first dinner,' David said. 'Not before sausage and mash night.'

'We promise,' Hannah said.

'It's getting there now we've got the venue, you know,' David said, as he walked to the hall and put his coat back on. 'Flowers, food, candles, cakes, décor . . . There's not much more left.'

'I saw on the spreadsheet!' Hannah asked. 'Nearly time to actually get married.'

'Scary,' Meg said.

'Not scary, exciting!' Hannah said.

'What Hannah said,' David added.

'I need to send the final designs round for the welcome sign, menus and table plan and things,' Hannah said. 'I'll do that tomorrow and then we're done!'

They really were. Meg had caught up with him earlier in the week with her laptop before they'd visited the pubs, and nearly everything was crossed off her list. Hannah had added all sorts of small details from her work in events that they wouldn't even have thought of, which had extended the partnership a little longer. David was hit with a wall of sadness he couldn't show them. He'd been quite enjoying this as a project. What happened when it was over? There was just one thing left on the list, of course.

'And your parents,' David said. 'Any news?'

'Nothing.'

'I've offered to speak to them,' Hannah said.

They were all standing in the hall awkwardly, and David leaned temporarily on the banister.

'Maybe that's a good idea,' David said. 'It's hard to know.'

He wasn't sure, in fact, that it was a good idea, but it felt like Meg and Hannah's remit, not really his own.

'I think I maybe hadn't realized, you know, how stressed it was making me . . .' Meg suggested.

'That's okay,' David said.

'And maybe that came out earlier,' Meg added. 'So, again, I'm sorry.'

'I'm sorry too.'

'I wasn't there,' Hannah said. 'But I'm sorry too. David. I'll see you when I'm back next week.'

'Have a safe flight.'

He hugged them both and began the walk home, and remembering Benji's success, texted him (they now had a steady stream of messages) to say thank you. Benji replied immediately, placing a thumbs-up emoji on the comment itself, like six hundred views was nothing. Six hundred customers! Imagine. He checked his calendar on the phone to triple-check he'd booked the pub for the right day and there it was, in black and white. Six weeks to go, more or less.

After that, David thought, *I'll really concentrate on the shop. After that.*

20

MEG

35 Days Until the Wedding

'So you have to outline. It's really boring but you simply have to, and it'll help later.' Meg looked out at everyone in the flower shop, and turned back to the easel she'd set up on the counter, where she was beginning to draw. Her pencil scratched against the thick card. 'Like this. It's not the exciting bit . . . You'll always want to get stuck into the parts that excite you the most, but do this first. I always picture it as scaffolding, if that helps. You need it to build the house. If you don't know how it's going to sit on the page, you can't do the details accurately. This is especially important if you were drawing, I don't know, say like a scene on a football pitch. If you get the dimensions wrong, soon enough, you won't have space for the goal for example and it'll be all squashed up and look . . . not very good. Worst-case scenario, you'd have to start all over again.'

As she drew, she could see the faces turn from boredom to intrigue. *What is she making?* she imagined them thinking. *Could they create the same?* She hoped they were itching to get started, as it was always more entertaining to try yourself than to be told how.

'So, get the scaffolding down, ideally in pencil and then you can rub away the pencil as you go, and it'll look like you just did this from scratch, which will seem really impressive. Give me just one moment on this, and I'll show you.'

Meg turned back and started scribbling, now going over the pencil lines with a mix of her Sharpie and her biro. She hadn't wanted to add colour this early, but thought thickness of line might not be intriguing enough for the group. Soon, she was getting closer to what she'd intended.

'Sorry, I'm not great at talking and drawing . . .'

'It's us!' Salma said.

'No it's not,' Benji said.

'I think Salma's right,' David said.

Meg smiled and allowed them to keep guessing. Someone else said it was a beach, and someone else guessed it was the dog groomer's down the road. Instead, as she added a few more people in, everyone seemingly agreed that she had drawn exactly what she could see in front of her.

She turned back to the group and they were there, like she'd brought them to life from the paper to the shop. Nine children sat around the huge table in the middle, the one David usually made displays on. A couple of other kids, including Benji, were sitting at the individual tables David used for classes. David, Mark and Jacob were in a line at the front of the shop near the door, looking on, leaning against the surface at the back. There wasn't a lot of space. They were all watching pleasantly as the group hung on Meg's every word and her and Hannah's friend Ailie who was up to visit stood next to them, smiling too, wearing a bright striped jumper and her hair tied up in a ponytail. In the background of Meg's drawing, you could see the beginnings of the large houseplants in the window, and the tiniest hint at the houses opposite the shop, which you could see through the windows. Despite being late afternoon, it was still pleasantly light in the evenings now.

'You're right, it's all of you guys,' Meg said. 'It's not perfect, there's not much detail, but that would come later. After the demonstrations, everybody's going to have a go at drawing the florist's from where we're sitting, or rather, where you're sitting. We'll come round and help with scaffolding, and then we can talk about the detail and whether you want to use pens, or paints, or shading, or anything you want. How does that sound?'

The group cheered, and Meg gestured to Ailie to come forward, before flipping over the easel to give her a blank page. Ailie had been on their university course and they'd all been friends ever since. She had definitely begun as, and was still, better friends with Meg, and had offered to do live illustrations of guests at their wedding as a gift to them. Though she had planned on a social visit and to talk weddings, Meg had thought she might also be a good fit for the night the youth club had asked for. It was lovely to have time together, away from Ailie's boyfriend and Hannah, and just to be with each other.

'Everybody say hello Ailie,' Meg said, stepping back to where David, Mark and Jacob were standing. 'And listen to what she has to say. She's brilliant.'

Once the youth group were off, the main job was trying to slow them all down. Everybody wanted to see the final result, not the planning, and so Meg felt like she was playing that arcade game with the moles, jumping between each of them as soon as they leapt past the early steps she and Ailie had described. Ailie and David were better at softly making suggestions, and letting them make mistakes. She and Mark were more likely to physically grab the pen from somebody's hand.

'That's good!' Meg said. She was pointing to Fred's sheet, who was shaping areas of flowers and plants instead of immediately starting to draw leaves. A girl to his left was currently drawing half of David's face, which was being squeezed onto the page, and had gone from unfortunate to startlingly unflattering. On the other side of the table, Mark was suggesting someone use a pencil instead of a pen – 'like Meg told you' – and David was pointing at Meg and explaining something about her that he was trying to get one of the kids to draw on the page, which she was trying to pretend wasn't making her self-conscious.

'How are you getting on?' Meg asked Benji, who was sitting on Fred's right.

'Good,' Benji said. His tongue poked horizontally out of his mouth when he was concentrating, and Meg noticed he'd drawn squiggles of what looked like animals and fireworks all down one of his arms. He put his pen down and looked back. 'I think I actually am ready to go. Am I?'

She looked at his page, where he'd drawn the basics of the table, five people and the background in alarmingly strong proportions. Every person looked like a real human and he had even included small details that brought the whole thing to life, even in its simplest form.

'Yes!' Meg said. 'Well done, this is . . . You've really got an eye for this, Benji.'

His mouth glitched into a smile involuntarily. 'Do you think?'

'Definitely,' she said.

'Cool, thanks, man.'

'Do you do art at school?'

'No, I didn't have space,' he replied. 'You only get three other subjects.'

'Well you can always keep this up in your own time. You're good.'

'Thanks, Meg.'

'Do you know what you're going to do, after your GCSEs?'

'I thought about doing English,' he said. 'But the teacher's really strict.'

Meg couldn't help herself. She knew she shouldn't be asking questions like this and yet she found herself saying: 'What's her name?'

'Mrs Kirby.'

Meg paused. 'She's actually my mum.'

'Shut up, Meg!'

'No,' she said laughing. 'She is!'

'I can't imagine her having kids,' Benji said. 'She's so . . . I dunno, that's mad that is! How old are you?'

David looked up from who he was helping. 'Benji! Why are you shouting? And you can't ask people how old they are.'

'It's okay, David,' Meg said. She turned back to Benji. 'Would you believe me if I said I'm twenty-one?'

'I'm not shouting! And *you're* not twenty-one. I'm not stupid,' Benji said, to the room who were now listening. He scowled at someone else in the club who looked away. 'Sorry, Meg, it's just crazy!'

'Why is it crazy?'

'Cos you're so different. You're so . . . I don't know. Chill.'

'Well people can be different from their parents,' Meg said. 'Sometimes on purpose.'

Benji looked deep in thought and didn't say anything. She wasn't sure anymore if she wanted to hear her parents talked about in positive or negative ways or at all, so instead Meg asked Salma how she was getting on. She was wearing an oversized sweater and a short skirt, and the top seemed to have some band on Meg hadn't heard of.

'I'm okay I think.'

'You've made my head massive,' Benji said, leaning to take a look.

'Yeah, I know,' Salma said. 'She said to draw it to scale.'

'Guys, you've both done well,' Meg said, standing between them before they started to bicker. 'I reckon add some colour, some shading. Here are the felt tips, but you can use whatever. Oh, hi!'

As she was speaking, Angie arrived, bustling through the door with a bag under her arm and two cake boxes stacked on top of one hand.

'Somebody help me!' she shouted, and as always, or perhaps because they could see it was cake, Benji, Fred and Salma bolted to the door to take things off her, and lay them down on the counter. There was no chance now; everybody was too distracted.

'They're for after!' David shouted, but Meg wasn't sure if he could be heard, and she heard the rustling of the boxes opening.

'We're just looking, man!' Benji shouted.

* * *

The next assignment, set by Ailie, was for everybody to draw something which was not in the room, entirely from memory, which she said would give them more freedom to be creative. 'Some of the great art is of things that don't exist,' she told them, and it might be, she said, that they'd prefer this style of drawing and illustrating over the other.

All the adults agreed to be involved as well. They were sitting at a small table near the counter. Meg was working on a flyer for the suggested flower subscription package, and Ailie was drawing another of their friends who would be at the wedding. From where she was sitting, Meg couldn't work out what David and Mark were drawing, and Jacob seemed invested in some kind of wizard or goblin whose outline Meg could see from upside down.

Meg had set a timer for half an hour, and she checked it again, seeing there were only ten minutes left. The initial burst of concentration set by the timer had made every member of the youth club completely silent. Now, as some finished, not utilizing the full half an hour, and some got bored or felt too challenged, the mutters of conversation in the room increased in volume. To set an example, the adults' table – outnumbered – stayed completely silent, concentrating on their individual projects, which meant they were mostly listening, unnoticed, to the club's conversations.

'What's that?' Fred was asking, and somebody told him they were drawing a lake in Scotland they had been to on holiday.

Benji got up from his chair to walk around everybody's work, and asked Salma what she was illustrating.

'That's my uncle,' she replied, pointing down at her art on the table. 'At his wedding last year.'

'You've drawn so much,' he said.

'Well that's his husband, and I had to draw guests.'

'I've only done one thing.'

'It's good though, so far,' Fred told him.

Meg peeked at the drawing Fred was working on, of a Tesco meal deal, in slightly cartoonish style, detailed and coloured in bright, exaggerated felt tip. Meg then noticed David staring at Salma, who was now holding her work up to show somebody else. There was a glint of something in his eye; was it sadness or confusion? She tried to remember to ask about it later.

Angie nudged the table suddenly as she got up, and she quickly apologized, before moving to the counter to portion out what she'd brought. Meg peeked at her drawing, which seemed to be a group of children sitting, watching the television. 'I've done as best I can with drawing,' she said. 'But I'll go and do what I'm good at.'

'Do you need a hand?' David asked, before getting up to help. He, too, was finished. Meg knew she should offer but she wanted to give David a great option for his flyer, and felt relieved when Benji instead got up to divide the cakes with them. She watched as Benji asked Angie questions about her process, about the design of the cakes, whether she had any social media for her shop. Meg played with a couple more elements on her flyer and then Benji came to sit with her.

'Sorry if I said anything about your mum, or upset you.'

'You didn't, Benji, but thank you.'

'Your mum's chill sometimes,' he said. 'Kind of like my dad.'

'What do you mean?'

'Like, he's not a bad person.' Benji was playing with a napkin he'd taken from the table. 'He just thinks things have to happen in a particular way and that there's a right and a wrong. He doesn't like it when we think differently about things.'

'You think my mum's the same?'

'You should have seen when Paul said the mockingbird was the best character in the book. She went crazy.'

Meg smiled. 'That sounds like my mum.'

'It's not his fault he hadn't read it. The Euros were on.'

'Anyway, Benji, I heard you went on a date,' she said.

Benji suddenly went silent. 'No I didn't.'

'Oh, I thought you did,' she said. 'I was just wondering who they might be, but you don't have to tell us . . .'

'Who told you?'

Fred and Salma looked up from their spaces on the table.

'It doesn't matter.'

He muttered something that might have been a swear word under his breath before shaking his head at David and going back to sit down.

'No swearing, Benji,' Mark said. 'Come on, you know the rules by now.'

Confused, Meg mouthed an apology to David, and they both looked over at Benji who was now sitting with his arms crossed, glaring at them, knocking his feet against the table legs.

The night was complete by six-thirty, and so Meg and Ailie went to the pub for dinner after shepherding the club out of the shop and joining David and Mark to tidy, despite their refusal to accept help. Benji had taken a picture of everybody's work, and had been one of the last to leave, his mood lightening with each slice of cake Angie gave him. By the time he walked out of the door with Fred, cookies in their hands, he seemed to have forgotten what he'd been annoyed about.

They both ordered veggie sausages and mash, which arrived at the table with thick brown gravy and whole roasted chunks of red onion, and the waiter seemed confused by Ailie's faint Scottish accent, worn away by years in London. He didn't seem to know where she was from, or how to ask. They began to eat, and Meg felt grateful for a moment of silence, like she'd been speaking for an hour, running Ailie through everything that had happened since they'd moved back just half a year ago.

'So you said in one of your texts you were worried about Hannah?' Ailie asked, sipping from her glass of water. 'If your parents don't come.'

'Not worried, exactly,' Meg said. 'She just has to comfort me when I get upset about it, which feels so often now, and her work is so busy. I just feel like it's a strain we don't need.'

Meg told Ailie how she wanted an answer about the wedding, but was dealing with capricious and infrequent messages from her parents.

'But you're not worried?'

'No, not worried, maybe that's not what I meant,' Meg said. She'd been having so much trouble figuring out how she was feeling recently, and neither texting nor talking seemed to help clarify. 'Hannah's so great and we'll always be fine. I just think we're having to adjust what we thought we were having for a wedding, compared to what we are having. Sometimes I feel so sad about how it is with my parents; other times I'm having such a fun time planning it with David that I completely forget that this isn't what people normally do. Hannah offered to go and talk to my parents, but with how they are I don't know if that will make it worse. I worry that it's because she just wants an answer, for my sake. Rather than the uncertainty.'

'Do you want an answer?'

'I do, of course,' Meg said. 'Part of me wants to go round every day and just talk it out. I guess I'm not hurrying it, because what if the answer is . . . no?'

'Yeah.'

'I don't know what that would even feel like. At least now, I don't know . . . at least there's some hope.'

'So you've got, like, a month to go?' Ailie said, checking a calendar on her phone.

'Yeah.'

'I think you might have to ask, or yeah, get Hannah to. You don't want to be upset on or close to the day.'

'You mean if I'm going to cry, I should get it all out of my system well before?'

'Well yes!' she said, before adding: 'Sorry.'

'We have a rehearsal a few days before, so I could see if they come to that,' Meg said, putting down her knife and fork. Suddenly, she felt less hungry than she had. She sighed. 'It's such a mess.'

'Yeah but, Meg, it's not your mess,' Ailie said. She had finished eating too and reached a hand out to Meg across the table. 'So don't take that on as something you've done.'

'Okay.'

'Did you see Patty from uni got married?'

'Oh yeah, I did see that.'

'Go on her profile. I want to show you something.'

Meg knew what this was going to be but she followed what her friend said anyway. She shuffled up the banquette seating Ailie was on and they both swiped through her most recent post, caption: *BLISS* and a bride emoji. There were ten pictures of her wedding, all made up of people: her, her husband and a variety of group and candid shots, of grandparents and children, and of a different dress later in the night.

'I don't know how she's picked two,' Meg said. 'I had enough trouble picking one.'

'No, look. That's not what I meant. You know she doesn't know her parents,' Ailie said. 'And look how much of a good day she's had. Family, as in blood family, isn't everything.'

She was right; there were photos of all kinds of people, all smiling or laughing. All the styles and tropes of all the posts Meg seemed to usually see, that even Matty had mentioned when they talked photography – of families in a line, of brides with their two parents and grooms with theirs, all lined up identically – were not present here.

'So, whatever happens, your wedding day will be amazing, Meg, trust me,' Ailie said. 'I can't wait. I've got my trains and hotel booked and everything.'

'Yeah, it is exciting.'

'I was watching some documentary . . . what do they call it, chosen family?'

As Ailie talked, Meg's mind drifted to all the new people in her life since this had all started. David and Mark, Martha and Carl, Matty, Angie, the youth club, Susan. Gus and Ramon, even. Meg clicked out of the profile, just in case she liked anything else by accident, and saw a new post from the Savage Lilies account. Benji had posted a series of the group's pictures of the shop, in a video montage to Stormzy's 'Rainfall'. Underneath, he'd simply written, *nine-thirty to five-thirty, fresh every day, savage lilies.* In contrast to his somewhat frantic personality and his excitability, the voice and look for the flower shop was a kind of classic elegance, with modern touches like the music. It was really distinct and having worked on so many social campaigns with work, Meg knew how hard it was to get these things right.

'Looks like they enjoyed the session,' Meg said, passing the phone to Ailie. 'Look at this.'

'Oh that's great,' Ailie said. 'Wait, isn't that the shop's profile?'

'Yes but one of the kids from the club is doing the social media for a bit, showing David how.'

'That's so sweet,' Ailie said. She was perusing a dessert menu that had just been delivered to the table. 'It's so nice round here, Meg, all the community action. It's like living in some lovely old film. I can't believe you used to knock it so much.'

21

DAVID

24 Days Until the Wedding

David had never been able to resist one of Angie's cakes, unless it involved beetroot or courgettes, and today was no exception. After politely refusing a coffee, carrot and raspberry loaf (not that offensive, David just hated carrots) he was served a bowl of jam roly-poly with custard. He didn't know if he'd ever had a more perfect morning.

'So why did you want to meet?' Angie said. 'It's unlike you to want to discuss business so seriously.'

'Well it's hardly that serious,' David said, brushing crumbs off his lap as he ate. 'Not with us. I just wondered a few things, like how you went about making sure you stay afloat, with the prices of everything going up. At Lilies, we did so well to modernize, and we have the reasons to get people inside, but recently I've noticed a dip in the floristry side of things, and there's not much more we can try.'

'Why are you talking like that, all defeated?' Angie asked. 'You're good, David. You've been going for ten years. You just gotta keep changing, I reckon. Keep adding stuff. Always keep it fresh, and different.'

As Angie said it, David could feel in the back of his throat the pastry range Angie had had for a few weeks one autumn, the matcha custard tart that had smelt and tasted like snot.

'But what if those things . . . don't work out?'

'Then you try the next thing! Like when I finally got rid of courgette cake – it just didn't sell.' David smiled. He hadn't seen it – or smelt it – in a long time. 'If you weren't doing anything, then I reckon you'd have a problem, but you've done new things before. You're creative.'

'You can't just assume all gay people are creative,' David said. 'You sound like someone describing a gay man in the Eighties: "*ooh he's creative . . .*"'

'Shut up you,' she said, throwing a crumb at him. 'Tell me what you're doing, and if it's working.'

'I've got a plan for a subscription service, you know, pay thirty pounds a month for a different bouquet delivered to your door. Offering twenty per cent off the first month to customers in the shop. They can also collect it, if they'd prefer.'

'That's good,' she said. 'That might work.'

'Maybe,' he said. 'I've been doing the seasonal bouquets for ages as well, around times of the year – Christmas, Easter, Pride month. They do okay. I could do with being in a few more places, finding people who don't walk past the shop. I wonder if anywhere else would stock us, like we do with you.'

'That's a great idea,' Angie said. 'Why don't you try to get into some of the wedding shows? You could ask on that group you asked me to join. I'm sure someone in there would know.'

'Thanks, Angie,' he said. 'That's a good idea. I'll have examples from Meg and Hannah's. Then I've got Benji from the youth group getting us on social media; that's the other big thing.'

'That's good. David, you're doing loads.' Angie put her elbows on the table. 'And changes don't translate to cash overnight. How is Benji? He seemed like a good kid the other day when I met him.'

'He is,' David said. 'He's doing okay, I think. I keep getting told the number of followers is still going up. A woman came in and said her daughter had showed her the shop's TikTok page, so that's why she came in, but then she didn't buy anything. He also keeps telling me about something called Snapchat but I've only just got my head around all the others . . .'

'So modern, David, moving with the times, you talking about followers. Do you even know what WhatsApp is?'

'Why is everybody acting like I was born during the war? My hair is only slightly grey! Are *you* on social media?' David asked, aghast. 'Why did nobody tell me?'

'We did tell you! I even sent you the links.'

'I know . . . I never knew how to open them.'

Angie raised an eyebrow. 'We do okay, but it's more me just posting photos to remind our regular customers we exist. I'm doing bits and pieces when I remember, and it's good to have a page to show opening hours and a phone number so people can contact us, but ideally we'd have someone who understands it, the kind of nuts and bolts of it. I think that works particularly well to get out-of-towners ordering online and stuff.'

'You're doing online orders?' David said.

'David, David, David . . .'

'One thing at a time!' David said. 'Rome wasn't built in a day. In terms of the social media, I think it's working . . . something the other day ended up with a thousand views, imagine if they all came in.'

'Well you wouldn't have space,' Angie said. 'You gotta remember, sales are made by less than one per cent of online activity.'

'Really?'

Angie nodded.

'Gosh, that's depressing.'

'See if it works,' Angie said. 'Just always have new plans on the go.'

'I don't know what else we could do.'

'Well is there anywhere you could make savings? We switched who we get our flour from; that's saved me a couple of grand over the whole year. It's like pennies a day, but it all adds up. Look, it's hard . . . It's tough for everyone.'

'I . . .' He paused, unsure whether to say it to her. 'I think we might have to cut back on cakes and things, maybe just offer really simple things I can buy in bulk. I don't want to do that though! It would be a last resort.'

Angie looked at him, and he wondered if it would have been better to lie than to have come to ask for business advice and suggested cancelling his contract with her.

'If you need to, you need to,' Angie said. 'Don't worry about me. I'm not some romantic fool.'

'Only if you're sure? We already don't open on Mondays, and I'm staying open late to catch last-minute sales. I've even started doing reduced yellow stickers like in the supermarket rather than just giving flowers to Mark. People seem to like that.'

'Hey, you gotta do what works for you and the customer.

We won't let business get in the way of a friendship, and you've got me quite a few wedding contracts, so I'm never going to be mad at you. I couldn't.'

'Okay,' he said, his stomach making loud gargling noises from the bucket-sized cup of tea he was drinking, along with the cake. 'Thank you. It's hard. I don't just see this as business, it's my life. Mark says I should be more cut-throat.'

'Maybe he's right,' she said. 'But don't lose you in the process.'

'I won't if you don't.'

'Oh I couldn't lose this,' Angie said, laughing, gesturing to herself. 'It's possible to be a nice person and have a business that makes money. I've got faith in that, if nothing else.'

David glanced out from the back room where they were alone to the front of store where it was a hive of activity. A couple of mums were sitting with their kids, and people were coming in for end-of-day treats or bread for the evening, forming a short queue. He knew her margins were tricky, but she seemed like she was doing okay. Maybe it wasn't difficult for everyone, maybe people just kept saying that to make him feel better.

'Thanks, Angie,' David said. 'You're even more wise than Mary Portas.'

'I don't know about that,' Angie said. 'But I'm honoured you'd say it.'

The next day, Meg had insisted on joining David on a trip to the shopping centre in Milton Keynes to pick out what he'd wear to the wedding. They parked a while away from the centre, and Meg kept laughing at him on the walk over.

'Trying to get your steps in, are you?' she said.

'How are those driving lessons going?' he said back and Meg smiled.

'I'll book them, at some point . . .'

On the walk across the underpass, they made a plan. Three shops only: a department store, a specific suit store and a general men's clothing store that he thought was a little young for him, but that Meg encouraged him to try. 'Let's not overwhelm ourselves,' David stressed.

Despite the fact it was a random weekday, the centre was incredibly busy. Inside, the glass panels that made up the huge building, once the largest indoor shopping centre in Europe, let in rectangular blocks of sunlight that warmed your skin. Meg told him about how the centre had also been used in a Cliff Richard music video – something he'd never heard before – and he was reminded, with a note of sadness, how much his mum had loved Cliff Richard.

In the first shop, the department store, it took a while to find the suits, and David tried on three different ones he thought he might like.

The first suit, when he came out to show Meg, was too bright under the lights, and he said he wanted something more understated. Meg looked disappointed, but he brushed her off and got changed. The second was ill-fitting, and though Meg suggested getting it tailored, that felt like an unnecessary expense considering everything going on with the shop, and he said he'd think about it. The third was itchy, and he hated it, and didn't even come out to show her.

In the second shop it was too hot in the changing rooms, like being heated from within, and he felt trapped in every outfit they tried. Every time he buttoned a shirt up to the top around his neck, he felt like he wanted to rip it off. It couldn't have been the weather, not the way this summer was going, and so he knew it was a mental thing. The man in the suit shop definitely thought he was a father of the bride, and with Meg becoming insular and quiet, David decided they needed to leave.

'Are you okay?' he said as they re-entered the main concourse of the shopping centre.

'Yeah, I just worry . . . if my dad doesn't come, who'll walk me up . . . You know, all the same things I'm worrying about, all the time really.'

'Do you want to talk about it?'

'Not right now,' Meg said. 'Let's do the next shop and then we can get a coffee.'

By the third shop, David felt like he had got himself into what Mark called his Goldilocks state of mind; everything became too difficult to choose, and everything would be too much one way, or the other, but never perfect. With Meg, he felt like he couldn't say that and so he muddled through a couple of the boring suits he had selected, before humouring her on three of the younger-looking fun outfits she suggested.

The first was patterned, and it definitely was too much. It had floral print, and he worried he'd look like some kind of plant-obsessed lunatic. It would be like Martha coming dressed as a violin, or Angie arriving at the wedding in a Battenberg costume. Meg had since suggested he try the suits with a T-shirt underneath, and the second suit, a light baby blue in a checked pattern, he actually liked. He stood inspecting himself in the mirror before Meg said anything and eventually he turned to her.

'What do you think?'

'I really like it,' she said. 'Do you?'

'I think I do. I feel really . . .'

'Comfortable?' she said.

'Yes.'

'I think it's great,' she said. 'It's a summer wedding, it's nice colours, it goes with the shoes you mentioned.'

'Do you think?'

'Oh definitely.'

'Hmmm.' David wasn't so sure. He felt good, but it was outside of his usual wheelhouse, and he wasn't sure of the attention he might get, particularly from Meg's parents if they came. He also wasn't convinced he and Mark had any occasions where he would wear it again.

'What are your reservations?' she asked. 'Do you want Mark to see it?'

'Maybe,' David said. 'It's a bit . . . more than I'd usually do.'

'But if you feel good, get it,' she said. 'You'll be among friends.'

David paused. 'I'll get it but I'll keep the receipt and think about it.'

'Okay, good idea.'

He went back into the changing room, and said he was going to try the jumper on he'd found as well, and so Meg said to pass her the suit and she could put it behind the till. He tried on the jumper once she'd left, and actually after the suit, it felt like a boring choice, so he gave it back to the person manning the changing area, and went to find Meg.

He couldn't see her anywhere, so did a lap of the store and then moved towards the stairs and lift, where she was standing with a huge paper bag.

'I've bought it for you,' Meg said. 'Hannah and I wanted to. No arguing!'

'You really didn't have to do that,' David said. 'And you tricked me! Let me send you the money, or half? You're already paying for a whole wedding.'

'This is part of the wedding,' Meg said. 'I refuse your money. The option is there though if you decide you want to swap it or get something else. I just wanted to give you some good news.'

'I really don't think you had to pay for that, Meg,' David said. He was holding his coffee cup in both hands, and watched a family pass by as they sat outside a large café, which opened out onto the park. 'But thank you.'

'I didn't have to,' Meg said. 'But we wanted to. You've done so much that I could never thank you, but I hope this says some of that.'

'Okay,' he said. 'I really appreciate it.'

They sat in comfortable silence. Some people were on their own, branded bags or their own rucksacks heaving with recent purchases, hurrying to their next shop or maybe their car. Some groups were wandering slowly, limited in speed by pushchairs, or walkers, or tiny toddlers taking three steps for every one of their accompanying adult. There were a number of kids in buggies that were made to look like cars, and one child passed closely to David, clapping his hands together in joy at being in charge of a vehicle. *Adult life is hard,* he wanted to tell the child. *Don't wish your life away!* He wondered if the children were better at parking than him.

'Can I ask you a question?' Meg asked him.

'Of course,' he said. 'No need to ask permission.'

'Did you speak to your parents?' she said. 'I've just been thinking about it with my own parents. I know they passed away, but before that . . . I was wondering if you felt like you wanted to, or if they did, and what happened? I noticed you looking at Salma at the illustration evening, when she talked about a gay wedding. Were you thinking about them?'

He thought seriously for a second about how to answer this question. Was Meg looking for closure, or hope, about her own relatives? Maybe he should just answer the question, speaking for himself, rather than worrying about what Meg might need. He remembered that he had felt funny at the illustration evening at Lilies because he'd been thinking about several things, but mainly Mark's clear direction that he needed to think about the possibility of their own wedding.

'I think about them all the time,' he said. 'If they hadn't died, if they'd got older, I like to think I'd have got in touch. They never did though, not properly, or not in the way I wanted. They sent the exact same Christmas card every year. I wrote back with a thank you card and told them every time I changed address. That was it. I always thought, well *you're* the grown-ups. *You* should be looking after *me*, you know.'

'And nobody else ever interfered?'

'My family was tiny,' he said. 'They were both only children, and so was I, so there were never siblings, cousins, aunts or uncles, which I am really sad about. There was my mum's mum but she didn't do anything, and she was getting on. I wonder all the time if I have any family out there now. I did an Ancestry test hoping I'd find a surprise someone, but there just wasn't anyone. That would have prompted me to try to make amends, I think, if I'd found that and shown them. Dad would have loved stuff like that.'

David went silent for a minute.

'I've got to make peace with the fact that we didn't reconcile before they died, you know, but I don't know if I ever will.'

'So you think I should reconcile with my parents?'

'Not if they're not going to treat you right. You only get one chance at family but you don't have to put up with being treated poorly.'

'I know,' Meg said, smiling at him. 'I mean the rehearsal's basically three weeks away. If they don't come to that, I'm going to insist on an answer for the wedding. Dad needs to come to the rehearsal anyway if he wants to walk me down the aisle, so it's all resting on that really.'

David had noticed Meg actually tense up when the shop assistant had said something earlier about her walking down the aisle, and he could tell it weighed heavily on her mind.

'Yes, of course.'

'So, yeah.' Meg put down her coffee cup. 'I'm not begging them to come, but I'm not shutting them down either, if they do need a little time.'

'That sounds like a good plan.'

Meg smiled at him.

'Do you think he will walk you down the aisle?'

'He said yes at Christmas when we announced we were engaged . . . I'm not very traditional but I do want that to happen. I'd be so embarrassed, I think, everyone wondering why he's not there, or sitting down but not walking with me.'

'You don't need to worry about what anyone else thinks.'

David winked at her. 'I know saying that's annoying, but it gets much easier to put into practice as you age, I promise.'

'I hope so . . .'

'Three weeks to go,' he said. 'I can't believe it.'

'I know!' she said. 'Unbelievable. I need to concentrate on my skincare, make sure I don't get any spots.'

'Me too,' David joked. 'Not sure the five o'clock starts help with that. Shall we head back?'

Looping her arm through his, Meg started their walk back to the van, and David couldn't help but thinking how it certainly was true that he had no biological family left, but he now had something, whatever it was, that might just be even better than that.

22

MEG

22 Days Until the Wedding

Meg sat down in front of the television to watch something mindless after the busiest day she'd had in a long time. On the screen in front of her, a group of women were at a dinner and dramatic cuts were getting faster until everybody was shouting and somebody threw a drink over somebody else. While watching, she was trying to make a caramel chocolate bar last but each of the six parts only made her want to eat another and soon it was finished. Hannah would be home soon; maybe she should message her to bring something else back?

She'd had a deadline to meet, so that morning she had woken up at half six to work on designs for some children's bedding based on the characters from the show she used to work on, and she hadn't looked up until ten o'clock when the grumbling coming from her stomach was impossible to ignore. Quickly, she had showered and eaten to be ready for David to come over, since they were meeting the man who would marry her and Hannah.

When the celebrant, Caleb, arrived, Meg couldn't get over how tall he was.

She had found him through David's online group, which now had over thirty members. In his post advertising himself to the group, he said he was queer, and had officiated over a hundred weddings, so Meg felt like they were in good hands. He was young, which she felt was important, as she and Hannah didn't want the ceremony to feel formal and she really did think they should have a man rather than a woman, though she couldn't work out why.

Seated at the kitchen table, he had run through the different options and some of the practical things he needed from the couple. Meg knew Ailie would be doing a more personal reading during the ceremony, so she told Caleb they were happy with the quickest and simplest ceremony script. He passed them the usual one, saying it could be tweaked where necessary, and there were a couple of places he usually inserted somewhat more personal touches.

David had gotten really into this section of the meeting, for some bizarre reason. Meg had felt bad when Caleb said how nice it was for the father of the bride to be this opinionated, and she could see him looking oddly chastised for his enthusiasm. It wasn't, of course, that she didn't want his help, just that this bit, more than anything else they'd had to arrange, felt so extremely personal. After five minutes of quiet, he had got involved in how they would exchange rings and sign the legal documents, and Meg had had to jokingly tell him it wasn't his wedding. The meeting came to a close fairly soon after that, and Meg felt happy that they had decided on what she and Hannah would want.

Later, David's friend Carl came round as David had suggested he, a copywriter, could help with the problems she was finding writing her speech. They all caught up briefly standing in the hall and Carl told her how excited Matty was to be her photographer. Meg had been so glad he had agreed, as she wanted somebody who came recommended and had left it too late to find many people who would be available.

Carl asked after Savage Lilies and David said how the online group had led to him hosting wine tasting classes on Tuesdays. The shop next door needed more space, and would give David a cut of their takings. He suggested he leave houseplants out for sale, and he had sent a text to Benji to advertise the night online and the wine bar had done the same.

Soon, David made his excuses, something about filing expenses, and left them to it. She told David as he left that at least her speech would be one of the few surprises he'd have on the day.

She and Hannah were both keen to have simple vows but to have time in speeches to speak about each other more informally; of course, Meg was nervous, but she wanted to do a speech, for Hannah and for herself. Carl was more sarcastic than David, and harsher. Where he didn't like something she had written, he said so, or aggressively scratched it out on the sheets she had paid 5p a page to print at a local computer café, but his harshness was ultimately helpful. He gave her a couple of better turns of phrase for things she had already written, but she still only had down half of what would be needed for a full speech, and she wasn't even sure she wanted to keep all of it. He kept suggesting she make these bold and dramatic statements of love, talking about the entire universe, and many lifetimes, but it all felt different to what she loved about Hannah, which was small details, simple pleasures and lazy days.

She kept imagining speaking, her hands sweating and her parents glaring at her, and every time it stalled all cogent thoughts in her head. Nothing spilled onto the page, and this had happened every time she had tried to write the speech.

'What's the block, do you think?' Carl had said. 'David told me about your parents.'

'I think it's them,' she told him. 'What will they think, or say? How will everyone else be thinking about the situation with them too? I know what I'd say to Hannah alone in a room, but . . . it's the public aspect.'

'Well then, just pretend it's Hannah and you alone, at home, and write from the heart,' Carl said. 'Remember, it is a wedding. It's not you just sitting talking. There's an audience, but it's not the public, it's people who love you and who want you to be mushy and romantic. It's a celebration! When Matty and I got married, at the start of his speech, I thought he was going a little overboard, but then I started weeping and people *loved* that! The photos are hilarious.'

That made sense, Meg knew, and yet when he had left to go and catch up with David in the shop afterwards, she still couldn't get anywhere. What was too much? Some of how she felt about Hannah was so deep and so huge that to say it might sound melodramatic. To try to put it into words felt impossible. Could she just draw it instead? Words weren't her strength, and Carl could help edit, but he couldn't write it. Could he? No, that was going too far.

As she was watching the television that evening, thinking about the day, the familiar sound of a key in the lock caught her attention, and she got up to go to the door to welcome Hannah home. It was a silly little tradition, one of the many tiny routines that make up a relationship that had its roots in a first time she couldn't even remember. It was so nice though, and she was glad they had it. It warmed her soul every time, whichever side of the door she was coming from.

'Hey,' Hannah said, nuzzling into Meg's neck. She could feel Hannah's frizzy hair mould to fit as Meg rested on her too.

'So I was thinking . . .'

'Let me put my suitcase down first.'

'I just wanted to say, please don't contact my parents,' she said. 'I like the offer, and I appreciate it, and I've thought about it a lot, but I'm going to remind them of the rehearsal day, see if they show up, and go from there. That's when I'll either know they are coming to the wedding, or, if they don't come to that, I'll tell them not to.'

'Okay,' Hannah said, pulling back from the hug to look at Meg's face. 'Whatever you want, if you're sure.'

'I am,' Meg said. 'They've got as much information as they need. I love *you* and *we're* getting married. They need to just decide.'

'Okay,' Hannah said, taking something out of her bag. 'Also, I'm home now. No more travelling, no more suitcases. I'm here with you.'

Meg kissed her. 'Good.'

'I missed you.'

'I missed you too, Han. No more travelling. Except the honeymoon.'

'Except the honeymoon, of course!'

'What's that in your hand?'

'Just a little souvenir,' Hannah said, and passed her a tiny box. Inside was a ring, a kind of cobbled silver, indented with impressive detail. It was only cheap, the kind of random thing you'd find in a gift shop, but it was lovely. 'I know you've got a ring, obviously. But I saw this, and thought of you and . . . I'd buy a ring and get married to you a million times if I could.'

Hannah leaned in for a kiss.

'Welcome home.'

23

DAVID

15 Days Until the Wedding

David was sitting behind the counter in a T-shirt, trousers and, ambitiously, sandals, looking at a folder of documents his accountant had left him to go through. He and Harry had had their latest catch-up in the hour before the florist's opened and despite David soothing himself with a large coffee and a cinnamon roll, he had felt miserable throughout. What she laid out was stark. There were no positives, only negatives. The accountant had heard through the grapevine – the sort of pun Mark would love, but not in these circumstances – that a new café might be opening down the street and might take some of their sit-in custom too. Basically, everything she had to tell him was bad news, and there was even a small business tax hike he'd had no idea about that had come into effect from April.

He'd thought she'd be impressed with his entrepreneurial spirit: the uptake in events, the queer business network and the collaboration with the wine bar next door. He thought that would all be valuable, but she crushed his hopes.

'Those little things, fifty quid here and there, often it's more about community than money,' she said. 'Probably took you longer than it was worth. These partnerships are good, but they take such a long time to see real benefit and even then it's usually small.'

He had never thought it was this bad. He was dreading telling Mark. He knew Mark understood how hard he tried every day to make the shop a success, but with Mark being so practical and methodical, he knew he would think he'd been too . . . David. Too idealistic, too creative, too focused on feeling rather than the hard reality of the numbers.

What was it he loved about Savage Lilies, and what would he miss the most? It was the ability it gave him to live his life how he liked. He did not have to sit at a desk in smart clothes anyone else made him wear, and pretending to some straight boss he wasn't who he was. Also if it were gone, they wouldn't be able to host the youth club anymore, and he'd have less reason to be involved in community projects. He'd feel a little less himself.

What was he without the shop?

He would hate to make Mark move out of the flat they loved too. It was their home and they had their routines. Neither of them, he knew, felt like they wanted to start again.

The accountant had advised him to wrap things up in a couple of months and, though David had kind of brushed the comment away, saying it wasn't over till it was over, a small voice inside of him told him that was stupid. *Cut your losses,* the voice said. What would he say to Benji? He was coming in shortly. He'd been so happy when Benji texted telling him three people had enquired online about the subscription. He'd thought that a huge step, but the accountant had been so dismissive. Maybe Benji was the answer. *Maybe children are our future,* sang the voice in his head. Stupid.

It was getting way past David's lunchtime – eleven forty-five – and there was no sign of Benji. Although he knew there'd be an innocent excuse, and that he was just a child, David wanted to feel annoyed at somebody, and until he arrived, Benji would be that person.

He came eventually, bouncing into the shop at a quarter past one, wearing a long-sleeve T-shirt and with a small bum bag worn on his front.

'Hey,' he said. 'Sorry, man. Needed to eat. Forgot, ate, didn't have my bike so had to walk.'

'That's okay,' David said, calm after having had a sandwich. 'These things happen. Do you want a Coke?'

'Yes please,' Benji said, coming behind the counter to sit next to David.

'I thought we'd go there,' David said, pointing to a table away from the counter.

'Okay, whatever suits.'

Once they were sitting down, David noticed Benji was checking his phone, and when he put it back down, he began to fiddle with anything he could: the spray bottle on the table, the keys in his pocket. He hoped it wasn't anything he had done, or any annoyance David had shown him. Often, he and Mark had seen Benji berate himself for small mistakes, and they or others had had to talk him down from real fury. It had been hard, often, to see him treat himself in that way. Today, that feeling seemed to be coming out in small tics.

'Are you okay?' David asked as Benji bounced his index finger on the sugar pot.

'Yeah, man,' he said. 'Why?'

'You seem, I don't know, a little worried. You don't have to tell me anything, but do talk to someone if you need to. Jacob's always around.'

'Yeah, I know. I'm fine. Just my dad being . . . him,' Benji said. 'I can't wait to move out.'

'Oh, Benji.'

'Or I wish I just had a proper job so I could get my own place.'

'I know that feeling.'

'Do you actually?'

'Yes!' David said. 'Of course I do. I wasn't always in my fifties.'

'I just can't imagine that,' Benji said. 'You at my age.'

'Why?'

'You're so confident. You just do whatever you want.'

'Doesn't feel like that sometimes, I'll tell you that.' David thought about other times Benji had let him and Mark in, those times so rare. 'You'll be okay. Childhood doesn't last forever. What's your dad doing?'

'He just gets home from work and it's always like I've done something wrong, like something's dirty or we've run out of something. I'm just a kid. I don't know what he wants.'

Benji looked at him and, perhaps done with this outpouring, got out his phone.

'Well I'm always here if you need to talk, and—'

Benji spun round in his chair, as if that was the end of it, and he wanted to move on. Sometimes, if David mentioned their relationship, or the idea of being helped, Benji would switch off, and he knew he'd done it again.

'Shall I show you what I've done?'

'Yes please, Benji,' David said patiently. 'If you're ready.'

David sipped at his cup of tea, impressed as Benji quickly scrolled and swiped and showed him videos and photos he had posted of the shop, clever captions (he must have stolen some puns from Mark) and a follower list of nearly three hundred and forty people. His presentation skills could be improved, since he dashed wildly between different topics, but his eye for making everything look great was remarkable. This was some of the best advertising David had ever had for the company.

'You've done amazingly.'

'It's only been a couple of weeks,' he replied. 'But I have so many ideas for what's next.'

'What are you thinking?'

'You could do a competition, get other businesses involved,' he said, scrolling through his phone to find an example. 'Maybe find someone through your gay network. See, look at this. If you ask people to share something, then their followers see it, and theirs, and so on. It's all an incentive. Like a pyramid scheme.'

'I think pyramid schemes are supposed to be bad.'

'Okay, then this is like that but good.'

'But what if we run that competition and then nobody posts?'

'Then people feel like they have a higher chance,' Benji said. 'And anyway, somebody always posts.'

David had to excuse himself quickly to help a customer. The shop was nicely busy for once – he wished the accountant had stayed to see this – and he was keeping his eye on the groups of people taking a look. He had rejigged the shop's front slightly and it seemed to be bringing a few more people in, curious about the subscription service and the events schedule that were now posted on the window.

'Do you enjoy this?' David asked, coming back to sit with Benji. 'Social media?'

'Yeah, man,' Benji said. 'I see businesses post stuff that's like, completely stupid. Sometimes stuff that actively makes you not wanna go there or whatever. I don't know how they get it so wrong.'

'That's right,' David said. 'You are good with that; you're good with people.'

'I don't feel like I'm good with people,' Benji said, in a way that broke David's heart.

'You are,' David said. 'Benji! Come on! That time you made sure Salma was okay when she came in and wouldn't tell anyone what was wrong? You made Ailie and Meg feel really welcome at the drawing class? I'm sorry, by the way, that I told anyone you went on a date. Maybe I'm not that good with people. I can keep a secret; I just didn't realize you wanted that to be private.'

'Nothing's secret forever,' Benji said. 'I know that. I just don't want anyone finding out yet.'

'All right.'

David knew when not to push, and so he kept silent.

'That's Meg's mum there,' Benji said suddenly.

'What?'

'Mrs Kirby.'

David twisted to look behind him, and walking into the shop was an older woman. She was wearing a matching top and skirt, in a dark yellow colour, and her hair, noticeably greying, was pinned up haphazardly on top of her head. She was methodically going through every shelf and display in the front window. David looked back to the table quickly.

'How do you know that?'

'She's my English teacher,' he said. After a minute, he added: 'She looks miserable.'

'You'd better get going. Thanks for all your work on the shop,' David said. 'Let's give it another couple of weeks then let's talk about handing it back to me.'

He was desperate to pay Benji, to show him how brilliant this was, how he could make this his job if he wanted, but knowing what he knew about Lilies' accounts, there was nothing he could do. Instead, Benji fist-bumped him (David had learned what to do now) and left the shop, greeting Meg's mum as he left, who looked startled. He noticed gladly Benji didn't try to fist-bump her. Back behind the counter, David was sitting, heart pounding, pretending not to look.

It was ten minutes of her walking round, inspecting things, somewhat anonymously amongst the eight or so people who were in, until she was standing near the counter. David was so confused. Did she know whose this shop was, and was she here to spy on him? This was where they were supposed to meet so she must know at least that Meg had planned to get flowers from him. He thought she and Meg hadn't spoken in weeks. Did this mean she was coming? Or could she be planning to send flowers to apologize for not coming?

Ava. That was her name. Of course. He remembered Hannah mentioning it one of the times they had all discussed the situation together. She was Ava; he was George. From afar, she seemed exactly how David expected. Even from a few feet away, he could smell a flowery rose perfume, and a sense of purpose carried around with her, in a way that felt intimidating.

'Could you help me for a second?' she said.

Suddenly they were interacting, and David stood up to come next to her. 'Of course.'

'I'm looking for flowers, something for my daughter's wedding.'

'Oh,' David said in shock. 'Congratulations. To you and . . . them.'

'Thank you.' Ava walked slightly away towards the front windows and David followed. He noticed she passed quickly past the queer bouquets, their pride-flag wrapping his own personal victory.

'So what does she want?' David asked, without waiting for Ava to steer the conversation. He wondered if he should say he knew who she was, but she spoke so quickly, he didn't have time to think clearly about how to navigate the situation.

'Just your usual wedding flowers,' Ava said. 'I like these.' She gestured towards today's mixed bouquets, which had pink roses but also a mix of white and red flowers of different varieties squeezed in amongst spring-style twigs and foliage. 'The roses, not the rest.'

'We can certainly do white roses,' David said. 'We do bouquets, arrangements, table features, arches even.'

'Okay, great.'

There was another pause, and David could suddenly understand how Meg found it hard to go against her parents. Ava was someone you wanted to please, or at least not disappoint. She had a sharp edge you wanted to get away from. What was she doing here, anyway? Should he break the artifice of whatever game they were each playing?

'Again,' he asked. 'What exactly is your daughter after?'

What would Meg want him to do in this situation?

'It's more for me to look,' she said, defensively. 'And then I'll tell her what I see.'

'Okay.'

'She's at work,' Ava added quickly, as some sort of decoy. David, of course, knew she wasn't, but he imagined this woman wouldn't respond well to being challenged.

'I'm not sure on these. Do you have them in a more . . . subtle colour?' she said, pointing at some of the buckets of flowers on the floor by the window.

'Not really,' David said. 'A lot of couples now . . .' He couldn't work out how to say it, but these were the flowers and colours Hannah had chosen. He knew they would be at the wedding and he felt he must defend them. 'They like a burst of colour, untraditional mixes, you know. People don't generally only have roses anymore.'

Ava pursed her lips in a way that made David feel uncomfortable. Was she testing him?

'It's true, of loads of things,' he continued. 'I mean, being a florist's . . . I've really had to move with the times.' Maybe this would change her mind, an admission of everybody having to bend with the changes in society. He gestured towards the photo booth, the cakes, the houseplants hanging from baskets above the door. He was aware his hands were shaking slightly. 'That,' he said, pointing to the coffee machine. 'Never thought I'd be a barista, but here we are.'

He waited for her to respond but she didn't.

'All the events, the weddings, funerals, any celebration isn't what it used to be, which I guess is good. As long as people can do what they want, they come in and we see how we can work together. I've done the flowers differently for all sorts of things, which makes it exciting.'

'I think we'd probably want to stick with roses and nothing other than pink and white. That's what I had at my wedding. My daughter always loved roses.'

David wasn't sure if this was true. Meg had barely mentioned roses and been open to much more interesting options. If it had been true at some point, it showed how much she didn't know her daughter, and it discounted Hannah's opinions, perhaps on purpose.

'I went to a wedding recently,' David persisted. 'Where they just had massive sunflowers.' He was thinking back to Carl and Matty's wedding, which admittedly had been nearly ten years ago. 'That wasn't traditional at all, but it was so them. Sunflowers meant so much to them and their story. You have to follow the couple, I find, as a florist.'

'Sometimes a couple doesn't know everything,' Ava said. 'I say that as a *parent*. Why have an older generation if you're just going to ignore them?'

'The world's changing all the time.'

'Right.'

He wanted to mention the grooms at the wedding he was thinking of but felt like he couldn't.

'You could always have a think and come back,' David said. 'Here's a flyer about our new subscription service as well.'

'Thank you,' she said. At least she took the flyer. She seemed to pause, looking at it for a second, and he wondered if she might recognize Meg's new illustrations. Suddenly, she seemed very small in the shop; an old woman, who perhaps David had been too harsh with. Perhaps he had brought too much of himself to the conversation. 'When I've spoken to her and her . . . partner, I'll be in touch.'

'Okay, thank you!' David said, smiling. 'Have a good day.'

He watched her walk away and down the high street, before getting in a car and driving off, and David stood stunned, not noticing a couple at the till waiting to pay, because he was too consumed trying to work out what type of interaction he'd just had, and whether he'd helped at all, or made everything much worse.

They were eating stir-fry again. Of course it was easy, but Mark's work had been really busy the last few weeks with late-afternoon appointments, and David was comforted by some sort of routine and similarity every day, with all he had going on too.

'I can tell what you're thinking,' Mark said, chopping spring onions into much finer slices than David ever could.

'What?'

'You're thinking we've had this a lot.' Mark raised his eyebrows as David smiled.

'Well we have,' David said. 'But that's fine!'

'There are much more harmful things to be addicted to!'

As soon as David had got home, he had discussed with Mark how odd it was to see Meg's mum in his own space. Mark kept checking he was okay and that it hadn't upset him too much, but it felt more like he finally had insight into how Meg might be feeling.

Since then, they had begun to cook. David felt like he did understand Ava a little better, in a way others might not be able to. He still did not condone her behaviour, and thought it genuinely shocking as a parent, but she was conveying thoughts and feelings he recognized from his own life. It was easy to shut away homophobia as something happening far away, or something that was a belief held by people who weren't in your life, but that was very rarely the case. It was much harder to think about the concept with people you knew, or loved.

While Mark and Hannah had been happier to write the parents off, David felt more in line with Meg, who understood the fear of a parent. Like his own mum and dad had implied that one horrible day, Ava didn't want Meg to face barriers, discrimination or to not be able to do certain things. Both David and Meg's parents knew, and it was true, that life could be harder if you were gay, but what David couldn't understand was Ava and George making the burden heavier. What mattered was having more people on your side, than against you.

To give in and admit you must be wrong took a lot of strength, and would mean admitting you didn't know as much as you thought about the world. David could see, even from their brief interaction, how Ava's world view was built on the foundations of tradition and respect for your elders. It was hard to let that go.

Perhaps if his own parents had lived longer, the world would have changed enough that they'd have seen that too. You couldn't think thoughts like that though, David always reminded himself, whenever his mind strayed into what-ifs and maybes. Nothing could be done.

'Do you mind if I mention the "C" word?' Mark said, as he dished up the meal.

'You never swear.'

'Christmas.'

'Even worse,' David joked, nudging Mark out of the

way so he could get into the cutlery drawer and lay the table. He had always felt slightly left out of Christmas, and joining Mark's family's festivities still felt like being a plus-one, even all these years later. It was worse when people tried really hard to make him feel like part of the family. David preferred for nobody to notice him or how he was feeling at all. New Year's was more his sort of thing, spent with the friends who were his real family, and looking to the future.

'My parents think we should do it at my sister's,' he said. 'They think it's too much to host everyone now, now there's grandkids and with how old they are.'

'Isn't it so incredibly early to even be thinking about this?'

'Yes,' Mark said. 'It is, but they think you and I should stay at a hotel nearby, and they don't want it to fill up so they suggested we book.'

David kept quiet; this was his best-case scenario, having a little bit of distance from Mark's family. He usually had the excuse of the shop to avoid the longest stretches of a family Christmas, but what if he didn't even have that this year? He couldn't face telling Mark yet what the accountant had said. He'd forgotten all about that with Ava coming in.

'Okay, if that works,' he said. 'I guess.'

'I can see you're smiling.'

'Well you know how I feel about Christmas.'

'Well it's win-win then I guess,' Mark said. 'You get a hotel room with a bath and the breakfast is rated nine out of ten. Are you happy if I book? When's the shop closing?'

'Oh don't worry, we can always get someone to cover.'

'Are you sure? You don't normally—'

'Yes,' David said, interrupting. 'It'll be nice to have a break.'

After the day he'd had, David wished he could just sit in silence or maybe zone out in front of the television, but that wasn't something they did so instead he sat, watching Mark eat, struggling to think of what to say that wasn't about the two main things in his brain: Meg's parents, and the fact that downstairs could be something entirely different by Christmas.

24
MEG

One Week Until the Wedding

Then, before anybody was acclimatized, or perhaps ready, it was Sunday night, and just one week to go until the big day itself. David and Mark were sitting at Meg and Hannah's kitchen table, and she and Hannah were holding hands, after they'd all finished as much of the three huge pizzas they'd ordered as they could. It was warm inside, the body heat of the four of them making Meg sweat a little under her jumper; the heat of June had finally arrived, but coming with it rain and clouds, the heavy muggy kind of summer you didn't want.

David and Meg were talking about all the people they'd met so far on the adventure of planning the wedding and joking about whether they might have missed anybody from the invite list. Hannah, drinking wine from a mug, because they had to remember to buy glasses sometime soon, was talking to Mark about their upbringings. The two were praising their families, but Meg could hear there was an edge to the conversation where they spoke about what it was like to have supportive parents in a relationship with somebody without that same support. Just as she was listening in, David asked her about her parents.

'I just wondered if you'd heard from them yet?' he asked. 'Sorry to—'

'No, nothing.' Meg shrugged her shoulders, topping up their glasses with the last of the wine. 'I asked about Thursday and they didn't say anything so we'll have to just wait and see.'

'And *whatever happens*,' Hannah said, leaning over, 'it's going to be okay, and the day's going to be amazing.'

'The day's going to be great,' Mark agreed.

'You've become a bit of a celebrity in the shop you know,' David said. 'Everyone asks after you.'

'No they don't,' Meg said.

'They do!'

'Don't stress her out, David,' Mark said.

'Have we run out of alcohol?' Hannah asked, standing at the fridge looking at what they had left. Initially, Meg and Hannah had invited the pair round for a mini hen do, without calling it that. Music had played softly in the background when the evening began, but Meg had turned it up a couple of times and now they were definitely having to speak louder to be heard above the noise.

'Unless I pop out and get more,' Mark said.

'Unless,' Meg said, looking at Hannah. 'We went out to celebrate?'

'Well, I have a day off tomorrow,' David said. 'And the shop's closed . . .'

'Interesting . . .' Hannah slowly closed the fridge, and it became apparent from everybody smiling very quickly that they were all game. 'Shoes on?'

Before they knew it, or could believe it, they were out the door.

Pink Punters was the nearest, and only, gay bar, and they managed to quickly get inside despite a short queue. They were quite early, it turned out, because the place was mostly empty when they arrived, though after half an hour, it seemed like big groups were flooding in after them. Nobody was able to believe they had all, as a group, made it onto a night out, and everybody kept individually saying how surprised they were, how long it had been, and had they all forgotten how to do this?

'Meg, did you come here when you were young?' Hannah said.

'No, no, we were all scared of this place.' At that point the DJ started playing Madonna, and her vocals rang through the speakers. 'I'm not sure why.'

It was an odd place, a large white building with original beams everywhere, as if it used to be a large hotel, but now was fitted inside with metal and plastic and a number of different rooms that would make it able to hold the masses of queer people who were there nearly every night of the week, and all that came with crowds being out until the early hours. There was a big half-in, half-out terrace that had large firepits behind metal grates to provide warmth, and groups were standing around them chatting and drinking. The four of them headed inside to dance.

They moved self-consciously at first, until the first drink was finished and Hannah returned from the bar with her round. Then, there was a not unpleasant blur to proceedings that made Meg barely notice the fact there were other people in the room. As if in a mirage, she noticed Gus in a group on the other side of the floor, and she shouted his name. She was sure it was him, though she doubted herself as she got closer. His hair seemed shorter, and it wasn't until she had manoeuvred in front of him that she could confirm it was him.

'Meg!' he screamed and hugged her, and waved to the others. 'This is my first girlfriend!' he shouted, to laughs from the group. 'And last!'

'Gus! Your hair!'

'Do you like it?'

'A new look!' Meg said. 'It's amazing.'

'Oh my God – one week to go!'

'Less than!'

'What are you doing in a club?'

'Having a spontaneous hen do,' Meg shouted. 'I'm so glad you're here!'

'We'd better get the hen a drink!'

He grabbed her by the hands and marched her out of the room and back outside towards the chilly bar. Drinks in hand, Meg blurted out everything that had happened since she'd last texted Gus: the message to her parents left ignored and her mum going into Savage Lilies. Gus could barely believe it.

'What did David do?' Gus asked.

'He tried to defend me and work out why she was there, but I think she just . . . I don't know, wanted to pretend she was involved in her daughter's wedding. Which I gave her every chance to do! It just makes me feel so low.'

'I know,' Gus said. 'I know you were really close growing up.'

'I was an only child! I tried to pretend nothing changed when I came out but . . . I guess I'm realizing it hasn't been the same in so long. I can't remember the last time we had a proper conversation.'

They spoke more, quickly and excitedly, and Gus tried to lift her spirits, asking about her dress and all the details he didn't know about the wedding. She asked him about texting Ramon, and Gus admitted he liked him, and that though they hadn't had a chance to meet up, they were looking forward to seeing each other at the wedding. Gus made her promise she wouldn't tell him any of what he'd said, and so like when they were teenagers again, she pinkie-promised. Soon, she felt good again, and excited about this new chapter.

'We need to let the past go,' Gus said, shouting, as they headed back to the dance floor. 'There's nowhere better to do it than a gay club!'

The evening was passing in a series of tiny fragments as they drank more: dancing here with them, dancing there with them, toilet, bar, outside, and back again. Meg didn't really go out in this way anymore. Even two glasses of wine was a rarity, yet she felt like after the months she'd had, nobody would begrudge her the type of night she and Hannah had had when they were younger. All they were missing was Hannah's old digital camera, and the pretence that they were 'just good friends'.

Back inside, David had amassed a crowd around him. Of course he had. It seemed to be a mix of people he knew already, some of whom were familiar from David greeting them in the shop, and then genuine strangers he had managed to charm. Together as a group, they went back out to one of the fire pits and Meg ended up talking to Mary, a trans friend of David's, who spoke about her experience in the local area and her transition when she had first moved. She had beautiful blonde hair and was wearing a shiny mesh top with short-length dungarees in a way that shouldn't work, and yet did. Her hair was in pigtails.

When Meg shared her journey with her parents, Mary grabbed her hand and said, 'Things might just take a while . . . but everything works out.'

'*If it's not okay, it's not the end,* is that what you were going to say?' Meg said.

'No, that's rubbish,' she replied, batting the words away with her hand. 'That's stupid, Meg, whoever told you that. Sometimes it is the end, of course. Only if you want it to be. We're all in charge of our own lives.'

Before Meg could get a chance to thank the woman for her wisdom, Mark gathered them together with a new round of drinks, and they raised a toast to the wedding. When Meg turned around again, Mary had quietly disappeared, back to the friends she had come with, and part of Meg felt like maybe she had made enough friends, maybe she didn't have room for more. Another, drunker, part of her wondered whether she'd just met a fairy godmother.

'To old relationships,' David said.

'To new friendships,' Hannah added.

'And new beginnings,' Meg added, and they all cheered, whilst Hannah came round to give her a hug.

'My hen,' she whispered in Meg's ear, her hot breath warming against the chill of the night.

'My wife,' Meg whispered back.

25

DAVID

Three Days Until the Wedding

David knew that that Thursday, he and Mark were on hand to make the day as smooth as possible for Meg and Hannah. It was their only real role now. He had put Ray in charge of the shop from lunchtime. Though he thought he would have had more time to mentally prepare, the last few days had passed in a blur of deliveries and now the rehearsal dinner was here.

He was preparing a small bag of things that he worried Meg might need, which included water, tissues, lip balm and those small calming sweets, which were surely more of a placebo than anything. He also had a raincoat for her, since the rain was forecast to continue, and a few snacks in case she was hungry.

All week, David had been obsessively checking the weather app on his phone, and it kept changing for the next days until the wedding on Sunday, sometimes showing brilliant sunshine, sometimes telling him it would be overcast or even showing him alarming flashing storm clouds. He kept telling Mark that those signs often meant a bigger storm was coming, but Mark, eternally positive, had told him to focus on the things he could control.

'Are you ready?' he called to him from the kitchen.

He could hear Mark pulling hangers from the wardrobe and putting them back. 'Nearly! I thought you said we weren't going till three!'

'I know but we could always go early.' David was tying his shoelaces. He knew it was one of his most annoying habits, to have got ready early just in case and then been itching to leave.

'I'll be out in five!' Mark shouted.

David waited patiently, checking himself in the mirror one last time. It was a rehearsal of the ceremony but it was also about some of the vendors coming to drop things off, so it wasn't a full dress-up occasion. However, Meg had mentioned staying in the pub for dinner afterwards, which David was looking forward to, so he had made sure to dress up more than he would for a day working in a florist's, whilst still being comfortable. He'd never liked fancy clothes. He had on a thick patterned jumper and soft chinos, paired with his trusty Skechers that saw him through twelve-hour days on his feet.

'Right, I'm here,' Mark said. He emerged into the kitchen wearing the exact same outfit. His jumper was a slightly different colour of green, and he wore boots not trainers, but otherwise they were like twin toddlers dressed up by their mother.

'Oh no,' Mark said. 'Shall I change?'

'One of us has to,' David said. 'Imagine her parents come and the first thing they see is this!'

'Okay, give me two minutes.'

David checked his watch and phone constantly as he waited for Mark to get ready.

'What a bad omen,' David said when Mark re-emerged into the room wearing a shirt. He moved to show Mark the weather app on his phone.

Mark was smiling, shaking his head. 'It'll all be fine – stop worrying,' he said, sitting down next to David on the sofa to put his shoes on again, before deciding not to and stopping.

'I just wanted to say,' he began, turning to face David. 'Maybe I was too blunt about the wanting to get married, and how I said it. I can't underestimate how your family will have made you feel, and I want to be sensitive.'

'Thanks.' David touched Mark's knee. 'That means a lot.'

'I really mean it,' he continued. 'Seeing Meg and you the last few weeks, I don't want to add any stress onto life for you, especially with everything happening with the shop. It's important to me but we're also a couple who have been together like this for years and years. If marriage isn't right for you, then it's not right for me. I shouldn't have been . . . I don't know, those ultimatums have never been very us.'

'Thank you.'

'You're not saying much.'

'Oh, I'm just thinking about the next few days,' David said. 'But I appreciate that. Really, I do.'

'All right, shall we go?'

Out the front of the shop, David noticed Gus, Meg's ex-boyfriend walking past. They quickly said hello but David insisted they were in a rush, and Gus waved him off.

'No worries, David,' Gus said. 'I'll see you later.'

* * *

The parts of the pub they were using looked plain and tired, but David felt confident they'd be transformed in a matter of days, particularly when Jacques had arrived to decorate and bring to life the designs he'd emailed over. David was just glad to be out of the drizzly grey weather. He reminded himself, as they greeted Meg and Hannah, that their job was to do whatever was needed, but also to keep everything calm and ticking on, to make Meg feel like everything was going to be okay.

Rod showed the four of them to the marquee outside, which they had ambitiously set up for the beginning of summer. It was flapping slightly with the wind, and David worried about the noise on the day, whether they'd be able to hear the speeches. Rod ran through the plan for the benches and chairs, which would be bought in the next couple of days and moved inside after the ceremony. He ran through the timeline for setting things up the day before, like what his team would sort and what was Meg and Hannah's to arrange. Hannah told Rod about her parents coming on the Saturday to help, and how they'd be around for all the last-minute details early Sunday morning. Meg stood awkwardly, with no updates from her own parents.

Next, they were shown the storage area in the basement, reached by the same set of stairs at the back of the pub where you went into the marquee. The room was painted white, but you could see dirt and stains on it, and David made a paranoid note in his head to put everything in plastic bags and be careful with anything delicate.

'I guess I'll leave you to it then,' Rod said, swinging a set of keys around his fingers. 'I'm upstairs if you need anything.'

'Thanks, Rod,' David said. 'We appreciate it.'

Over the next couple of hours, David and Mark tried to keep light-hearted chat going with Meg and Hannah who actually both seemed nervous in different ways. David was sure they were both affected by the wait to see if Meg's parents arrived, but whilst Meg had gone into a silent sort of trance, Hannah was jittery and particular, getting irritated with people for how they carried things, or if they said something slightly negative that might add to Meg's stress.

Jacques arrived, enlisting them all to carry boxes from his car into the storage area, which they stacked on the floor. David noticed how Jacques somehow ended up not carrying anything. The seamstress from the bridal shop, Susan, arrived, delivering one huge box with one of the most important things inside, Meg's dress. Everyone hovered around it, and Hannah even told Mark to go and wash his hands before touching it, though Meg wouldn't let her even take a peek. David stacked it on a table, protected it with bin bags and reminded himself to take it home to his that evening.

David checked the schedule Meg had given them all, a printed copy each with their name on the top, running through essential items and jobs, and the schedule for today and the day itself. David ticked everything off in his own head, anything that needed to happen before Sunday. Angie would be dropping the cake off on Saturday, Ramon was parking the truck later tonight and there were some deliveries of their drinks and special glasses coming on Saturday. Just before five o'clock, the celebrant arrived and David was again surprised with how tall Caleb was. When he extricated himself from his smart car, it was like he was being unfolded.

‘Hello! Back again,’ David said, shaking his hand.

‘Nice to see you,’ Caleb said, getting a small briefcase from the back of the car. ‘This must be the place?’

David showed him the pub and took him through to the back where everyone was hovering in the marquee.

‘Hi, everyone, I’m Caleb,’ he announced. ‘I’m just going to sort some things, then we’ll start at five-thirty?’ He put his briefcase on the side and started sorting papers.

David checked his watch, noting that it was five minutes past five.

‘Is that okay with everybody?’ Caleb looked round at the group. ‘No need to look terrified – this is the easy bit.’

Meg looked nervous but smiled back at him. Hannah put her arms around her.

‘So we’ve got the couple, that’s the important thing,’ he said. ‘Hannah, you’ll start up here as discussed. Meg, are we still waiting on . . . your dad was walking you, is that right?’

Nobody said anything, and it seemed Caleb suddenly remembered what he’d been told when he’d come to visit.

‘He’ll be here. Let’s give it till half past,’ David said. ‘If not, Plan B!’

‘All right,’ Caleb said, and David checked his watch again. ‘I just need to get something from the car,’ he added. They all said goodbye to Jacques who said he’d see them on the day. David kept glancing to the door and then looking away. *A watched pot never boils,* or Mark’s version: *A watched pot never sprouts.*

At twelve minutes past, Meg’s parents weren’t there. Everybody was standing in the marquee, waiting, and the occasional asides people had been saying to keep up the good cheer had got further and further apart until David couldn't remember who had been the last one to speak.

'Is that rain?' Mark said, and indeed, there were the tiny incremental drum noises of rainfall against the tarpaulin.

'Oh, that's annoying,' Hannah said.

'Best let it clear before Sunday,' David replied.

'Hello, everyone!'

David couldn't believe it. He spun round to see Meg's mum enter the marquee, closely followed by who he presumed was Meg's father, George, who up till now he'd only seen in photos of a much younger version of the couple.

'The man upstairs told us where to find you,' Ava said, marching over to Meg, ignoring everyone else in the room, no awareness of the silence she was breaking dramatically. They had both dressed up for the occasion, he in a suit and tie, her in a dress, no hat, despite Meg having insisted it was casual. Maybe that message had got lost with everything else that had gone on. While Ava was trying to take control, as she had in the shop, George looked awkward, as if embarrassed by the situation. They got closer and David could see that whilst Ava seemed older than him, George couldn't have been more than a year or two older than him and Mark.

David saw Meg looking lovingly back to Hannah, before approaching her parents.

'You came.'

'Of course we came.'

Meg hugged her mum, and then shook her dad's hand, and everybody in the room stared in silence. Meg looked happy but tears had begun to fill her eyes, and David was sure she was running through a whole range of emotions.

'Well, this isn't exactly a wedding party,' said her

mum, her voice slightly higher-pitched than David had remembered. 'Where is everyone?' She said it in a jovial tone, and despite the fact every hair on David's body was standing on end, he tried to pretend this was all normal, or in any way manageable.

'It's just the rehearsal, Mum,' Meg said quietly, following her parents as they approached Hannah, who greeted them kindly, as if nothing untoward had happened.

Ava turned towards David, before a flicker of recognition entered her face. 'You're that florist! What are doing here?'

David heard Mark draw an intake of breath behind him.

'How do you know David?' Caleb asked Ava.

'I know you went to Savage Lilies, Mum,' Meg said. 'David told me.'

'I—'

'I know you too!' George said, turning to Mark. 'From St Helens?'

'Yes, I'm the school counsellor,' Mark said. 'It's nice to meet you both, properly and outside of work.' He reached out a hand. 'We're friends of Meg and Hannah's.'

George coughed and Ava seemed to be slowly realizing they might be a couple.

'David's been helping Meg out,' Hannah said.

'Right,' Ava said. 'Is this it then, Meg, us and these . . . men?'

She gestured toward Caleb, who was staring awkwardly at the floor, and Mark, who was watching with a serious expression on his face.

'Yes, Mum,' Meg said. 'It's literally just to run through the day. I did text . . .'

'Oh I know, but texting can be so confusing.'

'Okay.'

Was that going to be her cover for the last four months? Was that anything near an excuse? David pursed his lips.

'We've got some bits from the car,' she continued. 'A few surprises. Will you all come and help?' Before anybody could respond, she was climbing the stairs.

Intrigued, David followed the group as Meg's mum kept up a steady stream of comments about the weather and if the clouds would last, and how you didn't want it too hot, and how the pub food seemed okay, and obviously it was a different kind of wedding. You wouldn't have a wedding ceremony in a pub in her day! She delivered it all with such confidence, David was nearly taken in, before realizing that what she was saying undermined all of what he and Meg had done and what they'd had to do. He had performed a role that she and George always should have taken on. Suddenly, in an anger that coursed through his body, he wasn't sure why they were all standing in the car park now, or why they had listened to her. He felt Mark touch his arm and mouth to him: *Just let this play out*.

At the car, a large purple people carrier, Ava started to tell people to take boxes of things out, and carrying one or two each, the group did as she said. Due to the rain, nobody wanted to stay outside or question anything, and so they were soon back down in the storage basement.

'Mum, what on Earth is in these boxes? You know I've planned—'

'Sorry we're coming in a little late, but we've spent the last week sorting lots of things you'd need for—'

'I think we might have—' David began.

'David . . .' Mark said, warningly.

'Ever since I came into the shop . . .' Ava said.

'We wanted to . . .' George added.

'It's like your dad says. Everything you—'

'I think what everybody's trying to say,' Hannah said diplomatically, 'it's the wedding is in three days, so I'm not sure what we . . .'

'I can see there's resistance.' Ava sighed, her voice louder like David imagined her admonishing a class of thirty. 'So I'll just show you.'

Ava seemed absolutely fine to interrupt anybody and so David stayed silent for fear of being spoken over again. Hannah rolled her eyes. Meg looked again like she was going to cry and David took a step closer to her.

'Your mum's been very busy this week,' George said. 'Please listen to her.'

From the boxes, Meg's mum was unwrapping all sorts of things.

'I've got décor, here, candle wrappers to stop the wax and you'll need serviettes, and an arch here that needs to be put together. There are balloons somewhere. They all match.'

David watched as George said nothing. He couldn't tell if George agreed with how his wife had behaved, and the message was a clear one from both of them, delivered by Ava, or whether he was just following his wife's lead. David hated him for either one.

'Mum, where did you even get all of this?'

'Hello?'

There was a new voice, and David wondered who else could possibly be added into this unique scenario. Would they be able to make it better or worse? Surely not worse. As David was thinking this, a short man was coming down the stairs, and Meg's mum introduced him as an old family friend, and a florist. David felt his arms tense with stress. *This was worse.*

'William sorted it all.'

The man entered, and began to look at what was already in the basement; everything Jacques had brought earlier was commented on, or moved out of the way. David had to stop him putting a large mud-covered plant pot on the wedding dress box. He started to talk about the flowers he'd buy in, what Meg's bouquet would look like, and how early he'd have to come here on Sunday to do it all. He mentioned the elegant table flowers he'd do, not whatever was on the planner sheet he seemed to have picked up without anyone noticing. David desperately wanted to snatch it from his hand.

The man suddenly had a pen and was leaning against a table, scribbling away, murmuring something about how you couldn't have speeches before a wedding breakfast.

'I can't believe you've left it all this late,' he said, finally taking a breath. Looking around, he must have suddenly realized five people were staring at him open-mouthed, and that maybe he should tread more softly. He took a step back towards Meg's parents.

'I haven't left anything too late.'

Meg was turning red. David willed on that she would get mad, rather than upset. He realized she hadn't spoken in a long time; none of them had.

'I've sorted everything on my own, and with the help of David, because you, my parents, were ignoring me! Why have you brought all of this stuff? Three days before . . . this is . . . crazy.'

'I'm not going to be called crazy. I'm your mother. If you're going to get married,' Ava said, 'you're going to get married properly. You may have set your sights on this . . . public house, but I'll be damned if I'm showing my friends photos of a wedding that looks like a night at the local boozer.'

'Well, I'm surprised you're even showing them any photos! Since you're so ashamed of me!'

'Darling, of course we're not ashamed.'

'Then why do you keep ignoring my texts? Why didn't you mind when I said we didn't have space for any of your friends?'

'I—'

'EXACTLY!' Meg was shouting now, unable to keep a lid on whatever had been brewing for the last few months, or indeed, David thought, her entire life. 'I had flowers. I had—'

'Darling, we called William as a last resort, after going into your shop—' she shot a filthy look at David '—where all I got was attitude, and I presumed you'd told some stranger about how terrible we are—'

'I was just defending the flowers they'd already chosen . . .'

Mark was tutting behind him.

'Are you tutting at me?' David said.

'No!' Mark said. 'At them! How dare you both come in here—'

'Look, we really don't need more flowers,' David said. 'We've sorted all of those from my shop a long time ago, and actually I'd be losing money if—'

'Well isn't that brilliant, Meg,' Ava said. 'The one family friend I do bring and you won't even let him help. This is *not* how I brought you up.'

Meg was now staring at the ceiling trying not to cry,

and Hannah had an arm around her protectively. 'What's happening . . .' she muttered.

'Is this what I think it is?' While they were shouting, Mark seemed to be peeking into other boxes, and then in horror, seemed to be pulling out a second wedding dress in a huge plastic sleeve. 'I didn't know you were doing an outfit change, Meg.'

'Mark, I think . . .' David was shaking his head at Mark slowly. Mark suddenly looked mortified, before realizing this was one of the boxes Ava and George had brought.

'Mum . . .'

'It's my wedding dress,' Ava said, putting her hands on her hips. 'I think it would be a nice family tradition if you wore it. I don't mind if you need to alter it. Obviously you went ahead and got rings without asking anyone . . .'

There was a pause before anybody spoke, and David was sure he'd heard Caleb actually gasp.

'Over my actual dead body am I wearing that,' Meg said.

'Meg!' George said.

'Hey, leave her alone,' David said. He knew he should be keeping quiet but he couldn't bear it.

'Yeah, this is . . .' Hannah began.

The stairs creaked – seriously, who now? – and suddenly Gus was in the room. That must have been why he'd said something earlier about seeing them. David hadn't realized they were that close again.

'Hi, everyone,' he said. He was wearing a shirt and chinos. 'How's it going? Thanks for having me, Meg.'

'Sorry, Gus, what are you doing here?' Hannah said. 'Said with love.'

'Ava texted me, about the dinner tonight.'

'Mum, why?' Meg asked.

'I thought your ex-boyfriend should be here. You were always very close . . .'

'He's like a friend of the family,' George added.

'You haven't seen him in ten years!' Meg was back to shouting. 'You didn't like him at the time, *actually* – sorry, Gus – you were just happy I was living what you thought was a normal life. Oh my God!'

'Sorry,' Gus said, taking steps back towards the stairs. 'I really thought I was invited, if your mum texted me.'

'No, that's fine, Gus,' Meg said. 'It's not your fault. You weren't to know my parents are *crazy*!' She was staring at both of her parents, who looked aghast. 'Gus is gay, anyway!'

David saw Mark open his mouth to comment but he stopped himself.

'Angus is not gay,' Ava said. 'He was your boyfriend.'

'He is, actually,' Hannah said.

'Me and Meg actually was the phase,' Gus said.

'Angus is *not* gay,' Ava said. 'I saw you in the ASDA last year and you didn't say a word.'

'I actually go by Gus now . . .'

'Well why would he tell you?' Mark said.

'He is gay,' Meg said. 'He's dating a boy who makes tacos.'

'Well we're actually only texting.'

'He's not,' Ava said.

'I really am,' Gus said, shifting his weight awkwardly.

'Okay,' Ava said. 'Whatever.'

'You thought you'd bring my ex-boyfriend, and I'd suddenly swap out my fiancée for a man, didn't you?' Meg rubbed at her temples. 'Wow, you actually really thought that would work.'

'We didn't think *anything*,' Ava said. 'Like I've mentioned – and I don't know why you're shouting – I think if you're going to go ahead, we should be involved. You should have a proper wedding the family can be proud of. We're your parents. Now, have you thought about food?'

This seemed to be the final straw, and Meg burst into tears. Hannah and Mark stood either side of her to comfort her.

'Of course I—' Meg began, before convulsing into sobs.

'Why doesn't everybody go upstairs?' Hannah said. Nobody moved. '*Now*, please. I think there needs to be a family discussion here to sort everything out.'

They all filed out, and David wanted to smile to Meg, to assure her it would all be okay, but even he wasn't sure. She was sitting down now, shoulders heaving as she cried, and he knew he couldn't help. She wouldn't even look at him. He followed the others up the stairs silently, and wished, with everything he had, that this week could go differently for Meg, whilst feeling a sudden shame in his own guts that he couldn't place to any thought except one. *What if everything I've done has actually made this worse?*

26
MEG

'You can't just do all this without us! It isn't fair!'

Meg's mum was unrelenting. No matter how Meg approached the topic, how logical or emotional her arguments, her mum could not see sense. She was standing, arms flailing around her, as if trying to grab onto an argument that would suddenly make Meg docile, obedient, and a child again. Her skin was flushed with anger and her feet, whenever she paced as she spoke, were making tapping noises on the concrete floor. It was a response Meg was used to, a few times a year when Ava used to get this mad, sometimes at her husband, sometimes at Meg, once or twice at someone random in a restaurant or at the shops. It was one of the first changes Meg noticed in herself when she moved to university, the feeling of release at not being scared anymore of what her mother's mood might be.

'Mum!' she continued. 'You weren't here, you didn't reply to me, you didn't come to any of the things you were meant to come to. What were you expecting me to do? If we're going to talk about fair, let's talk about that! No, let me speak! You were the ones being absent parents when I had loads on my plate, and actually could have done with the help.'

'We've brought help; we've brought William!'

'I don't give a damn about William!'

'Well! That's charming.'

'Please don't swear,' her dad added.

'He's gay too, you know. Your rules, whatever your belief system is, I don't get it! Why is he okay? Is it okay until you get married? Is it okay to be gay but only in private? Otherwise you get banished from the family.'

'Why don't you take a minute and calm down. We're worried about you . . .' Ava said.

'Nobody,' George said, 'is saying anything as dramatic as anybody being banished.'

'You are! If you were going to disown me, you should have just done it when I came out to you! Doing it right now, in the middle of my wedding? It's so cruel.'

Nobody seemed to know what to say.

She felt Hannah twitch next to her. 'I think we maybe all need to take a minute.'

'Darling,' her dad began.

'We're not disowning you,' Ava said. 'We're *here* aren't we?'

'I wish you weren't!' Meg shouted back.

The room went silent, and although the situation involved her by necessity, she wished she were a bystander, or that someone else was talking for her. Every word pulled out of her was torture.

'We were just worried, darling, which is actually our job as parents.'

Hannah looked irritated. 'Ava, I need you to listen to me, this—'

'Hannah, with respect, you've said your piece. I'm going to say mine,' Meg's mum said. 'For a lot of people, it is a phase. I've read about it online.' Hannah was shaking her head, but Ava continued. 'So it's not out of the bounds of imagination that as parents we want Meg, and you actually, to consider whether you want to go through with something this serious.'

Hannah took another protective step towards Meg.

'And, you have to understand, we are not your generation. We are worried about your life, and your job opportunities, and with a ring on your finger, all of this is going to be very hard to avoid.'

'What do you mean *all of this*?' Hannah said, making air-quotes with her hands, though Ava hadn't when she had said those words. 'We are getting married because that's what we want to do.'

'What I mean is you'll have to say it at work, and people, I'm not saying they're right, people might make assumptions.'

'What assumptions?' Meg said suddenly. 'I actually work freelance and literally never have to say anything personal to anyone, ever. What you're saying, it's just . . .'

Hannah looked between them both. 'Ava, George, I want to marry your daughter. I don't know how you can still have a problem after how long you've known me,' Hannah said. 'We need the wedding to happen, ideally with your blessing.'

'I know, which is why I've shown up here, and your father too, to make sure that if you are doing this, you're doing this properly. All of this—' Ava gestured around at her boxes. 'Is being thrown back in my face.'

'I'm having the wedding I, *we*, wanted to have,' Meg

said, looking at Hannah. 'You would have had your input if you'd shown up to any of the things I asked you to. You haven't even seen the dress I've chosen! I probably would have compromised loads if you'd—'

'Well I don't think that's healthy either, Meg,' Hannah interrupted. 'It's our wedding, Ava. *We're* a family and a wedding isn't just something you do to please your parents.'

'Yes, but weddings are family things, so,' Meg said.

'I know, babe, but you know what I mean.'

'Oh great, now you're fighting,' Ava said. 'Look, are you sure about this?'

'Oh, Mum, will you just stop it?' Meg asked. 'Please.'

Ava looked at George. 'Are you going to let her speak to me like that?'

'I don't know where you've picked up this attitude,' George said, before turning his gaze onto Hannah.

'It wasn't me.'

'What?' Meg said to Hannah.

'It wasn't me!' Hannah protested. 'What he said!'

'I know that.'

'Well tell your parents!'

'Life is hard for gay people,' Ava said. 'That is what everyone says, that's what William tells me, that's what happened in *EastEnders*. Your florist, for example, has a real chip on his shoulder. I don't want your life to be hard, so yes I would still rather you were marrying a man. My expectations won't change overnight.'

'It's been ten years!'

'You're going to tell me life isn't hard?'

'Life is hard for everyone!' Meg said. 'The only person making my life harder because I'm gay right now is you! Everyone else is happy for me!'

Again, the room fell silent. Meg wondered briefly if their conversation could be heard upstairs in the pub. She wondered if David could hear her; she wondered what he thought.

'You know what, you're uninvited, just don't come,' she said. 'You obviously don't want to celebrate our marriage, and you obviously don't care that I've spent months planning my wedding, so just don't.'

'Uninvited from my own daughter's wedding . . . well, that's quite something.' Ava was shaking her head, speaking at low volume. 'Are you sure you want to behave like this? Your poor dad . . .'

'Am I sure I want to . . . Are you . . . I never want to see you again,' Meg said. It was out before she'd thought to say it, and she knew had she shouted, had she screamed, it would be something she regretted later. The words would be something said in the heat of the moment that she'd feel contrite about later, something she spoke to her parents in soft tones to apologize for, like coming down the stairs to the kitchen as a hormone-fuelled teenager who had finally tired of whatever she and her mum had been fighting about. As it stood, it came out from Meg as a disappointed sentence, thrown out, that she really did feel. It just was what it was.

Her mum stormed out of the room, and her dad followed. At the bottom of the stairs, George paused, as if to say something. Meg thought that he might say sorry, or apologize for Meg's mum, or give her some reason to hold out hope. Instead, he turned his face away and followed Ava.

Meg's body went into overdrive, and started feeling a way she had never felt before. It was like her heart was getting too big for her chest. A migraine formed at her temples, and she felt like she needed to take her shoes off. She was too hot but her hands were frozen to the bone, and she couldn't catch breath from the air to say any of the hundred things going through her head. She looked at the boxes of wedding things, hers and her mum's, dumped in this room. Was any of this worth it? Was Hannah worth losing her parents over? Had she lost them already?

Overwhelmed by the strain this must be putting on Hannah, she felt like she needed to get away from her too. Meg couldn't see Hannah in pain because of her family. She felt too responsible, and she was tired of the one person she was meant to be spending the rest of her life with just seeing her as a sad, crying person. She wanted Hannah to see her as something other than this, as beautiful, or funny, or even comically stressed, or any of the things people were meant to feel in the run-up to their wedding. Once again, she wished this were all normal.

'I need to get some air,' she said, before running up the stairs and out of the room, leaving Hannah alone in the empty room full of all the wedding paraphernalia, all the boxes they did and didn't want, of a wedding as they wished it to be, and the special day someone else supposed was right for them.

27
DAVID

David was sitting with Mark at a table in the pub listening to what he could from downstairs. You couldn't hear much of it, which was good since he was sure Meg would want privacy, but you could hear snippets when their voices went high or when anybody shouted. Rod was behind the bar drying glasses pretending not to hear, a couple of other lone patrons drinking as if they couldn't hear a word.

A couple of times Mark had touched his hand, as if to say, *I know it's hard to hear.* He knew in his heart Hannah was there to protect Meg, and that Meg could handle herself anyway, but he felt so protective over her that it was near unbearable to stay in place. He wanted to storm downstairs, perhaps scream at them in a Barbara Windsor moment to *get out of his pub.*

He began to pace. Tactfully, Caleb had made his excuses and gone to wait in his car, and Gus had got himself a drink and sat at another table, looking sadly at his phone. It must have been hard for him too, to see childhood relived like that, and David felt the same. David felt, like most of the ongoing issues with Meg's parents, that he wanted to do what he could to stop it, so that she wouldn't have to go through what he did. It wasn't his place to cut her off from her parents though. Only she could choose that, if that were what she wanted. He could feel a pain in his leg, the tendon to the outer side of his right ankle. Was his body responding to the financial stress of the shop or the emotional stress of this wedding? Perhaps it was both. Perhaps it was aware, like his overactive mind, that he owed Mark an answer soon on the idea of their own wedding. The clock was ticking.

'Just stay here for now,' Mark said. 'It might be good for them to get everything out.'

'Okay.'

'Nobody's stormed out,' he said. 'It's not over yet.'

David sat back down. They were sitting in a small alcove near the pub's fire, which seemed to have been lit in order to counter the unusually tempestuous June weather. David wished this was a regular quiet weekday, and that he had a glass of red wine in front of him, and Mark ready to tell him a funny story about his day. Instead, he felt out of sorts. Winter in summer, rain on your wedding day. At least he was here with a partner, not alone. Partner. What a ridiculous word, he thought, for what Mark was to him.

David couldn't imagine today was a particularly strong advertisement for the idea of marriage. He could understand Mark wanted to get married and to do so while his parents were alive to see it and young enough to enjoy it. For Mark, it wasn't just about the romance but he had also spoken before about the practicalities, of being a legal next of kin and money and all the things he said you don't want to think about, but that you should. The romantic side was so obvious a reason to do it as to become part of the wallpaper for Mark. No part of him thought anybody would think anything other than that it was brilliant. Mark's parents had been the biggest advocates for his sister's wedding five years ago, each going to the stag and hen respectively, and were front row on the day, cheering and throwing confetti, and even being the last left on the dance floor. He had only known support. If weddings were family events, Mark was ready.

Of course he understood where David was coming from, but of course he could never *fully* inhabit the same feelings. He could sympathize, but it was hard to empathize with the freeze David had every time some man came in the shop and seemed to judge any of the pride flags, or whenever they were on holiday and without even intending to, he found himself toughening up his exterior or taking a step away from Mark. None of those were things Mark did, not in the same way. He never really altered himself.

David didn't want that for Meg. He did not want it for himself, either, but perhaps it was too late for him. If he could save Meg, that would be enough.

'You seem deep in thought,' Mark said.

'It's nothing.'

From downstairs, suddenly, he heard Meg's voice, clear as day. *I never want to see you again.*

Mark gasped. 'Did you hear that?'

Then, there was movement and her parents emerged from the stairwell and walked in single file out to the car park. David heard their car drive off almost immediately. They didn't even notice David or Mark as they walked past, and he saw Ava scowl at Rod as she went, who ignored them and went out the back door of the pub. David couldn't tell whether Meg's parents had ignored him and Mark, or not seen them hidden where they were, somewhat in darkness.

Meg appeared next, eyes red and puffy, following them more slowly towards the exit.

'I think they're gone,' David said.

Meg turned back and saw where they were sitting.

'Oh you made me jump,' Meg said, wiping her face with her jumper sleeve. 'I didn't see you.'

'Their car just left; we heard it. Are you . . . ?'

'I just need some air,' Meg said, still speaking as she got towards the front door.

'Should I—?' David said, but she ignored him.

'Give her a minute,' Mark said.

David looked at Mark, unable to hide the fact there were tears in his eyes.

'Darling, why are you crying?'

'It's just . . . what she shouted . . .' David started wiping at his eyes, sleeves bunched in his fingers to dry himself. The tears kept coming, and he could not wipe them away fast enough.

'That she never wanted to see them again?' Mark said.

'That's what I shouted when I . . . What happened to me is happening to her,' David said. 'And she doesn't deserve it.'

For the first time since Meg had come into his life, David sat down next to Mark, and leaned his head across Mark's chest, and felt all the feelings he had pushed to one side trying to help. Finally, properly, he cried.

'No one deserves this,' Mark said, stroking his head. 'Not you and not her.'

'I know.'

'I know you know it, but I need you to believe that about yourself, David.'

'Yeah.' David wiped his eyes on his jumper sleeves.

'It'll be okay, I promise.'

'Do you think?'

'Yes,' Mark said. They were facing out to the rest of the pub, which, now completely deserted, gave the impression they were entirely alone. They had been sitting together for an amount of time David couldn't figure out. Had it been ten seconds, or forty-five minutes?

'It's normal that this, a big life event, would make you think about your life, and what's happened to you,' Mark said. 'It's really normal to feel upset. It's also really normal to hope you can help someone you care about.'

'I know,' David said. 'I think because I'm rarely an angry person, I just get so frustrated at how unfair the world can be, and so when it happens, all the rage points inwards.'

'Well stop that,' Mark said. 'Because I think you're brilliant, and it's other people who are the issue.'

'But aren't you desperate to make other people change?'

Mark paused for a second. 'I do, very often, wish I could have influenced your parents in some way, like, have given them a good shaking or to have met them with you, or . . . I don't know. Maybe that is anger too. I never met them though, and there's nothing either of us could have done. You tried, and you got nothing. It's always tricky, and delicate.'

At that moment Hannah came upstairs. She too had been crying, and her hair was frizzy. Evidently, she too was rattled by what had gone on downstairs.

'I'm just going to get Meg; she wanted some air,' she said. 'Thanks guys for staying.'

'Of course,' David said.

'No bother,' Mark added as Hannah left. 'Here if you need us.'

'Maybe in a minute we can get some food?'

'All right,' Mark said sadly.

'I'll be right back.'

'Do you think I've set her a good example?' David asked Mark as Hannah walked out the door. 'I really wanted to be a perfect father figure for Meg, but there's so many times I've been ashamed. When Rod was weird with me here, and I lashed out unnecessarily, when I was shopping for a wedding outfit and I just wanted to blend in. That's no lesson to teach, is it? Imagine if the youth club are picking up all my insecurities and thinking that's normal?'

'No parent is perfect,' Mark said. 'And the youth club needs you.'

'Your parents are perfect.'

'They're not!' Mark said, before laughing. 'They're *really* not. I don't want to sound ungrateful because they've been much better than yours were, of course, but maybe it's helpful to take out this idea that it's all black and white. They're not perfect, or they weren't always who they are now.'

'Tell me.'

'Oh, I don't know,' Mark said. 'It was the Eighties. I was going to school on a non-uniform day, my dad wouldn't let me wear a certain top, said it made me look gay.'

'Oh, I'm sorry.'

'But now he's great! He would never say that now!' Mark said. 'I'd forgotten that; don't think I've ever told anybody actually. Everyone can change though – that's my point, you know. If you feel like you still have some shame, then let's work on it.'

'You really think that stuff isn't just . . . me now? We're old, Mark.'

'I don't believe that,' Mark said. 'It's my job as a counsellor to believe otherwise, and in my heart, I don't think it's true either. Any flaws you see in yourself, I promise you. They're not noticeable to me at all.'

'Okay.'

'And David, if you stop helping at the youth club I will be so angry because we are both responsible for Fred becoming an astronaut. I need to be able to count on you.'

David smiled. 'Can I tell you something I've never told anyone?'

'Always,' Mark said, taking his hand. It was warm from his right side being closest to the fire.

'The reason what she said was so upsetting is when I came out to my parents, it happened how I said before, and I shouted I never wanted to see them again, and I stormed out. That is all true. I was so angry, but I felt it so deeply that I didn't want to ever see them again that I left, and stayed at a friend's house. I made some excuses to their parents, then went back a couple of times to collect my things when they were out, and I made plans and I left. They didn't kick me out, they didn't take my key, they wanted me back desperately, actually. It was me who sorted it all. Found somewhere to live and paid the deposit. Kept taking on shifts, kept saving. I didn't eat to make sure I could keep paying the rent. I know, unbelievable for me . . .

'They tried to get in touch with me, every now and again. It was only later, when it had been months and then years, that they kind of stopped . . . There were Christmas cards, defensive letters, things like that. It was me who put the barriers up. I knew if I went back I'd change, for them. I chose it, the whole thing. It wasn't something outside my control. I was nearly an adult and I chose every day to not let them in, not even later when I was so happy.'

'David . . .'

'I don't want Meg to make that mistake,' he said. 'I can't tell her that but she needs to know it. They were still my parents, I never actually didn't want them in some way, I just thought there was a way it would change one day . . . I thought there was time.'

David wiped at his tears again, the right sleeve of his jumper now a sopping wet mess of wool.

'Thank you for telling me,' Mark said. 'You know you can tell me anything, anytime. Day or night.' He hugged David again.

'I feel better now I've told you.'

'I'll bet!' Mark said. 'Had you told anyone that before?'

'Never.'

'Oh, Dave.'

They sat in silence for another minute, next to each other looking out at the pub, Mark's thumb stroking the top of David's hand.

'I can support you,' Mark said, turning back to him. 'Dealing with these emotions, and I, you know, I really get why perhaps you wouldn't want to get married. I think I understand it the more we go through this process with Meg.'

'But don't you want to get married?'

'I do, but only to you, and if you didn't want to, that would be fine, honest . . . I'm here to support you, David, and we're . . . our relationship doesn't need a wedding. I want one, but I don't need one. I'm here to look after you, till you're . . . well not old and grey, exactly, but greyer than now.'

‘Shut up.’

‘But us dealing with all of our baggage and fears, together, you opening up to me just now,’ Mark said. ‘That’s more important to me, that that happens every day, than one individual wedding day could ever be.’

‘I am still thinking about it though,’ David said.

‘Whatever you want,’ Mark said, and looking at him, David was desperate to give him what he wanted. This was the best man he’d ever known. He knew, could see it in his eyes, that Mark had somewhat given up hope on the idea, and maybe that was for the best. Maybe they were cursed, maybe . . .

‘Help! Somebody help! Please!’

The cry came from the pub doorway as Hannah burst back in, hair dripping from the rain, and her voice shaking with the cold.

Gus stood immediately from where he’d been sitting and rushed towards her. From where they were sitting, David could see the scene play out in awful slow motion. He instantly knew.

‘She’s gone!’ Hannah shouted. ‘Meg’s gone, she’s gone. I lost her!’

28

MEG

Meg was standing outside the pub, looking up at the clouds, the roof tiles, and the awkward guttering bolted to the outside of the building. What was happening? What had just happened?

She had prepared, she had thought, for all eventualities. In quiet time in the days leading up to today, her brain had been rushing through everything that might go wrong. If they came; if they didn't. Instead, this new thing had happened that she'd had no time to sort out in her head: her parents crashing down the doors of her own wedding, insisting and pulling rank that she do what they wanted, that if she wanted to marry Hannah, even that had to be under their terms.

She hated that she had shouted at them.

She hated that they'd come.

More than that, she hated that David, with all he'd been through with his parents, had maybe heard. She couldn't look at him properly when she'd walked out.

It was embarrassing for Hannah, the person who was supposed to love her the most, to see her like this. She worried constantly about when Hannah would finally say this was enough, that this was not what she wanted for the one wedding day she would get in her life.

It was far more embarrassing that Mark, despite his protestations that this was all okay, and her parents' fault not hers, was someone she had not spent that much time with at all and was seeing her act like a spoiled child.

She looked up. The sky was a pinky-grey, as if the sun was trying to break through but couldn't manage, and Meg felt cold around her neck and shoulders. She wished she was wearing Hannah's big pink fluffy jumper, something to comfort her. She felt restless and she felt adrift. She couldn't leave everybody and go home, even though she wanted to be there more than anything in the world. She wanted Hannah and a blanket and the breakfast they loved. A cup of tea, made by somebody else. A biscuit and a hug.

She wanted, more than anything, to be somebody who could have a hard day and run back to their parents' house and be made dinner and curl up in fresh sheets. She wanted a mother who would stroke her face and tell her everything was going to be okay. She wondered if she had ever had those parents.

If she went back in, they would be waiting for her to decide what to do, and if she went home, Hannah and maybe the others would find her there too. She would have to face the next three days. She would have to live them, in some form.

Breathe in for three, hold for four, breathe out for five.

She tried it but it didn't work.

The idea of returning to normal, and being forced to return to real life, felt too much. She let the panic take her over. Maybe this is what she deserved. Screw the breathing exercises, screw calm. Maybe her parents were in the right, and maybe this had all been so stupid to expect that she'd be allowed the wedding that everybody else had had. A car rushed past suddenly out of nowhere, and she pictured it driving into a puddle, the water splashing all over her. Surely, it was one of those days.

As those thoughts swirled in her head, a memory came to her mind.

Twenty years ago, two decades, yet clear in her head as if it were happening now. She was at St Helens, happy to be in a concert at school as part of the choir. She remembered weeks of practice after school and more hours at home, to make sure that she, surely one of the weaker voices she had thought, could keep up with everybody else.

She remembered, when the day had come, the noise out in the hall from where they stood behind the curtain, of all the parents come to see their children. Her parents already worked in the school, so of course it was easier for them to come than anybody else. They might even be in the front row.

The whole choir was in position, and Meg had been breathing, trying to get calm before the start of the song, making sure her first note would be free of the panic of her nerves, and come out completely perfect.

When the curtain lifted, they began to sing, and she felt her voice lose control every time she saw a new face that wasn't her mum or dad. She had eventually scanned the whole room and was sure they weren't there; by then, she was also sure the others had noticed she wasn't in time, in key, in line with everybody else. She felt markedly different, like she was under a spotlight.

Afterwards, milling around trying not to cry, a teacher,

somebody new who must have worked one or two days a week, asked her where her parents were, said that she could go to them, and having to explain that they hadn't come made the teacher speechless. Looking back, he should have said something comforting, but he didn't. Eventually, Gus's parents had waved her over.

She remembered the shame and she remembered the knowledge she was lying to them too, that they thought she was a nice friend of their son's, that they would think differently if they knew all the thoughts that were in her head day and night.

Now, Meg began to run. She didn't know where she wanted to be, but it wasn't here, and it wasn't with anyone, and it wasn't here in the street where anybody could see her, or three days before a wedding that was fixed in time and that couldn't just be ignored. The air braced her lungs, and there was drizzle on her face, all round her mouth as she tried to breathe. She kept going, her legs stamping on the pavement, her arms swinging, and though she felt dried out, the tears came again and again and again.

29

DAVID

Grateful for something to do, David had decided to make himself in charge of the control centre. They rushed back to Savage Lilies and made sure Rod would ring them if she showed up at the pub. Hannah had run to see if she'd gone home and, finding nothing, was back at the shop. They had all tried calling her, but she still wasn't answering. David wondered if her phone was off, and he thought it best if someone stayed in case she showed up and he immediately began to allocate jobs to the others.

'Right, Hannah, you don't really know the area, so why don't you team up with Mark and go on foot,' he said. 'Mark, you know Woburn, and can go down alleyways and things. Here, take this umbrella; the rain's picking up.'

'We'll call you if we find her,' Mark said. 'Love you.'

'I love you too,' he said. 'Gus, stay here a minute, maybe we should take my van . . .'

'Whatever you think, David,' Gus said.

David looked around at the shop, assessing. 'But I do think someone should be here.'

'Yeah, probably.'

'I know,' he continued. 'I'll use the business network to ask people to keep a lookout, then we've got eyes all down this street and beyond.'

'Good idea,' Gus said, as Mark and Hannah ran out into the rain.

'Hey, bye, hey, bye.'

There was a new voice coming from the door he couldn't even recognize, until he saw it was Ramon from the taco truck.

'I just parked in the agreed spot for the pub,' he said. 'Rod told me to come here. Is everything okay?'

'Meg's missing,' Gus said.

'Oh no,' Ramon said. 'Can I help?'

'Why don't you go together?' David said. 'We've got others on foot. Why don't you two go in the van, drive around, tell me if you see her. That sound okay?'

The pair looked nervous but David didn't have time for nerves. If this was going to be their first date, then so be it.

'Now?' Ramon asked. 'Okay.'

At the door, Ramon paused to let Gus out first.

'A gentleman,' Gus said.

'No, it's just so you're in the rain for longer.'

With that, they were gone and David was alone. He wanted to cry. He felt responsible and he could taste acid in his throat, the stress of worry. He stood at the door, and took his phone out of his pocket. He sent a message to the Work with Pride group, which now had a WhatsApp group for more immediate issues. He wrote: *Hey, hope everyone's okay. My friend Meg – she's short, dark hair, wearing a vest and cardigan and jeans – has gone missing. Will you all keep an eye out? Thanks.*

He received a text from Mark, saying: *No luck at the church, the tennis courts, or Gerrit Lane. Keep you posted.*

David looked out. The sun had nearly set. Where could she be? It would be harder to find her in the dark. The bright shop lights, strip lighting and spotlights, illuminated him like a ghost against the blackness of outside. He appeared bathed in light. His face looked lined and sad. There was real worry in his eyes and he hoped he hadn't made anybody more stressed than they already were. Was his plan going to work? Should he call the police? He knew they normally needed somebody to be missing for longer. What was it, a day? Twelve hours? It had maybe been fifty minutes. What was it on that police drama – people were nearly always somewhere they wanted to be found, somewhere that meant something to them?

He quickly formulated a message and sent it to everyone out searching, asking if they could think of anywhere with an emotional connection Meg might have chosen. After a couple of minutes, Gus called his phone.

'Gus?'

'ASDA.'

'What?' David said. He wasn't sure if he'd heard correctly. 'Gus, I—'

'The ASDA,' he said. 'There's a trolley park with a roof, to the side. No one ever uses it for trolleys; it's in a weird place. Anyway, we used to drive there when I got my car in Sixth Form. God, I should have thought of this earlier. I used to smoke there, or we used to go there if she was upset. From here it should be, like, fifteen minutes?'

'I'll send Hannah,' David said. 'I'll head there too. Thanks, Gus.'

30

MEG

'Meg?'

Suddenly, she wasn't alone anymore. Hannah was there, and Mark lurked behind her in the car park. They had found her. Of course that had been what she wanted. She had begun to feel cold, wet and even more sad, but then she felt silly, embarrassed even, and fearful of how it would be to tell everyone what she'd done.

She started wiping her eyes. The crying that had started outside the pub had stopped when she arrived here but now was beginning again. Hannah rushed towards her and hugged her tightly, and Mark moved closer under the cover as the rain continued to patter against the metal, pooling in dark reflective puddles dotted around them. Meg imagined for a brief moment the pools of water across the car park being made of her tears.

The trolley hut had been constructed with huge grey and green panels and steel connective arms, like scaffolding. Meg remembered some point during her time in Sixth Form when they had just stopped putting trollies there. As she'd been running, she had worried it perhaps might finally have been taken down. No, here it had stood waiting for her, after she'd run for what felt like forever. Her thighs still burned. It was the place she used to come and cry when her parents upset her, or another girl was mean to her, the place she used to come with Gus, everyone thinking they were kissing when really they would sit, sharing headphones, listening to Lady Gaga.

'It's okay,' Hannah said. 'We're here.' She nuzzled into Meg's side, as if she was afraid to let go. 'I was so worried. Please never . . .'

'Sorry,' Meg managed to say through the tears.

They stood for some moments longer, until Mark spoke.

'I've just texted David, told him you're here.'

'Okay. Thanks, Mark.' Meg wiped her eyes and Hannah led her to a railing just above the ground where they were both sitting.

'Why did you run, Meg?' she asked.

'It's all too much,' Meg replied. 'This was about us, and now I'm ruining everything.'

'Everything?'

'Yes, everything! You're being patient with me but it's rubbish! We should be enjoying ourselves and instead we have all of this. I don't know if we should even . . . I don't know, I don't feel like we have enough time to make a decision, I feel like life's just here, suddenly, happening.'

'None of this is your fault—'

'It is though, isn't it!' Meg said. 'They're no one else's parents, and I'm the one who keeps inviting them to things.'

'Which is normal!' Hannah said. 'You are not your parents, Meg, you are your own person. I love that you're optimistic. I love that about you, that you're not writing them off and you believe people can change.'

'Everything is too much. It's too much . . . What if they don't change? How stupid I've been . . .'

She felt slightly better, seeing Hannah, but she could feel her insides heaving against her ribs.

'I wish you'd told me you were feeling like this,' Hannah said. 'I thought you were happy and going to see if they came or not, and go from there? We discussed that together.'

'It's just never going to be normal though, is it? Never on my terms . . .'

'I never thought they'd show up and do that either; no one did. You can't control everything.' Hannah sighed. 'I think what we need is to make a plan.'

'I think we probably need them to just say whether they're coming or not . . . none of the in between. They come on our terms or they don't come at all,' Meg said.

'Okay.'

'But let me think about it . . . They're my parents.'

'I know, Meg, I know,' she said, rubbing Meg's back. 'You know if you want to postpone the wedding, that's fine too. Whatever you want, I'll do it. We can cancel everyone's invites and do it just us. I only care about us being together.'

'I can't make you do that.'

'You're not making me do anything.'

'We'll lose money though, Han.'

'I don't care about money!' Hannah said, laughing. 'Meg, let me be your partner! That wouldn't be ideal, of course, but it's better than this.'

'I just thought they'd pull through,' Meg said. 'I thought they'd do the right thing, because . . . they usually do. In the end, they're usually okay.'

'Well they've not necessarily done the right thing in the

past; they've done the minimum. They've not exactly been supportive, ever.'

'Do you really think that, Han?'

'Yes, I do,' Hannah replied. 'It's been ten years; it's never exactly been easy.'

Hannah looked at her, like she was considering telling her more, or feeling like she'd already said too much. Meg was grateful she didn't elaborate, not right now.

'Maybe I was completely blind and only saw what I wanted to see,' Meg said. 'I just thought we were just a family that didn't say sorry, or talk about things like that. I thought that on the inside, they had grown.'

'Maybe.'

'Should I just tell them not to come? They've given me enough reason. It's just . . .'

'I'll do whatever you want, and I'll support you,' Hannah said. 'Don't you ever think that's something I don't want to do. Nobody would blame you for cutting them out of the day, but I certainly don't blame you for wanting them there, at all. Nobody else does, either.'

'Okay.'

There was a rumble of a car and headlights passing through the gaps in the panels of the hut, and after the noise of footsteps coming towards them, David arrived. He stood just under the roof, shoulders wet from the rain, face wet with tears from his eyes, then, running past Mark, he came forward to hug her.

'Oh, Meg,' he said. 'You had us so worried! Never do that again! Promise me now, *please*.'

Meg couldn't help but laugh, that finally there was a real adult here, who could tell her what to do, and who could get them all in order. After they had hugged and he had let go, all of them looked at David, hoping for something. They were all dripping wet, and shivering slightly. What did they want from him? Maybe it was answers and an explanation, maybe instructions, maybe even a telling-off would do. He was their best hope.

While they all waited to see, David moved forward to hug her again, and Meg felt like he needed the hug as much as she did.

31

DAVID

David extricated himself from the hug. He didn't want to. He wanted to hold Meg until it was all okay and tell her this was the end of her struggles, but he was just happy for now they had found her and the rest could wait. Gus and Ramon were suddenly there too, and they moved forward to hug Meg after him.

'You're okay,' Gus said to her. 'We've got you.'

'I don't know if I can do this,' Meg said, leaning against a railing at the side of the hut, looking at them all. 'Sorry for running away. I don't know what I was thinking but . . .'

David couldn't figure out if Meg didn't feel anything or if she had so many feelings, she was having trouble articulating them all at once.

'I don't know what to do. I don't know if I need my parents there, or I need them not there,' Meg said. 'That sounds so selfish – you've all literally run through the rain – it's just . . . you only get to do it once. I don't know.'

David, too, didn't know what to say, but looking around the group slowly, it seemed everybody had turned their heads towards him, as if he knew how to solve the problem.

'Family, Meg, it . . . it can mean loads of things,' he said, taking a step towards her. He didn't know where this was going, but he knew this was a crisis, and he knew he wanted to help. 'I don't have parents, at one point through choice, and now I couldn't if I wanted to . . . but that doesn't mean I don't deserve love, or anything else I want to do. Mark is my family.'

'I know,' Meg said.

'So your parents are one part of the puzzle,' he continued. 'As a gay person, chosen family is everything. You've not relied on your parents in the same way . . . You want them involved, but look at the number of people here who are willing to help you. You've more than outnumbered the two of them. Think of everyone else getting everything ready over the next few days: travelling, getting their outfits, staying nearby. Think of how Hannah has supported you through all of this. You've got half the town excited about the wedding, people you don't even know who ask me every week about you. That doesn't compare to your two parents, but it makes a dent, you know. Not everybody could do that, and it's because you're brilliant, Meg. You're warm and funny and as much as you're lucky to have Hannah, she's lucky to have you too.'

'He's right,' Hannah said, holding her hand. 'He always is.'

'Your wedding will be incredible,' he said. 'We're all looking forward to it. It's basically the highlight of my summer. You can't control other people, and if your parents are going to be like that, perhaps they've shown you enough times who they are, and you can't do anything else. Not now. But you can't put your life on hold for them either. You're standing up for yourself and Hannah, and maybe that's your most important family, now. It's hard to accept that, but I did it.

'I never thought my parents would get on board . . . When they died, I hadn't spoken to them since being a kid, and I will always wonder what might have happened differently, if we'd had more time, if we'd talked more.' David scratched his head. 'It's worth talking to them, maybe, in a less stressful scenario, but then make your peace. When I first met you, I said there's so much more to life than what your parents want for you. Live for you, not them.'

Mark smiled at him.

'Life is so hard,' David continued. 'You need to do whatever's best for you to get you through all the days you have ahead of you, not behind you.'

'Thanks, David.'

'You're welcome,' he said. 'I should add as a stand-in parent that if you run away ever again, you'll be grounded.'

He pointed to Mark. 'Your other dad is incredibly disappointed too.'

Meg laughed, wiping tears from her eyes.

'Shall we all go home?' Mark said. 'I could do with a cup of tea and some biscuits.'

'Yes please,' Meg said, shivering. 'I'm so cold.'

Ramon passed her a blanket from his van.

'We can regroup tomorrow, see what you want us to do.'

'Thanks, David,' Meg said.

'Thanks, David,' Hannah said.

Out of some sense of duty, Mark, Gus and Ramon thanked David too.

'Ramon, can you drive Gus home?' David said. 'I've got space for us four, but no more.'

'Yeah, sure.'

Those two ran out into the now sideways rain, and David unlocked the van, telling Meg and Hannah to go in and get the heating on.

'Good chat there,' Mark said.

'I made that up on the spot,' David said.

'You keep putting Ramon and Gus together too . . . You've like the Cupid of Milton Keynes.'

David watched from the rear-view mirror, where he could just about see Ramon and Gus smiling and laughing, Ramon helping Gus with his seatbelt, then playing with the blanket Meg had given back to them.

'It's not all about Meg, you know,' David said, winking at Mark. 'You don't have to be married to be in love.'

In the car, everybody was too uncomfortably wet and tired to speak. Meg, noticeably, seemed deep in thought, until suddenly she grabbed the radio and turned it down, till the traffic announcer's voice faded to nothing.

'I've made a decision,' she said. 'Tomorrow, I just need a day to relax. No anything from anyone. I'm going to have a lie-in, turn my phone off, all of that. Digital detox, or whatever they call it. Saturday, Hannah, let's go to my parents, and I'll tell them properly and calmly how upsetting this all is. I'll ask them to come on my terms, but if they don't, they don't. We've planned such a special day and I deserve to have it, and so do you.' She began to tear up, and she and Hannah reached for each other's hands. 'So it'll go ahead.'

Mark cheered, and it echoed around the van, and he looked like he regretted it, reading the room wrong, but soon they were all cheering, and the mood was back to what it had been on the hen night. David turned the radio back on and turned up the music.

'Going to the chapel!' Mark began to sing to the rhythm of the song.

'Thanks for your speech back there,' Meg said to David. 'That was amazing.'

'If you want me to do one on the day, I will,' he said. 'And even if you don't, after a gin or two, maybe I'll try.'

'You've done more than enough,' Meg said. 'Above and beyond. I don't know how I'll ever thank you.'

David thought about wanting advice on him and Mark's situation, and the struggle with the flower shop, and how he would never get to go and tell his parents how he felt, but none of that was Meg's issue to solve, and certainly not today.

'Just have the best day in the world,' he said, turning onto the high street. 'For me.'

32

MEG

One Day Until the Wedding

Meg noticed, as she looked up at the plastic clock in their favourite brunch spot, the second hand ticking past the vertical alignment of the hands showing midday, that this time tomorrow she'd be walking down the aisle. Aside from everything else, she hoped the weather would pick up. It was a wet, windy and stormy Saturday morning, and the rain was lashing down against the windows, no mistaking whether you needed an umbrella or not. The café was sparse and empty, owing to most people likely staying at home. Anyone who was already there was reluctant to leave. It meant the piles of pastries in the window stayed high, and there was a pile of sodden shoes and umbrellas by the door.

'Do you think the rain is a bad omen?' Hannah said. 'Like, God, or the universe or whatever, is against us?'

'Well neither of us is religious,' Meg said. 'I feel like we've got enough on our plate without the universe having it in for us too.'

Yesterday had been much of the same in terms of

weather; grey everywhere, and fog and rain meaning you could barely see more than a few metres ahead of you, and yet Meg felt blissful. It was like home was her own personal little bubble and her day of relaxation had been perfect.

She had lain in, been treated to a coffee in bed from Hannah, then walked to the Lido she'd been meaning to try for weeks. A cold swim in the rain could fix you like nothing else, she had always found. After a quick lunch at home, she had taken the bus to the cinema, and though the film hadn't been great, the weekday quiet meant she had one of the greatest sleeps she could remember in a long time. That evening, a takeaway on the way, and Hannah returning home from work to greet her, she felt, as much as she could, back to normal. She had even booked the course of driving lessons she'd been talking about for so long. She felt hopeful, again.

'Excuse me,' she said to the waiter. 'Can we have another look at the menu?'

'Of course, let me grab one for you.'

'I haven't seen you in here before,' Meg added. 'Are you new?'

'Moved to the area recently,' the woman said. 'I'm at the Open University from September but wanted to get my bearings before that, so I'm here most days, then I'll probably go part-time.'

'You'll love it round here,' she said. 'Let us know if you need anything; we're in a fair bit. I sometimes come and do my work in here.'

'I will, thank you,' she said, smiling down at them. 'That's very kind. I'll just grab those menus for you.'

Meg looked around the restaurant and she realized Hannah was sitting staring at her, smiling.

'What?'

'You're like the local tourist board,' Hannah said. 'I feel like I'm with . . . I don't know, the town mayor or something. I feel like you've really made this home.'

'Well,' Meg said, feeling slightly shy. She hadn't even realized what she was doing. 'Everyone's been so nice to me, it feels, I don't know . . . It feels effortless to give that back.'

Meg was, considering all that was going on, feeling surprisingly optimistic now. Whereas a few months ago she might have feared having little to look forward to after the wedding, now she had so much. New community initiatives to get involved in, new work possibilities and new friends. She was considering formally getting involved in the youth club and the great thing about making her own hours was that she'd be able to commit to that. Also, she had seen that the fairly new local Pride needed volunteers, for on the day but also on the board throughout the year, and she knew that might be a great way to give back. She knew she'd be good at it. It was still on her mind to set up a regular drawing and illustration club in the shop, but she didn't want to get ahead of herself.

'How are you feeling about this afternoon?' Hannah asked.

'I feel okay,' Meg said. 'Having just that day to collect my thoughts was really worth it. I know what I'm going to say. I've actually written it down.' She patted her bag, in which she had her notebook. 'So I can say what I want without them changing it, or without having to follow what they want to talk about.' She took a huge breath in. 'Thank you for coming with me.'

'Stop it!' Hannah said. 'Obviously I'd come with you.'

The waitress dropped the menus back in front of them.

'Do you think we'll get a pudding?' Hannah said.

'It's not that I want to delay going round there but . . . yes, let's.'

'And the rain.'

'We don't want to trip and fall . . .'

'Could we split a French toast?'

'Do you think most brides have a two-course breakfast the day before their wedding?' Meg asked.

'Well luckily for you, it's a non-traditional wedding,' Hannah said. 'So we almost have to . . .'

'I'd get French toast or that banana bread.'

'We can't get both.'

'We can't have both.'

'Can we?'

'Could we?'

'I'll order.'

Meg had not been to her parents' house since Christmas when she and Hannah had told them they were engaged. It looked exactly the same. Stone-cobbled white front, and roof tiles that she was sure could do with a clean. Her parents were intensely house proud, and yet with her dad's mild arthritis, it was clear that the outside jobs – roof, garden, patio – had fallen by the wayside. The garden was ever so slightly overgrown, the hedge veering perilously into the pavement, in a way she hadn't realized in the winter.

She and Hannah stood for a moment too long at the door, long enough that she was sure her mum would know they were there and open the door anyway, but their hands brushed against each other for a second, and then Meg grasped Hannah's hand in hers. They had a second alone.

'Ready?' Meg asked Hannah.

'Yes.'

Meg knocked three times and the door opened quickly.

'Hello, darling. You came,' her mother said, smiling but on edge. Everything about this kind of meeting belied what her mum thought families should be: obedient, agreeable, showing that everything was fine.

Ava opened the door wide to let them both in and showed them to the living room. It was all as it usually was, but there was something sad in the house now they were a family in the situation they were in. The striped wallpaper seemed to make the room feel cramped, and her mum's insistence on not having harsh lighting seemed to make the place seem dim and deserted. A window was open and a cold breeze was flowing through the house. On the coffee table, she had laid out a variety of biscuits and she asked if they wanted a cup of tea.

'I'm all right actually,' Meg said. And she was. She knew what she was here to do. 'Han?'

'I'm okay too.'

'Okay, well your father and I did want a cup of tea, so we're going to make—'

'Mum,' Meg said. 'We actually won't be here very long.'

'I said we were having a tea. That's what we planned.'

'No,' Meg said, firmly, louder than before. 'Let me say what I want to say.'

There was a moment she felt her mum was going to continue to argue, but then she came through from the kitchen and sat on the sofa next to George. The sofas were perpendicular to each other and Meg felt grateful she didn't have to stare across at both of them in such a confrontational way. She started speaking, staring at a spot just above the fireplace. She was holding her notebook open in her hands and she knew she was shaking.

'I feel like you've said enough about how you feel,' Meg said. 'Some of that, I would want to change. Some of that, I don't know if I can, but I need you to listen to me.' She took a deep breath. 'It is the day before the most important day of my life, and I need you to hear me and hear how I feel and how what you've said and done affects me and Hannah. I'm not coming to you angry, or sad, or expecting anything. I just want to give you all the information you might need for you to make your decision about tomorrow, which is our wedding as we have planned it.

'First, I want to tell you how I feel about Hannah. I love her. Deeply. I think she's brilliant. She's kinder and smarter and funnier than I ever really thought I deserved. We talk about everything, and she treats me with the care and respect I always thought you would want a partner to treat me with. She loves me, and I love her in the ways I always saw you two loving each other growing up. I always thought we'd got past my teen years and you'd seen the light, or whatever, and that you were happy for me. I thought you saw, with Hannah, how lucky I was. I gave you all the allowances of the time you grew up in, and where you'd lived, and who you'd known, and I said, even recently, it just takes people time. Now, you've had enough time.'

'Meg,' her mum said.

'No, Ava,' Hannah said. She didn't look at her mum as she said it, but her meaning was clear. *This is Meg's turn to speak.*

'Growing up was really, really hard for me.' Meg wiped at a tear. 'This place was all people like you and I felt every day like I was an alien who'd been dropped on a planet that I wasn't built to live on. I'd go into school and try to carry on but you were there too, and I knew, before I knew anything about being gay, I knew that to even think it would disappoint you. Do you understand what a pressure that is to put on someone? Don't answer.

'You were teachers, and I know you weren't allowed to say certain things at school, but at home? You could have. Nothing was stopping you, except yourselves. I was never a girly girl, you could have suspected . . . but it's not even about that. It's how you treated others. It's not like you ever said something homophobic about me; it was the things you said about gay people on the television, or if you saw people holding hands in the street, or whatever. That had an effect on me that pushed me back further into myself, struggling to deal with those two parts of me. I had no control. I had no way to leave and I had no way to tell you the truth. I genuinely thought that if you knew, you'd kick me out onto the streets. The one saving grace was Angus, Gus he goes by now, and our friendship, and you turned even that into something so pressurized that as soon as I went to university, I barely spoke to him. And he'd needed me to stick by him, and I didn't, and I'm only just making up for that. You see, silence just breeds silence.

'I don't, for a second, think you knew what you were doing or wanted that result. But now, everything you've done this year? It's been the same. You've seen the effect on me and you've still done the same thing.

'Actually it's been worse, because you don't have the excuse of the time you lived in or what other people are saying or that I was a child. I'm a grown adult, making decisions and living my own life and you're constantly making me feel like I'm not good enough. And I am! I know I am.' Meg willed the tears to stay in her eyes for just moments longer. 'I want to get married because I deserve love and I deserve the day that everyone else gets. That's why people fought for this, for years. Everybody I've met in this community through David, they've all shown me I'm more than enough. I find it hard to believe, sometimes, but they think I'm brilliant, actually.

'You have to respect my life now, please,' Meg continued, closing the notebook. 'I want you there but I want you there celebrating me, not the idea of me as a child. Me, as I am now. I can't be anyone else; trust me I've tried.'

Hannah shifted in her chair.

'Now, it's the day before my wedding and I don't want to hear anything negative, so unless you're going to sit and say you're coming and everything's fine, then I don't want to hear it. You can come to the wedding we're having, or I'd rather you stayed at home.'

They sat in silence. George was watching Ava, waiting for her response. It felt like a lifetime, before her mum slowly opened her mouth, Meg's dad watching.

'There's nothing much for us to say to that,' Ava said.

'Okay,' Meg said. She hung on for a moment longer, expecting perhaps *because we're so moved, of course we're coming,* or *nothing much else to say because we're so ashamed of what we did.*

When neither came, she nodded at Hannah.

She wanted to say bye, but she knew her whole body was shaking.

They left the room and the house in silence. It was still raining and Meg braced as they walked out into it. When they'd walked far enough away, far around the corner onto the next street where there was no way her parents could see them, Meg collapsed into Hannah, and cried and cried. She had to stop a howling noise coming from her mouth, though she hoped any noise was hidden by the rain. This was worse than she had imagined. She had felt okay speaking, but it had felt so painful, cruel even, for them to sit there in silence. They stayed like that for a few minutes. Meg noticed somebody on the street look at them and she buried herself closer into Hannah's neck and hair, which were soaking wet.

'I'm sorry,' Hannah said. 'Are you okay?'

'I will be,' she said. 'I will be.'

'All right.'

It would be okay. They would potter around for the afternoon doing last-minute jobs, and then they would have dinner together and get an early night. Their last night, as girlfriends or partners, before the rest of their lives began, and there was only one word to choose from: wife. Closure, at last.

'And I've decided something,' Meg said, wiping wet hair from her face. 'I want David to walk me down the aisle.'

33

DAVID

Saturday came and it brought with it customers in abundance. Where had they all come from? He could have done with a quiet weekend. He'd had a delivery that morning, including the wedding flowers, and had gone over to the pub to take Meg's mum's dress back to their house. Meg had said she didn't want it anywhere near the event, but didn't want to give it back.

He was astounded as even more people came in. Whether this was a new uptake for a reason David couldn't identify, or some kind of karmic reward for the last few days, he didn't know. He knew the soles of his feet hurt, and he knew he hadn't had a chance to wash his hands since nine-thirty that morning. The wrinkled lines on the backs of his hands – when did that happen? – were crevices filled with dirt, and under his fingernails needed a good brush.

'Do you think it will brighten up?' Benji asked. 'For the wedding tomorrow?'

'I hope so,' David said. 'Or I'd be worried about that marquee lasting the whole day.'

'You always worry,' Benji said.

'No I don't.'

He had arrived bright and early, asking David if he could interview him and take photos of him in the photo booth for that week's social posts. David had skirted around the issue, and sensing resistance, Benji had instead used the time to take control of creating David's online shop in order to allow subscriptions to be ordered. 'It's not the twelfth century,' he had said, when David asked if it was necessary. 'I'll get it set up now. Give me your card.'

The weather outside was miserable. A continuous downpour David had heard throughout the night and hadn't relented since. The noise of the rain, happening out there, was somewhat comforting. David always thought that when it rained it felt like they were in a rainforest, and today was no different. It was like the air was heavier, and everything far away was slightly blurred, like Meg had illustrated some intricate beautiful portrait of rain and stuck it to the windows.

David busied himself with restocking what had been sold that morning. They'd had a run on the celebration bouquets, so he had to put out his sign that read MORE BOUQUETS AVAILABLE – MADE TO ORDER – ESPECIALLY FOR YOU. The wording made him think of Kylie, and he suddenly remembered a new song for the Plant Playlist. How had he never thought to add 'Where the Wild Roses Grow'!

At lunchtime, Ray and David were just about managing together, and Benji was in taking photos and videos of how busy it was, which David supposed must be something that helped online. He was weaving in and out between people and kept referring to something called an algorithm. David was just about to suggest he come to the back room for a tea and a rest, since he still wasn't paying Benji, when he cornered him to ask him to film a video.

'Again?' David said. 'All right. I'm surprised you've got space for all these things on your phone. What do you need me to hold?'

'No, I want you to be *in* a video,' he said.

'Doing what?'

'Like a "meet the owner" kind of thing,' Benji said. 'I've prepared questions and we can always redo them, but it would be fun to get your genuine reactions. I bought this microphone so it's good quality.'

'Let me see the list,' David said. 'I'm quite busy and I'm also completely filthy.'

'It's *authentic*, David,' Benji said, passing him his phone, which had a small list of questions. 'People want their florist to be dirty! Like they want a chef to be fat.'

'Okay, I'm not sure I need to identify as a gay man in this video,' David said, reading Benji's questions.

'But that's *you*. The whole point is to get to know you.'

'Can I think about this, Benji? I'm a little—'

At that moment Hannah came inside. Her hair was wet, and she shook her raincoat uncomfortably over the doormat.

'Hey, you,' David said, walking towards her. 'How are you?'

'Erm,' Hannah said.

Benji was watching her curiously now from the counter, and David followed his lead. Benji always knew when there was something up with a person.

'Are you okay, Hannah?' David asked.

'Yes, it's just . . .' Hannah began. 'Meg's parents again. I don't want her to know I came in but I needed to . . .

We went round earlier. I don't think they're going to come. Meg gave them this big speech, about not wanting regrets, how she grew up, and they just sat there.'

'Oh, poor Meg.'

'They said there was nothing to say and then we just awkwardly left,' she continued. 'I don't think they're coming and I've been the one the whole time saying it doesn't matter, it doesn't matter, it'll all be fine. It *does* matter though. I think Meg wanted to insist on an answer but in the moment . . . I want Meg to be happy and I think the only way she'd be happy is if they came. It will kill me tomorrow if they don't, and we've got no way to know.'

Benji stepped forward. 'Should—'

'Benji, don't worry, you've missed a bit of the story,' David said. 'It will be fine, Hannah, I promise. Just keep supporting her.'

'You think?'

'Yes, definitely,' David said. 'It's really hard with her parents, but she'll get through it. I did.'

Benji walked away to the back room.

'As soon as it's happening, she won't have time to think of her parents,' he said. 'We will make it a wonderful day. I'll do everything I can.'

'All right,' Hannah said. 'I'd better go back. Said I was getting milk but I needed a little offload. Thanks, David. Bet you could do with a lie-down after all this.'

'Me?' David said. 'Not on my sixth coffee I don't, so don't worry about me. It's your day. Take this milk.' He handed her a carton from the fridge. 'Go home to Meg. Relax. Nothing's going to happen now.'

* * *

The rush continued into the afternoon and so Mark came down from upstairs to help. He was good behind the till, David always found. His wide smile always invited customers into the shop but they never found him overbearing. It didn't hurt that he didn't require paying, either. But Mark needn't know about the shop's dire money troubles, not yet. David felt too awkward to tell Mark, and he needed to get to Monday before he properly looked at what they should do, then he could tell Mark what the plan was. He wanted to present him with a plan of action, not an admission of defeat.

He had half-hoped the stir of custom today would be the end to their problems, but he knew from experience a busy day would often be followed by days of tedium. Everyone had just happened to move their day of shopping to the same date, and it often didn't mean anything. Nobody today had bought a subscription, no matter how often he mentioned them.

No, what was he doing? Mark was there for him for everything; that was the whole point of them. They could sit together and Mark could help. Mark's skills and David's knowledge complemented each other, and what reason should he ever have for keeping anything from him? Mark would do anything for him. He wanted Lilies to succeed just as much as he did. Why else would he have given up his Saturday afternoon? He watched Mark behind the counter having a spirited conversation with an older gentleman who always bought lilies for his wife. He was brilliant, Mark, he really was. There was no more thinking to be done.

'I just—'

He couldn't get the words out, and Mark looked over at

him quizzically. Shouting over all the other voices, he said, 'Was that for me?'

'I need to go and pick something up,' he said, hurrying to find his keys. 'Sorry, I completely forgot. You two can manage for the last hour?'

'I guess I can,' Mark said, looking confused. 'Are you okay?'

'Yes,' David said. 'I'm brilliant. How nice that it's busy. We're over the rush; I'm sure of it. You'll be fine. Just something I need to do before the wedding.'

'If you say so.'

'I love you!'

'Go on, if you're going,' Mark said. 'See you tonight. Can't wait for the takeaway.'

'Me neither,' David said. 'Bye, petal.'

'Hello?'

On the other end of the line, Mark's voice sounded tired. He could hear no background noise, other than the low hum of a song – perhaps Guns and Roses – so he presumed the last of the day's customers had petered out.

'Sorry, it took much longer than I anticipated,' David said, before taking a breath. 'Then, you'll never believe it, I got a flat tyre!'

'Oh God,' Mark said. 'Have you done anything?'

'Well I haven't changed it myself if that's what you're imagining. Mark, you've known me for long enough to realize that.'

'No, I know, I mean have you called anybody?'

'No,' David said. 'I mean yes, yes I have, I was on the phone to them for ages actually. Sorry that's why it's taken so long. They can't come till tomorrow. They said to leave it parked up here. Will you come get me? I'll send my location.'

'Do you want me to call the insurance?'

'No, no, nothing like that,' David said. 'We can do that later. Definitely don't call them, just hurry up! It's raining!'

'All right, I'll be there,' Mark said, pausing as the location was sent. 'I'll be there in fifteen. You don't mind if I leave the shop? I've not closed up or anything.'

'No, that's fine,' David said. 'Just lock up and put the sign on the door. See you soon, love.'

When Mark arrived, David waved him over to where he stood. The van was pulled over on the side of the road, parked up next to a small brick wall on a hill. Parked up was a generous term for being stopped diagonally across the road. There certainly wasn't room for an actual car to pass but luckily nobody had come along to try.

From where the van was, where David had been sitting inside in the driver's seat, you could see the sun beginning to dip towards the crest of a hill, broken through the clouds, in that hazy way it sometimes managed despite even the most belligerent sky. The insistent rain, present all day, had finally cleared and the sunlight reflected off sodden grass and drenched concrete roads.

'Hi!'

'Hey, come here.'

The road was near-deserted, and there was a tiny area curved off by stones where David was now standing. Mark crossed the road and came to him.

'What a nightmare,' he said. 'Poor Daisy!'

'Well yes,' David said.

Mark glanced at the wheels before walking round to the other side, and then all the way back round to David.

'Do you know what a flat tyre is?'

'Mark—'

'You don't have one, David.'

'Can I show you inside?'

'Is that flat tyre in the vehicle?'

David pulled back the door of the van and invited Mark in.

'You're not supposed to trust men in vans, you know.'

'Mark, shut up,' David said. 'Get in.'

Mark climbed up inside the van and saw a dinner laid out in front of him. There was a tiny table (made of an upside down Dutch bucket with a tablecloth on) with a picnic on top. There were olives, and cheese, and bread. To the side, in another bucket, was a glass of non-alcoholic wine, in ice. He handed Mark a small bouquet of roses.

'Bought these from the petrol station,' he said. 'So you wouldn't be suspicious.'

'Wow, David. I didn't expect this at all.'

'Surprise date night.'

They sat together in the van and started to eat. David was hungry, after all. They caught up quickly about the day and then got onto talking about how they'd met. For about half an hour, until most of the food was gone, they reminisced and Mark even got a couple of photos up on his phone he'd found recently, showing the first time they'd gone on holiday together, to Greece, and photos of the first Christmas they'd spent together.

Suddenly, David's ringtone blared from his pocket.

'Sorry, I'll . . .' He checked the screen. 'Oh it's Meg, let me just get this.'

He shuffled slightly and opened the back doors of the van, so he was sitting looking out at the countryside. He listened as Meg explained the unfolding situation. The sun was closer, inches it looked like, from the surface of the skyline, green and blue and yellow all stamping their way through the clouds, which marked everything with a dark black edge. Shadowy black rippled in the grass with the movement of the wind, which David could hear, safely tucked away in the safety of the van. The view was beautiful; what he was hearing was not.

He turned back to Mark to tell him the news.

They needed to go, he said, because the wedding venue had flooded with the day's rain and not only was the venue ruined and the marquee broken, but all of the things in the storage room destroyed too. Meg was freaking out, but David had turned instantly into action mode, and wanted to go and help, but in his head he wanted to tell Mark the truth, which was that it was a shame on many levels, because he'd very nearly, finally, plucked up the courage to finally ask Mark to marry him. He held on to the ring in his jacket pocket and thought, *well I've waited nearly twenty years. What's a day or two?*

34

MEG

Meg and Hannah rushed to the pub as soon as they heard the news. It wasn't that they didn't believe Rod, or wanted to see the damage, but that it felt so strange to suddenly be alone in their home with the new information. They both felt like they wanted to do something.

When they arrived, a sign on the door, hastily printed out in Comic Sans and stuck with Sellotape, read: FLOOD DAMAGE – CLOSED FOR FORESEEABLE. David and Mark were standing with Rod on the raised area that seemed to have escaped the worst of the damage, but Rod was filling them all in. It was bad. Everything was waterlogged, even the beer pipes, and it would be a health and safety issue to have customers. Water had got in through the roof, pooled in the pub's beer cellar, and wrecked the storage room downstairs. He didn't know when they'd be able to open. David looked flushed and upset.

'Rod, I'm so sorry,' Meg said.

'It's me who needs to apologize,' Rod said, shaking water from the bottoms of his trousers. 'I can't believe tomorrow's off.'

'I know,' David said. 'It's crap. Have you got insurance?'

'We'll be fine,' he said. 'I thought everything was safe. I was following the alerts, we were prepared, but . . . that marquee is a little old, and I guess this building is old enough that maybe it's finally given up. I won't show you the marquee, but it's . . . I'm really sorry too. The stuff in the basement storage room, it's ruined. Did you take anything out of there?'

'No nothing,' Hannah said. Meg thought about everything that was there – the nonsense from her parents but also the décor, Angie's cake would be in there by now, and even her dress. She'd asked David to take her mum's dress home so she wouldn't have to see it. If only she'd got him to take hers too. Though she wanted to ask about the dress, she knew there were more important things.

'You need any help?' Mark said. 'I feel bad us turning up and adding pressure.'

'It's okay, we've got the staff that were meant to be in helping, and these are my sons here.' He pointed at two boys carrying sopping cardboard and beer bottles upstairs in plastic buckets. 'I don't know when they'll get shifts back so I want to give people work. We've got enough people, but thank you. It's not glamorous, but we should be fine.'

'Well call us if there's anything we can do,' Hannah said.

'I really wanted to host the wedding, you know,' Rod said, turning to Hannah and Meg. 'It was really important to us, that you picked me, even after our little hiccup. I was so happy you . . . you know, I was so behind it all. You're a great couple.'

'It's okay,' Meg said. 'And thank you for saying that; it means a lot.'

'We'll get out of your hair,' David said.

'Maybe you can just do it anyway, in the flat or something.' Rod looked at them blankly. 'Go to the park or do it over the phone or however you do it now.'

Mark laughed. 'What do you mean?'

'Well, me and the missus, we didn't have a big wedding,' he said. 'She didn't have a big family and we didn't have any money so we just went to the registry office and came here for food and a dance. I broke the council's volume limit that day, but it was worth a little fine. All you need for a wedding is your wife and a drink in your hand.'

The entire group stared at him.

'Maybe you're right,' Hannah said. 'Meg?'

David smiled. 'Thanks, Rod. Wise words.'

'I try.'

Meg was silent.

'Do call us,' Mark said, as they began to walk out. 'For anything.'

They got outside the front of the pub, weirdly bright end-of-day sunshine peering through the clouds after all that had happened.

'Are you thinking what I'm thinking?' David said, turning to the group. The streetlights were turning on, which David had always thought was lucky, to see the switchover.

'David, we don't have a venue, or a dress, or a cake or . . .' Mark was shaking his head. 'I didn't want to say in there but . . .'

'Yeah, David,' Hannah said. 'There's just so much to do. I don't know if—'

'We have two brides,' he said. 'We know so many people who want this wedding to happen.'

'I don't know, David,' Meg said. 'I've been looking for signs and maybe this is one . . .'

'What if it's a sign the other way?' Hannah said.

'What?' Meg said.

'That all of the stuff around us doesn't matter, and that it's us getting married that's important.'

'It's entirely your choice,' David said. 'But the taco truck is fine. That's one thing – the food is sorted. I've spoken to Angie; I've spoken to Martha. Everyone's happy to muck in, even if it wasn't what was planned.'

'David . . .' Mark said. 'I knew you were up to something.'

David looked curiously at Mark, in a way Meg had never seen before. 'I just thought it would be such a shame, after all our work. They're on hand, if you want them to be. We can sort it. I don't have all the answers, or barely any of them actually, but I never do and things usually turn out all right.'

They were both staring at him, and Mark too.

'Basically, if you both trust me, and you want to get married tomorrow, in a different way than you thought, then I can sort it. You two try and sleep, try and relax, and in the morning I'll have some form of a wedding for you. If that's what you want – it's entirely your call. It might not be perfect, and you might just want to wait, but we'll have you and we'll have guests and really those are the only things you need, and the celebrant obviously.'

'What do you think, Han?' Meg turned to her.

Hannah smiled sheepishly. 'I think . . . we should do it? I don't want to wait any longer. I want to marry you and I don't care how we do it.' She took Meg by the hands. 'I just want to get married.'

'Thank you,' Meg said quietly. 'I do too.'

'And of course we trust you, David,' Hannah said. 'You're family.'

Meg thought back to her engagement to Hannah, a moment between the two of them sitting by their favourite canal in London. It wasn't flash; it was a bench with rotting wood and bent cans littered all around them. Meg had been certain, at some point, she saw a defiant fox in the bushes, but it was where they rested for a second on a walk and with solitude and quiet, Hannah had pulled out a ring and asked her. It wasn't what a lot of people would want, but Meg wasn't a lot of people. All she'd cared about was Hannah.

'Let's do it then,' Meg said. 'David, tell us if you need any help. We can't just—'

'No need,' David said. 'I've got this. Count it as your wedding present. Go get some sleep. We'll see you brides tomorrow.'

'But I have so many questions . . .' Meg looked stunned, and stood unmoved. 'What if something else goes wrong? What if my parents come but they hate it? Oh my God, what am I going to wear? Do you think we could dry-clean the dress?'

'Meg,' Hannah said, touching her face. 'We'll be becoming wife and wife. I don't need to know anything else.'

'Are you sure we can do this, David?' Mark asked.

'We can do anything,' David said. 'And everything.'

35

DAVID

16 Hours Until the Wedding

From the window of their flat, David could see Rod's pub at the bottom of the hill. By sheer luck, his own shop was okay. It was complete chance. He wondered if there was anything he could do for the pub, but everything had been completely ruined by the water. Would it be appropriate to set up a fundraiser? He thought about posting in Work with Pride.

'Stop thinking about Rod,' Mark said. 'You can't solve that too.'

'It's times like this I wish I was a superhero,' David said, sitting back down at the kitchen table.

'You're not though,' Mark said, irritably. 'Now, where were we?'

The kitchen table had become a planning station. David had found a comically large notebook downstairs, some kind of sketch pad, on which they were writing out all the things they knew of the wedding and everything that needed to be sorted, fixed or arranged. The time was nine-thirty but David was sure they could do it. Nearly everything that had been planned had gone through him so he knew they wouldn't need to trouble the happy couple in the final days, and it worked now to be able to get in touch with everybody with just hours to go.

A tiny and, he knew, overly optimistic side of him thought that perhaps they could do it all by midnight and still get a good night's sleep. This was about making Meg and Hannah's dreams happen, and David knew he would pull an all-nighter if he had to. He, Mark, Gus and Meg's friend Ailie were sat around the table, mismatched mugs in front of them, all equally bedding in for the long haul.

'So, the first bank of things are done,' David said. 'Check! Tick! Well done, everyone. Now, let's move on to the more . . . difficult ones.'

There had been a few things that were easy to sort or would stay largely the same; they had called Caleb the celebrant to make sure he knew he'd be heading somewhere else, but his job remained unchanged. Ramon's truck – Gus had called him, and David had heard him call him 'babe' – would be fine, and he should continue any preparations he had planned for. On the phone, Ramon had mentioned a friend who had a mobile drinks van, who could come wherever they needed, so they had booked that in too. Martha's sound equipment was at her home, so all was fine for music, and Angie had said she could make batches of cupcakes with a simple design on. It wouldn't be a wedding cake, she said, and she seemed a little miffed that the cake she had dropped off just that morning had been soaked through, but in the end the drama of it was too appealing and she agreed to work all night.

David had tried not to let other people's comments stress them out so every call had been as brief and to-the-point as he could manage. It was only the call to Angie that had gone over ten minutes.

'There is the table plan to think of,' Ailie said. She was wearing pink dungarees with a pocket in the front and he had felt comforted by her sense of practicality when she had arrived to help. At least her illustrations would be fine as she had the supplies with her. 'I know they're being very casual but there was a clear plan for seating. Wherever we go with, all the tables will be different . . .'

'Let's leave that for now,' David said. 'Until we have the venue, let's not think about it. Any luck on places?'

They didn't yet have a location, but they would update everybody on that when or if they had one. *When* they had one, David kept reminding himself. They had all been calling venues or anywhere at all that might take a wedding. Everywhere was fully booked. There was nowhere willing to cancel their usual table reservations or already-ordered food for a last-minute wedding. People seemed confused by the request.

'Nothing,' Mark said. 'Sorry.'

'The best thing I have is a Chinese takeaway that would give us until seven o'clock, but I don't think that's any use.'

'I thought of Pink Punters,' David said. 'They've had flooding too though, and they have a special night on tomorrow night that they've already sold tickets for, if they can even open.'

'Do you have any more favours you can pull, David?' Ailie asked him. 'Meg said you knew everybody. Is there anywhere we've not tried yet?'

'I'll keep thinking,' David said. 'Angie's bakery is out; she has classes in tomorrow morning and she'd lose money and we can't do that.'

'The other pub still have that event on?' Gus said.

'As far as I know.'

'Shall we get some other bits done?' Mark said. 'Time's ticking.'

'Okay,' David said. 'Oh and Matty's still fine to do photography so that's not a problem at least. I text him.'

'What about décor?' Mark said. 'Everything down there was ruined.'

'We still have all the flowers we planned,' David said. 'They're downstairs.'

'Will you need more things?' Ailie said.

'What about the youth group?' Mark said, sitting up suddenly. 'They all loved the illustration class. What about if they put some things together? You've got paint and the back room downstairs, where they can make things.'

'That's actually a good idea,' David said. 'It's a Saturday night; they'll all be up. Will you call Benji?'

He took the Sharpie and ticked another bullet point off the list.

'What about the wedding dress?' Ailie said. 'That's a big one.'

'And she only really liked that one, right?' Gus said. 'In the shop?'

'It was so stupid of me, when I went to remove her mum's one I should have just brought hers too.'

Ailie sighed. 'The dress will be the thing to set her off tomorrow if that's wrong.'

'She did the same with prom,' Gus added.

'Hey, what happened to us all staying positive?' Mark said. 'David, get the good biscuits out. I was saving them for eleven but I think we need them now. Why don't you call Susan, and see what she can do? Maybe they stock duplicates. Will someone call Campbell Park? It's not a hundred per cent going to be sunny but maybe we need to start thinking about outside venues.'

'Gotcha,' Gus said.

David walked off into the bedroom for a moment of peace. Could they do this? There was so much left to do.

'Yes, hello, Susan,' he said. 'It's David Fenton. I called earlier . . . Right so, you'll never guess what's happened . . .'

An hour later, the notepad was now full of words, criss-crossing and written over and over each other. More things had been confirmed, and David was doing an okay job at keeping people on track, but he knew the question of the venue kept rearing its head and was unavoidable. Meg and Hannah's flat was too small, as was theirs. Neither had a garden.

'Do you think her parents would open up their house and garden?' Mark said. 'Hannah told me where they live. Those houses there aren't tiny, not for the number of guests we have coming.'

'I just don't think we should meddle,' Ailie said. 'It sounds like it's still a mess.'

'I agree,' David said. 'Let's leave them to decide if they're coming.'

'Any other luck on venues?' Gus said.

'I think I've called every pub in the county,' Ailie said. 'Nearly every single one is playing the rugby and won't move it.'

'How boring,' Gus said. 'Maybe it's camp to have it in a manly pub while the rugby's on?'

'Do you want to go to a manly pub?' Mark said.

'Not really.'

'Are there any other places on this high street we could have it?' Ailie asked.

'Everywhere's too specialized,' David said. 'The hairdresser's has those sinks in the way, the bridal shop is too small, the supermarkets can't move their aisles, not that they would . . .'

'What about downstairs?' Mark said. He put both his hands out on the table. 'Oh my God. How have we not thought of that at all? David, you don't mind being closed for a day do you?'

'Of course I don't.' He did, really, or he *should,* but not for this occasion.

'Okay,' Mark said. 'Well that's it then?'

'I didn't even think of the shop because . . . well that big table can't actually move out of the room, and it's all dirty, it's not exactly the place for a lovely white dress. And it's small. What are they going to do, sit on the counter?'

'Well firstly there might not even be a lovely white dress . . . Second of all, I just checked your weather app,' Mark said. 'It's saying now it will actually be dry all day. Sunny, even. People could sit outside too, and if we have Martha's sound system, they'll be able to hear on the microphones.'

He saw Gus and Ailie looking up at the clock surreptitiously.

'I just . . . I wanted them to have it somewhere special.'

'Lilies *is* special, David,' Gus said.

'I think we might be out of time,' Mark said. 'This is a really good option but it's also kind of the only one we have. We can make it special. We have time to do that, if we agree now that it's there.'

'It's too late to cancel the orders for tomorrow though,' David said. 'So they'll all arrive and be in there too.'

'What if they become part of the décor?' Gus said. 'The

flowers spill out into the street, so it all feels like one space, even if some people are inside and some are outside.'

'If it's half outside,' Ailie said, 'you'll need loads more décor.'

'Benji's messaged me,' Mark said. 'They're all coming in five minutes to make some decorations downstairs, and they say they can do the morning as well. Jacques said he can come wherever, so he can supervise?'

'It sounds like it's happening,' David said. 'Whether we like it or not.'

'I think we should get food in,' Mark said, standing up to get his keys. 'Keep everybody going for a couple of hours. I'll go see what's open.'

'The shop is a mess,' David said. 'We'll need to clean it too. I can't ask the kids to do that.'

'We've got four of us here,' Gus said. 'Ramon could come too. I could text him.'

'Good idea,' Mark said, patting him on the back. 'I'm sure Carl and Matty would come too.'

'Do we need to tell everyone then?' David said. 'Do we even have everybody's contacts?'

'I think let's just put a sign on the pub in the morning, then it's just a short walk,' Mark said. 'We don't want everyone texting Meg and Hannah now and freaking them out. As far as the guests know, everything's happening tomorrow as planned.'

'Okay,' David said. 'Then let's go downstairs I guess.'

At the doors to the flower shop, five or six of the youth club including Benji and Fred had already arrived.

'Thank you so much for coming,' David said. 'It's very good of you to give up your Saturday night.'

'Mark said there'd be beers,' Fred said. 'On the text.'

'I'm sure he didn't say that, but nice try.'

'Is Meg okay?' Benji asked.

'I think so,' David said. He checked his watch – ten minutes to eleven.

'She should be sleeping. I've told her to leave it all to us and we'll sort it.'

'Wow, scary,' Benji replied.

'Not scary!' David said. 'It'll be fine. I can't believe all your parents let you out.'

'Well mine like you two, and they heard about Meg and Hannah's wedding, and they said they didn't mind,' Fred said.

'My dad was out anyway, so I was at Fred's,' Benji said.

A couple more kids arrived and David let them all into the shop, showing them where the cardboard and paints were. They all got started, excitedly talking about what they were going to paint and, rather than try to manage the situation, David let it pass over him. It would sort itself out. Whatever they could do would help. He noticed Benji was filming everything.

'Do we need all of this on camera?' he asked him.

'It's in case you need it,' Benji said. 'I was filming at the pub too . . . I don't know, feels like a big moment. You want footage so you can show how you managed to make it all right in the end.'

'Okay,' David said. He didn't feel like it was beneficial to show anybody how gross the flooded pub floor looked, nor what a disaster Meg's wedding had turned into, but Mark always said you had to pick your battles with Benji, and this felt like one of those times.

'Anyway, in you go,' David said. 'Hopefully it won't take long. Benji, can I chat to you for a minute?'

'Yeah?'

'So, I just wanted to say . . .' They were standing outside the shop and he wanted to make sure Benji heard him, without him feeling like he'd been singled out again. 'Sorry for treating you like a child the other day in the shop. I didn't realize you'd left and I'd hate for you to feel unwelcome. I should have let you into that conversation with Hannah.'

'That's okay.'

'Well it's not really,' David said. 'You are still young but you're sixteen and you deserve more respect, same as when I told Meg you'd been on that date. Anyway, I wanted to say that and that what you've done with the shop's online presence is amazing. I'm not going to be able to pay you – I don't have the cash, so it might have to stop soon – but I think you've done wonders.'

'Why do I have to stop?'

Benji was looking at him, completely confused.

'Well, it seems unfair to me,' David explained.

'Do you get paid for helping with the youth club?'

'No, I don't.'

'Then how is this different?' Benji said.

David stared at him blankly.

'You're doing me a favour, giving me stuff to put on my CV and that. Let me keep doing it? Please?'

David peered into the shop and saw Ailie and Jacques directing the kids with what he knew must be an incredible vision for what they wanted. She was taping huge boards together and had found few wooden pallets that he could see she was imagining becoming something else. Jacques was holding a giant love-heart neon sign.

'Okay, Benji, we'll carry on for now. Why don't you post about tomorrow so people know the shop's closed?

It would be great, actually, if you could tell the shops either side of us what's happening and that there might be noise and disturbance in the street. And maybe tell people nearby – you could door-knock, or you could get some of the local news pages to post? I'll tell everyone from Work with Pride.'

'Okay,' Benji said walking back into the shop. He turned and shouted: 'But only if I get a beer!'

Mark arrived at the shop with the fish and chips he'd picked up from down the road – that beautiful forty-two-second journey – and he kissed David softly on the cheek as he passed. The night was fresh with the falling of the rain and now the clouds had fallen, you could see perfectly through the night and up to the stars.

David stood, indulging himself, just for a moment. The stars always made him think of his parents. Not that he thought they were up there or anything like that, but that those stars were there long before his parents were born, and would be there long after him or anyone he knew. The lights on the other side of the street made a line of yellow down to the bottom of the hill. There was the sound of cars in the distance, people heading off somewhere, or returning home to loved ones, and David could feel the chill of the night in his nostrils. Maybe it was time for another coffee. There was no telling how long this would take, and if this was going to be the shop's last hurrah, he wanted it to be something incredibly special.

Life could still be really exciting, it turned out. Even in your mid-fifties.

36

MEG

Five Hours Until the Wedding

Seven in the morning. Meg was in the bathroom getting ready. She was having what she called the warts-and-all. It was usually a Sunday night routine but instead it was now a morning ritual, which she imagined would help her both look and feel amazing for the day ahead.

First, she wrapped her hair in a hair mask and cling-filmed the lot. This kept it warm, and increased the efficacy of the mask. She had music playing from her phone and got through the list of tasks – cutting nails, plucking hairs, squeezing spots. Often, she flossed or used those expensive interdental brushes. Then she'd shave, use a face mask, then body-scrub her entire body before washing and conditioning her hair. She didn't want the shower to end; it was the last moment of peace she was likely to have.

As she got out, she commenced the next stage of preparations. A Vitamin C sheet mask, body butter, hair serum. There was always so much to do.

Once she'd completed most stages of the getting-ready plan, she threw on a tracksuit to meet David who was coming round to theirs, hopefully to explain all that had happened overnight. She had to put that on, since she didn't know what she was wearing, or where she was going. She stood close to the window to look out at the street, and though it wasn't raining, she could feel the early morning chill through the glass. She'd felt bad when Hannah had left at six in the morning to get ready at her parents' hotel.

'Was it a late one?' she asked David when he came in the door of their home.

'No, no,' he said. 'It was surprisingly easy.'

She wasn't sure she believed him but knew she would show her gratitude later.

The door went again and David went to go and let in the hair and make-up artist, Stacey.

Now they were there together, David, fully dressed in his baby-blue suit, began to make drinks and Stacey started laying out her equipment.

'Exactly the same as the trial, is it, Meg?'

'Yes, please.'

'Perfect.'

Meg was glad now they'd decided to hire someone, as it meant she could sit calmly and think about the other parts of the day. Yes, she wished she knew about her parents, but there were so many other people making their way to be there for her and Hannah, and so many other unknowns now, that they were one of several worries.

'Do you need anything, Meg?' David asked, handing her a coffee, and reminding her to be careful with it. 'I know it's weird not to know anything.'

'I . . . I wouldn't know where to start. We can just go with it. I've got a couple of backup outfit options, depending on what you planned. Just in case.'

'No worries,' David said. 'I thought you might have done that.'

Meg looked at herself in the mirror. Her skin looked calmer than it had this morning when she had showered, and her hair was being put up in rollers to set before it would be let down and finalized.

'It's looking, I think, eighty per cent sun,' David was saying. 'Maybe seventy-five, to be conservative.'

'Okay,' Meg said. 'Well that's good. Is there anything I need to know about . . . everything?'

'I want to tell you all of it,' David said. 'I'm rubbish at keeping secrets. But, if you're happy not to know anything, then just rest assured. We've thought of everything. You'll eat, you'll drink, you'll dance and, most importantly, you'll get married. That ticks everything off I think.'

'Okay.'

'You've got ages, so you can relax.'

'Okay.'

Though it wasn't the only thought in her head, it was one of the bigger ones. What were her parents doing right now? Her hand itched towards her phone, but she resisted. *Stay calm,* she told herself. *Whatever happens will happen.*

37

DAVID

Two Hours Until the Wedding

David felt nervous but he psyched himself up because Meg needed to know what she was wearing. Her hair and make-up was now mostly done, and he was sitting patiently on the sofa, fiddling with his phone.

'Okay,' David said, getting up. 'Meg, can I show you your new dress?'

'Oh, yes, okay.' Meg spun round excitedly in her chair. 'So it *is* a dress? Okay, for this I am perhaps a little nervous.'

'Don't be,' David said. 'It's fine.'

He walked into the hall and came back holding the bag with the dress in.

'Close your eyes, and I'll hang it on the door.' She placed her hands over her eyes. 'Okay, open.'

'Oh my God.'

David watched as Meg took it all in. It was her mum's dress, or at least it had been. Susan had been working all night but David hadn't wanted to tell Meg the idea in case she was instantly turned off. With a huge number of tweaks, what had been a traditional sort of dress now looked amazing. It was a thick white silk, with a see-through wrap over the decolletage and down to the wrists. The train had been old-fashioned, too long and heavy, but had now been completely taken off. Where there had been some damage, Susan had sewn blocks of colour in triangles at the bottom of the dress, which were hidden but opened up as the dress moved. The bottom of the dress would only just skirt her knees, but at least there was space for her to move properly, and that was more like the type of dress she would wear out somewhere anyway. The colours at the bottom were simple pastel versions of the pride flag.

'David, this is . . .'

She looked at him and seemed to lose her train of thought. He had no idea what to say, or what she thought. 'If you hate it, or you want to wear something else, we can, well I don't know . . .'

'Okay.'

'Susan said trying to dry yours would have completely ruined the material.'

'No, no, it's . . . David, I think it's perfect.'

'Do you really?' He could have burst with happiness.

'It's completely perfect,' she said. 'I would never have thought . . . I want to put it on right now.'

'Put it on then!' David said as Meg stood up.

'And we did check with your mum,' David said. 'She'd said alterations were fine, but Ailie messaged her to make sure. She said she didn't have use for it anymore.'

Meg looked like she wasn't sure what to say. He wondered what that meant for today. 'Can I put it on?' she asked, turning to the make-up woman, Stacey.

'Yes, of course,' Stacey said, checking her watch. 'But be careful of the lipstick!'

Meg ran away to the bedroom and came back with the dress on.

'This is so great,' she said, bending to look at herself in David's narrow mirror in the hall. 'I think it's . . . it's definitely more fun than before. I never would have thought to wear something like this. It's so short.'

'Are you happy?' David asked. 'I was worried it was a little short or that you would think it doesn't look like a wedding dress, but I guess that's good for later on when Martha . . .'

'I'm ready to dance now!' Meg said. 'You were right. Thanks, David, I . . .'

She moved over to hug him and squeezed him tighter than she ever had.

'Can I ask you something?' Meg asked.

'Yes, of course.' David checked his watch. 'But make it quick; you've not got long.'

'Well it's something important . . .' Meg said. 'I wanted to know . . . Where's my wedding?'

They both laughed. 'Do you want to know?'

'I do, but it doesn't even matter at this stage.' Meg looked at the ceiling as if trying not to cry. 'The one thing I do want to ask is whether you'd do me the honour of walking me down the aisle?'

'Meg! I . . .'

'I spoke to Hannah about it after we'd visited my parents, and it seems so obvious now, that it should be you. You've been by my side every step of this journey, and I wondered . . .' She paused. 'Whether you'd take the last few steps with me?'

She looked at David and David looked at Stacey, who looked like she was going to cry.

'Of course I will.' David touched Meg's shoulder. 'I'd love to!'

'Are you sure? You don't have to.'

'I really want to, Meg. That's lovely, thank you so much for asking.'

'Well thank *you*,' she said. 'For everything.'

38

MEG

The Wedding

People always said, when you told them you were getting married, that some parts of the wedding day would be nerve-racking. They would preach advice like you were undergoing some endurance test or like the stakes were the highest you could imagine. They said you had to remember to eat something and not to drink too much because people were constantly passing you fizz. Make sure you have water, often, and eat, she had been told. People had said to her, in the months since their engagement, that the moment everybody looked at you as you walked up the aisle was tear-inducing and scary, at first, and people had also whispered at her about after the day itself, the days where it was finally all over and you felt some kind of grief about it. People were so obsessed with weddings she had even been given details like when to go to the toilet, or how to manage your make-up over a twelve-hour day. Nobody, however, had told Meg about the minutes before the wedding ceremony.

People had popped in to say hi – Ailie, Mark and Martha had all been there – but now they had left, and with secrecy around what they told her, she felt quickly panicked. What was she doing?

She asked for a second in the bathroom and was breathing, three-four-five, to bring herself back to the present. It wasn't fear or cold feet that brought her here, but an overwhelming feeling of *life*, the fact she was living through a milestone moment. The idea of being wedded to Hannah forever took her breath away. It was in a good way, but it was still more intense than any average day tended to be.

Every now and again when she moved, she could smell her mum's dress. Though there was a dusty smell – it had been in their attic for decades – there was also a perfume she couldn't recognize, maybe one her mum had worn before Meg, or bought specially for the day. She felt a bit dizzy if she thought about that, like her eyes were watering. She tried not to think about her mum.

Her hands were clammy and she had to remind herself not to, as usual, wipe her palms down the front of what she was wearing. She was sweating beneath her hair, which after heavy styling, felt heavier than it ever had. Meg's heart was thumping in her chest in a way where it felt like it was trying to escape, to run away or to run to Hannah. She wondered how Hannah, likely standing right now at the top of an aisle (did they even have an aisle?) was feeling.

'Meg?'

There was a light knock at the door.

'Yes, David?'

'Can I come in?'

'Yes.'

David poked his head round the door, and then seeing her, hands clasping onto the sink, white with terror, came in and closed the door behind him.

'Here,' he said. 'Sit on the toilet. Take a second.'

'Why have I done this?' she said. 'What was I thinking?'

'You kind of chose this,' he said, grinning. 'Sorry.'

'I know, it's crazy,' Meg said, her chest heaving up and down. She felt instantly calmed by David's presence. 'You had the right idea, you know; we should have just stayed as we were. Nothing wrong with just being partners.' A pause. 'I'm sweating so much.'

'That's okay.'

'Am I making weddings seem appealing?'

He smiled. 'I'll decide on me and Mark after you've done the whole thing,' David said. 'Which starts with us getting in a taxi, where you are due, minus two minutes ago. You've got this.'

Meg heaved herself up.

'Do you need an emergency wee?' he asked.

'Maybe.'

'I'll be outside.' David smiled at her, walking into the hall. 'Take your time; it's your day.'

When they walked together out the door she saw that Mark's car was the taxi, with 'about to be married' written on cardboard on the back. They left, and soon they were on the high street, a now familiar place, and the car stopped abruptly. Because of blacked-out windows, Meg couldn't tell exactly where they were, or see out of the windows.

'Are we here already?'

'Time to get out,' David said.

When she did, she was confused. It looked like there was some kind of event happening in the street, and then she realized they were outside the flower shop. However, she'd thought it was somewhere else because there were rows of people sitting outside on tiered seating made up of wooden pallets, painted in bright colours. Had they planned their wedding on the same day as . . . ?

There was a general sort of intake of breath as people realized one of the brides had arrived.

'Meg, the wedding's here,' David said, gesturing to Savage Lilies, whose signage had been covered up with a huge banner that read MEG AND HANNAH. 'It's in the shop. Let me show you.'

She took his hand and he led her towards the door. The music she'd wanted to walk down the aisle to was playing, but not the right part of it, but she was too taken in with what David and the others had got done that she couldn't really think about anything as insignificant as what music was playing. She was so happy. The view in front of her was perfect.

'Just smile,' she said, more to herself than any advice for David. His arm steadied her shaking hand and she was able to walk slowly but surely. The waves of people standing to see her felt like a Mexican wave. Any sort of guest list had gone out of the window. All of the youth group were seated in chairs outside at the back, followed by a number of each of their work friends, and Ailie and the rest of the university girls were sitting in the last front row with their boyfriends and husbands, before she reached the doorway to the shop itself. Sophie and her husband waved to her and she saw the woman who collected for the food bank.

Someone, or everyone, had managed to make outside feel like inside. There were huge card drawings of flowers and pride flags lining the banks of chairs, making it feel completely natural that there was the glass window of the building dividing the area into two. Flowers were stacked in buckets out to the sides of the chairs. Where beautifully specific arrangements had gone out of the window, instead, the sheer bulk of what seemed to be the shop's entire stock meant the street and the shop felt full of colour. Like the shop, she felt full, but her eyes began to scan, to see if two people in particular had come. She couldn't tell.

The windows, she noticed, as she took a deep breath and walked inside the shop, had been cleared of their usual foliage. In a white marker-pen, someone, probably Ailie, had scrawled in decorative writing: *Love Wins* and a huge love heart. The big table was hidden behind the counter so you couldn't get there, and short rows of three chairs were on either side of an aisle that was littered with tiny decorated pieces of cardboard that looked like flowers. It was cramped, for sure. A variety of plants and flowers hung from the ceiling and all around; at the front, on the counter, was a tiny arch that reached Caleb the celebrant's head, but only just. The whole room smelt of cleaning fluid and flowers, and Meg noticed a neon love heart propped up on the counter.

Forcing herself to walk slowly, Meg saw Hannah's parents and family, as well as Mark, Carl, Gus and Ramon. Everybody had stood up, and her eyes scanned for her parents, though she could barely distinguish anybody, given how watery her eyes were.

She kept walking and it wasn't till she hugged Hannah and turned quickly out to look back at the crowd that she could look properly, and there, in the front row, turning slowly, were her mum and dad. Her mum wiped at her face with a tissue. As she did so, she broke into a massive smile, and Meg smiled back, before finding it too intense and looking away. Her dad waved at her.

They came.

'Thank you,' she mouthed to them, as she stood next to Caleb, and Hannah, who she looked at properly now. She was wearing smart, polished, black shoes, and her hair was down entirely, flowing in its curls onto her chest and down her back. Her striped suit, a faded brown, was oversized and suited her style perfectly. Meg glimpsed a floral pattern on the inside lining. On the lapel, a tiny gardenia from Meg's bouquet was pinned to her. Her hands were folded in front of her and Meg could see her fingers fiddling with themselves.

She took another look at the crowd. More people were crying than she expected; she saw Gus's parents, his mum crying, and Ailie and the girls were all dabbing at their eyes with tissues. She saw her mum take in her dress and start to cry more, and Meg didn't know whether that was out of appreciation or because her dress had been torn in half, but she put it to the back of her mind.

She said thank you to David, who went to go and find his seat, getting a laugh from the crowd when he waved at everybody and announced his name. Meg reached across to grab Hannah and they hugged briefly.

'Hi.'

'Hi, Han.'

'All okay?'

'More than.'

Meg hadn't even noticed but Matty, holding one camera and another strapped on a belt to his body, was following her, and now sat on the table behind the counter to take photos through the flower arch. She glanced again at her parents, and noticed they, like everybody else, were wearing small pride-flag ribbons round their wrists, made from the wrapping David usually used on his special bouquets.

'Right,' Caleb said loudly through a microphone. 'We got here.' There were laughs from the audience, which seemed to break any tension. 'Everybody, shall we begin?'

To cheers, they did.

After Ailie's beautiful reading of a poem, there was just one tense moment when Caleb asked whether 'anybody here present knows of any legal impediment . . .' There was a brief moment of silence, and a laugh. She heard Benji shout something from outside, which she supposed Caleb should have taken seriously, but had let it slide. It had sounded like 'Obviously not, man!'

All Meg was trying to do during that moment was avoid her parents' eyes, since a tiny part of her, a single percentage, wondered whether they had come just to object. They didn't though, and she breathed a sigh of relief. Everything was going to be okay.

'You never know,' Caleb had joked to the crowd. 'There can often be a lot of last-minute surprises.'

There really had been.

Eventually, and Meg kept reminding herself to *take in every second* as people had told her, Caleb paused before announcing that he could now proclaim them wife and wife, and that they might now kiss each other.

They kissed, somewhat self-consciously, a brief peck on the lips, but Matty muttered for them to do it for longer so he could get the photo so they did and people cheered again, louder than the last time. Meg couldn't help but smile. It was a cacophonous noise that echoed in the busy space, with a tailing sort of cheer from outside, which sounded abnormally loud, like that too was playing from a speaker.

'Now, I want you to all cheer the happy couple outside, and into the rest of the day,' Caleb said. 'This has been one of the most unique weddings I've officiated; I'll tell you that. I wish the happy couple the best and it's now over to all of you—' he gestured to the crowd '—to make the day as special as possible. I know a lot of you have already contributed to getting us here so on behalf of the couple, thank you.'

Meg looked at Caleb, tearing her eyes away from Hannah for a second. She had always thought he was somewhat serious, too formal for their vibe as a couple, but she was beginning to like him. Even more so when he added: 'It looks for the people outside like the sun is slowly creeping out so here's hoping that stays for the rest of the day. Go and enjoy the weather. June weather can be tricky, but I guess that's Pride month for you.'

He was smiling now, in on the ridiculousness of the whole day, when he announced: 'May I present . . . Meg and Hannah!'

He winked at them and they set off down the aisle, Meg awfully aware of her feet and what her face was doing. She tried to look forward for Matty's camera as flower petal confetti fell on them, in reds and yellows and oranges. Meg could feel the petals getting caught on her dress and hair, but she didn't mind, and they walked out the front of the shop where more people were lined up throwing more.

Hannah looked at her and whispered to her. 'They're from all the broken-stem roses David has. He's been collecting them for months.'

Out on the street, she was blinded by the light before her eyes adjusted, and she kept walking, hand clasped in Hannah's, but suddenly they seemed to have kept walking for ages. Meg realized it was because behind the rows was a crowd of people standing, who hadn't been there before, or had they? The crowd had definitely got so large, there was no way to even reach the end of the it.

'What on earth . . .' Hannah said under her breath.

As far as the eye could see, people were cheering. There were perhaps a hundred more people than there were guests.

'What's happening?' Meg said. 'Did you . . . ?'

'I don't . . .'

People continued to throw petals. David must have been collecting for ages. Meg could see Ramon waving from his taco truck. She noticed quickly he'd finally implemented her branding suggestion, and the truck's new name, Taco Chance On Me, was lit up on the top. Leaning out of the serving hatch, he was blowing on a horn. Next to him, there was a bar on wheels called Pink Drinks, and next to that was a raised platform where Martha was waving, headphones around her neck, playing a Hall and Oates song. It was magical and it was queer and it was all theirs. Now, not because she had to, but because she wanted to, she kissed Hannah again to even louder cheers. As it happened, despite the crowds that were all there for them, Meg could have sworn they were alone, together, finally wife and wife.

39

DAVID

'So you've got to tell me, how the hell did this happen?' David said, throwing his arms wide at the crowd that must now be upwards of two hundred people. He was standing with Mark, talking to Benji and Salma, who had done a teenage version of dressing up, Salma in a dress and Benji in a smart jumper with a school shirt underneath.

'There's so many people,' Mark said.

'People just wanted to come!' Salma said. 'We made sure people on the guest list had that pride ribbon, so you know who's here from the wedding and who's extra.'

'And it's public so I think people have just stopped, interested to see what's going on,' Benji said. 'It's not exactly bad for the shop.'

'We only knocked on a few houses to let them know, but everyone just wanted to come see,' Salma said.

'And people knew you were involved, which helped,' Benji said. 'The GOAT.'

'Who brought a goat to a wedding?' David said, looking around.

'No,' Salma said. 'You're the GOAT.'

David looked at Mark.

'It means Greatest Of All Time,' Mark said. '*Obviously.*'

David took a look around. Everybody was mixing and having a nice time. The taco truck could never have served everyone all at once, so there was a happy queue of people lining up patiently for their food. Ramon had only catered for the guests, so he'd called a couple of people he knew from the food festival and now there was a semicircle of food options, and another drinks cart, for everybody else. Two conjoined trucks were called Meat Me Halfway and Boom Boom Bao, and David was struck by the constant presence of the Black Eyed Peas, reminding himself to request them later on the dancefloor. There was another vendor, Coq Au Van, and Ramon had told David that, if needed, he was going to call somebody called Carbonara Tara.

In the middle, Martha had set up her decks on a series of brightly painted pallets, and was playing mid-tempo love songs, dancing away behind the speakers. People weren't dancing yet, but groups of people were swaying to the beat.

Where was Meg? David had not had a real chance to speak to her since he'd taken his seat in the ceremony. He could see her now, talking to a group of friends in the distance by the bar. She was holding a pink cup, and was laughing. She looked free and relaxed. And the dress! He was not exactly a fashion expert but it seemed to convey everything she might want at a wedding: some tradition, the pride colours, a burst of personality, so modern and so her.

'I'm going to go ask Martha about being a DJ,' Salma said. 'I think I could do that,' she added.

'Shouldn't you call her Miss Apoline?' David said. 'She is technically a teacher.'

'Oh, she doesn't care about things like that,' she said, before running away into the crowd.

'I'm going to go check Matty's okay,' Mark said. 'Maybe take him some food.'

'So how did this happen, Benji?' David asked, turning to him. 'Tell me your secrets.'

'Loads of people wanted to come,' he said. 'Once we'd posted. You said to do everything to make it special, so first off we knocked on a few doors this morning to make sure people around here wouldn't mind the noise, but also to invite them. A few people said they'd stop by but it was as soon as it went online, it went mad. Everything got a bit carried away as soon as I posted.'

'Wait, is that a news truck?' David said, looking over to a van with some sort of satellite on the top, and a woman in a pale purple blazer and skirt standing next to it fiddling with a microphone. 'Benji, what?'

'Oh they're here!' Benji said. 'I need to go speak to them.' He spun round to walk off.

'No, slow down,' David said, grabbing his arm. 'It's like you're running the day! That's meant to be my job!'

'They messaged the flower shop page, look.' He held out his phone to David. 'It's a feel-good story, right? Local community, ordinary people. They love stuff like that. The pub is getting donations in.' As Benji spoke, David couldn't believe the boy he'd seen grow up from a shy ten-year-old who couldn't control his emotions was now co-ordinating a national news team. 'You've gained five hundred followers today.'

'Five hundred?'

'Five hundred.'

'As in half a thousand?'

'I should have got you to help with my maths revision,' Benji said.

'Are you sure?'

'I don't have my results yet but I'm pretty sure I can halve a thousand.'

'That's so many followers.'

'It's nearly a thousand on TikTok,' Benji said.

'Well that's . . . that's amazing,' David said. 'I really can't thank you enough.'

'I even got Mrs Kirby to come.'

He looked over in the distance to Meg's parents, who were standing with a drink each. They weren't talking to each other, and looked slightly sheepish, but occasionally Ava was pointing out details in the crowd to George.

'What? That was you?'

'When we were knocking on doors, I didn't know she lived there, so I knocked and then I explained what had happened.'

'Did she ask many questions?' David said.

'She asked if Meg was okay,' he said. 'I didn't let on that I knew, you know, what had happened. She didn't say she was her mum either.'

'But you don't know what's happened.'

'I've picked things up,' Benji said. 'I'm not stupid.'

'No you're not,' David said. 'Sorry. So, what did she say?'

'She just asked what I thought about it,' Benji said. 'She asked if all the youth club were coming and what we thought of a same-sex marriage and I just told the truth. I said Meg had been teaching us all and that she was great, and that I wasn't thinking about a same-sex wedding. It's just a wedding, you know. Then, well, I told her I was bisexual. I think she was a little bit shocked by that.'

David paused, aware of the magnitude of this moment.

'Oh, Benji, well done,' he said. 'And I'm proud of you! You've never told me that.'

'I know, well . . . It's recent.'

'Then what did she say?'

'She just said everyone deserved a happy wedding day and she said she'd be coming. She looked really emotional.'

David looked over at Meg's parents again and for the first time, felt a real hint of sympathy towards them. Their lack of bravery, to go outside what was normal, or what they assumed was normal, here in their town. The way she had been in the flower shop, almost seeking approval from others. How it had taken half the neighbourhood to be going to her daughter's wedding before she agreed to come. It was a start, at least.

'Who else knows about you then? Am I last on the list as usual, like when nobody told me skinny jeans were over, or knowing what a GOAT is?'

'Well, I'm only just telling people, you know. Starting this week. You're actually the first.'

'Ah, I see,' David said. 'I'm proud of you, you know.'

'You said that already.'

'Can I hug you?'

'You don't need to hug me, man; it's not a huge deal. But thank you.' Benji grinned. 'Anyway, I need to go. Fred was getting us tacos, and I need to speak to the news people. You need to talk to them too, and make sure you mention the subscriptions! You've got nothing to sell today but that will get people booking online.'

'That's such a good idea,' David said. 'My business manager.'

'Of course it's a good idea,' Benji said, rolling his eyes at him and walking off into the crowd. David walked across and down the high street in the other direction looking for Mark, and realized at some point the area had been zoned off by cones. Suddenly, Mark was there tapping on his shoulder, eating a taco from a small paper cone.

'There you are,' David said.

'Can I—'

'Can I talk to you inside?' David interrupted.

'That's what I was going to say.'

Without argument, they walked together towards the shop, passing Benji asking the news people how they got their jobs, and past Ailie's illustration stand, currently drawing Mary, who was asking her to draw her ten pounds thinner.

'Right,' David said, closing the shop's door behind them as they went inside.

'Right,' Mark said, putting his hand in his pocket.

David raised an eyebrow at him. 'What?'

'David, for over a decade . . .'

'No stop, wait.'

'What?' Mark said.

'Mark, ever since I met you . . .'

They were talking over each other and David couldn't reach inside his jacket pocket quick enough. Instead, he scrambled down to one knee, and in front of him, Mark did the same. Mark opened a small silver case, and David held the ring for Mark between his fingers; he had thought the bulky case in his pocket would be too obvious, but he hadn't even noticed Mark's.

'Are you joking?' Mark said. 'I can't believe it.'

'Are *you* proposing to *me*?' David asked.

'Are you, David Fenton, proposing to me, is the real question?' Mark shook his head. 'This is unbelievable.'

'I thought you were waiting for me!'

'I was, but you've done so much for so many people, I wanted to surprise you to show you how nice being proposed to is!' Mark said. 'And because you've had such an intense few weeks.'

'Mark, this is amazing. Wait, let me—'

'I love you David,' Mark said. David sighed. 'No, let me go first! Since you've got me a ring, I'm presuming you're going to say yes, but you didn't have to. I just wanted . . .'

'No, I wanted to . . .' David fumbled for the words he'd prepared in his head. He raced through in order to get them out before Mark. 'I can't control a lot. Not what people's parents do, or what mine did, or what happens with the shop. I know that I can do this, though, and that I want to.'

They kissed and slipped the rings onto each other's hands. The words could wait; they knew how they felt.

'I was going to wait till later,' Mark said. 'Or tomorrow.'

'So was I.'

'I wanted to find somewhere secret.'

'Me too.'

'But I couldn't wait,' Mark said. 'And I'm not sure it's that secret.'

Mark nodded towards the window, where two news cameras were pointing through the glass filming. Salma had a hand on either cheek in shock, and a crowd was gathering. Benji had his thumbs up next to the camera, like he was directing the scene. Even with the door closed, David could hear the news travelling backwards into the crowd. He had really thought they were hidden in here, and in normal circumstances, they would have been. He hadn't banked on the fact that with half their stock gone outside or moved, they were essentially in a glass box.

'Help me up,' David said, reaching out to Mark. 'My knee's gone.'

Standing, they clasped each other's hands.

'Better go greet our public.'

'I feel like Charles and Diana,' Mark said.

'That's not a great reference point for the start of an engagement.'

As soon as the door was open, they were hit with a wall of sound and applause from those close to the shop, but then it seemed news had travelled even further and Martha announced on the microphone that there'd been an engagement on this special day and could everybody please cheer for David and Mark. Everybody joined in, and the sound was deafening.

They didn't know what to do so David led Mark out towards Martha and suddenly Meg and Hannah were there, looking on in shock. There was a second when David thought they might be annoyed but then they were running towards them, and the four of them were holding hands and jumping up and down.

'Oh my God, oh my God!' Meg said. 'I can't believe this!'

'This amazing news!' Hannah shouted. 'How did you keep this a secret?'

'Sorry we didn't mean to do it today,' David said. 'We really didn't.'

'Don't be silly,' Meg said. 'We're ecstatic for you!'

A car's engine revved behind the crowd and Angie stepped out, shouting something that nobody could hear.

'What, Angie?' David shouted across to her.

'I said it's time for cake!' Angie said. 'Been baking all night and morning. Now somebody come and help with these boxes.'

'David and Mark just got engaged!' Meg said.

'It's about time!' Angie replied. 'But today of all days?'

'It's untraditional!' David yelled to her.

At the car, Benji and Fred were there helping too; Benji was smiling oddly at David.

'What?'

'It's a big day for you, David, and the shop.'

'What do you mean? You know I just got engaged.'

'Not that,' Benji said, resting his head on the top of a huge square box in his hands. 'The news want to speak to you, at six o'clock. Now they're here, they think it can go on the national news. Live! Can you believe it?'

He couldn't believe it. At least the shop, the thing he'd loved most in the world after Mark, was going down in style. With the butterflies that now seemed to have resided permanently in David's stomach, he continued taking boxes out of the car, thinking to himself: *what a day.*

40

MEG

'Ahem, right, can everyone hear me?'

Time for the speeches. Usually, these were Meg's favourite parts of a wedding, but given today it was her who had to speak to a crowd of people in the hundreds, she felt sick with nerves. She tried to pretend the crowd wasn't there and concentrated instead on those she could see immediately in front of her – Hannah, Ailie, Angie, David and Mark – and not her parents who were somewhere to the left, slightly out of focus. She still hadn't spoken to them.

She put her hand down on top of one of the speakers to steady herself. 'I never thought my wedding would look like this,' she said to polite laughs. 'Obviously. I don't think any of us did!' Her fear had been that once she started speaking, people would start shouting from the back of the crowd that they couldn't hear her but luckily it seemed like the last-minute rigging Martha had done had worked.

'When I was younger I never really knew what my wedding would look like,' she said. 'Initially, I imagined what every little girl imagines when they're playing with the dolls they're given. A nice man, tall and handsome. When I got a little older, double digits, I realized maybe that wasn't what it was going to be. Hannah is still quite tall though.'

She looked at David and Mark, smiling and laughing encouragingly.

'It wasn't even possible for me to marry Hannah a decade ago, when we met. A wedding wasn't always on the cards.' She took a big breath in. 'I'm so glad it is, now. Against all the odds, and throwing away everything we thought might take place today, here we are. You and me, Han. People have said this isn't normal, or it's too different, and you know what? I'm glad this isn't normal, because whatever we have, and whatever this is—' she gestured out to the crowd '—it's better than whatever normal is. I feel a lot of Pride, today.'

She looked at the people in front of her, the community she had found, and it was this, the antidote to loneliness she had found through David, that made her begin to well up. *Come on, Meg,* she told herself, *you can get through this.*

'When I grew up, just around the corner,' she said, 'I never realized there was so much love around here. You can be quite in your head as a teenager, I guess. The community and its people have changed and I've discovered that putting yourself out there, well . . . It's given me more than I ever thought I deserved. Hannah, I can't wait to make our life here.'

As the crowd applauded, Meg knew there would be just one hard part of the day left. She could see her parents clapping politely, standing in front of a chicken van called I Just Fried in Your Arms.

'Thanks, everybody, again for coming,' she said. 'Hannah's up next, and she's going to do the thank yous, because we thought I would cry too much!' Meg added, before coming down from the platform and bursting into tears. 'She was right!'

David looked at Meg as Hannah reached the end of her speech. 'No, you didn't have to!'

Hannah's voice came booming through the speakers: 'We've actually got some flowers for someone who absolutely doesn't need them but certainly deserves them. Meg wanted to do this but thought she might be too emotional . . . If everyone can applaud or raise a glass to David, our . . . what shall we call him? Father of the Pride seems appropriate.'

Meg presented the flowers to David and they both hugged to cheers from the crowd.

'Now, Meg, don't worry I was coming to you.' Meg jokingly hid her head under her hands. 'The thing with Meg, the first time we met, it was in a café at university and Meg moved to make space for me. I kept going back, not just because I had a hell of a lot of work to do, but because I hoped she would be there. Looking back, we were both doing that, but it took months to figure out what we were to each other. Were we friends, or something more?

'I think with Meg, she brings people together. Little did she know it but by the February after the Christmas break and our first exams, we were together and we had a group of friends around us that we've had ever since.'

There were cheers from the girls, standing in front of the taco truck, some of them holding two drinks each.

'That's what you do, Meg, even when life's hard you're still a beacon of light, and people are drawn to you, and if I have to spend every day of the rest of my life making that clear to you, that's what I'll do. It's no surprise you've somehow got hundreds of people here to support you, and us. We could be doing this in Wembley Stadium and the crowd still wouldn't be enough.

'So, before I get Meg to myself for the rest of our lives, I'd like everyone to raise a glass to my wife, and to love, and to community.'

Meg smiled, embarrassed by all the attention. She tried to hold back her tears, and instead look as though she was smiling at people. She could see the shop full of people, whether official wedding guests or not, taking photos in the photo booth, and the plants that were still in the shop looked amazing with the light from the sun streaming through the windows.

Out of the corner of her eye, she could see the youth group hovering near the bar, working out who could try and get served, pushing each other forward one by one. Not long to go, she thought, watching them. A couple more years.

There were people she'd seen in the shop whenever she'd been in speaking to David, or the girl who worked with Angie, or Salma's parents she had seen picking her up from the shop once, there with her uncle. Hovering near one of the food trucks, Jacques, despite all his décor being ruined, had come, and he was trying not to spill ketchup on his suit.

Standing under the awning of the shop were her parents. Though she had not been avoiding them, she felt somewhat uneasy about what they might say, after everyone else had said so many wonderful things. She walked over, and before she had said anything her mum grasped onto her and hugged her so tight she had to push her arms off a little bit.

'Congratulations,' her dad said.

'You look . . . beautiful.' Her mum reached out to touch the fabric of the dress. 'This . . . They've done an amazing job.'

'Thanks,' Meg said to her parents, standing awkwardly apart from them.

'Shall we have a little talk somewhere private?' Ava said, her eyes full of tears. 'Is there time? If you can.'

'There's time,' she said. 'I've got a couple of things to do, and people to talk to, but yes I'd really like to talk.'

'Okay, darling,' George said, hovering awkwardly next to his wife. 'You can't do everything. Whenever you've got a moment.'

41

DAVID

It was hard to move amongst the crowd, and even crossing to the other side of the road seemed to take twenty minutes. Everybody was trying to clear a space, led by Ailie and Martha directing people with the microphone. Rather than being an MC, Martha had become some kind of crowd control, telling people about cars parked in the wrong place or lost clothes found on the floor in between the songs.

'Hi, David,' Meg said as he joined her group of friends. 'Was the news thing okay?'

'I was made for the cameras,' David joked, flicking non-existent hair behind his ear. It had been okay. He thought he'd done well, given how out of his comfort zone the whole thing was. He'd talked about the shop and the street and what it was like to live and work here. He'd followed Benji's lead, mentioning the subscriptions and talked about his engagement to Mark while the footage captured earlier had played over the top of the segment.

'I think they want to talk to me in a minute,' Meg said. 'Apparently they're re-packaging it for the morning show as well.'

'At least you don't have to speak live!'

'But first,' Martha's voice boomed from the speakers, which seemed to be getting louder, 'can I invite you all to watch the couple's first dance?'

Soon, Meg was being led by Hannah into the middle of the circle. Martha began to play their first dance song, 'Can't Help Falling in Love'.

David was now standing next to Meg's parents watching the couple, and he was deliberately trying not to look to his left. After a while of them dancing, Meg's arms on Hannah's shoulders, and staring into each other's eyes, whispering things the crowd couldn't hear to each other, Martha invited 'the newly engaged couple' to join them. He couldn't see Mark and was scanning the crowd for him when Ava touched his arm.

'Congratulations,' she said.

'Thank you,' he said, pausing to say something else before Mark's hand was in his and, seconds later, he found himself spinning Mark round in front of the crowd.

'Do the *Dirty Dancing* routine!' Salma was shouting.

'Not with his knees!' Mark shouted back.

He felt somewhat self-conscious but it felt like the crowd was there to support them rather than just observe, which buoyed him up. He could see out of the corner of his eyes that a lot of the flowers seemed to have been made into flower crowns, giving the entire crowd even more of a festival vibe. Soon, everyone had joined and was dancing together.

'Do you think our wedding will be like this?' Mark said into his ear.

'Well the shop will be a cheap venue,' David said. 'We know we can do it.'

'Stress-free, right?' Mark said.

'Maybe we can put the extra time into choreographing the dance?'

'What are you saying about my dancing?' Mark said, breaking off from David to try out a new move.

After a couple of songs, swapping partners with Hannah and Meg, David genuinely felt his knees needing a rest.

'Do you want a drink?' he asked Mark.

'Espresso martini?' Mark said, pointing at the drinks bar, which seemed to have a rather extensive cocktail range for what was essentially a camper van.

'That's what I was thinking,' he said. I've barely had a coffee today.' He took Mark's hand in his, leading his fiancé through the crowd. He looked up to see, faintly, what looked like a rainbow.

'Surely not.'

'It can't be,' Mark said. 'That's too much – surely not.'

'I think it is,' he said, and there were gasps from the crowd as people realized, and soon, the music was playing to a crowd of people, nobody talking, all looking up to the sky.

One of the businesses, was it Chilli Con Barney or Anneka's Rice, he wasn't sure which, had laid out café-style chairs and tables, and David and Mark now sat with Carl and Matty as the dancing continued. The sun was still up in the sky and they were in that peculiar part of a wedding where nobody knew what time it was. The crowd, initially more of an older crowd out for the day, was replaced by the festival atmosphere led by groups of teens and people in their twenties enjoying the last of the sun with a drink or two.

'Are we tired?' Carl said. 'I could do with a lie-down. Did you not think of a lie-down area for the older gays, David?'

'You're welcome to take a second upstairs,' Mark said. 'But you may become afflicted with what I believe is called FOMO?'

'Fear of missing out,' Matty said.

'Fear of my oldness,' David added.

'Very nice,' Carl said.

'Make sure you go and get an illustration of yourself from Ailie,' Matty said. 'She's stopping soon.'

'Yeah we need to,' Mark replied.

'Do you think we were ever like that when we were young?' David said, pointing out the groups of young people around, them dancing in circles. The youth group had formed a circle and people were occasionally entering the middle of the circle to dance.

'I wasn't,' Mark said. 'Much too shy.'

'I wouldn't have had my ears pierced either,' Carl said. 'I'd never have been allowed.'

'I wouldn't have worn these clothes,' Matty said. 'Dad would never have let me out the house.' He got up to continue taking photos of the conga line that had now started down the street.

David sighed, whether with sadness or resignation. You couldn't change the past, Mark always said, only the present. You couldn't even control the future either; nothing was guaranteed.

'They're all so . . .' David said. 'I don't know, they're still teenagers and awkward and acting in ways they'll be mortified about in years to come, but not in the same way. They've all got a sense of self. I don't think we had that.'

He looked out at the group who seemed to feel completely unwatched, or perhaps not caring. He noticed Benji dancing with Fred. Their heads were getting closer and they kissed quickly. It was the first time, it seemed, that others in the group knew about it too. David hadn't even made the connection. A couple of the others made noises at them, but they smiled and shoved them away. Benji looked instantly lighter, a secret unburdened.

The rest of the group, David observed, which included others he hadn't seen before who must have been from the school, were dancing in pairs, holding each other, opposite and same-sex pairs. Rod's sons were dancing with the group. Rarely was David able to observe life like this. Nobody else was watching, and nobody else cared. Looking left and right, he realized it was only the four of them who were watching, contemplatively.

'We can't let them have all the fun,' he said. 'Shall we go and dance?'

Charli XCX made way for the wedding classics of ABBA, and soon they were again on their feet, lining up and entering a circle with Angie and Martha, who had left Salma in charge of the decks. She kept having to go back to tell her to stop playing Dua Lipa deep cuts.

David's knees were hurting, but he didn't want to stop this moment, so he stayed in the circle dancing till his knees, calves and feet couldn't take it anymore. They all cheered as Ramon, finally done serving food, walked into the circle holding Gus's hand, and he realized he had more energy in him yet.

42

MEG

While everybody else was dancing, Meg led her parents back to the flower shop. Finally in the shop, months after they were meant to be there together. Her mum was looking around at the room, the chairs neatly stacked now and the majority of the plants outside or against the walls. It was the barest and most lifeless Meg had ever seen it.

'So,' she said. She didn't want any awkwardness but she also wanted her parents to lead the conversation. She was so glad they came, but it needed to mean something. They had to understand why. Meg felt like she had said her piece, and said enough, for them to know what the situation was.

'I noticed we weren't in your speech,' Ava began.

'Well, I didn't know for sure you were coming.'

Her dad was standing next to her mother, his arms crossed over his chest. 'That's fair.'

'I know, Meg,' her mum said. 'We wouldn't expect to be. It just made us sad, about how the last few months have been. I also know that it's our own doing.'

Her dad reached out to her. 'The first thing to say is we're really sorry.' He looked at Ava.

Without meaning to, Meg was aware she had taken a sharp, painful breath in, like her heart was caught in her throat.

'We are really sorry, Meg,' her mum said, and her lip started to wobble. She reached out a hand toward her. 'We truly are and we really hope you can accept our apology.'

'It might take time, and not be fixed today, but our intention is to fix this,' her dad added.

Meg didn't know what to say.

'You look absolutely beautiful,' her mum said, now dabbing at her eyes with a tissue. 'I like what you've done with the dress . . . It was so heavy on my wedding day, I was worn out by eight o'clock.'

'I wish we'd had late-night carbonara at our wedding too,' her dad added.

Meg laughed.

'Nothing is as important to us as your happiness,' Ava said. 'This side of your life, it makes you so happy. Hannah makes you so happy. We should have supported that—'

'And not got caught up in . . . stupid stuff,' George added. 'Nonsense, really.'

'It's not a side of my life, Mum; it just is my life.'

'Sorry, I know. That's what I meant. We shouldn't have taken this long to realize how right this is for you.'

'But what took you so long?' Meg asked. From the speakers outside, she heard the Spice Girls play, and she heard Benji on the microphone shouting to the crowd that this one was a *big tune*.

Her parents were looking at each other, unsure what to say.

'We all need to be honest,' Meg said.

'I know, darling,' Ava said. 'We know Hannah and we

really like her; it's nothing to do with . . . It's stuff . . . our own issues from our own era we should never have saddled you with. That's what everyone talks about now, baggage, right? We didn't understand and it shouldn't have taken the kids from the school to show us how *our* views were the abnormal ones. The idea of missing your wedding, it killed us, Meg. We had to come.'

'It's like when you showed us the rings when you'd got engaged, I . . .' Her mum's voice trailed into nothing. 'We'd just have liked to be involved.'

'And we're sorry,' her dad said. 'For showing up on Thursday and making everything more stressful.'

'It's not easy being a parent, you know,' Ava said. 'I don't mean defensively, I mean, to be vulnerable. It's . . . it's not an easy time and as a child you just think your parents are perfect. We're not, and none of our parents were. You expect all these things, and that your child is going to turn out in some sort of way you can control. It's nothing to do with you, really, who your child is, though people like to claim the good bits for themselves.'

'All your good bits are just from you, Meg,' George said.

'And those good bits are, well they're brilliant,' her mum said, starting to cry again. George put his hand on Ava's shoulder.

'Are you going to stay?' Meg said. 'Dance the night away?'

'You know dancing was never really our thing,' George said, and Meg smiled. 'But we've got another drink in us, I think. Why don't you pop round tomorrow? Or we can come to yours. A cup of tea, a debrief. We'd like to apologize to Hannah too but we don't want her day to be about us.'

'That sounds nice, Dad,' Meg said. 'We go on the honeymoon tomorrow, but when we're back?'

'Sounds perfect,' George said.

'We'll have to get the good biscuits in, George,' Ava said. 'Or some of these cupcakes you have here, Meg. They're delicious.'

'Well,' George mumbled. 'Some of them. Not the vegetable ones.'

Each of them hugged her and for the first time in years, it didn't feel like a formality but like the walls were down and she was being comforted by the parents who should always have been able to comfort her. They started to walk towards the doors of the shop, and to rejoin everybody. Meg felt several stone lighter.

'Can I just say,' George said, looking out at the festoon lights that were now slung across the street between the shops, and the disco ball Martha had rigged above the decks, 'I've never been to a wedding like this in all my life.'

43

DAVID

Benji found David in the crowd and asked if he could show him something. David could barely hear him through the music but followed him to the side of the main throng.

As the sun had started to falter after its ardent support all day, it was people's phones, the occasional streetlight and the hastily erected lighting above them that made it possible to see, just enough that it did not feel too dark. It certainly felt too loud, and now David couldn't tell how many people were around, other than simply loads. He had heard rumours the police had come with a noise complaint, and Martha, who was now attempting to break dance, had sent them on their way.

'Have you seen this?' Benji said, thrusting his phone into David's hand.

'What?'

'Your orders page.'

He showed on his phone how he was on the back-end system of the website. Since the subscriptions and orders had only come into the shop in person, he hadn't needed to learn how to do this yet, but as Benji scrolled, David could see pages and pages of orders, some individual, some signing up on a monthly basis.

'What the . . .'

'The subscription mention worked,' Benji said. 'The news, you know like millions of people watch the national news? I don't know why. Anyway, I think you've got nearly two hundred orders, and counting. Well, we don't have to count, it's . . .' He squinted at the screen. 'Okay, it's two hundred and sixty-one.'

'Shut the f—' he looked down at Benji '—front door.'

David quickly did the maths; if the cheapest option was thirty pounds, they'd have more than enough to be back in the black this month. That was seven and a half thousand pounds, an amount he hadn't seen in years. He grabbed the phone and looked again, as if it might be a trick. If this was just the start, or if the bulk of these orders were subscriptions coming in the next month as well . . . He didn't want to get too excited, but maybe . . .

'Thanks, Benji, for all of this,' he said. 'This is amazing, and you're . . . you're just great! Great work!'

'I know.'

'And you and Fred?' David said. 'I knew you were being secretive about something.'

David looked at him, now a young man, instead of the boy he'd once known.

'I dunno,' he said.

'I think it's very brave,' David said. 'If your dad's ever funny, you know . . . I'm here to talk to.'

'As if I care what my dad thinks,' Benji said.

'That's a fair point,' David said diplomatically.

'He's actually . . .' Benji seemed to relax as he spoke. 'He's been better, the last few weeks. A bit lighter. I dunno if he's got a girlfriend or whatever, but . . . we're getting on. I'm out more doing the social media stuff, seeing friends. I think he knows about Fred coming round but he doesn't mind; he hasn't said anything.'

'Well whatever happens, Benji, I still think it's brave, and I'm happy for you both.'

They stared at each other for a second.

'Are you happy to stop being soppy now?' David said.

'Yes, man,' he said. 'Let's go get Salma to play something good.'

They moved to walk through the crowd.

'You know, Benji, you need to be careful calling everyone man. It might get under some people's skin.'

'David,' Benji said. 'Come on. Salma calls everyone girlypops. How is this different?'

'I guess . . .'

Benji turned back, facing away from the crowds. 'It'd be *weirder* if I had specific terms and was guessing for certain people. I call everyone man. Well, people I like,' he added, before looking thoughtful. 'I treat everyone the same.'

He couldn't really argue with that, so David continued walking with Benji through the crowd, trying to think of songs they'd both enjoy and could ask for. They probably wouldn't play any Tracey Thorn, and 'You Don't Bring Me Flowers', his favourite by Barbara Streisand, was probably not the right vibe. Benji was humming something.

'What are you singing?' David asked. 'Shall we request it?'

'It's Fred Again.'

'Aw, you're obsessed with him!'

David looked at Benji who was looking up at him, annoyed.

'It's a band, David . . .'

EPILOGUE

Two Weeks After the Wedding

Parking at the airport was going to be a nightmare. He didn't know why he'd offered. He tried to slide into the parallel-parking bays in the complicated loop system they'd introduced, but he knew people behind him were having to move in increments through the tiny gap he'd left for them to pass. Mercifully, nobody beeped. He pretended not to see them as they drove closely past his window.

It was both because he was excited to see Meg and Hannah and so he could finally drive away from the space that he screamed their names as he saw them emerge from the glass of the airport exit.

'Get in, get in!' he said through the window and, suitcases secured, Meg took her place in the front and Hannah in the back. They both had bronzed skin and Hannah had a new set of freckles covering her face. It seemed Greece had been good to them. They appeared relaxed and comfortable, even after a three-hour flight.

'Welcome back!'

Meg put her seatbelt on. 'Thanks so much for picking us up!'

'You're a lifesaver,' Hannah added, turning on her phone which buzzed into life.

'No problem, no problem.' David turned out onto the main road. 'How was it then?'

They caught him up quickly, on snorkelling and sunset boat trips and surprisingly amazing Mexican food they'd found on the islands.

'I've finally got my texts . . . Gus just sent me one,' Hannah said. 'Him and Ramon are finally going on a date!'

'They took their time,' David said.

'I think Gus wanted to not rush into anything,' Meg added. 'He told me that's always his mistake.'

'They have our wedding to thank,' Hannah said.

'Well I'm still coming down from the wedding,' David said. 'What a brilliant day.'

'I realize they didn't play any Black Eyed Peas, David,' Meg said. 'Were you okay?'

'Well apart from *that*, it was great! Salma's fault.'

'What other news have we missed? We've tried not to be on our phones all week.'

'Oh God, what have I got to share?' David asked himself. 'Angie's given Benji a job, you know.'

'Really?'

'That's amazing,' Hannah said.

'She was so impressed with what he did for Savage Lilies, she's got him in a day a week, and then another place in the queer business network has done the same. He's made up.'

'He deserves that,' Hannah said. 'He's great.'

'Are the orders still rolling in?' Meg asked.

‘Still! I don’t know if they keep replaying the news clip or what . . . the accountant’s eyes nearly popped out of her head.’

Meg touched his knee. ‘I’m so happy for you, David.’

David thought back to the live news clip that he had recorded on his phone from the TV; him stumbling over the subscription details and how shocked he was by Mark’s proposal. *Never in a million years, or in my wildest dreams, would I have imagined today,* he had said. The emotion must have got people subscribing quickly. It was theatre. He was being sensible, reinvesting the money into the shop, and the accountant was getting involved in a way she hadn’t before. Jacques was going to come and redesign the back room so he had more space for events, and as he paid the deposit, he’d felt like he was securing his and Mark’s future.

‘And you know about Benji and Fred dating?’ David asked. ‘That they became official?’

‘Obviously, David.’

‘Why obviously!’

‘Could you not tell?’ Hannah asked from the back.

‘Not at all!’ David said. ‘Maybe I’m too old.’

‘Not too old to get married though,’ Meg said. ‘I feel like we’ve not spoken about that properly . . . I’m so happy for you both. You just . . . what . . . changed your mind? I didn’t get a chance to ask on the day.’

‘It sounds like a lie but it was you guys,’ he said. Now they were on a main road, David could relax slightly. He took one hand off the wheel to drink from a bottle of water. ‘You just showed me how good it can be. Not some family pressure or something stressful for no reason, but about you and the love you have for the most important person in your life. And a million things can go wrong and you still want to, because it's for both of you. I feel like if I can make Mark that happy, why shouldn't I?'

'I'm glad I could do that for you,' Meg said. 'You've done so much. I, we . . . There's no way to thank you.'

'You've said thank you already.'

'But I can keep saying it; that's all I can do,' Meg said. 'Oh and I can give you this.'

Meg took out a small frame she had in her backpack. Glancing away from the road for just a second, David saw it was an illustration from Ailie. It was instantly recognizable; he had seen people holding them all day at the wedding but hadn't had a chance to sit with her and get one himself. It was a beautiful line illustration, with watercolour detailing, of him and Meg wearing their outfits from the wedding, standing in front of the shop. David had his arm round Meg, who looked at the camera with her arms crossed, and they were both smiling.

'This looks so much like us.'

'Ailie's good!' Meg said. 'I asked her to do one specially cos I knew neither of us would have time to sit with her for long enough.'

'Oh, Meg, thank you, this is . . . This is so special.' David turned the radio down slightly. 'How's everything with your parents?'

'Good,' Meg said. 'They were . . . I don't know, different. It's not like we're fine, but I don't feel like we're going to be bad anymore. We've laid it all out on the table to sort through; that's what I feel like. I'm just so glad they came.'

'Your dad was one of the subscribers to the flower subscription, by the way,' David said. 'I spied his name on an order, which is nice.'

'Maybe he's buying them for your mum, Meg,' Hannah said.

'And your mum's helping Mark out with some peer support thing at school, Mark told me,' David added. 'It's not a gay thing but a lot of the queer kids use it, I think.'

'That's amazing,' Meg said. 'God, they really are changing.'

'It's all from your special day,' David said. 'I really think you made an impact.'

'I'm so glad we did it,' Meg said. 'And glad we trusted you.'

'I wish my parents had lived to see something like that day,' David said. 'I really think they could've changed their minds.'

'I think so too,' Meg said.

'That first day you came into the shop, I just . . . was a little bit lost, with the shop and myself and now . . . I'm getting married, I've got even more wonderful friends, and the shop's going from strength to strength. I'm reminded of who I am again.'

'For what it's worth,' Meg said, 'I think your parents would be very proud of you.'

'There's no way to know, I guess,' David said. 'I'm proud of myself though.' David clipped the kerb. 'You know at one point, I suggested our wedding present to you could be driving lessons. Mark told me no.'

'I think that's fair.' Hannah laughed from the back seat.

'We'll have to find new ways to spend our time though,' Meg said. 'This can't be the end. We have to make sure we still do stuff together, like pizza night, the youth club, our night out dancing. You weren't just a stand-in, you know.'

'Well you actually can't get rid of me for another year.'

'Why's that?'

'Well Meg, I'm getting married too,' David said smiling. 'And the best woman usually has a fair bit to get on with at someone's wedding.'

Acknowledgements

It takes a village! Thanks to everyone at Avon for their support getting this novel from idea through to finished manuscript and into readers' hands.

Firstly, the biggest thank you to Rachel Hart, the best editor with the most insightful suggestions, even when I'm making absolutely no sense on the page. I very much enjoyed figuring out what was a reasonable level of swearing given Meg's circumstances! In Editorial, I'd also like to thank Helen Huthwaite and Amy Mae Baxter, Jess Zahra for helping me shape the book you're holding, Helena for copy-editing and Penelope for proofreading. Apologies for all the commas.

In the Audio team I'd like to thank Molly Robinson and Molly Lo Re, and thank you to Hannah Lismore in the Digital team.

The cover is down to illustration from Mallory Heyer and design from Sarah Foster, who have brought Meg and David to life wonderfully.

Internationally, my thanks go to Angela Thomson, Jean-Marie Kelly, Sophia Wilhelm and Emily Gerbner. In Rights, thank you for the work of Aisling Smyth, Zoe Shine, Ashton Mucha, Anda Podaru and Helena Font Brillas. In Publishing Operations, thank you to Melissa Okusanya and Hannah Stamp, and in Sales, very warm thanks to Emily Scorer and Katie Buckley.

For getting this book into the hands of readers, I can't thank Emily Hall and Jessie Whitehead enough, and I send a big thanks to Francesca Tuzzeo for managing production.

To my agent Andrew James, thanks for your constant support.

A special shout-out to Matilda Cracknell for her help in floristry accuracy early on in the process and teaching me about roses and broken stems.

Thanks to Ewan Newbigging-Lister for his support in all things writing, including celebrating the wins and talking me down on the long and arduous process of trying to get published. We did it!

My family were always big readers and I can't thank them all enough for encouraging my reading and buying me books for decades, including my auntie who this book is dedicated to.

And finally, a thank you to my own found family who I couldn't do anything without. You're the best.